Praise for *The Ghost Hunters*

'Surprising, serpentine and clever'
Sunday Times

'Close the curtains pull up a chair, open a book –
and prepare to be pleasantly scared'
Metro

'A deft, spooky psychological drama based on a true story'
Daily Mail

'Engrossing . . . a chilling English ghost story'
Fortean Times

'Spring weaves a dark web of romance, deceit
and a lingering curse'
Metro

'I was gripped by the supernatural menace and the gradual
revelation of mysteries and secrets'
Fortean Times

'Genuinely spine chilling . . . an excellent blending
of fact and fiction'
Light Magazine

'A gloriously spooky tale, perfect for dark autumn nights'
Netmums.com

'A roistering paranormal adventure'
Radio Times

Neil Spring was born in south Wales in 1981. He started writing at the age of twenty-eight. Between 1999 and 2002 he studied philosophy, politics and economics at Somerville College, Oxford. In 2013 he published *The Ghost Hunters*, a paranormal thriller based on the life of Harry Price. *The Ghost Hunters* received outstanding reviews and has been adapted into a major television drama under the title *Harry Price: Ghost Hunter* for ITV. Neil is Welsh and lives in London. *The Watchers* is his second novel. You can contact him on Twitter @NeilSpring or visit him at www.neilspring.com.

Also by Neil Spring

The Ghost Hunters

The WATCHERS

NEIL SPRING

Quercus

First published in Great Britain in 2015 by

Quercus Publishing Ltd
Carmelite House
50 Victoria Embankment
London EC4Y 0DZ

An Hachette UK company

A CIP catalogue record for this book is available
from the British Library

PB ISBN 978 1 78429 063 4
EBOOK ISBN 978 1 78429 062 7

10 9 8 7 6 5 4 3 2 1

Typeset by CC Book Production

Printed and bound in Great Britain by Clays Ltd, St Ives plc

For Guy, Lord Black of Brentwood.
A dear friend and a great man.

Note

This novel was loosely inspired by the UFO sightings that took place in Wales throughout the late 1970s. However, all the characters appearing in this work, as well as all details of the story itself, are entirely fictitious. Any resemblance to real places or persons (living or dead) is purely coincidental. For more information on the historical background of the sightings, please see the author note at the back of the book.

The "Broad Haven Triangle"

RAF Brawdy

US Naval Facility

St Brides Bay

Broad Haven

Broad Haven Primary School

Haven Hotel

Stack Rocks

Giant's Point

UFO landing site

Little Haven

Ravenstone Farm

Lighthouse

'We are a haunted species. The spectres are among us. They continue to come. They rattle their chains. Yet it is us who have chained them.'

Ralph Noyes, former MOD official

Prologue

DELIVERY OF THE PARSONS REPORT

BY JONATHAN HARRISON, FORMER
SPECIAL ADVISER TO THE PRIME MINISTER

Wednesday 22 May 1979, 10 Downing Street, London

Perhaps it was the prospect of meeting the new prime minister that accounted for his ashen expression; perhaps it was the weight of history which lay behind that famous black door. Whatever it was, the young man looked fearful. I might even go so far as to say tortured.

Smiling, I gestured him forward. 'This way please, Mr Wilding.'

Many visitors to 10 Downing Street react with something close to awe, but this shabby, unkempt gentleman was different. He was not taking in the grandeur of the entrance hall; he was focused on stepping carefully across its chequered black and white floor.

'Is that it? 'I asked, eyeing the slim blue file in his hand.

He nodded without looking up, and I hurriedly guided him to the corridor that ran to the back of the house and up the grand stairs. He did not admire the gilded banisters. He did not eye the portraits of previous prime ministers. But when, as we reached the landing of the first floor, he glimpsed through an open door a vast oval table surrounded by vacant chairs, he stopped.

'There?' he said.

I nodded.

He stared into the panelled room, and I let him have a moment. It's not every day a former parliamentary researcher is invited to attend an extraordinary meeting of the National Security Council.

'You followed the instructions in my memorandum?' I checked.

'Yes.'

'You told no one of this meeting?'

'I told no one.'

'And you understand that – '

'That what is said here today remains a secret, yes,' he snapped, finally meeting my gaze.

'The prime minister is waiting,' I said, and I guided him along. I did not add that our new PM was not a lady to be kept waiting. Nor did I point out that he had just one hour to tell his story – to convince us – before the council members arrived. He did not look like he could take the pressure.

We arrived at the door to her study and I knocked once.

'Come in.' Her voice was calm but stern.

The prime minister looked up as we entered her office. I gestured Wilding to a chair before the desk, but before I could make the necessary introductions our guest had turned back towards the door I had just firmly closed.

'Mr Wilding, are you all right?' I asked.

He had gripped the door handle and was rattling it: once, twice, three times.

'Mr Wilding?'

He looked at me with embarrassed, apologetic eyes and nodded, yet proceeded to perform the exact ritual a second time.

In all my years as a private secretary in Downing Street I had never witnessed a guest behave so peculiarly, especially before a prime minister. I was nervous to see her reaction – intrigued too, for this was only her second week in office.

After a third cycle of rattling, I ushered Wilding towards the chair once more. 'Please, won't you sit down?'

He did. Carefully. Perched on the edge of the seat as if ready to leap up at any moment.

The PM studied him. His hair was unruly, a shock of dark curls. His eyes too were dark and set deeply in a gaunt face. Haunted is the word that comes to mind. He looked haunted. And if the stories about him were true, that was understandable.

'You are a difficult man to find,' said the prime minister at last. 'Two years?'

'I needed to get away. I needed to recover.'

'Remind me who you worked for?'

'Paul Bestford. Member of Parliament for Pembrokeshire.'

'Ah yes.' She nodded, only once but her tone spoke volumes. 'Paul's loss of self-respect was sad to see. But his loss of self-control, *that* was unforgivable.'

The observation was cuttingly smooth. I wasn't surprised when Wilding flinched. But his eyes remained locked on hers.

A beat passed, another, and still they stared. The silence was loaded with tension.

Finally, the prime minister began again. 'Mr Wilding, I am so terribly sorry for your loss,' she said with an empathy far removed from her public persona. 'And so grateful for all you have done.'

'Thank you,' Wilding murmured. Quickly, he looked back over his shoulder to the door, then back at the blue file he was still holding in his right hand.

'I want to reassure you that a full investigation into what

happened in the Havens has been under way for some time,' the prime minister said. 'And the guilty parties are being sought.'

Wilding nodded. A gesture of reluctant acceptance, or grief perhaps.

'Help me understand,' she said, 'what compels a man to act as your grandfather did?'

Wilding looked distressed. Dropping the blue file onto her desk, he said, 'This. The recurrent power of evil.'

She didn't reach for the document immediately, just eyed it steadily. 'You have no idea,' she said, drawing a breath, 'for how long the intelligence services have sought this information. Beyond the Vatican Library, only a few copies exist, and we had no lead on any of them. Until now.'

But Wilding was no longer paying attention. The high windows that overlooked Horse Guards and St James's Park were like a magnet to his eyes. *What on earth is he looking at?* I wondered. Finally he tore his gaze away, pulled in a deep breath.

'Has Dr Caxton arrived yet?'

'He is expected shortly,' the prime minister answered. 'We are in desperate need of his assistance. Yours too. Now go on. Tell me, please, Mr Wilding, how did you come by this document? From the beginning. Leave nothing out.' She gave me a quick glance. 'My secretary will take notes.'

'I . . . I don't know where to start.' He paused, then added, 'Prime Minister, I think the questions you really want to ask are, "Did those things actually happen? *Could* they happen?"'

She tilted her head to the side, just as she had during my briefing to her earlier that morning on the plague of phenomena that had occurred two years ago in the distant community of the Havens, St Brides Bay, in west Wales, an area the newspapers were calling the Broad Haven Triangle. The events had made national headlines: mutilated animals, tormenting poltergeists, dancing lights in the sky, unidentified flying objects and menacing silver-suited figures watching, watching.

Wilding hesitated. 'What now? I mean, what happens to me?'

'We will establish a unit to investigate these matters.'

'Yes, but will I be safe?'

'That rather depends upon you, Mr Wilding.' The prime minister gave that noncommittal smile that I would live to see her give many more times. Her gaze dropped to the title of the blue file before her: The Parsons Report. 'This document couldn't have come to us at a more important time. The Soviets are hell-bent on world dominance, and they are rapidly acquiring the means to become the most powerful imperial nation the world has ever seen. They are among us. And this could make all the difference.' She paused. 'I want to hear your story. There will be time afterwards for you to write it down.'

Wilding leaned forward and rested his tented fingers on the desk's dark leather surface. 'Prime Minister, there's something I'd like to know before I begin.'

'By all means.'

'Do you believe we are alone in the universe?'

Margaret Thatcher's eyes widened. 'Mr Wilding, my national security advisers inform me that it is no longer a question of belief.'

Wilding released a troubled sigh. It was hard to tell whether he agreed with her or not.

'Well then,' he said, leaning restlessly back into his chair, 'my story begins in west Wales sixteen years ago. At a place called Ravenstone Farm.'

Robert Wilding's Statement

I

Secret State

'The Earth is a farm. We are someone else's property.'

Charles Fort

— 1 —

Friday 6 December 1963, Ravenstone Farm, west Wales

I remember the first time I laid eyes on the farm, rocking and jolting in the back seat of Grandfather's truck, struggling to ignore the overpowering stink of damp dog fur as we passed down a narrow potholed lane bordered on both sides by skeletal trees.

We had travelled some ten miles from my family home in Brawdy, across St Brides Bay, near the military base where my father had been posted, and as the truck laboured through the many winding lanes and huddled coastal villages to bring us here, I watched the sun sink ever lower to the horizon and felt my spirits drop with it.

My parents had died in an accident and I was to be taken in by my grandfather, a man I had met only a handful of times. Mum and Dad had never brought me to the farm, even though we'd lived only a few miles away. Now, as we made our way down the narrow lanes towards the house, I couldn't help wondering why.

'Well, boy, here we are,' said Grandfather, trying his best to be cordial with a grandson he hardly knew. 'Home.'

The word sounded painfully hollow. I already knew that nowhere would ever feel like home again.

Hanging from the rear-view mirror: a small silver cross, attached to a beaded chain. I looked past it, through the dirty windscreen and saw the gloomy lane open into a small clearing, saw the wide fields slope down towards the cliff edge beyond. Directly ahead were dilapidated cattle sheds of corrugated iron, brown with rust, and immediately to the right, behind a low crumbling stone wall, the farmhouse. It had stood here at the edge of the Atlantic for hundreds of years, he told me. Once, perhaps, it had been gleaming white. Because I was a child I never thought to ask why my grandfather might be living somewhere so lonesome: miles from anywhere, in a place without road names, shops, a pub or even a phone box.

His truck crunched to a halt on the gravel next to a grey Hillman Hunter that had seen better days. I climbed out, feeling an odd pang of nervousness. Looking doubtfully around me, I scrunched my nose against the stench of manure. Listened. Somewhere beyond the fields the ocean roared, and from behind the farmhouse a bull groaned as if in pain.

'Don't mind 'im,' Grandfather muttered, his rough voice offering scant comfort as he climbed down from the driver's seat and opened the back of the truck.

Despite his age – mid-fifties – he was a strong man; he had to be to manage the chores of Ravenstone Farm alone. He had a fresh scar, jagged, on his left cheek, which caught the eye, and he was tall with a quiet confidence about him. Though on that crimson evening he inspired little confidence in me.

'You like swings, boy?' he asked awkwardly.

I didn't but I nodded yes. Grandfather was staring to the side of the farmhouse, where rising from the overgrown weeds there was a slatted wooden seat suspended by two twists of rope on a rusty frame.

'Your mother used to love playing on that thing.'

A sudden memory: me in my school uniform, eating breakfast in our kitchen, watching Mum in her jeans kneeling over a placard emblazoned with the slogan BAN THE BOMB.

Grandfather's voice jolted me back to the present.

'That'll be your room.' Hunched in his shabby greatcoat, he was pointing with a hand that was red raw from the cold to a narrow window directly over the small arched porch that led into the farmhouse. 'There's quite a bit of damp. I'll sort it.'

But I wasn't thinking about the damp. I was thinking about the thick iron bars fixed over the glass. They weren't just on my window. They were on *every* window.

'This way, boy.'

I followed him into the narrow hallway, where the lingering animal odour was even stronger, the carpet hard and brown, and the wallpaper so cloudy yellow you could almost taste the cigarette smoke. Hanging next to the front door, a camera and a brown leather binocular case, and leaning very near this, in the corner, a double-barrelled shotgun.

Grandfather's eyes fastened on me. 'You're not to touch that. Not ever!'

His face had turned stony. He watched carefully as I shuffled down the hall and peered into the small front room, where an enormous bookcase was filled with musty tomes. His study.

I took a deep breath, filling my lungs with the stale air. I was intrigued by the newspaper clippings that plastered the walls, partly because I had never seen such a thing before, mostly because of the many black headlines screaming about 'mysteries in the sky'. And that wasn't all. A great picture hung over the mantelpiece, da Vinci's *St John the Baptist*, immersed in shadow. An enigmatic smile touched the great saint's lips as his right hand pointed skyward.

I gasped as a dark shape suddenly sprang from the shadows towards me. But it was only a spirited black Labrador, alert and lovable as he pushed his nose against my leg, tail beating furiously.

'What's his name?'

'Jasper.'

'Can I take him out, Grandfather?'

'Not now . . . It'll be dark soon.' His hooded gaze shifted to the window and the purple sky beyond. 'Upstairs now. Unpack.'

Waiting for me in the shadows that lingered strangely at the bottom of the rickety staircase was the small trunk my parents had given me the previous Christmas. Packed inside: history books and my new school uniform but none of the toy guns and army uniforms I used to play with. My childhood dream to be a soldier had died with my father.

'Hurry up, boy!'

I did as Grandfather instructed.

God help me, I went upstairs.

That evening, as I lay on the steel-framed bed under woollen blankets that made my skin itch, I longed for sleep while unfamiliar sounds kept me from my rest: creepy, insistent, croaking rhythms that might have been frogs in the pond, high-pitched shrieks that might have been the cries of prowling foxes and, just to the side of the house, another sound, riding on the pitiless wind – *creak-squeak creak-squeak.*

Perhaps Mum had come to hate the farm where she grew up. She had certainly never mentioned it, and whenever I had asked her about her childhood her answer was always the same: *Better left in the past.* The memories brought stinging tears to my eyes and churned my stomach. These days I'd often wake up crying, and I had been dreaming a lot about my parents and all the things we'd never do.

My knees were tucked up to my belly as I stared at the ceiling, at the rough wooden crucifix nailed over my bed. Downstairs, I could hear Grandfather moving about, singing a hymn to himself, pleading for the souls of 'unbelievers'. I closed my eyes and felt myself hardening against him. Against the undeniable fact that this man was all I had left in the world.

I woke to the birds' dawn chorus chirpily greeting a new day and the distant rumble of a tractor. Grandfather was in the kitchen, leaning over an enormous Aga.

'We're going for a walk this morning,' he said without turning. His attention seemed divided between the latest edition of the *Church Times* and the sizzling bacon in the blackened pan. 'Down to the coastal path. I want to show you something.'

I had been hoping he might ask me how I was, how I had slept.

The truth was I'd slept badly. Since my parents' deaths I'd been haunted by the same strange dream about a dark-haired girl with an oval face and a lighthouse throwing its yellow beam across the sea. Pulsing. I'd woken shivering with fear, too scared even to try to sleep again. But now, in the light, it all seemed very distant.

After breakfast we set off with Jasper down a muddy rutted track across the fields which surrounded us for miles. I sighed, wondering why I already felt a closer bond with the dog than I did with my own blood relative. But the truth was Jasper calmed me in a way that Grandfather did not. I would grow to love that dog, really love him. On a desolate farm far from anywhere, Jasper was one of the greatest gifts that a lonely little boy could hope for.

I could smell the sharp salt of the tide. As we reached the lower fields, near the cliffs, Grandfather quickened his pace, regularly glancing over his shoulder as if to check we weren't being followed. Or watched.

Then, suddenly, he stopped.

'Grandfather?'

His lead-coloured eyes were fixed on a large rocky outcrop half a mile offshore.

'Stack Rocks,' he whispered. 'This is the nearest point. You're not to come down here, not ever.'

'But why?'

I felt his reproachful eyes on me. Something else was there too. Was it fear? Why should he be afraid?

'Stack Rocks,' he said again. 'Sometimes the kids in the village ask the fishermen to take them out. But you must *never* go there – you stay away!'

My gaze followed his. The outcrop was barren except for a ruined fort on its highest point. Grandfather told me that in the last century the squat structure had been built to defend the shore. Later it had been abandoned and left to decay.

'It is a dangerous place, boy. You understand?'

I didn't, but I nodded anyway, and an uncomfortable shudder crept over me as I watched him, for his eyes were now prominent and strained. Hunching forward to drop a hand on my shoulder, he continued speaking in a voice not much more than a whisper. 'Our planet is haunted. And there are those who would do us harm.'

Suddenly, a distant memory – burning rubber. A yellow beam cutting through the darkness.

'I don't know what you mean?' I said. 'Why are you looking at me like that?'

'The forces of darkness are forever present. You must not hunt them or seek them. Understand? You must *never* invite them in!'

He was standing close. So close I felt suddenly overwhelmed by his presence, by his fierce and rapturous face. 'Please, I want Mum and Dad.'

'Your father?' His tone turned bitter. 'The mistakes he made will cost us dearly.'

'But . . . but he was my dad!'

'He was a monster!'

My heart was pounding. I wanted to strike him for talking about my father like that, but I didn't dare.

'The Book of Revelation tells us that fallen angels would strike thrice between the eyes and cause great suffering.' He looked broodingly across the fields, the sea, and at Stack Rocks, then gave me a look so dark it made me shiver. 'You must be protected, boy.'

Protected from what? From whom? We weren't likely to have visitors at Ravenstone Farm – it was too isolated. I hadn't even heard the telephone ring.

'From the forces of darkness and the tricks of the Lawless One,' he shouted above the rising wind. 'From the fires in the sky and from the heat below.'

The cold seemed to rise from the sea and strike at my face. *Someone help me*, I thought. *He's gone mad.*

Suddenly, as if in answer to my plea, a figure passed into view on the coastal path. A man in farmer's clothes. He raised a hand in a gesture of hello.

Grandfather's eyes held my gaze for a moment or two, then, ignoring the walker, he crossed himself, turned sharply and strode back towards the farmhouse.

I'm pretty certain it was at this precise moment that I decided I couldn't trust my grandfather, couldn't trust anything he told me.

The months dragged by. I enrolled at the secondary school in Haverfordwest but made few friends. I felt different to the other children. Not only were they oblivious to what life had dealt me, I also knew that none of them would be welcome at the farm and I would be ashamed to take them there. Grandfather never fixed anything or cleaned, so the farmhouse fell ever further into neglect, until even the television gave up the ghost. After school and at the weekends I was forced to create my own entertainment. So I began to explore. And what child isn't intrigued by what is out of bounds?

I quickly found a favourite spot: down to the lowest field, through the barbed-wire fence and into the tangled bracken overlooking Stack Rocks, the best viewpoint over the Atlantic Ocean and RAF Brawdy.

I was scared of what Grandfather would do if he knew I went down there, but curiously not scared of the place. On the contrary, I felt strangely drawn to the spot. Connected somehow.

Stack Rocks Island pulled my gaze. Held it. Rising from the waters in three humps, the large outcrop resembled a mythical creature. None of the fishing boats went near, nor any birds. None I ever saw. Sometimes it seemed as though even the rain itself didn't touch those rocks. And there was something odd about Ravenstone Farm itself, I had come to realize. Not the isolation of the place, but the way it *felt*, the way the air, even on the coldest days, warmed the skin, the way it pricked and crackled and made the hairs stand on end.

My mother and father were arguing again in our house on the base. Screaming at one another as I sat hunched at the top of the stairs wishing they would just STOP!

The perspective changed, and suddenly I was cold. Freezing cold and hunched in darkness, screaming to get away. But get away from what?

Suddenly, in the distance, across the rough sea, a pulse of yellow light: flashing, flashing.

A lighthouse.

I woke with a jolt. The first thing I heard was the window rattling against its bars. And when my eyes adjusted to the early dark, the first thing I saw was the wooden crucifix above my bed.

An uncertainty flowed through me for a moment, irresistible and overpowering, and then hardened into a single concern: the front door – was it locked? Grandfather always locked it; he locked all the doors when we came in. But perhaps he'd forgotten. I would go and check for him.

I had one foot on the rough bare floorboards when a low earthy drone filled the air. The hairs on the back of my neck shot up and blood pulsed in my ears. At that instant I heard it: *thud thud thud.* A visitor at this time in the morning? I knew something was wrong the instant I creeped downstairs into the shadow-haunted hall. Something was amiss in Grandfather's study.

I went in, flicked on the light.

'Hello?' I whispered. 'Anyone there?'

No one I could see. And yet clearly someone had been there because the thick brown rug that should have been in the centre of the floor was rolled to the side, all the way back to the enormous bookcase packed with ancient texts. Yet the furniture that rested on the rug – the wide desk, the rickety armchair – remained in its proper place. Then I noticed the picture over the mantelpiece, the one of St John the Baptist pointing enigmatically at the sky. It had been turned on its nail, one hundred and eighty degrees, so that it was hanging upside down.

Again: *thud, thud, thud.* It was coming from the front door.

I went back quickly into the hall. Fumbled with the lock chain, opened the door.

'Hello, young man. Are your parents at home?'

I was looking up at a tall, spindly man in a black suit, probably in his late twenties. My stomach tightened with fear.

'Umm, I think my grandfather is here . . . He's asleep.'

The stranger looked at me steadily. 'Not your parents?'

His square black glasses gave him a studious air and an easy authority. But there was nothing sincere in his sharp smile and nothing genuine in his pointed, gaunt face. And why, I wondered, would such a young man colour his hair that brilliant shade of white?

'They're not here.' My right hand went instinctively to my wristwatch, fumbled with it. 'They're . . . they're dead.'

'Dead?' His head tilted slowly, and when he spoke again it was without a trace of sympathy. 'How inconsiderate of them to leave you behind. Alone.'

Those words were like a knife in me. Yet I felt a sudden strong impulse to invite him in. I felt dazed by his eyes . . . eyes that remembered midnight. And his skin . . . waxy white, smooth like a child's, though there was nothing childish about him. A shiver ran up my spine.

'May I come in?'

'I'm not supposed to talk to strangers,' I answered, watching my words turn to frost on the air and suddenly wondering why his did not. 'I ought to get Grandfather.'

The Black-Suited Man's face hardened. 'Your grandfather won't thank you for waking him.' He leaned forward. 'Please, let me in.'

As I was about to step aside, the stamp of feet above made me swing round. A shock of relief shot through me as Grandfather, in his dressing gown, launched himself down the staircase.

'Well, hello again,' the visitor said. His lips pulled back over his teeth. 'I've come to collect. Where is it?'

'Oh God!' rasped Grandfather, still in motion. He grabbed my shoulder roughly. 'Get back, Robert!'

To see my grandfather, always strong, so desperate at the sight of this man with plastic skin, wasn't just surprising, it was terrifying.

He slammed the door on the visitor and shot the chain.

'The Black-Suited Men, messengers of deception, harbingers of death,' he whispered. He sounded afraid, he sounded insane.

Slowly his head swivelled towards the open door to his study. He saw the carpet rolled back, saw *St John the Baptist* hanging upside down. He lunged for me, dragged me after him into the study. There, still clutching me, he stared into my eyes. I would *not* disobey him, he insisted. For my safety and for his, I would do as he said, and the good Lord would keep us safe. But I didn't feel safe; I just felt confused and scared to death as he righted the painting, then yelled at me to get down on my knees and pray before it.

'Grandfather, no –'

Something struck the back of my head, and I pitched forward, stunned. The shock was worse than the pain, shock as I realized that he had actually thrown his Bible at me, shock that now he was towering over me, crossing himself.

'Hear, Holy Father . . .'

After what felt like an eternity he got off his knees and looked warily at his desk lamp. It was flashing on and off, on and off.

'You've been down to the lower fields. Haven't you, boy?'

I wanted to explain that from there I could see the hangars at RAF Brawdy across St Brides Bay, to see where we used to live, to see the watchtower that Dad used to love. But I was too frightened to say anything, so I just nodded with a slowness that felt exaggerated.

'I told you to stay away from the cliffs,' he said after a long moment. The naked lightbulb on his desk was flickering harsh light across his expression. 'Do you know why?'

I shook my head.

'There are giants in the ground there. Watchers.'

It seemed such a peculiar remark for a serious, intelligent man. But I could tell that he believed what he said and was keen that I believe it too. 'Their existence flickers on the edge of this world. Mischievous, dangerous beings.'

'Why are they dangerous?' I asked, wide-eyed. 'What do they want?'

'To open the mind of man . . . and flood it with horror.' When he continued he spoke softly, as if he feared being overheard. With every word, my heart pounded harder. 'The Watchers were judged by God and bound for seventy generations. Their faces are made of shadows, and those who look upon them shall die.'

I kept thinking, *He believes this, he actually believes this. Is that why Mum never mentioned her childhood, why she never brought me here to Ravenstone?* Had Grandfather scared her away with such stories?

'You trust me, don't you, boy?' A keen Atlantic wind rattled the window, and as I looked upon his saturnine face, my eyes pulled to that angry scar, a shiver ran through me.

'Because one day, boy, the giants will return. Doesn't the Lord's good book tell us so?' He nodded with the fervour of a fanatic. 'And there will be wars and rumours of wars between nations . . . signs in the heavens – '

'That man at the door,' I interrupted, 'who was he?'

But the question I really wanted to ask was, *What had he come to collect?*

Suddenly, the desk lamp, still flashing, exploded with a shower of glass.

And again came the knocking. Not knocking, pounding. A terrible noise that shook the house – shook us.

One.

Two.

Three.

'Grandfather, what's happening?' I was trembling all over.

From outside a hum of voices. Trampling feet crunching over ice and gravel.

That was when I saw them through the parted curtains: five or six men swaddled in thick dark coats, cameras and binoculars looped around their necks. One man carried a map. Another a shotgun.

Grandfather ignored the men outside, his whisper so low I could barely hear him. 'The Watchers appear at times of change. At times of danger. They are returning, boy. And we must be ready.'

– 2 –

Friday 4 February 1977, Westminster, London

It was just gone six thirty in the morning when the jangling telephone in the hall dragged me from the depths of sleep.

'Get that, would you, Robert?' Selina called sleepily from her bedroom across the hall.

Only half awake, I saw in my mind my hand reaching for the phone. I had a vague idea who it was, that this call was important.

My eyes snapped fully open. I sat upright, rubbed the night-mares from my eyes. This was it – the penultimate day of the select committee evidence sessions. My stomach twisted with anxiety as I thought of the shit storm that was coming.

'We're going to be fine,' Bestford had said the night before as we were leaving his office in Parliament.

But I knew my boss was wrong. No amount of preparation could be enough because the future of the British government depended on what happened today.

'Robert, the phone!'

Somehow getting out of bed at that moment was easier than usual. But it was the window that held me back from going out into the hall to the phone.

'Robert!'

'Just a second.'

I did try to resist the urge to check the window, like I tried every day, but it was too strong. My gaze focused on the catch, making sure it was still in place. Then I tapped the frame, left side first, then the top, and finally the windowsill. It had to be done strictly in that order, otherwise I'd get as far as the bedroom door before going back to do it all again. And again.

Ringgg . . . ringgg . . . ringgg . . .

I padded across the wood flooring of our narrow hallway, taking care to avoid Selina's half-unpacked suitcase, and plucked the telephone from its cradle on the wall.

'Hello?'

The line crackled. No one spoke.

'Hello?' I said again.

The muffled static sound continued for another five, perhaps ten, seconds before three loud clicks sounded and the line went dead.

Three clicks.

Good. That means he wants to see me.

'Who is it?' Selina asked from her bedroom.

'No one,' I answered.

I went into the living room and sat down in the semi-darkness on the small yellow couch Selina's parents had given her before she had rented me her spare room. Everything about the flat was yellow and orange and brown, and though I hated the modern decor and the claustrophobic feel of the space, its location – Vauxhall – was perfect for work, and to share with Selina, even just as flatmates, was its own pleasure.

There, before me on the coffee table, next to two empty wine glasses, was the thick file of local newspaper cuttings Selina and I had discussed before bed.

We're getting reports every day now, Robert. Twenty-two in just twelve months. All from around St Brides Bay. Even the coastguard doesn't understand . . .

I opened the file. The lurid headlines screamed up at me: SCIENTISTS BAFFLED BY MYSTERY RUMBLINGS . . . EXPERTS PREDICT MORE SIGHTINGS.

I tossed the cuttings aside, unfazed. During my time on the Defence Select Committee I'd become something of an expert on military activity in our skies. Balloons, unusual plane manoeuvres, aircraft observed in unusual atmospheric conditions; so many prosaic explanations for 'unexplained aerial phenomena'. I could still remember my grandfather's voice warning me about dark forces, fires in the sky. I hadn't yielded then to his fanatical paranoia that mischievous beings were watching us from above, and I sure as hell wasn't about to do so now.

I switched on the radio; Johnny Rotten's voice filled the room. The Sex Pistols were singing that Britain had no future, and I was wondering if they might have the right idea. I snapped it off and went instead to the television: crowds demonstrating outside nuclear power plants, Jimmy Carter addressing the United Nations on mounting tensions with the Soviet Union. Nothing but wars and rumours of wars, missile proliferation, arms treaties. The new US president was going to have his work cut out.

We all were.

'It can't have been no one, Robert. At this hour?'

I looked up to see Selina framed in the living-room doorway, slender as a willow, a blue towel rather disappointingly covering her breasts, though the sight of her still-damp thighs was pretty gratifying.

I said, 'Wrong number, that's all,' not seriously expecting her to accept that answer but knowing I had to say something.

'But that's the fourth call this week.'

'We'll sort it. Selina, listen, there's something I need to ask – '

'You think it's intentional?' she interrupted, going to the kitchen counter. 'Someone making trouble?'

She looked straight at me as she flicked the kettle on, working her jaw slightly, the way she always did when something was bothering her. I gave her my best smile, which she usually met with her own wonderfully calming one, but not today. Concern lingered on her face, and there was an unfamiliar glimmer in her eyes.

I heard myself say, 'We mustn't forget to lock the flat when we leave today, OK?'

'OK.'

'But really, we must lock the flat.'

'I know, Robert.'

I managed to swallow the third iteration. She saw my tight jaw and looked away. Sorry for me or just weary of me?

Shit. I wanted to punch myself. I wanted to tell her how traumatizing it was, to convey some sense of the isolation never being certain about something as simple as locking a door or window caused. Doctors had used all sorts of words to describe the way I was – words like obsessive and compulsive and paranoid – but no matter how hard they searched for some reason, some trigger, they could find none.

Even if there was a trigger, I wasn't sure I wanted to know what it was.

What I certainly did want was to make Selina, anyone, understand. It didn't matter how long I searched through my mind for reassurance or how long it took me to carry out my checks, the answers would never satisfy my uncertainty. It was like suffering from bowel cancer but only having the vocabulary to describe a mild stomach ache.

'I'm sorry,' I said gently.

'Take a break when the evidence sessions are over, please. You need to let out the frustration. Trust me, I know.'

Selina had a job interview in the City today. I wished her well, of course, but I'd miss her terribly if she got it. We had worked together for Paul Bestford, chairman of the Defence Select Committee and MP for Pembrokeshire, since leaving university. And during those three years I'd come to rely on her calm common sense and support.

'What time's your interview?'

'Three o'clock.'

'But you'll miss the start of the committee session.'

'This is *your* crusade, boyo.' A playful attempt to remind me of my Welsh connections. 'You don't need me. You'll be fine.'

I wasn't so sure. There was only one thing worse than dealing with unreliable witnesses: an unreliable committee chairman whose relationship with the bottle was becoming the subject of whispers in the Palace of Westminster's many bars. In Parliament the gossip flowed as freely as the wine, and I could tell from the way the other researchers muttered about our boss that they thought his time was limited. And I needed Bestford.

It was easy to remember the first time I met him. He'd come to our school after the 'Great Flood' and given a talk about all the reinforcements to the sea walls that would make the Havens safe again. I carried that memory with me into adulthood. And by the time I had left university at twenty-two, he was chair of the Defence Select Committee. I got the job as soon as I applied. Partly because I understood the constituency and its issues, mostly because I was passionate about scrutinizing defence policy.

'Call in afterwards, if you have time. Please?'

'I'll try my best. Robert,' she said after a pause, 'do you think I'm making the right decision?'

I nodded and said encouragingly, 'It's your time to move on,' even though I felt the opposite.

I saw her now with me: the countless hours together on the campaign trail in Broad Haven, pounding pavements, knocking on doors. She'd had that natural way with people that made them smile and talk about their problems as though they really believed we could help. Her entire life was politics, no doubt about that, but on those doorsteps she had so easily shown interest in television chat shows, music and supermarkets. Me, I dealt in facts, numbers and statistics, and the Campaign for the Accountability of American Bases. It had come to divide us: Selina was afraid Bestford was losing touch, that the Cold War and his work with me on the committee was two steps too far from the rugged realities of country living for farming folk to demonstrate their understanding at the ballot box.

Still, today was a very important day. And still we were a team. We had to be. Parliament was an odd place, perhaps not quite the madhouse you saw on television, but certainly the only environment where you might catch an MP throwing a punch at a bar or happen across the prime minister dabbing a coffee stain from his tie. I'd grown sick of the smiles and handshakes that concealed hidden agendas and the constant tensions about the issues bringing the country to its knees. After the late-night votes you would overhear MPs in the bars muttering glumly about the forthcoming 'collapse'. I was tired of hearing that too. It wasn't just the picket lines and fear of the country's lights going out again; it was something more profound. We had lost our way.

Selina looked straight at me. 'You could leave too, you know. Pursue a proper career.'

I smiled at that even as I was trying not to remember Mum saying the very same thing to Dad when we lived at RAF Brawdy. She had hated everything the military stood for, not just the wars, weapons and lies but the injustice. It was an era when America kept nuclear weapons on British soil, just in case the Cold War turned hot. She argued that criminal activities were taking place on our own soil, that American bases in the UK were accountable to no one but the Pentagon. And these days I mostly think she was right.

'I mean it, Robert. Perhaps it's time for us both to get out.'

As Selina waited for me to say something in defence of our dubious profession, I found myself staring at the photo of my parents on the mantelpiece, a family snapshot, creased and faded. All at once I was a child again.

The photograph had been taken outside RAF Brawdy's main gate. Dad's face was stonily set as he frowned at the middle distance, behind the photographer. I was distracted by something in the sky. Mum, meanwhile, was wearing a smile that did nothing to conceal her defeat. Her anger. She was also wearing a patch that covered her left eye.

On the morning of Thursday 8 February 1963 – ten months before Mum and Dad lost their lives in the Havens Great Flood – peace activists surrounded RAF Croughton, a US Air Force base and CIA relay station in Northamptonshire, and cut through the perimeter fence. Their mission? To draw attention to the deadly nuclear arsenal they believed was illegally stored on the base. RAF Croughton was one of the most important bases in

NATO, and though my father had known Mum was attending the protest, he hadn't known what she and the others intended to do. Had he known there's no way he would have allowed her to go. Trespassing was still trespassing, even if the protestors only wanted to plant a peace flag. Except something went wrong. Something terrible. I remembered Mum leaving the eye department at the hospital in Haverfordwest. Back when the Beatles were top of the charts. I remembered her complaining for months about nausea, vomiting, diarrhoea and weakness. She used to say her eyes were burning, as though they'd suffered sunburn. By the time December came, painful blisters were forming on her skin, and she had lost clumps of hair.

What had happened at Croughton? There were rumours of an incident on the base that night, an explosion of some sort, and Mum, along with the others, was arrested for criminal damage. Precisely what had happened remained a mystery, partly because Mum didn't remember, mostly because the British and American governments hadn't accepted the need for an official inquiry. They were stonewalling. They had been stonewalling for fourteen years, and I still wanted to know why. I wanted to know why Mum's medical records from that night had gone missing. I needed justice.

It was what I had been working towards all this time – since Ravenstone, since I was old enough to believe I might make a difference – finding out something about that night that others had missed. Today was the day I might finally get to the bottom of it.

'Selina, I need your advice.'

She nodded, smiled.

'Remember those military expenditure figures I mentioned?'

'You mean the classified figures?'

I nodded and watched her eyebrows draw together. It was the same look she gave me whenever I suggested us drafting a politically bold – which meant risky – speech for Bestford.

'I'm thinking of using them today in the session. Taking Colonel Corso by surprise.'

She shifted uneasily. 'Robert, I don't know where you got them, but those figures are highly classified. Inadmissible.'

But still evidence, said a voice in my head.

'Thirty million spent on upgrading security at RAF Croughton since the protests! Something called Project Caesar. I don't know what it is, but it's some sort of black operation – has to be. It could help me find out what happened that night. They're hiding something. Selina, I need to know what it is.'

Her smile had vanished. I think it was starting to dawn on her that I might never let this drop.

For weeks Bestford and I had rehearsed the questions he would put that afternoon to Lieutenant Colonel Conrad Corso, the last in a very long line of American military witnesses who stood accused of covering up whatever had happened at RAF Croughton in February 1963. For reasons of 'national security' the inquiry had been delayed again and again. Any longer and we might never have discovered the truth. But now we were finally making progress. If we were lucky, the secret memo in my possession could be the smoking gun we needed.

I tried to make her see. 'Without those figures, all we have to go on is rumour and speculation. Mum would have wanted me to do this. I need to know why she was injured, Selina. I have to prove they were keeping nuclear weapons on the base!'

'Where did you get this document, Robert?'

I held my tongue as she stared at me.

'Does Bestford know you have it?'

'No.'

'Well, you need to be damn sure he has your back! No risks. Remember, you signed the Official Secrets Act.' She considered me for a long moment with an expression somewhere between frustration and admiration, all the while fingering the delicate silver crucifix around her neck. 'You do a lot for him. More than you should – you know that?'

I felt a need to acknowledge the ongoing issue to which she was referring – Bestford's shaky appearances on the floor of the House; his raging moods when he woke from his drunken sleeps – but there was nothing I could add that Selina didn't already know.

'You can't allow his behaviour to go on for much longer, Robert. The risks to you and the party are enormous.'

She was right. Problem was, I didn't care much for the party, a ramshackle collection of loud, aggressive old union men. I didn't feel part of a group, not in Parliament, not anywhere. I was in this for answers, that was all.

Suddenly I felt my heart pound, and deep within my brain the distracting rhythm of another thought began to beat: *Did you lock the office door before you left yesterday?*

Yes, I answered. *I remember doing it.*

But you might be wrong, came the cruel taunt.

Once again that awful, familiar frozen feeling in my head made me doubt myself, to imagine the worst. What if I hadn't locked the door? What if someone had broken in, stolen all our files? What if? What if? What if?

'Robert, are you all right?'

Was I? I wasn't sure. I squeezed my eyes shut and returned to Selina's concerns about Bestford's drinking. I knew our boss was far from perfect and wanted to help him if I could. There weren't many MPs who would tolerate my doubts and anxious distractions. He had been good to me.

'Robert?'

I nodded and tried to smile. *She must think I'm crazy.*

'You know, sometimes I think you need something else to care about, something other than your work. You could get away for a while, go back to the constituency?'

I shuddered, remembering with a chill the loneliness and isolation, the indefinable feeling of danger, of being watched. Even though I had not been back to the Havens since I left my grandfather's farm at eighteen, I saw it clearly. That lazy seaside community, the green hill which sloped down to St Brides Bay, the cluster of houses stranded around the choppy steel-grey waters, serpentine roads clogged with fog, fishing boats tethered in a tiny cove. And, in the distance, half a mile out to sea, Stack Rocks rising menacingly from the waters.

Selina had given up and was again sifting through the newspaper cuttings strewn across the coffee table. My gaze touched her bare shoulder again, the blue towel, her necklace, before skimming over the sensational headlines. One from late December read, YOUNG MOTHER AND CHILD IN FLYING FOOT-BALL PERIL. 'Not exactly your typical constituency casework, is it?' I said, picking up the cutting. Hoping the article would lighten the mood, I scanned down to the body of the story.

> A single mother described yesterday how she and her daughter were followed for more than a mile by a 'flying football' in the latest in a spate of UFO sightings in west Wales.
>
> Ms Araceli Romero, proprietor of the Haven Hotel, said she was driving near Little Haven when her ten-year-old

daughter Tessa spotted a light dropping from the sky towards their car.

Ms Romero accelerated under the falling object. But Tess, watching through the back window, saw it stop and then charge at the car. She described the phenomenon as a yellow ball, about the size of a football, with a torch-like beam coming from its base . . .

'I was petrified, we both were,' Ms Romero told our reporter Frank Frobisher.

'It's a scam,' I said, laughing. I expected Selina to laugh as well. She didn't.

'You seem very sure.'

How many wild stories had I heard about flying saucers? Publicity seekers or people who were just too keen to believe, zealots like my grandfather deriving pathetic self-importance from fantastic tales. 'Trust me. This woman's just trying to drum up some bookings for her hotel.'

That seemed likely. The Haven Hotel was a converted fortification stranded on the cliff above St Brides Bay and looked like a place of nightmares. The children at school used to say it was haunted by the ghost of the White Lady, that ancient smuggling tunnels ran from its basement through the cliffs down to the beach below. But to me the greatest mystery was why anyone would want to stay in such a grim establishment. Run by a strange Italian woman who didn't mix with the villagers, the building, with its dusty Gothic windows, some of them broken, didn't look anything like a hotel; it looked like the newest residence of the Addams Family.

I studied the cutting again. The photograph beneath the headline showed a sad-looking young woman with a narrow face and long dark hair. She was holding the hand of a thin girl with terrified eyes.

Something about that woman . . . A memory almost sparked, connected to the lighthouse from my dreams. Its yellow beam pulsing, pulsing before the image slipped away. As it always did.

'Well, this Araceli Romero wants our help,' said Selina. 'Phoned the office twice this week.'

'And she expects Bestford to do what, exactly? Demand the aliens pay landing fees?'

'She's in a state, and so are many of the locals. There's been a whole spate of reports about lights in the sky and strange things appearing out of nowhere. Not helped by this reporter, Frank Frobisher.'

'Never heard of him.'

'He's with the *Western Telegraph*,' Selina said. She rose and stood beside me. 'And when you think about it, the locals have had their fair share of uncertainty after what happened with the Jacksons.'

I nodded absently. I didn't know much about the disappearance of the English couple who had stayed in the area last summer. Only that dealing with correspondence on the issue had become an almost full-time job for Selina.

'Any developments on the case?'

'Don't get me started.'

According to the police report, Thomas and Joan Jackson were gentle churchgoing wildlife enthusiasts who knew the Pembrokeshire coast intimately. On the day of their disappearance, beneath the morning's honeysuckle heat and the bluest sky, they'd set off for a walk along the coast to a remote beauty spot on a footpath running over the cliffs of St Brides Bay. They were never seen alive again.

Selina sighed. 'If I get this job, you'll have to stay close to the police investigation.'

I had no wish to stay close to the case. 'My grandfather lived near that footpath. Ravenstone Farm,' I said quietly.

I'd had no contact with the man since the day I left home. Dead or alive, wherever he was made no difference to me.

'You've never spoken about him,' she probed gently.

'No . . .' I trailed off. The truth was, I'd blocked out much of my time at Ravenstone Farm. And I was thankful for that.

'What sort of man was your grandfather?'

Cruel. Extremely paranoid. Those were the words that leaped to mind. *A man of nightmares.*

'He had religion bad,' I said, remembering the rosary in his truck, remembering the shock as his Bible struck the back of my head. 'He thought there were hidden dangers everywhere.'

'What do you mean?'

I hesitated. How much to say about the guardian who had raised me to be the man I was? 'As a young man he was in the air force. He quit, became a farmer.'

She nodded encouragingly. Smiled

'When I lived with him he would scare me with fairy tales about fires in the sky and giants in the ground, watching us. He said their faces were made of shadows.'

Selina's smile vanished. 'What else did he say?'

And suddenly, from long ago – the worst time – I could see the wild contempt in my grandfather's eyes as we stood together on the cliffs overlooking Stack Rocks; could see him crossing himself; could hear his rusty voice: *Your father was a monster!*

Dad had deserved better. Much better.

I stood up abruptly.

'Robert?'

'I'm sorry. I need to focus. Big day!'

Before I could reach the door, Selina grabbed my arm and said, 'You take care of yourself when I'm gone. Promise me.'

A sort of prophecy. I see that now.

– 3 –

The journey to work took barely fifteen minutes, but on grimy mornings like this it felt much longer. I walked swiftly along the Albert Embankment through a thin low-hanging mist, crossing Westminster Bridge, dodging one of the new Silver Jubilee buses.

Weaving through the crowds on Parliament Square, I couldn't ignore the weary realism in everyone's eyes. It looked nothing like the hopeful optimism the police said we needed to get through this difficult time. The IRA West End bombings the previous year had left a black cloud over London.

The Houses of Parliament loomed grandly before me as I joined the procession of young men and women filing into St Stephen's Entrance. Parliamentary researchers, we were easy to spot in our ill-fitting suits and scuffed leather shoes – glorified bag handlers weighed down with thick files and bundles of papers.

I didn't know anyone who wasn't intimidated by the grandeur of Parliament; the mantle of history that weighed on your shoulders in a complex of buildings that felt both like a cathedral and a museum; an eight-acre maze of stone where a hundred staircases connected three miles of passages and over one hundred rooms. But today it wasn't the building intimidating me. Under my left arm I was carrying a folder packed full of notes on the inquiry: witness statements, official letters, everything except the pivotal document mentioning Project Caesar. That was tucked safely in my inner jacket pocket.

'You know where you're going, sir?' The question had come from a young policeman.

'Yes, thank you.' I flashed my parliamentary pass and hurried on my way. The admiral would be waiting.

I paced past the darkened library that was my second home, heels clipping on the ancient flagstone floor, until eventually I came to the octagonal Central Lobby on the principal floor, the heart of the palace. Ahead of me and on either side symmetrical corridors lined with frescoes stretched away to the debating chambers of the two Houses: the Members' Lobby and Commons Chamber to the north, and the Peers' Lobby and Lords Chamber to the south. And there, in the far corner, was the stairwell leading to the roof.

What made the roof garden at Parliament special aside from the fact that hardly anyone ever went up there was the view. It hit me now with the same force as the plummeting temperature as I stepped out into it on that iron-cold morning. On my right the Thames wound its dark, permanent course through the city; on my left and directly ahead were Westminster Abbey, Whitehall and Horse Guards, the last once the headquarters of the British Army and the scene of countless parades and ceremonies since the seventeenth century.

'Remarkable, isn't it, old chap?'

The admiral was just a few metres away, his leather-gloved hands gripping the railings and his head tilted back in appreciation of the view. I had expected to find him here.

'Democracy,' the admiral said quietly. 'Whenever I need to remind myself of what we're defending in this endless war of attrition, I come up here.'

He was immaculate, refined – as always. Silver hair neatly side-combed, gold cufflinks catching the sun as it rose over the glittering buildings on Whitehall – the cogs and gears which ran our country: the Cabinet Office, the Treasury, the Ministry of Defence.

'You must be freezing,' he said, scanning my thin suit jacket. 'We'll make this quick.'

'Thanks for your call this morning,' I said.

He nodded cryptically but didn't smile. 'I have something to discuss with you. But first it's a vital day for you. I know that. How are you faring?'

'Fine. Selina's helping.'

'Will she be at the evidence session this afternoon?'

I felt sure she would make it and told him so. The admiral didn't know Selina personally, but he always expressed interest in her work and her relationship with me.

'Still, you really don't look well, old chap. You haven't skipped your pills?' Curiosity in his voice, and concern.

'No, still taking them.'

He raised a sceptical eyebrow. Perhaps he knew me too well. I had been skipping my medication for weeks. The tablets made me feel drowsy and unfocused, but without them . . . that was when the dreams began. Dreams about the lighthouse and the beat of its peculiar yellow light.

'You're afraid of lack of control. That's the heart of the problem. But you must keep faith, never give in.' He dropped a hand on my shoulder. His face was pinched red from the cold. 'Remember what I told you. Keep a tight hold on your thoughts, or they'll take control of you. When it gets too much, close your eyes. Breathe deep.' He inhaled, breathed out slowly. 'And keep taking your medication.'

Lord Hill Bartlett, one of the highest-ranking members of the military: chairman of the Military Committee of NATO, with an impressive office located in the north-east turret of the MoD Main Building on Whitehall. He had entered the Royal Navy as a cadet in 1928 and served as an officer in various ships in the Far East and Pacific Fleets during World War Two, being promoted to lieutenant commander in 1944. But my high regard for him had nothing to do with his military credentials. The admiral was my anchor in a sea of stress. Less of a mentor, almost a surrogate father.

From somewhere on the Thames sounded the hooting of a passing tug. The admiral produced a pipe from his pocket and gave me a sage smile.

'I'm concerned about Paul,' I blurted, burying my hands in my pockets. 'If the fight's going out of him we may not have much time. I need something else to go on now. Something solid.'

'Under the circumstances I've given you all I can,' he said, keeping his watery blue eyes on me. It wasn't what I wanted to hear, but still there was something reassuring in the admiral's appraising stare, a familiarity born of his many attempts at professional and personal counsel.

I found myself remembering the embarrassing day we had met three years earlier. I had just started as Bestford's researcher and, fresh out of university, was naive and drunk on the need to find out what had happened. We were getting no answers from the MoD or the Americans about RAF Croughton despite the scores of letters that I had written and Bestford had signed.

The admiral must have seen those letters and the many parliamentary written questions Bestford had put down about the Croughton arrests and protestors' injuries, because soon after I was asked to attend a private meeting in his office. Although he was forty years my elder, we became friends quickly, and he taught me the value of the long game. It was, he said, 'the gentleman's way', like succeeding in a chess tournament.

I produced from my inside jacket pocket the document mentioning Project Caesar, running my finger down a column of numbers. 'See here, thirty million pounds allocated to a black project run out of RAF Croughton for the last fourteen years. What is it – a secret unit, a weapons storage facility?'

'Ah yes, you've brought me back to why I wanted to speak to you in the first place. This is a little awkward, Robert. I'm sorry. I know I gave it to you, but I'm afraid I can no longer allow you to show this document to Bestford today. Or anyone on that committee.'

That came as a shock. Since I had first been summoned to meet the admiral, he had been nothing but accommodating. He had been respectful of the Defence Committee, of Bestford and my loyalty to him even as he had illegally passed me sensitive intelligence about Project Caesar. I was never entirely sure why he had taken an interest in me. I suppose I might have wondered if he was homosexual. Even if he was, I didn't care. I liked him, trusted him. And his help with the Campaign for the Accountability of American Bases meant far too much to me to risk.

'You know I have always assisted where I can.' The admiral inhaled on his pipe, taking his time, then lowered his voice to a confidential tone. 'But new intelligence has come to light, even since this report.'

'What intelligence?' I asked with more hostility than I intended.

'Something that would make any mention of this money, this project, deeply unwise.'

'But you gave me these figures. They could make all the difference! Please, you have to tell me what it is.'

The admiral frowned and brought his face closer to mine. 'Robert, you know as well as I do that there are forces in this country of which we know little. People watching, all the time . . .' He paused, shook his head, then looked away.

I turned my back on the admiral's stony expression, wondering what he was holding back.

He laid a heavy hand on my shoulder. 'Project Caesar does not exist, old chap. It never did, and you never heard about it. All right?'

It's very far from all right, I thought, fixing my eyes on the Cenotaph in Whitehall. I was so close, and this was way too important for me to fall at the last hurdle.

'Why don't you stay away from the inquiry today? Let Bestford handle it?'

'I can't do that.'

Suddenly he grimaced, jerked as if pricked with a needle in his side.

'Admiral?'

'No, no. I'm all right. You know I want the best for you,' he continued, now walking towards the exit. 'But I strongly urge you not to attend this afternoon's session.'

I turned, opened my mouth to speak.

But the admiral was gone.

– 4 –

Committee Room 10 is the grandest of the committee rooms, all high wooden benches and deep green carpet. Located on the first floor of the House of Commons, it has an arresting view over the Thames, but at this time of year the room possessed a gloomy atmosphere, thick with dust and the scent of political blood.

'Right, that's enough rehearsal,' said Bestford just as Big Ben struck four o'clock. He didn't thank me for the time I had just spent coaching him for the afternoon session, but when did he ever?

My boss removed his spectacles and pinched the top of his nose, and as he did so I recognized the strain in his face.

'You're sure you're up to this?' I asked.

'Just about.' Today he looked every day of his fifty-three years. His voice was husky, his eyes red.

I hope he hasn't been drinking.

'As soon as this is over, we need to focus on the constituency. There'll be an election soon; a new political generation is preparing to take power, and every day the newspapers bring more depressing news. Just look at what's happening in Northern Ireland! And last year in Lebanon, more bombings. People think we're out of our depth. They want law, order. I can't risk look-ing out of touch.'

'It's not just about how you look,' I said sharply. 'This is about what matters.' I could have added, *It's your duty too.*

It was Paul's role, along with twelve others on the commit-tee, to scrutinize the policies and expenditure of the Ministry of Defence. Not bad for a man whose maiden speech had focused on the problems of poverty within farming communities. Since then he had grown quickly into the role of Pembrokeshire's Member of Parliament, piggybacking on the expansion of RAF Brawdy in his constituency to help secure another election vic-tory. New houses were built; a runway was added. A winning move for Bestford and the local economy.

I tried adopting a more reasonable tone. 'Paul, outside that door is a pack of journalists who'll be hanging on every word uttered this afternoon. You must make Corso confess to what happened at RAF Croughton – somehow.'

'Don't forget, that base was made available for use by United States visiting forces under the terms of the NATO Status of Forces Agreement of 1951. Whatever happened at that base, we need to show some restraint.'

'We're not here to show restraint; we're here to make a difference!'

His eyes flashed. 'Our relationship with the Americans. Do you know why it's special? Why it matters?'

'It's not special if it's illegal.'

'It matters for our morale, Robert. We're not at war with the communists, but we soon could be, and the UK is utterly dependent on the Americans. The public need to know that Britain could repel an invasion from the Soviet Union.'

He was right about that, unfortunately. I thought of the

leaflets explaining the different emergency sirens, how to protect yourself from radiation, how best to dispose of dead relatives' bodies, but my patience was shot.

'Their bases are out of control, Paul! They're putting innocent lives at risk. If we don't prevent serious violations of international law, who the hell will?'

I expected him to come back at me, but at that moment there was a rapping at the door. A policeman entered, ushering in our star witness, Lieutenant Colonel Conrad Corso. Bestford stood and extended a welcoming hand to the American officer while I took my seat behind a long table at the side of the committee room, opposite high leaded windows and wood-panelled walls. My notes and files on the inquiry were spread out before me. Every document. Except one.

I thought of the admiral's warning with deepening unease.

All thirteen members of the Defence Select Committee filed into the room, taking their seats around an enormous horseshoe table. John Myers, Labour Member for Lewisham, drummed his fingers impatiently on the table; Joanna Winterton, Conservative MP for Eastleigh, raked her hand through her limp brown hair. Here were my boss's challengers and colleagues. You could see the mix of emotions on their faces as they exchanged private mutterings. Hope. Uncertainty. Fear. In their own constituencies they were in control. Not here. The shadow of the Cold War and other geopolitical tensions had forced this inquiry on them, and there was no telling the extent of the damage that it would wreak.

'We should make a start,' said Bestford, watching as journalists and members of the public took their seats on the rows of benches at the back of the room. Then, with relief, I spotted

Selina – she had been seated on her own, near the windows. She had made it just in time. I smiled fleetingly but thought she looked nervous. Was it the job interview?

'Welcome, Colonel Corso, to this evidence session on the defence implications of American activities on British soil. You are the deputy base commander of RAF Croughton in Northamptonshire.'

'Correct.' A thick drawl from one of the southern states of the USA.

'Colonel, this committee has the power to compel any witness to swear an oath. Now, I assume or rather hope I don't need to remind you that the NATO Status of Forces Agreement requires that US bases on British soil be fully accountable to Parliament and compliant with British law.'

'I am very well aware of the law, sir.'

'Well then, over the last few months we have been examining evidence relating to various United States bases in this country suspected of illegal activity. This has led to a specific allegation against your own base, which, we have heard, was the site of a deeply worrying incident in February 1963, during an anti-nuclear protest. An explosion on the base. And a series of violent arrests outside the perimeter fence.'

He paused briefly, and I felt a sadness so intense it was equalled only by my hope.

'Civilians were seriously injured. As a result of direct action taken by serving American officers. This is the reason we have asked you to come here today. We need answers. We need accountability. You understand?'

Corso smiled confidently, fixing his eyes on my employer. And for a long moment said absolutely nothing.

My hope turned to anxiety. *Answer him, answer him!*

'Colonel . . . perhaps it would be fitting for you to begin with an apology?'

'An apology?' Corso squared his shoulders. His face was heavy and lined, the battle scars of a difficult career, but his smooth uniform and polished medals lent him an easy authority. 'For what, exactly?'

'People died that day – a woman blinded – all British civilians. And you have the audacity to stand before us and question the reason for an apology? Sir, have you no respect at all?'

Over poised pens and raised heads my employer's question rolled across the room all the way to the pack of journalists at the back. For all his faults, Bestford could be powerfully arresting when he concentrated.

He raised his voice. 'Who authorized the security team to carry weapons and apprehend the protestors?'

'That I do not know.'

A wave of muttering swept through the room. My eyes fastened on the nearest window.

'You don't know who gave the order?' The question hung in the air. 'Or do you deny that they were carrying weapons, that shots were fired?'

'What I deny,' Corso snapped, 'is the improper insinuation that US Air Force personnel acted inappropriately. Croughton is a Strategic Air Command base. The protestors were a security risk. They breached the perimeter fence nearest the hardened armament barracks. We needed to act.'

In my head familiar images flashed: Mum leaving the hospital with dressings over her eye, the scabs on her face.

'Then you're saying your actions *were* justified.'

'I'm saying it was necessary to exercise sufficient force.' Colonel Corso was leaning forward, defiantly tilting up his chin, and as I watched him, feeling my own fury burn, all I could think about was the secret document in my possession. How it could make all the difference.

'Colonel Corso,' Bestford continued, 'please tell us precisely what sort of weapons are stored within Croughton's hardened armament barracks.'

The witness dropped his gaze. At the far end of the room a huge portrait of Winston Churchill glared down upon him.

'Our security systems are classified.'

Bestford bristled. 'Then tell us the *nature* of the work carried out at Croughton!'

'The activities of US Air Force bases are determined by the Pentagon. Perhaps your question would be better addressed to them, Mr Chairman?'

Bestford straightened in his chair. 'Tell us then how can the British government sanction the presence of bases like your own when we have no idea what you're doing on them? There is a broader point here, the significance of which should be noted by everyone present. The world is just the push of a button away from Armageddon. Need I remind you that if only a small proportion of the nuclear arsenals possessed by our countries or the Soviet Union were to detonate, the entire northern hemisphere would be plunged into nuclear winter.'

'We all have our fingers on the red button. That's why no one presses it. You're an intelligent man, Mr Chairman – I assume you understand the concept of mutually assured destruction? Bases like mine are the first line of strategic defence, for your country and for ours.'

The pencil between my fingers snapped. How could a soldier who was a guest in our country dismiss these concerns with such casual disdain?

Beyond the latticed window, out on the Thames, a distant siren wailed.

'US nuclear-armed bombers operate from the UK,' Bestford continued. 'One bomber caught fire on the runway at Croughton in February 1963. The day of the protest. Is this true?'

It wasn't. The truth was far worse.

'February 1963?' Colonel Corso hesitated. 'No, no, I'm sorry. I don't recall.'

'But you . . . ' Bestford hesitated, and I felt the colour drop out of my face. His knuckles were turning white from gripping his fountain pen tightly to prevent his hand from shaking. He'd promised me he wouldn't drink this week!

He found his voice again, but it was a shade quieter, or perhaps the siren outside was louder. 'You . . . are the base liaison officer. You *should* know!'

'Ordinarily, indeed. I would agree with you.'

'Ordinarily?'

Bestford then turned and looked at me with some anxiety – a sudden realization surfacing there – and my stomach swooped. Had I missed something?

'Mr Chairman,' said Corso, 'I did not arrive at Croughton until two weeks after the protests.'

Suddenly the admiral's warning about the secret document clenched between my fingers was as distant as the winter my mother had joined the protests. *No matter! Thirty million spent on upgrading your base since the disaster – new runways and secret armament barracks!* I wanted to shout. *What are you hiding about what happened there? What the hell is Project Caesar?*

I was struggling not to stand up and hurl these questions at him. Would I have risked my job and my relationship with the admiral to breach parliamentary protocol and intervene?

Considering the heat of my anger, I honestly believe I might. But it's senseless speculating about that now because what happened next eclipsed everything.

A policeman dashed across the room to one of the windows and pressed his hands against the glass, peering out.

'What is it, what's wrong?' asked Bestford as the thundering beat of a helicopter somewhere above us filled the room.

'Get out!' the policeman yelled. 'Everyone out!'

No one moved. No one said a word.

'Get out, now!' shouted the officer, in motion, grabbing the nearest journalist and shoving her towards the door.

The room erupted. Cries of alarm rose. Chairs crashed down. People were trampled in the scramble for the door.

Someone screamed, 'Call the sergeant-at-arms! Get away from the windows!'

'Robert, come on!' Bestford yelled at me. He had made it to the door.

I should have run. But from what?

I turned. A powerboat was throwing up a great white plume of spray as it carved through the choppy grey waters towards a row of boats tethered immediately below the Houses of Parliament. It was burning. Out of control.

'Robert!'

This is the end, I thought.

I leaped for cover behind the nearest bench and braced myself for the impact.

– 5 –

An iron taste in my mouth. I could still feel the heat from the blast on my face when I opened my eyes and squinted into the chaos. My head was throbbing. I saw the door and wanted to go to it, but somewhere near me a woman was crying out, 'Help me, please!'

The thud of the explosion had pressed painfully on my ears. I struggled to my feet, coughing against the fumes, staring into the flames licking at the tables and green-leather chairs. A terrible acrid smell hung in the air, burning my throat.

I might have staggered to the door, to the safety of the Committee Corridor. Instead, I saw her. The slim young woman in the dark blazer lay on the carpeted floor like a broken doll. There was a deep wound on her forehead, and her face was covered with so much blood that I didn't recognize her. Until my eyes fastened on the silver crucifix around her neck.

Crouching down at Selina's side, I squeezed her hand and pleaded with her to say something, anything.

'What's happening?' she managed. 'I . . . I can't see you.'

'Help's coming,' I said confidently while looking frantically around me.

No one was coming.

'Robert, please . . . I feel like I'm drowning.'

I looked down to see . . . blood, blood everywhere, an open wound in Selina's stomach, and in her hand a huge splinter of glass she had pulled out. I pressed my hand against her body to stem the flow of blood. The nights I'd dreamed of touching her, tenderly, gently. Not like this.

One bloody hand flew up to clutch at her necklace. She hesitated, as if struggling to remember something, then, gasping for air, managed to say, 'Robert . . . I've seen them.'

'Don't try to speak.'

'Their faces . . . Robert . . . their faces are made of shadows.'

Those words, that familiar phrase, struck a new kind of fear into me. Was she hallucinating?

'Robert!' Bestford's cry broke in suddenly from behind me, and I turned to see him emerge from the billowing smoke.

'Selina,' I said. 'We can't move her . . . ' I was fighting a losing battle with the pulsing wound, blood gushing through my fingers. If I moved her, she would die. I knew it.

Bestford was coughing. 'We must get out!' he gasped.

Selina was trying to talk, panic etched onto her face, but I shushed her. 'I won't leave you,' I told her.

I looked around desperately. I couldn't see Bestford now, but someone was coming towards me out of the smoke and orange glow thrown out by the tangled wreckage. A man. I could see his mouth moving, but all sound was dead. I seemed to be suspended underwater, watching his movements as if in slow motion, observing every line on his face, his uniform, his badge.

'I won't leave her,' I yelled at the policeman.

More figures moving slowly through the smoke, mouths forming words I suddenly couldn't hear. Then I passed out, I think.

*

My vision was hazy, my head pounding as I squinted into the harsh light.

Where am I?

In a few seconds my eyesight adjusted, sharpening into focus: bright sterile walls, a row of beds and a strong scent of medicinal alcohol.

'Welcome back,' said a rough voice. 'You had me worried.'

Bestford was sitting at the bedside wearing an expression of intense anxiety. The sleeves of his white shirt were rolled up. His tie was loose.

'How long have I been here?' I asked in a hoarse voice.

'Two hours, perhaps.'

I tried to move and found that I could, pretty easily, but that didn't stop my heart from racing. The adjacent bed was empty.

'Where's Selina?'

'No more questions. Try to rest.'

'Where is she?' I shouted, jolting upright.

He gave me the sort of look I hadn't seen since the day my grandfather told me of my parents' deaths, and a terrible realization stunned me into a long silence.

'I'm sorry, Robert. I'm sorry.'

Selina was dead. And it was my fault.

My fault.

Bestford was talking to me, but I wouldn't listen, I couldn't. Selina, she was all I could think of. It didn't seem possible that she could be gone.

'Robert . . .'

I saw her now, standing in the living-room doorway that morning, a blue towel covering her chest, her hair tumbling loose to her shoulders, her lips curving in an easy smile.

'Robert!' Bestford's face loomed over mine. 'She's not responding, but they have her under constant surveillance.'

For a moment the words just hung there. 'Then she's alive?'

'In a coma,' he said quietly, stepping back.

'But I . . . It's my fault. I asked her to come to the inquiry after her interview.'

'Don't be ridiculous. You couldn't have known. No one could.'

I swung my feet out of the bed, only now realizing I was wearing a hospital gown. No matter, I had to see Selina. She would be here somewhere. I stood, but a sharp pain exploded in the side of my head and made me pause.

'Take it easy now. You took quite a blow. Flying glass and debris.'

Defeated, I sank back onto the bed. A thought struck, and I grabbed Bestford's arm. 'What happened to Colonel Corso?'

Bestford shook his head. 'Vanished. We're trying to trace him.'

'Listen to me, Paul. We need to talk to Corso. Immediately.'

Before I could move, Bestford reached into his suit pocket and produced the slim document I had kept to myself. Only Selina and the admiral had known about it.

He saw my questioning expression and said, 'They found it on you when they brought you in. Robert, what the hell were you thinking?'

'It's everything we need,' I said, meeting his watery eyes. 'Something called Project Caesar, run out of RAF Croughton. I'm sure it's linked to the incident in '63. We have to find out what it is.'

He looked at me despairingly. 'You just don't give up, do you? You're a man obsessed. You've made your mother's battle a crusade.'

'This inquiry was always going to take time.'

'And we've run out of that.' Bestford's face had closed off.

'Paul, this means everything!'

'And we have nothing!' he said, standing abruptly and crossing the room to the window. 'No evidence that nuclear weapons were stored illegally at Croughton, no real information about what happened that night in '63. And I am under considerable pressure to give an accurate picture of what *did* happen to the Secretary of State for Defence, who's very quickly beginning to suspect that the whole thing is nothing but a wild conspiracy theory cooked up by left-wing campaigners drunk on their own imaginations! Don't you get it, Robert? It's *my* credibility on the line, not yours.'

He shook his head, looking away from me, perhaps thinking, as I was, about the long hard months we had spent pounding pavements together on the campaign trail in the Havens.

This was a crisis. If Bestford gave up, how would I ever learn the truth about the protests at the US base at Croughton back in February 1963? How and why Mum was blinded, what had caused the explosion that had scarred her face.

'Robert, the inquiry will be postponed until further evidence comes to light that more convincingly demonstrates the illegal operation of American facilities on British territory.'

'But the biggest clue you'll ever have is in your hand!'

He looked down at the secret document I had procured, the only evidence we had that might explain the explosion that had happened at RAF Croughton. 'If the ministry knew we had this . . . we'd be finished.' He fidgeted nervously with the document.

And then I had to look away as he meticulously shredded my every last hope.

– 6 –

Monday 7 February 1977, Westminster

Only two days had passed since the hospital let me out, and already I was losing control. Out of bed five or six times in one night, just to check the doors and windows. Then I would curl up in a ball on the bed, my mind churning with thoughts – Selina's final words to me: *their faces are made of shadows*, the admiral wishing me luck the morning before the explosion, Bestford postponing the most important inquiry Parliament had conducted since James Callaghan became prime minister.

I dragged a hand through my hair, staring at my reflection in the bathroom mirror. *You look dreadful, Robert.*

Abruptly, I turned away, out into the hallway, away from the man in the mirror with the deadened eyes, but there was nowhere to go. Without Selina, this wasn't home. Every room in the darkened flat echoed with an eerie silence. I needed to get out, some fresh air, anything to take my mind away from the guilt gnawing in my gut, but the front door remained closed. The loneliness was insufferable. My dedication to my work had come at a price; I just hadn't felt it until now. Selina had always said I should have made more of an effort with the other researchers in Parliament. They had their friends, the late raucous nights in Bellamy's Bar. I had my work. And beneath it all a nagging sensation of something left behind, unfinished. Something waiting for me.

I went into her bedroom, flicked on the light. Her bed was made, her clothes hung in the wardrobe. Neat and orderly. Just like her. *But how well did you know her, really?* A large space in the row of books on the shelf above her bed caught my attention. And on the bedside table a thick volume with a brown leather cover. The Bible.

For obvious reasons I didn't like being around Bibles these days, but I picked this one up, and it fell open to a dog-eared page. A passage was underlined, the Olivet prophecy in Matthew 24 – Jesus' prediction of the signs that will precede the end days: 'The sun will be darkened, and the moon will not give its light; the stars will fall from Heaven, and the powers of the heavens will be shaken.' I thumbed through. Underlined in the Gospel of Luke:

'And Jesus asked him, saying, "What is thy name?" And he said, "Legion": because many devils were entered into him.' And again in Matthew: 'The demons begged Jesus, "If you drive us out, send us into the herd of pigs." He said to them, "Go!" So they came out and went into the pigs, and the whole herd rushed down the steep bank into the lake and died in the water.'

I knew Selina had been raised a Catholic, but why had she marked these specific passages? Confused, I went back to bed, my eyes itching with tiredness, and eventually fell asleep. That night I dreamed again that I was eleven, on my knees, hands clasped together in prayer as Grandfather loomed over me. The memory morphed suddenly, the way it does in dreams, so that I was at once in his study and somewhere else.

Somewhere outside. The wind in my face, the sensation of motion. The lighthouse —

The shrill ring of the telephone jolted me awake. I went out into the cramped hall to answer it, reciting in my head, *Somewhere, we went somewhere . . . but where?*

A voice I couldn't immediately place said, 'Can't sleep, Mr Wilding?'

'Who is this?'

A pause.

'Mr Wilding, I must meet with you. Tonight, while there is still time.'

Ah. That American drawl.

'What the hell do you want?'

'To help,' he said quietly.

For some reason I couldn't fathom, Lieutenant Colonel Corso wanted to talk.

Midnight struck as I arrived at the small bridge spanning the lake that dominates the centre of St James's Park. A greyness blurred the outline of the trees, beyond which, across a stretch of dark glassy water, Buckingham Palace glowed brightly through the gloom.

'I thought you weren't gonna come,' said an abrupt voice.

At the other end of the bridge Lieutenant Colonel Corso was detaching himself from the shadows. We met in the middle, keeping a cautious distance.

I studied him carefully for a moment. This was a different Corso to the man who had given evidence to the inquiry: agitated, smaller somehow. The skin around his eyes was stained with dark rings, and the determination that had characterized his face was missing.

'Mr Wilding, I need to talk to you about the inquiry – about what happened at Croughton.'

I was going to say, *But you weren't even there*, except it was obvious now that that had been a lie.

'Why come to me now?'

He shook his head. 'I've held my silence long enough.'

'Why should I believe anything you say?'

'Honestly?' He dropped his voice. 'Because my life is in danger, and because I believe that your colleague, Miss Searle, was injured because of me.'

For a moment I couldn't process the words. 'Because of *you*?'

He nodded. 'Miss Selina Searle came to see me at Croughton some weeks back. I also visited her in your employer's constituency, in the Havens. She wanted to discuss, off the record, what happened that night back on base in '63.'

'Before the inquiry?' I didn't even attempt to hide my disbelief. 'No way! She would have told me.'

'Miss Searle already knew too much. Because the truth is something they will do anything to protect.'

I turned my back on him, staring into the strange ghostly fog that hung low over St James's Park. 'Do you mean the IRA?' I asked, thinking of the car bomb that had exploded outside Parliament just a year earlier.

'This *wasn't* the IRA,' said Corso.

'Then who?'

'Ask yourself who would lose the most from this inquiry?'

I thought about it. 'The victims, the campaigners who went to Croughton and who are still waiting for justice?'

'The Americans, Mr Wilding. The NSA, the CIA. Don't think they're not capable of it. Yeah, sure, suspicions will be laid at the feet of the IRA, but the explosion will be ruled an accident. The truth is, that boat was remotely controlled.'

'How do you know all this?'

'I'm in a position to know many things. About our nations. Their secrets.'

He sounded more human than he had during the committee session and I sensed that he wanted, perhaps needed, to unburden himself. He came a step nearer.

'Your colleague, Miss Searle, was one of a number of targets. She was very troubled when we met and wanted to talk about something she had seen. She thought I might be able to help. She showed me a drawing given to her by a constituent, Mr Wilding. She wanted to make sense of it.'

'What sort of drawing?' She had never mentioned any drawing to me.

From somewhere beyond the park came the wail of a police siren. Corso threw a quick glance over his shoulder before continuing in a low voice. 'In 1963, the night of the protests at RAF Croughton – I have to say your boss Bestford was right – there was an accident on the runway. A warplane loaded with a bomb caught fire. Thankfully, our men managed to extinguish it, but not before the bomb was scorched and blistered.' He lowered his eyes. 'Only God knows how close we came that day.'

'How did Selina know about that?' *And why the hell didn't she ever tell me?*

'Somehow, Miss Searle discovered there had been other events on base that night,' he declared. 'Certain unexplainable events.'

'Like what?' I demanded.

His eyes turned up to mine. 'Lights in the sky, hovering over the forest near the base,' he said at last, quietly but with absolute conviction. 'We had nothing on radar, but these lights were perfectly visible. Just hanging over the trees. I sent a team of men to investigate, and they came back with abnormal radiation readings. Terrified.'

I opened my mouth to speak, but he held up a hand.

'I'm nowhere near finished. There had been bad static on the radio all night. I was alone in the control tower when I heard the noises – quiet at first, just faint whisperings, but gradually getting louder, like twigs or stones lashing on the roof. Then an odd humming noise. And I saw it. An odd light on the horizon. Just hovering, burning orange, like . . . like a fire in the night sky.'

I glanced up. The phrase had momentarily brought an image of my grandfather to mind. 'A star, perhaps?'

'The brightest light I ever saw.'

'Or a planet? Certain atmospheric conditions at night can make it seem as though – '

'The thing flew at me.'

I stared at him.

'It flew straight at me, towards the tower.'

'Colonel – '

'Listen to me,' he said, gripping my arm. 'There was a huge blast of light, and I saw it clearly – a huge black triangle. I had to duck as it swooped overhead.'

I'd heard of flying saucers . . . but flying triangles? I felt conflicted. This was not some wide-eyed believer. I was staring into the eyes of a professional whose occupation depended on maintaining a clear mind. Corso was a trained observer.

'So what was it? Some sort of experimental aircraft? A drone?'

'Every aircraft I know of makes some sort of noise. This was silent.'

'Was it tracked on radar?' It must have been, if it was as large as he claimed.

'No. Radar said the skies were clear.' He released my arm before continuing in a slow, deliberate voice. 'Listen, this was a structured craft under intelligent control. Unreal. As it passed overhead a whiney, hissing sound came from the radio. The air was filled with electricity and the whole place shook. My coffee mug jumped off the desk and smashed on the floor. Seconds later, the plane on the runway caught fire. Electrical systems all over the base malfunctioned. And it was then that the perimeter fence was breached.'

'By a protestor.' I didn't ask if it was my mother, but it's what I was thinking.

He shook his head.

'I don't understand. Then by whom?'

'By *what*, Mr Wilding.' His face darkened. 'It was a man but like no man you've ever seen. Must have been seven feet tall. And shimmering. Silver.'

I wanted to laugh. I wanted to leave.

He held up a rough palm. 'Now, I know what you're thinking: I was tired, asleep maybe, dreaming or worse, drinking? But other men saw it too. The personnel standing watch at the armament barracks. With the protestors beyond the perimeter fence south of the fighter wing, they were on high alert. The thing didn't walk; it floated. Passed right through the metal fence. And instantly all the electrical equipment failed all over the base, a fire broke out in the officers' mess, and the plane on the runway caught fire. The protestors were caught in the middle of it all.'

The story sounded absurd. All I could think was, *Why are you telling me this?*

'What were you keeping on the base?'

'Cruise missiles,' he replied at once. 'Their transporters, nuclear warheads.'

It was the answer I had long suspected, and if I'd heard it during parliamentary business it would have vindicated my hard work, and I'd have been celebrating. Because my mother had been right, even though my father had mocked her, belittled her belief that the US Air Force was using Britain as a base for nuclear weapons. But now I didn't feel like celebrating, not in these circumstances.

'And it wasn't only the perimeter fence that was breached,' he added. 'The hardened armament barracks were found unlocked and opened. The warheads were exposed.'

'Jesus . . .'

'Mr Wilding, something invaded our airspace that night, invaded the base,' Colonel Corso stated in the stern self-assured fashion of a man who believed his actions were just. 'So you'll understand why my men fired at the thing, but also why the entire event had to be kept secret.'

'Did the protestors see it too?'

'Some of them did. Some of them were close to the plane when it caught fire. They were burned either by that fire or whatever the hell it was that visited us that night. They didn't remember much,' he said shakily. 'You see now why our men acted to contain the situation. We had to get the protestors away. And we couldn't risk the story getting out.'

Strange objects in the sky? Shimmering silver figures? Mum had never mentioned any of this. She had returned from the protest badly injured and disorientated, her memory shot. 'Colonel, people died that night. Were injured. My own mother was partially blinded.'

'I regret that. I truly do. But we were totally unprepared for what happened.'

'Someone must have leaked it, surely?'

'The airmen, engineers, scientists, even the cleaners were sworn to secrecy. Their oaths were sacred. Working at Croughton was an honour and a privilege.'

'What happened to them?'

'Redeployed to American bases all over the world. A new

runway was constructed on base, more weapons were brought in, and security stepped up. More land was acquired and a new facility was built at the northern end of the base. Officials flew in from the air force, the CIA, the National Security Agency and the Atomic Energy Commission. The whole project – the event, its cover-up, the investigation – was codenamed Caesar. No one outside the project, absolutely no one, knew about it.'

I pulled my coat around me, watching his words frost on the freezing night air. This all sounded as fanciful as one of Grandfather's stories. The monsters from his fairy tales lived only in stories by the likes of M. R. James and H. P. Lovecraft; the real monsters were the men my mother despised, the men who funded, manufactured and stockpiled nuclear warheads. Men like Colonel Corso. But I couldn't believe his tale. Not one word. Except, if he was lying now, I had to wonder why.

'What are they doing at this new facility?'

'Couldn't tell you. It's off limits, even to me. But somehow Selina knew all about the events that led to its construction. The sightings, the cover-up.'

How did she know? Selina only dealt with constituency business.

'What was she looking for?'

'A connection with recent sightings in your employer's constituency. The Havens.'

'You're seriously asking me to believe that what happened in Parliament was an assassination attempt because of all this?'

'That's what I'm saying.'

'I don't believe you,' I muttered. Although now I wasn't sure.

'I envy you, Mr Wilding,' Corso said slowly. 'You have the luxury of remaining fixed in your purpose to protect and promote peace without ever having to know the consequences of that mission.'

'What about you? You went along with this.'

'I've paid the price, believe me, Mr Wilding. I've lost . . . so much. My family. My daughter. Now I believe they're monitoring me. Watching me. That my life is in danger.'

'Who's "they"?'

Suddenly we heard nearby the sound of feet crunching on gravel. Corso grabbed my arm and pulled me to the end of the bridge. In the grey murk that shut out the view of the Mall beyond the park we waited in silence for the footsteps to pass.

'How do I know you're telling the truth?' I whispered.

He waited until the only sound was of the Union Jacks lining the edge of the Mall in celebration of the Silver Jubilee billowing and snapping in the wind, and then he said, 'You don't. But even now you're wondering, aren't you?'

I knew that Selina had been looking into supposed UFO sightings in the constituency, one of so many odd tasks that lands on the desk of a parliamentary researcher. But she was aware of my personal interest in the anti-nuclear protests at RAF Croughton, and it seemed impossible that she would have pursued such a line of inquiry without telling me. And if there was another link between RAF Croughton in Northamptonshire and the Havens in west Wales, I sure as hell wasn't seeing it.

Studying my face, Corso reached into his pocket and took out a folded piece of notepaper, which he handed to me. 'Miss Searle gave me this. Take it.'

I unfolded the paper and looked down but had to strain to see in the darkness.

'I can't explain it,' Corso added. 'I doubt you'll find anyone who can.'

Tilting the paper into the moonlight, I could just make out a rough pencil sketch drawing of a bulky figure with a square shaded area where its face should have been. It vaguely resembled an Apollo astronaut, but the figure's arms were too long, its head too rectangular.

'Miss Searle, you and Bestford – all of us, everyone in that committee room – almost died because of this,' Corso said. He kept his eyes on the drawing. 'Whatever was seen on my base in '63, I think Miss Searle saw it too. Or knew someone who had.'

'Why on earth would you think that?'

'Something she knew, from speaking to people. Something she told me.'

'What . . . what did she tell you?'

His answer made me straighten. Made me go cold. 'She said their faces were made of shadows.'

– 8 –

'Unexplainable events,' Corso had said. But I had learned long ago that there was always a logical explanation to be found.

One evening in the depths of winter – I was thirteen, I think, or fourteen – and just home from school, a door banged in the wind. I crept out of the kitchen into the hall to see my grandfather hunched in his overcoat in the porch, his gnarled fingers gripping a camera. His head was tilted back and his eyes fixed on the cloudy night sky. I came and stood beside him and saw the focus of his attention, a brilliant flashing white light. Somewhere in the farmyard Jasper, my only friend, my only source of comfort, was barking madly.

'Get inside!' Grandfather ordered. 'You must not look at it, do you hear?'

I heard but I didn't understand. The light was strikingly bright and, by my estimation, very high in the sky. But it seemed to be coming nearer. As it approached I saw that it wasn't just a light but a burning cross radiating points of light from all angles. It was flattish but with rounded edges, and there was no engine sound. No noise whatsoever.

'Boy, I said *inside*!'

I obeyed but only for a moment. My feet took me through

the hall, into the kitchen and out the back door. I stood in the cold and looked up again into the sky.

The fiery cross was still visible, though it had slowed, was hovering. It then moved across the sky, and as it passed over the lower fields, towards the cliff edge where I was forbidden to venture, I had to run across the yard to the cattle sheds to keep it in view. Jasper was at my feet, growling, his hackles up.

Now the cross was hanging over St Brides Bay. There it lingered for a few more seconds, the dark waters around Stack Rocks reflecting a deep red glow, before it flashed brightly and dissolved into darkness.

Grandfather turned and saw me, and I hardly had time to frame the question on my lips – 'Did you get it, Grandfather; did you get it on film?' – before he threw an arm around me and dragged me back to the farmhouse, muttering under his breath about fires in the sky, signs in the heavens and imminent danger.

The next morning, watching as Grandfather trawled the newspaper for other reports, I began to wonder if perhaps there was something to his curious tales. Even though nothing had shown up on the photographs Grandfather had snapped, I had seen it too. I hadn't imagined the fiery cross. And if he and I were deluded that night, so were many more people.

Over the next few days there were numerous other sightings of things in the sky, including reports of a fiery cross from six police officers in Glossop, Derbyshire. In the ensuing investigation the closest airbase to the incident, RAF Chivenor, denied radar confirmation of any unknown object.

I couldn't help it, but I began to wonder whether Grandfather was right.

He wasn't; there aren't any such things as flying crosses. But planets and stars? Meteorites and satellites? Sure, there's an abundance of those. Turns out that's what we saw – a Russian satellite re-entering the earth's atmosphere. It was in the paper a few weeks later. As the satellite's altitude decreased, atmospheric conditions made spikes of light, beams and sparkles shoot out in all directions. Tricks of the light.

Soon after that news report, I formed some pretty strong views on flying saucers. They weren't craft from outer space. They were night-flying aircraft, weather balloons, comets, car headlights, stars seen at unusual angles through trees and mist. They were explainable. And I was extremely relieved, even if Grandfather did refuse to accept rational explanations. I would never be like him, would never be dragged into his wild superstitions.

Selina was similarly sensible and logical, I'd thought. I remembered the UFO reports she'd shown me but didn't for a minute think she was actively investigating them. The issue bothered me as I sat, alone, in her flat the day after my meeting with Corso.

It was Tuesday. I knew I shouldn't have been drinking, given my state of shock, but I needed something to take the edge off. Selina's parents had been on the phone three times that day, questioning me about the explosion. Every detail. And I was beginning to doubt that I would ever again be able to close my eyes without seeing Selina lying bleeding on the floor.

I didn't believe Corso's tale any more than I believed in flying saucers. I certainly didn't believe anyone would launch an attack on Parliament to cover up such an absurd story. At the same time I couldn't shake from my mind something Selina had said to me the morning of Corso's evidence session: *You think it's intentional? Someone making trouble?*

I had assumed her agitation that morning was because of her job interview in the City. But now I was beginning to wonder how close she had been to the reports of peculiar sightings back home. How long had she been investigating the Croughton connection?

My thoughts turned to the admiral. He had first told me about Project Caesar and then warned me to leave it alone. My pulse quickened. I had never felt more isolated. I reached for the phone and dialled the only number I had for him at the Ministry of Defence, letting it ring once, twice, before the line clicked dead.

Keyed up, I returned to Selina's bedroom, feeling very much the intruder as I dragged open the desk drawer and rifled through three or four slim folders, wondering whether I might find a clue here. All I could see was the usual flood of constituents' letters from farmers, residents' associations and charities, much of it demanding Bestford's 'urgent attention'.

Why had she brought so much constituency correspondence to London? With mounting curiosity, I reached to the back of the drawer and found a folder of cuttings, most of them sensationalist crap written by the journalist I vaguely remembered Selina mentioning, Frank Frobisher.

Was it any wonder the residents of Little Haven and Broad Haven were joining 'flying saucer walks', given reports like this? Tutting, I tapped the cuttings into order in the folder, ready to replace it. A face peeped out from a cutting at the back of the pile. The haunted hotelier Araceli Romero. The mother who'd reported a flying football of light and wanted Selina's help.

At the sight of the picture, I felt something that made me wonder, *Do I know her*? I was sure not, but something kept me looking into her wide frightened eyes.

On the back of the article, scribbled in Selina's handwriting, were the words 'Haven Hotel' and a telephone number. I checked the time – 9.45 in the evening – and decided I would call anyway. I let it ring for almost a minute. Eventually, a woman's voice answered and at once I felt cold, exhausted. I couldn't explain the sensation, the light-headedness, but couldn't ignore it either.

'Is that Miss Romero?' I asked. 'Araceli?'

'I'm sorry, we're closed for the season.'

'Actually, I was hoping you might speak to me about your recent . . . sighting?'

Silence. A long pause.

'I read in the newspaper – '

'Don't you people have any respect for our private lives?' she cut in.

She thinks I'm a journalist.

'I work for your Member of Parliament,' I said, trying to adopt a reassuring tone, 'and I read in the newspaper about what happened to you, the light that chased your car. When I was young I saw something very similar, but it turned out to be a satellite. Perhaps you saw something else, some meteorological anomaly?'

'Who the hell do you think you are?'

'Someone who can help.' Then I found myself adding, 'I used to live in the area.'

'I said all I'm going to say about this to Mr Frobisher at the newspaper. And to the military.'

'The military? When did they contact you?'

'Aren't you listening? I don't trust officials, and I won't be ordered to be silent.'

I didn't like what I was hearing. Silent about what?

'Please,' I tried, 'I need to ask you about my colleague, Selina Searle. I believe she had information that could explain what you saw. I think she might have contacted – ' The line became crackly. 'Hello? Hello?'

I pulled the phone away from my ear as a high-pitched metallic whine filled the room. Then the line clicked dead.

– 9 –

My conversation with Araceli Romero had left me shaken. I poured myself another drink. On the television were images of police boats patrolling the murky waters of the Thames. My hand clutched the glass as a thin greying detective appeared on screen. He spoke with the slow, deliberate consideration of a man imparting bad news. 'Although no bodies have yet been recovered, in the absence of any further evidence we are treating the event as an unfortunate accident.'

An accident? His voice was ringing in my head as I plunged out of the flat into the murky night. Feverishly I headed along the Embankment, over Westminster Bridge and found myself in Parliament Square. Across Whitehall, the grand windows of the Foreign Office glowed through the fog.

I hurried to a public phone box, paranoia making the blood pound in my ears. Thank God Corso had told me where I could find him; if he was right, if there was a connection between the explosion on the Thames and the sightings in west Wales, and someone knew I knew . . . well, there was a chance I could be in serious danger.

The telephone box was empty. I slotted in a coin, dialled the number. 'Room 9, please.'

I waited ten, perhaps twenty seconds to be connected to his room.

Come on, come on . . .

A man with a stiff English accent came on the line. 'Hello?'

'Sorry, to whom am I speaking?'

'This is James Stevenson,' said the brisk voice, 'hotel manager.' Before I could decide whether to hang up, he cut in with a question: 'Are you a relation of Colonel Corso? Do you know where we can reach him?'

'I was hoping you might tell me.'

A pause. 'We haven't seen him in two days, and well, he was due to check out yesterday. His belongings are still in his room.'

Corso had said his life was in danger.

'Did he leave a note?'

'No, sir.'

'Did anyone leave any messages for him?'

'Only one message, sir,' said Mr Stevenson, 'from a Frank Frobisher.'

I remembered the byline on the newspaper cuttings in Selina's room. 'Can I have his number?'

'I really shouldn't give it out.'

'Please,' I said, clutching the receiver close, 'a lot could depend on this.'

'Who did you say you worked for, sir?'

'Paul Bestford MP. Chair of the Defence Select Committee.'

It took some persuasion, but the manager eventually gave me the number. I found a pen and a scrap of notepaper in my pocket and jotted it down then hung up.

'Hey! You gonna be long in there?'

I looked up to see a fat middle-aged bloke rapping on the rain-soaked glass.

'Hey, come on! I'm waiting here!'

I turned my back on him and slotted in another coin.

'Hey!'

I ignored the guy beyond the glass and punched in the number that the hotel manager had given me. Frobisher had been trying to reach Corso too. I needed to know why.

The phone rang and rang. I was about to hang up when a gruff Welshman answered.

'Mr Frobisher?'

'Yes,' he sounded agitated. 'Who's this?'

I explained my connection. 'I understand you've been trying to reach Lieutenant Colonel Conrad Corso?'

'Oh, good. You've located him, have you?' I heard the rustling of paper over the line. Then Frobisher said, 'I'm trying to cover this flap down here. My God, since we published that story on the flying football everyone's started reporting sightings of strange lights! I want a quote from a US military source. Want to make sure they're not testing something around St Brides Bay that they shouldn't be.'

Something didn't feel right about this. Frobisher could have asked anyone from the US military about the sightings. Why Corso specifically?

'Corso's spent a lot of time down here, been seen in the Ram Inn quite a bit.'

That intrigued me, partly because Corso's base – RAF Croughton – was over two hundred miles from the Havens, but mostly because it tallied with what Corso had told me about visiting Selina in the constituency.

'If you ask me, the military are taking all this more seriously than they're letting on,' Frobisher added. 'Whenever I dig, the witnesses clam up.'

I asked him to clarify.

'When I approached Araceli at the Haven Hotel – to ask her if she'd seen anything else – she said she'd been threatened.'

'By whom?'

'Some men who came to see her after my article was published, warning her not to talk.'

'Did she describe these men?'

'Tall, dressed in black. She said their skin was like wax.'

A shadowy memory tugged at me. 'Mr Frobisher, I have something I think you ought to see. Can I send it to you?'

'You should get down here, man, come see me.'

Grandfather's craggy face, the scar like a crooked smile, leaped into my mind, and I felt a shiver of fear as a familiar thought surfaced: *Somewhere, we went somewhere . . .* 'No, I can't do that.' I hung up.

Pushing out of the phone box past the waiting man, my mind was fixed on getting home, making myself safe. My world was turning into shifting shadows. I could not allow myself to become lost in them. But I had taken only a few steps before I was halted by a name called out from behind. My name.

Oh God, they've found me.

I was relieved when I turned and saw it was just a lone man, black-suited, professional. Until I registered the serious authority in this pale stranger's demeanour.

'Yes? What do you want?'

'Your attention.'

I looked around. There were other people in sight close enough to give me confidence to fire back, 'Like you wanted Colonel Corso's attention?'

He nodded in the direction of Trafalgar Square. 'Come with me, Mr Wilding.'

I stood very still and replied, 'I generally don't go anywhere with strangers.'

'It's your choice, of course.' He reached into his pocket and brought out a packet of cigarettes. 'But if you value your safety, you'll come with me now.'

'Why?'

'The men I work for require your assistance with a project.'

'What sort of project?'

'The sort that doesn't exist. Not in any official sense.'

We were standing a little way down from the MoD Main Building, where on many occasions I had attended briefings and conferences in its grand Pillared Hall. In the distance the towers of Westminster Abbey loomed.

'But why me?' I demanded, finding my mouth dry with anxiety.

He lit his cigarette and inhaled deeply. 'The project concerns the committee inquiry, your boss, your home. What happened to Miss Searle. We've been watching her for some time, watching you too, until we knew the time was right.'

'I don't know what you're talking about.'

'You will. If you come with me.'

'Where?'

No reply.

'Who sent you?'

'A friend.'

'This is bullshit,' I muttered.

'Bestford has cancelled the inquiry.' His voice turned eerily cajoling. 'He had his reasons. And no one will ever know the truth about what happened at Croughton.'

I should get away, right now, I thought, but instead heard myself saying, 'OK. I'll come with you.'

– 10 –

My heartbeat picked up noticeably as the man in the black suit led me not to the MoD building we'd been standing opposite but to the Hotel Metropole just down the road from Trafalgar Square. We passed through a great revolving door into a splendidly decorated lobby – all marble columns and red carpets. The place was oddly deserted. Not a guest in sight. Not even a receptionist.

The man led me across the lobby towards an old-style lift next to which was a sign that listed a basement, a ground floor and five floors above us. 'Where are we going?'

His only response was to produce a small brass key. The lift doors slid closed behind us and I felt my anger rise, for I was certain that he was enjoying this.

'Tell me!'

'Room 800,' he said as he inserted the brass key into a tiny hole at the bottom of the lift control panel.

My gaze jumped to the buttons. 'But this building only has five floors . . .'

'We're not going up, Mr Wilding. Room 800 is located eight floors down.'

He turned the key. The lift jolted, and we descended into the ground.

Understanding dawned. 'The hotel is a front?'

He nodded silently.

'For what?'

'You'll see.'

I had no idea how deep we were going but my ears popped as we descended. The evening's events were taking their toll: I felt weak and nauseous, and it was becoming increasingly difficult to focus.

'What you are about to see is classified at the highest level,' said the stranger as the lift shuddered to halt. 'What you learn here, you leave here. Understand?'

I nodded.

He dragged back the door to reveal a further steel door, pushed a button, and I heard a locking mechanism turn. Then the door swung open, revealing a wide white-tiled tunnel that ran straight into the earth as far as the eye could see.

'What the hell is this place?'

'This city has its fair share of hidden histories and quiet corners. You're standing in the very best: an underground fortress, Mr Wilding, constructed after the crisis in Cuba to meet the needs of a government and Parliament in hiding. We use it now primarily as a crisis management and communications centre.'

'How deep are we?'

'Two hundred feet below ground.'

Buried alive, I thought.

The man in the black suit led me deeper into the facility. The air was thin, processed, and thick pipes and cables lined the walls.

'One kilometre long and six hundred metres across, this bunker can house four thousand government officials. It's totally self-sufficient, blast proof and radiation proof.'

'Who works down here?'

'People without names. One hundred senior civil servants. Rotating teams. Three months on, three months off. It's a way of life for them.'

I had been in nuclear bunkers before, when Bestford had toured some military bases in Scotland. I had been on three such trips, but I had never seen anything quite like this. As the stranger led me along the corridor, the sheer size of the facility became ever clearer: my eyes roamed from the green linoleum floor, to the gleaming tiled walls, to the many turnings into separate tunnels. A sign immediately up ahead was marked with an arrow and read TUNNEL F: POST OFFICE TOWER, 350 YARDS. HOUSE OF LORDS, 1,700 YARDS.

'This is impossible,' I muttered. 'An operation this size?'

Legends of underground connections between government offices were rife in Parliament. But no one I knew seriously believed these places existed. Something so large could never remain secret, could it?

'The Germans managed it,' said the man in the black suit when I asked him. 'The secret rocket factories at Nordhausen were four miles deep, huge facilities joined by enormous tunnels constructed forty years ago. I can assure you that modern tunnelling technology is more than up to the job, Mr Wilding. Some bases near the coast join with natural caverns and passages, even extending under the sea.'

Why are they showing me all this? I asked myself. *And what can possibly be so important, so sensitive, that it needs to be examined under two hundred feet of concrete?*

A solid steel door up ahead indicated there was more yet to see. And as my intimidating guide proceeded to open it, I was wishing I had taken the precaution of telling someone what I was doing that evening.

Not that I had anyone to tell. *And they'd never find me anyway.*

The enormous door buzzed open. A switch flicked. Rows of lamps suspended from the ceiling above us cascaded on, and I gasped at the sight of a huge strongroom of boxes and files towering up to a ceiling that must have been one hundred feet above. In the centre of this steel-reinforced concrete chamber was a large mahogany desk and an old-fashioned drinks cabinet. The furniture looked distinctly out of place in this setting but fitted perfectly with the silver-haired man rising from his seat at the desk to greet me.

'Welcome, old chap, to Room 800.'

I moved swiftly towards the man I thought I knew, suddenly full of frustration. 'Admiral, what the hell is going on? Why am I here?'

A searing pain made me freeze. The man in the black suit had grabbed me, twisted my arm roughly behind my back.

'No, no. It's quite all right,' said the admiral. 'Let him go.'

He did so. I held still for a long moment, breathing deeply, waiting for the admiral to dismiss the man.

'Did you know about the explosion?' I demanded once we were alone. 'Is that why you told me not to go to the inquiry?'

The admiral came towards me slowly. 'We didn't know exactly where and when the attack would happen.' He saw my hand still trembling and said softly, 'Now then, I'd try to calm down a little if you can. You're going to need a clear head for what's coming.' He turned and his gaze roamed the enormous room. 'You are looking at the jewel in the crown, the details of British intelligence operations collected over decades.'

'I thought government documents are kept at the Public Records Office?' I said, taken aback.

'Oh yes, indeed. That's where they are *supposed* to be.' His smile was furtive. 'These are the cases no one knew what to do with – propaganda projects, assassination targets, acts of bribery. Every difficult decision ever faced by successive Cabinet secretaries. If certain issues were too difficult, too sensitive, they were locked up down here.'

Almost involuntarily I reached for the nearest box slotted into place on a metal shelf, but the admiral's hand shot out and fastened on my wrist. 'No, no. I cannot sanction that. Some secrets must remain secret.'

I nodded, momentarily embarrassed at my own impetuousness, but I couldn't help asking the obvious question. 'Then why bring me down here?'

'To give you a sense of the overall picture. There is much the people of this country do not know, a secret history that would stun minds: Soviet defections, covert operations. You wanted to know the truth about that night in 1963 – what happened at RAF Croughton, about Project Caesar, why it must remain secret.' He led me to his desk, sat and leaned back in his chair, studying me closely. 'I apologize if my friend was a little rough with you. How about a cup of tea? Something stronger, perhaps?' He nodded at the drinks cabinet and smiled knowingly. 'Belonged to Churchill. Lends a certain charm to the place, I think.'

'You run this facility?'

He said nothing, but the answer was in his tantalizing smile. As he lifted his glass, I clocked his perfectly manicured nails, his pearl-white cuffs.

I had assumed that he was a go-between for the MoD and Foreign Office, someone who transcended the endless manipulations of politics. I had assumed I could trust him, not just because he had helped my career, but because he had helped me personally.

It was the admiral who had first noticed my absent moments, the way my eyes fastened on doors and windows, and made me see them for what they were – a nervous condition that could cost me my career. It was the admiral who had given me the name of a doctor I could trust, a psychiatrist with a private practice in Harley Street. And it was the admiral who had paid for the first sessions. I had absolutely no reason to doubt the man, and yet the situation was making me uncomfortable.

'Where is Colonel Corso?'

'Now, now. Knowledge is a privilege, Robert. It comes at a cost.'

'I'll pay, whatever the price.'

'Are you sure? You must be very sure,' he replied, lowering his voice. There was an expression in his eyes I couldn't quite decipher, as if he couldn't decide whether to admire me or feel sorry for me. 'You will have heard things from Colonel Corso, incredible stories that will come to make sense.'

'How did you –'

'We listen to everything. Especially matters of national security.'

Selina had been worried someone was making trouble for us. 'Were your people monitoring her?' I asked the admiral and felt my anger rise as he nodded. 'Why?'

'We needed to know what she knew.'

'And the high-pitched noise I've been hearing on the telephone? At the flat?'

I thought he would nod, but the Admiral's face was blank. 'I don't know what you mean. Our main concern were Miss Searle and Colonel Corso. Weak man.'

'Did you kill him?' I asked.

He gave me a disdainful glare. 'His whereabouts are a

mystery, even to us. Kill him? You might as well accuse me of orchestrating the explosion on the Thames.'

'Did you?'

He met my question with the silence he clearly felt it deserved then said, 'Your committee inquiry risked exposure at the worst possible time.'

'For whom?'

The admiral fixed me with a look of great seriousness. 'For the Americans.'

'Our closest allies? *They* were responsible?' And yet I wasn't shocked. If Colonel Corso's story was true, our inquiry could have exposed a lot more than the illegal storage of nuclear weapons at Croughton.

The admiral motioned me to a chair at another desk, on top of which lay a slim black lever-arch file. 'Have a seat.'

I remained standing. 'Why didn't you tell me any of this before?'

'You had no need to know.'

'And now I do?'

He paused, staring directly at me. 'Yes, old chap. Now you do.'

'Am I in danger?'

'We are all in danger. A great shadow is descending upon our nation.'

'Admiral,' I tried again, 'Colonel Corso told me what happened at RAF Croughton. Project Caesar. The explosion, the black triangle, the silver figure that walked through the perimeter fence . . .' It was madness to ask, but the question was on my lips: 'Is it true?'

'Truth is a hazy concept, old chap. Certainly there was a troubling incident at Croughton in 1963. Events we didn't understand.'

'Then what happened? What did Selina know? What did Colonel Corso see?'

'Croughton was a strategic base for front-line fighter planes. Whatever happened that evening led to events that are in motion now and cannot be reversed. The Russians have got wind of it all and we learned yesterday from a source within the US Navy that the Sound Surveillance Project is tracking a Soviet nuclear submarine bound for the UK. Its current course puts it on a direct heading for St Brides Bay. Diplomatic efforts are of course already in play but the situation does not look promising.' He gave me a piercing stare. 'We need you, Robert. And we need *his* help too.'

'Whose?' I said dumbly.

Silently he plucked the file off the table, opened it and passed it to me. He didn't need to say a word: the answer to my question was frowning up at me from an official report.

Randall Llewellyn Pritchard.

My grandfather.

Overhurst Farm,
Broad Haven,
Wales
Monday 7 February 1977

Dearest Julia,

I understand that you have reservations about my trip to the Havens. Please know that I do too, but I'm not getting any younger, and – having finally learned the true identity of my father – please understand that it is truly in my blood to find the truth.

Sightings of strange objects in the sky continue daily. The locals are deeply superstitious and seem to fear these events. They even have a name for them – the Happenings.

One event in particular has caught the imagination. It occurred at the Broad Haven Primary School and involved thirteen pupils aged between nine and ten. Truly their report of their sighting is intriguing, and according to their headmaster school life is taking a rather long time to get back to normal. Not that Mr Howell Cooper believes the object witnessed by his pupils was necessarily a flying saucer on the ground. But after the event many reporters, photographers and television cameramen descended on the youngsters. Their descriptions vary widely, but the consensus of opinion is that the flying saucer was first seen at lunchtime on Friday, behind a bush about three hundred yards from the school.

The children made some crude sketches. Most gave

the object a classical saucer shape, though others drew it looking more like a pudding, or even a cigar. Some gave it a dome and windows, others a flashing light.

I know you will be smiling as you read this. And as much as I am inclined to look for a logical explanation for what is happening down here – you know this is precisely what I would urge my students to do – I have already promised myself that I will delve into this curious matter with an open mind, even chronicle the findings in a book, if it will find a publisher.

Indeed, I have already decided the title: 'The Mind Possessed: A Personal Investigation into the Broad Haven Triangle'.

I will write soon, I promise.

All my love,

Caxton

– 11 –

I watched with mounting intrigue as the admiral clicked the lights off. He took up a position beside a projector, which whirred into life with the flick of a switch and spooled out flickering images of the remote coastal village that used to be my home: the sweeping beach at Broad Haven, the cove at Little Haven and beyond, St Brides Bay. As a child I'd look at that vast expanse and think, *I'm going to get away. I'm going to be someone and finish what Mum never could.* Now I looked and thought about the lighthouse in my dreams, remembered Grandfather's warnings and superstitions.

'As far as we can ascertain,' began the admiral, 'the recent disturbances in the Havens began on Christmas Day with an unexplained humming sound, which came at night, rattling windows. Locals thought it was coming out of the ground.'

There are giants, Robert . . . giants in the ground. Dangerous beings.

'Complaints first reached us through the 14th Signal Regiment at the Cawdor Barracks, Brawdy, where your father was stationed. Miss Searle, working in the constituency office, would have known about all of this. She would have been keeping files, records. As she did on this young woman, Miss Romero.'

The image on the screen changed: the hotelier with whom I had briefly spoken. 'Miss Romero's was one of the more recent reports to make the newspapers. And while you were preoccupied with the committee inquiry, Miss Searle contacted RAF Brawdy directly to pursue the matter. They, in turn, dispatched Flight Lieutenant Webb, who visited Miss Romero at the Haven Hotel.'

'What did he find?'

'Aside from a very confused and frightened young woman? The roof of her car was scorched, burned with an intense heat, and the car wouldn't start. Webb concluded that Miss Romero and her daughter believed they had been confronted by something totally other.'

'Believed,' I repeated. 'Doesn't mean they *were*.'

The admiral nodded, but only for a moment. 'The following week there came six reports of unusual activity in St Brides Bay. Men in diving suits sighted just off the coast, near Stack Rocks Island. During the day and at night. And then this, just last Friday, the most intriguing report of all.'

The room blinked into darkness for an instant as the screen refreshed. Now I was staring at a flickering image of thirteen children huddled together in the playground of their school. Twelve boys and one girl. They looked dazed. Some of them were deathly pale.

'An entire classroom of children at the Broad Haven Primary School witnessed something extraordinary.'

Every child held a drawing of an object that looked like an upturned disc resting on the ground.

'You see, Robert,' he continued, 'you may find this a surprise, but we have known for many years that flying saucers, UFOs – call them what you like – are real.'

I just stared. His choice of words wasn't helping me. When I heard 'flying saucers' I thought of bug-eyed aliens and shitty B-movies from the 1960s. 'Now please. You're not suggesting that these things come from . . . ?'

'Another planet?' He smiled, shook his head. 'Just because people see something strange in the skies does not necessarily mean that the something strange is a vehicle controlled by an alien intelligence.' He paused, choosing his words carefully. 'But peel away the layers of myth and speculation and you have a phenomenon deserving of serious scrutiny.'

'It can't be true,' I whispered, eyeing the file of newspaper cuttings, police reports and other official documents.

'Would it surprise you to learn there was once a division within the ministry that served as the focus for UFO reports in Britain, that Churchill himself gave the project the green light?'

What could I say? Contradictory opinions were stirring within me, growing, because on the one hand the triviality of such stories after what had happened to Selina was offensive to me. But on the other, here was one of the highest-ranking officials in the British government, a sensible level-headed professional, telling me I should take this seriously.

'So,' I said cautiously, 'what are they?'

'Most sightings can be explained as misidentifications of normal objects, optical illusions, psychological delusions or hoaxes. The rest are –' he smiled at the image of the kids on the screen '– shall we say, rather more interesting.'

I studied him carefully, wondering how this connected with the explosion in Parliament, with Soviet intrigues and the mysteries in the Havens.

'To know the present you must understand the past.'

The room blinked into darkness again. Now the projected

image on the screen was of the front page of *The Times*. A head-line read, DOWNING STREET HIDING TRUTH ABOUT FLYING SAUCERS.

'When the first reports appeared in British newspapers in 1947, a war had been won; another was just beginning, a war on communism – a totally different way of life. The skies were ours to control and protect, but suddenly there were these flying discs that no one could identify, objects which ran rings around our fighters and slipped in and out of radar. Artificial objects under intelligent control moving at quite fantastic speeds. They represented extremely advanced technology, and the possibility that Soviet secret aircraft were operating in UK skies was very real indeed. We weren't the first to put a man in space. If the Kremlin could do that, what else could they conquer? Imagine,' he almost whispered, 'just one unidentifiable blip on the radar. Was it a Russian bomber, a guided missile? We needed to know. For that reason, personnel from the RAF and the navy were asked to submit reports for analysis, which were sent here, to Room 800. Witnesses weren't to discuss the phenomena they had observed with anyone except authorized officials. The most puzzling cases were locked away in this room.'

'So you're saying most UFOs are secret military aircraft?'

'That is what I believe.'

'And the black triangle that appeared over Croughton in '63?'

'A Soviet drone, probably. We couldn't let the public know that the UK's air defences could be breached so easily. Imagine the impact on public confidence!' The admiral was watching me closely from under his bushy eyebrows. His face seemed heavier under the facility's artificial light. 'You look doubtful, old chap?'

'I still don't see how this is connected with the explosion in Parliament.'

'I'm getting to that.' There was a long, long pause. 'Remember when the U-2 spy plane was tested, it looked very much like a disc, especially when flying at the highest altitudes.'

'But the U-2 was . . . American.'

'Well exactly.' The admiral smiled. 'Trust me; the NSA and CIA have played the game far better than the Soviets. Indeed, the US has taken a different approach regarding public hysteria over flying saucers: UFOs provided the perfect smokescreen under which to test highly advanced prototype aircraft.'

Suddenly I understood. 'You mean the Americans have actively encouraged the general population to believe in flying saucers?'

He nodded. 'It was essential. In this Cold War nothing is more in demand than better, faster, more invisible aircraft, but the military couldn't have their own people accidentally exposing their new weapons to the enemy.'

'How is this connected with the Havens? With my grandfather?'

'Our sources suggest that the Americans have been working on a top-secret aircraft, testing it in our skies without authorization.'

'Why test it in our skies?'

'Mission rehearsals. Our air defences are among the very best. They're putting their new toy through its paces, testing its stealth in foreign skies, testing foreign military reactions. And they are engaging in activity that is very dangerous. Imagine, if one of these objects was to crash or collide with an interceptor jet. That sort of disaster would trigger an international incident with unthinkable consequences.'

'You're sure it's the Americans?'

He nodded. 'They've built something that would defeat the

Soviets in speed, height and stealth. An aircraft that flies at ninety thousand feet and twenty-two thousand miles an hour. Soviet missiles wouldn't stand a chance.'

A very unsettling thought now occurred to me. 'You think the Americans are responsible for these sightings in Wales, don't you? That's why the Soviets are interested?'

The admiral nodded and sighed. 'We have suggested politely and indirectly to our friends in America that they should not conduct these flights in UK airspace.'

'And . . .?'

Up flashed the picture of the schoolchildren with their pictures of what they had seen. 'Clearly, they're not listening. It is clear that whatever happened at RAF Croughton in 1963, it was because something with this technology went wrong, and the Americans have done all they can to cover it up. We cannot allow that to happen again.'

'And why specifically in St Brides Bay? Why the Havens?'

With his gnarled hands knitted behind his back, the admiral went to the light switch, flicked it on, then crossed the room to stand before a huge Ordnance Survey map fixed to the wall. 'There are military installations all over the area,' he said, pointing to Broad Haven, which lay under a cluster of blue pins – reports of strange sightings? 'Here, a missile testing ground at Aperporth, and down here the military firing range at Milford Haven. And here, at the top of the bay, RAF Brawdy.'

'But none of those bases are American.'

The admiral moved on to another slide, an aerial photograph of a facility I hadn't laid eyes on since Mum and Dad were killed on the night of the Great Flood.

RAF Brawdy. My home before Ravenstone.

'Robert, this site here –' he pointed to a building alongside the base '– belongs to the US Navy.'

'But NAVFAC is just an oceanographic research station,' I told the admiral. I had reviewed the documentation on the facility myself. It was the first thing I had done when I started working for Bestford.

'A research centre?' The incredulity in his voice was unmistakable. 'Controlled by the US Navy and secured on all sides by a high, double barbed-wire perimeter fence, two lookout towers and a gatehouse? And for something so apparently innocuous, the Americans have been less than eager to share what exactly they're doing behind those fences. They had a fire recently. The firemen at RAF Brawdy went to help. They did not receive a warm welcome. In fact, the Americans denied them entry at gunpoint. Does that sound routine to you?'

I hesitated, wishing I had reviewed that documentation a little more carefully.

'That research facility is equipped with its own generator, its own security force,' continued the admiral. 'The guardroom has bulletproof glass. The terminal building has a series of heavy metal doors with an airlock in between each one surrounded by sound dampers and protected against electromagnetic snoopers. Totally blast-proof, built to withstand nuclear and biological fallout. The facility is manned by twenty-two USN officers and two hundred and seventy-eight other ranks. Believe me, the Soviets have rockets that can strike a target anywhere in the world. And now that they've got wind of what's going on there, Broad Haven is at the top of the list.'

'You look worried.'

He dropped his gaze. 'We don't have much time. Since the children went public with what they saw, news crews have descended on the village. They're going crazy for the story with tales of aliens and God knows what else. They're calling the area the bloody Broad Haven Triangle, for Christ's sake! Six months ago your grandfather told a newspaper reporter that an increase in sightings over west Wales was to be expected. Do you see, Robert? He *predicted* this. And we need to know how.'

'I don't see how he can help you. He's crazy! He thinks they're from outer space.'

'The admiral frowned. 'Be that as it may, we need to contain this situation before it escalates, before he starts a panic. And you, Robert, are uniquely placed to help us. You know the area, you know the people.'

I thought frantically, searching for any excuse that might buy more time. The very idea of seeing my grandfather again – indulging his mania – made me go cold.

'My closest friend is lying in a coma, and you want to send me on a wild goose chase to the middle of nowhere, talking to crazies and hunting lights in the sky?'

The admiral raised his eyebrows. 'I would have thought you'd understand. You're so passionate about campaigning for greater transparency on American facilities in this country, but so unwilling to accept how you yourself can play a part.'

His remark dangled in the silence that opened up between us.

'The parish council has called a public meeting this Friday to debate the phenomena. And your grandfather is planning to interview some of the children this weekend.'

My mouth was dry. Not just because I couldn't stand to think of Randall contaminating other young people's minds, but because I knew what was coming next.

'We want you to reacquaint yourself with him, find out what he knows.'

'You want me to spy on him?'

'We don't know what we're up against. I don't know how, but your grandfather seems to have some inside knowledge about the situation and is clearly intent on telling everyone he comes across about it. The exercise is pivotal to safeguarding the security of this nation, classified above top secret. I haven't even informed the secretary of state I'm consulting you.'

'Have you even told him about this facility, about Room 800 and its secrets?'

The admiral's face remained fixed.

'Does *anyone* know? The home secretary, the prime minister?'

'Only those with a need to know. As you, Robert, now most certainly do.'

He handed me the thick file of official reports, his eyes fastened on mine.

'Robert, I need you in the Havens. Help us solve this. Find out what your grandfather knows. Find out how he can predict the next wave of activity. And stop him from panicking people, stop him drawing Soviet attention. We don't have much time. I fear that the attack on Parliament was only the beginning!'

The penny dropped. My stomach did too. 'You're suggesting the Americans attacked Parliament to hush up what's going on in the Havens?'

'The National Security Agency,' he said, nodding, and I immediately remembered Corso's cryptic warnings. 'They're running some sort of secret experiment they will do anything to protect. And I'm offering you a unique opportunity.'

Return to the Havens? I remembered Ravenstone Farm, the squeak of its floorboards, the sea winds that rattled the windows behind their bars. I remembered my grandfather's menace, his iron-grey hair catching the light as he crossed himself and pointed skywards. I remembered him forcing me to pray beneath St John the Baptist's enigmatic smile.

I remembered all this and shook my head. 'I won't do it. I can't ever go back.'

The admiral gave me a hard look. 'You must, Robert. For all our sakes.'

– 12 –

My childhood was calling me.

As I watched the gentle rise and fall of Selina's chest beneath the crisp hospital sheets all I could think was, *I can't go back to the Havens. I won't.* Yet part of me wanted to go, was desperate to please the admiral. To help.

Also I was curious.

In two days' time my grandfather, the man who had so alienated me with frightful tales of fires in the sky, would interview those schoolchildren, would confirm their fanciful stories, maybe even add to them. Would they believe him? I had to do something.

But I can't go back to the Havens . . .

The window was half open. Although the fresh air was soothing, I couldn't stop myself getting up, crossing the room and fastening it shut. Checking twice. Three times.

I told myself not to panic. Without a clear mind I would have nothing left. But as I looked again into Selina's pale expressionless face, I felt the hollow fear in my heart open and threaten to swallow me whole.

I can't go back!

I focused on the beeping machines, the shallow rhythm of Selina's breath. Slowly reason returned. If I never followed up

on the events explained to me by the admiral, everything I had
worked for all these years would be for nothing.

I had a responsibility. I didn't know whether the admiral was
telling me the truth, if the US facility adjacent to RAF Brawdy
was caught up somehow in the mysterious events that were
unravelling in the Havens. But it was true – I remembered now
– that Bestford had been involved in authorizing the US to build
a facility in the area in the first place. 'It would enhance the
economy, contribute to important research,' he had told the
newspapers. And he had been invited to attend every major
meeting on the deal at the Ministry of Defence. Had Bestford
been hiding from me what he knew about the true nature of
the facility? If the US military was behind the incident at Broad
Haven School, it was possible that Bestford, a man I trusted, had
campaigned with, had kept me in the dark all along.

So the admiral's task, as strange as it was, also offered me the
unexpected opportunity to finish what I had started with the
parliamentary inquiry – without Bestford. A chance to hold the
Americans to account for their illegal activities, to complete my
mother's work, to get justice for the injuries she had sustained
three months before she and Dad were taken from me. I must
go, I knew it now.

I patted Selina's hand softly, got up and turned towards the
door. To my surprise, it was opening.

'Robert?'

Bestford. And I could tell from his glazed eyes that he had
been drinking.

'What are you doing here?' I said bitterly, and as he turned
away put one hand on his shoulder, halting him. 'You know
something is going on in the Havens, don't you?'

He regarded me warily, shoulders slumped, and shook his
head. His eyes had become windows to a dark place.

'It was you who asked Selina to investigate. That's why you wanted to delay the inquiry, why you tore up the document on Project Caesar after the explosion.'

'I was protecting us! I thought Selina might be able to find out more, that we could hush it all up before it got too public – '

Did I want to shake him, punch him? Of course I did. But I just pushed him away. 'The question is, what else were you protecting? What else aren't you telling me?'

He held up his palms in a defensive gesture, before turning to click the door closed behind him. 'Just keep your voice down.'

'I'll keep my voice down when you tell me what I want to know!' I looked down at Selina in the bed. 'Why the hell did you put her on something so dangerous?'

'Until the proprietor of the Haven Hotel saw something I thought nothing of the reports. But that same morning we were informed that strange lights had been seen in the bay, near Stack Rocks Island. The call came from Secretariat Air Staff 2A within the Ministry of Defence. They were extremely concerned. When the articles about the UFOs appeared, I began to have my suspicions and asked Selina to make subtle inquiries.'

He raised his eyebrows in wary expectation of my response. We both knew it was beyond procedure for a member of the committee to instigate such an investigation outside an official inquiry.

'Come on, Robert, get real. Bright lights that fall out of the sky, chase cars? I knew that it was a secret military facility, but it sounded as though they might be testing something down there, something we don't know about. We needed to take it seriously. Listen. If the Americans *are* up to something down there, and anyone finds out, it'll be me who gets the blame. Me!'

'Because you green-lit the US facility.'

He dropped his head and turned to look at Selina stretched out on her hospital bed. His hands were trembling in the way they always did when he had been drinking, so much so that I couldn't help but wonder how long it would be before he ended up in a place like this.

'That's why you tried to throw me off the scent. You don't want to be held accountable. Paul, wake up! We can't give up now! If I can prove these sightings are down to the US military, some illegal black-budget project, it might be all we need to reignite the committee inquiry.'

'Robert, I've decided. These aren't questions we have any business asking now.'

'With respect,' I snarled, 'you are the chair of the Parliamentary Defence Select Committee. These are precisely the sort of questions you should be asking!'

'Robert, really, what's your problem? What have you got to complain about? We're winning the Cold War, aren't we? We're richer than the Russians, more comfortable, better houses! What does it matter if the Americans are storing weapons – planes – near Broad Haven? It's not for us to ask.'

'It matters because the world could end at any day!' I shouted. 'One pushed button away from Armageddon, you said so yourself! I'm half-minded to go to the press – '

'If you do this,' he cut in, 'it's not just the base you're threatening. It's everything: people's lives, a community. Expose anything and you're only exposing us. Robert, that base is there *because* of us.'

Suddenly, I was struck by an alarming thought. 'Oh God, Paul. Tell me they aren't keeping nuclear weapons at Brawdy. Not on our own patch? Tell me that, please.'

For a long moment Selina's heart monitor was the only

sound in the room. Then I found my voice. 'How long? How long have they been there?'

'Almost two years,' he said quietly.

'American?'

He nodded.

'And *you* consented to this?'

'I was briefed. That was all.'

'You never mentioned nuclear weapons! Christ's sake! You thought no one would find out?'

'The Prime Minister had made up his mind.'

'He must have offered you one hell of a bargain.'

'That's politics, Robert. One day you'll realise that these weapons might actually have a useful purpose in keeping us safe!'

I turned away in disgust.

A part of me wanted to find the nearest telephone and call *The Times* and spill the story. Bestford deserved it.

Instead I thought about the frightened children at Broad Haven Primary, Araceli Romero alone with her daughter in the hotel on the cliff. I didn't yet know why, but I was particularly worried about those two, about what might happen to them if I didn't find out what was really going on.

I remembered Selina's drawing Corso had given me, the picture of the hulking figure with no face. The silver humanoid. I fished it from my pocket and unfolded it. I had to finish what Selina had started, but there would be no cover-up this time.

'I'm going to Broad Haven, to learn the truth about what's happening,' I told him.

'The Americans will not tolerate an investigation,' Bestford replied, his tone urgent.

He swayed on the spot, and I felt a flood of revulsion. I knew I had to ignore it and pretend I was addressing the old Bestford, the sober Bestford who had rescued me from a life heading nowhere in west Wales. I faced him with an intent stare.

'Paul, I have been at your side in this inquiry for six months, as I have been since the day I left university and came to work for you. Pounding pavements for miles to plead with people for their support, shoving hundreds of leaflets through people's doors . . . And all for *you*, Paul! When journalists call, it's me who covers for you – pretends I have no idea what they mean when they ask about your prolonged absences, your endless private appointments and periods of sickness. I chair your meetings when you're ill, I write your speeches, I celebrate when you win, and I'm here to clean up the mess when you don't. And when you make your speeches on the floor of the House, *I'm* the one in the backroom, hidden in the shadows, as the rest of the House looks at you.'

I stepped forward. He took a cautious step away from me.

'And now for the first time I have a chance to make a real difference, to find out what I came here for. And I won't allow you to take that away from me. Do you understand?'

'You don't know what it's been like,' he managed to reply, ashen-faced, before collapsing into the chair beside Selina's bed, head cupped in his trembling hands. 'I can't take it any more. I need a break. I need you to abandon this, to hold the fort here. After all we've been through, Robert, say you'll do that for me.'

The inspiring man I had followed all these years was a trembling husk before me. I saw now that my suspicions were correct: politics didn't just take your life, it sapped the soul, made good men great only to reduce them to a shadow of their former selves. *That could be me*, I thought, watching Bestford's shaking hands.

'You're failing me if you don't stay,' Bestford muttered feebly.

'And I'll be failing myself if I do,' I said. 'Consider this my resignation.'

FROM *THE MIND POSSESSED: A PERSONAL INVESTIGATION INTO THE BROAD HAVEN TRIANGLE*

BY DR R. CAXTON (CLEMENTINE PRESS, 1980) P.9

Genuine mysteries are rare, but there are occasions when some instances are so bizarre, so shocking, that no amount of time will diminish their impact. Conspiracy theorists thrive on such events. They keep us guessing and grieving, even more so when the people affected come from the most ordinary of places.

The Havens. A quaint community on the west coast of Pembrokeshire in the south-west corner of St Brides Bay. The Pembrokeshire coastal path passes right through the heart of the village, which in the summer months is a draw for holiday-makers but come winter is damp and freezing and windswept by the gales that rush in from the Atlantic. At this time of year the residents live a quiet life, suffering few intrusions from the outside world.

And after the tragic events of that winter, even fewer now.

The primary school at the end of Marine Lane is long gone, demolished. But its secrets linger. The public house – the Ram – has closed. Only the church remains, but its doors are boarded up, and of its enigmatic Catholic priest, Father O'Riorden, there is no sign.

The faces you meet regard you with suspicion, eyes empty. Because for all the scientific facts about the tragedy, there remain many questions some would prefer weren't asked at all.

Bruce Lawson, who ran the Nest Bistro, a popular fish restaurant, hasn't been back to the village since the events of February 1977. His establishment was demolished just a few weeks after the tragedy. 'You stop talking about it after a while,' he admits. 'People think you're crazy when you talk about weird things in the sky.'

– 13 –

Wednesday 9 February 1977, 11.45 a.m.

When it came, the morning was muggy and thick, barely stirring under a steely sky. Peculiar weather for February.

I put a case containing my few pairs of jeans, walking boots and thick jumpers into the back seat of my second-hand Ford Cortina, then climbed behind the wheel. The drive would take four hours, three and a half if I was lucky. Above me, as if in protest against my journey, a mass of clouds was stacking up, promising trouble.

The drive began well, with traffic flowing freely all the way out to the Hammersmith flyover. By the time my car slipped out onto the motorway the office blocks had fallen away and I was telling myself that my return to the Havens was for the best: a chance to uncover wrongdoing by a foreign government in our country, to help vulnerable people and to solve a genuine mystery. A nagging doubt remained. But then I could barely remember a time in my life when I hadn't been haunted by doubt.

I pressed down on the accelerator, clicking the radio on before quickly silencing the Carpenters singing 'Calling Occupants of Interplanetary Craft'. I swear the irony wasn't lost on me. On another station the weather announcer was suggesting listeners avoid long-distance travel. My spirits sank.

Keeping my eyes on the road, I thought about the Havens and wondered whether the place had changed. *Who are you kidding?* I told myself. *Places like Little Haven and Broad Haven never change. Which is why people like you run away.*

Now I was returning as an outsider. A fierce sceptic. To a community that was perhaps already caught up in Cold War paranoia . . . or something worse.

That the Havens were steeped in superstition I had known ever since school. I remembered the whispered warnings about the mad woman living in the hotel on the cliff almost as vividly as Grandfather's tales of giants in the earth and fires in the sky. Rumours everywhere. Publicans, shopkeepers, teachers, parents – all urged me in hushed tones to avoid certain parts of the coastal path and certainly never to walk down to Monks Cove, where the shore is nearest Stack Rocks Island.

And now these UFO sightings. What had Selina learned from speaking to the witnesses? And how had she connected the events in Broad Haven with Colonel Corso and the incredible occurrences that had taken place at RAF Croughton in February 1963? UFO sightings then, UFO sightings now. Nuclear weapons hidden all down the coast. Were the people seeing a secret American aircraft, as the admiral had told me, or was there something else besides?

I had to know, but as I glanced again at the drawing on the seat beside me of the strange helmeted figure with the blacked-out face, I was certain the mystery had nothing to do with flying saucers or people from other worlds.

I saw Selina's pale lips in my mind's eye, forming the words: *Their faces were made of shadows.*

I blinked to banish the image but it surfaced again almost instantly, the way my dreams had been doing since I'd begun to skip my medication. Dreams about my childhood mainly, the time before Ravenstone Farm when my parents were still alive.

I was seven when Dad was posted to RAF Brawdy. That was February 1959, before I knew anything about Ravenstone or how my life would change a few years later. I can still remember the view as we came down towards Newgale, waves breaking over the rocks and Newgale Hill in front of us. Mother would say that only God could create a setting so beautiful. I loved sitting on the cliffs overlooking the sea, the long hot summers of exploration, the bright yellow mustard field across the street from Brawdy's front gate, the evenings in our front gardens when my friends and I would wait to wave at RAF pilots as their Sea King helicopters came in to land – elated if they waved back at us. Sometimes our fondest memories are of things better left behind.

At school the other children would ask me about life on base. Any missiles? Any secret planes? The truth is, life on base was the only life I had known: regimented, disciplined, ordered. There were times when I might have convinced myself I was just the same as the civilian children, but never quite. Because at the end of the school day I went home to a removed, self-contained life. On base we had our own shops, our own tennis court, even our own indoor bowling alley! No wonder we felt important.

Brawdy soon became the place I called home, and for a time I was happy there. Dad was doing well; Mother found a job working as a nurse at the St Thomas Green GP surgery. Life was good. I began to think we wouldn't have to move, ever again. The Americans changed all that.

They came about a year later, planting their own bases up and down the coast. Mother hated them; she raged about them, was instantly suspicious about what they were doing. She joined the protests outside RAF Croughton the following year. The American bases in Britain were above the law, she said. The Campaign for the Accountability of American Bases with their placards and their marches became her obsession, and she never stopped questioning my father about what 'those bloody Yanks' were up to in Wales.

Dad, in contrast, was tight-lipped about his work, hesitant to speak out like Mum. After working on high-energy pulse theory, whatever that was, he was made public correspondence officer, which he said meant dealing with public concerns, but Mum translated that as 'turning bad news into good'. He was strict, entirely intolerant of dissent. I guess he needed to be. In the military a man's career can be blighted by the smallest mistake. He wasn't completely incapable of relaxing, though; he used to ride the most amazing Norton motorcycle and when I was good he would take me out on it, even if it was cold and raining. I think now that he *needed* that motorcycle, that somehow it helped him believe he could escape.

He did not escape west Wales. He died there. They both did.

In the lead-up to the protest Mum and Dad had been arguing for days about something he wasn't telling her. Some top-secret report he had read and wouldn't share. He said she would 'never understand', that she was too stubborn, 'like your father'. She had certainly inherited the old man's spirit. His conviction.

I thought about Dad shouting at Mum when he realized she was heading to RAF Croughton to protest against the thing it was his job to protect. I thought about her coming home from hospital afterwards, the patch over her left eye and the way she told us she couldn't remember. Even after her arrest, her injuries, she remained dedicated to her cause. Watching her struggle around at home, that was painful. I didn't like the expression of contempt on Dad's face when he looked at her either. 'You don't ever bloody give up, do you!' he shouted. She didn't. And maybe that conviction was partly responsible for their untimely deaths.

The morning of the day they died I had woken to hear them arguing again. What about? I wasn't sure I wanted to know. But I had a horrible premonition that it was about me.

That afternoon bodies were washed ashore in the aftermath of what became known locally as the Great Flood, the result of an unusually wet winter. The police found their car at Grandfather's house and muddy tracks leading down to the same field I was explicitly forbidden to enter. The field that opened onto the coastal path. There was a way down to the beach too.

Why they were out there in such terrible weather and what they were doing was a mystery to everyone but especially to me. Mum had never much liked the sea. She wouldn't have gone near the coastal path unless there was an extremely important reason. Or unless someone had forced her to.

Forced. That was how I felt now as my car took me back towards the scene of this nightmare. I thought I was probably inviting another avalanche of grief but I kept my eyes on the road anyway.

I drove until I began to feel hungry. I had left England behind me, crossing the Severn Bridge. And now, for the first time in my journey, I felt a serious change in the weather. Ahead of me the road stretched into the greyest horizon, and by the time I reached Cardiff that grey had faded into darkness and the storm was showing its true power, sending snaps of lightning forking across the heavens as distant thunder growled.

I was already planning my course of action for when I arrived in the Havens. There were some things I had to do, including speak with my grandfather and find out what he knew about all this. Either he was blessed with psychic powers, which I didn't believe for a moment, or maybe he was working with the Americans, helping to cover up test flights of a prototype aircraft? An equally unlikely explanation. Whatever was happening, I was curious to hear what the children would tell him. Curious too to hear first hand what they thought they'd seen. And then there was the journalist, Frank Frobisher, what did he know?

My fingers tightened around the steering wheel. Would I really have to go back to Ravenstone Farm – where pictures on the wall turned on their own, where something had *tried to get in,* where something had woken us in the night? Was that really what had happened?

Hard to remember. Not surprising, given I'd tried so hard to put the past behind me.

If only I could have remembered what happened that night, everything that was about to happen to me in the Havens would have made a great deal more sense.

My Ford Cortina was doing its best. Port Talbot whizzed by, then Neath and Swansea. By the time I reached Carmarthenshire, the wind had got up to a gale pummelling the car. The headlights flickered, dimmed. I peered through the windscreen into the hammering rain and worried what would happen if the vehicle lost power altogether, leaving me stranded miles from anywhere. Squinting at the road through sheets of rain barely hindered by shrieking wipers, I realized that I hadn't seen any sign of habitation for miles, not since I'd passed the lights of a small petrol station.

Something is coming, something is coming . . .

The thought came from nowhere.

Everywhere around me was in darkness now. A sign at the roadside gleamed in the beam of my headlights. Nantycaw Hill. A steep climb, but there was no traffic ahead of me, or none that I could see. To my right a grassy verge. I took the incline, shifting down another gear, pressing hard on the accelerator until I had just about cleared the hill.

And that was when I saw the light overhead. A globe – a ball – glowing red as it bounced swiftly across the sky.

I slammed on the brakes, heard a terrifying screech as the car skidded on the slippery road. I dragged down on the steering wheel, but too hard. There was an awful sensation of spinning, any sense of control lost. The Cortina spun on, on . . . until finally it shuddered to a halt at the roadside.

I sat frozen, listening to the rain drumming on the car roof, squinting into the pitch black. Finally my trembling hand tried the key in the ignition. Nothing. The headlights flickered and died. I tried the radio but got only hissing static.

What now?

Boom!

The ferocious sound had come from above. So loud that if you'd told me someone had punched a hole in the sky I'd have believed you.

What I didn't believe was the buzzing sound erupting all around – like nothing I had ever heard. It set every hair on my arms standing on end.

What was this, some sort of freak electrical storm?

Thud!

I held my breath at this sudden new sound.

Thud, thud. Something striking the car roof.

Hands on the steering wheel, knuckles turning white, I sat perfectly still, holding my breath and listening intently.

It would have been easy to stay in the car, because that's what common sense was telling me to do. Only there was nothing commonsensical about this event. And curiosity can be our own worst enemy.

Pushing open the door against the pressure of the wind, I let myself out into the wild and ragged night, my long dark raincoat flapping around me. The thudding, slapping sound was louder up ahead. I turned and splashed towards it, disorientated by the persistent low-frequency hum.

Where the hell is it coming from?

As if to answer my question, there came suddenly another booming retort that echoed across the sky. And my car came to life, engine growling, lights blinding me. And still the rain thudded down . . .

I stared uncomprehendingly around me.

Fish! Black fish everywhere. The ground was covered with them, scores of flapping, gasping creatures.

'That's . . . impossible,' I heard myself say over the hiss of the wind.

Something struck my face. I could feel myself about to retch as I looked down at a large fish at my feet. Then another, and another, pelting me from above.

I bolted for the car and locked myself in, drenched and shaking uncontrollably. Switched on the heater and reached for the wiper control to turn them off.

In moments the rainwater built up on the windscreen, hiding the impossible sight of fish falling from the heavens, hiding the sight of . . . everything.

Thick. Dark. Engulfing.

– 14 –

Thursday 10 February 1977, Nantycaw Hill, Pembrokeshire

The siren jolted me from a jagged sleep.

Drowsy, I opened my heavy eyelids and squinted against flashing blue and red lights.

'Sir! You all right?' the officer said loudly through my passenger window, rain streaming down his face.

I wound down the window and saw morning had come.

'Yes,' I managed to reply, looking down at myself. 'Yes, I think so. What time is it?'

'It's noon, sir.'

I started with surprise. And then I saw the fish covering the ground in front of the car.

'Strangest bloody thing I ever saw!' exclaimed the officer. 'You think birds dropped them?'

Is he for real?

'There was a storm,' I replied, remembering hazily. 'Birds couldn't fly in that sort of weather.'

His eyes were scanning the surreal mess. He stooped to pick a dead fish up off the ground, examining it at the side of my car with an expression of fascination and confusion.

I had read that sometimes, during severe storms, small tornados could form and come down over ponds and lakes. I told the police officer this, who dropped the dead fish and gave me a questioning glance. 'You spent the night out here? Alone?'

'I . . . Yes, I guess so,' I heard myself say. 'After the fish . . . I must have fallen asleep.' But I had no memory of falling asleep. No memory of anything in fact, after the extraordinary rain.

The police officer was shaking his head again. 'Bloody weird.' He looked at me contemplatively for a moment. 'And where are you heading, sir?'

I shook my head, clearing the haze. 'Umm, St Brides Bay. Broad Haven, Little Haven.'

His head jerked up. 'You live in the Havens?'

'No, no. Just visiting.'

'Aren't many visitors care to make it out to the Havens in winter. Unless . . .'

A radio was summoning him to his car. 'Take care,' the officer instructed as he backed away.

'I'll drive safely,' I assured him.

'No, I meant in the villages,' he said. 'Take care in the Havens.'

The ten-year gap that separated me from the Havens had closed within a single day. My head was thudding as I surveyed the community that had once been my home. I knew what I was feeling, homesickness – just a different type. I felt sick to be home.

The road ahead sloped down towards the cluster of houses around the bay. The sea beyond was so murky and grey it was impossible to discern where it ended and the sky began. And in the distance, half a mile out to sea, an outcrop of rock rose menacingly from the waters.

Stack Rocks. In the back of my mind I heard Grandfather's warning to me as a child: *You stay away from Stack Rocks.*

Then, on the far side of the bay, high up on the cliffs, something caught my eye. I rolled down the window, still murky despite the cleansing rain, for a better look and caught an icy blast. There it was again, a sharp flash of white light. This time I really focused and fancied that against the background of the sky I could now discern many smaller, twinkling lights arranged in a line along the cliff. RAF Brawdy. But it wasn't a runway I recognized. It was new.

At the bottom of the hill I turned left into the strong sea wind, driving past a small collection of seafront shops – a pub, an ice-cream shop, a cafe – all apparently deserted. This was Broad Haven. The rain had stopped but the road ahead was strewn with broken branches and leaves, which whipped and rolled with the gale. Putting the car into first, I powered up a steep hill, which fell away on one side into a rough cliff. And then, immediately on my left, a great rambling building stood out against the sky: the Haven Hotel.

After all these years the old place still struck me as having an air of foreboding, standing defiant against the elements, but weathered and battered and crowded with shadows. The winding driveway was in poor repair and the hotel's peeling wooden sign at the roadside had been badly defaced.

There were other stories about the hotel. Stories I had forgotten until now.

On many winter evenings the children who lived there would chase a yellow balloon through the woods in the grounds. It floated among the branches, back and forth, back and forth, bright and yellow and shining. Like a tiny sun. They tried to catch the thing, oh they tried, but it never allowed them to get near.

My car rounded the cliff before the road dipped again, bringing me to the tiniest of hamlets – Little Haven. Fishing boats tethered in the cove bobbed on grey waters. The place seemed deserted but for a smudge of house lights through the drizzle and sea mist.

Suddenly a sign of life. An elderly man appeared right in front of my car, crossing the road.

I stiffened. *Please, don't let it be him, don't let it be Randall.*

I was struggling to see and breathing hard. What would we say to one another?

It wasn't my grandfather. I expected to feel relieved. What I didn't expect was to feel a modicum of disappointment. *I'm still in his grasp. Even after all this time the old man is still messing with my head.*

The elderly gentleman who wasn't my grandfather but had still given me quite a jolt was heading towards a small shop with a sign in the window and a red postbox out front. The light from within kindled hope. I braked, jumped out of the car and followed him into the warmth, hopeful that I would find a public telephone. It would be a good place to start anyway; shops like this traded on local gossip.

The bell jingled as the door shut behind me.

'Hello. Do you know where I could find Frank Frobisher?'

The stout woman behind the counter eyed me warily over a stack of unsold newspapers. I guessed she was somewhere in her sixties, slow moving, with a puffy pillow face and beady black eyes. Those eyes were shrewd and unwelcoming, but it was her blue-tinged lips that I kept looking at. *Dead slugs.* 'You're not the first, you know, coming here this week, asking about him. Why's he so popular?'

I tried to ignore the thick scent of musk which permeated

the gloomy little post office and gave her what I hoped was my best smile.

'I want to ask him about the articles he's been writing,' I said cheerfully, 'about what happened at the primary school. Official business.'

The sluggish blue lips parted and her weighty gaze dropped to my stained shirt and creased suit. 'Funny sort of official business, if you ask me. Been some trouble?'

She already knows what's happened, I thought. *She just doesn't trust me.*

I noticed something else. She was wearing a small golden lapel pin with a wheel and the word ROTARY, which struck me as a little peculiar because she didn't seem at all the sort of woman who would donate her time to support good causes in the community.

'We've had quite enough trouble in these parts lately,' she continued, tilting her pillow face to one side. What with that Jackson couple, poor sods! Shouldn't be a wonder if they never find out who's behind it,' she muttered. 'Truth is, they just don't *know*. And with all these Yanks round the place, we don't know either. Bloody Americans! Overpaid, oversexed . . . and over here.'

I hadn't noticed any Americans. Had barely seen a soul, not on the wide stretch of beach nor outside the short strip of shops on the seafront. It was as if the entire village was asleep. But I did remember the Jackson case. The murder of the English holidaying couple was one of the last things Selina had mentioned: *The police are going to re-interview the locals. If I get the new job you'll have to stay close to this one.*

'Perhaps I could use your phone?' I said, thinking about the journalist I needed to meet.

The postmistress, looking sour, shook her head. 'The lines are down. Being so far west out here, we get the worst of the weather that blows in off the Atlantic. Ninety-mile-an-hour winds sometimes.' After a moment's thought she added, 'With all the so-called communications experts we have around here you'd think they'd have found a solution that works by now!'

'Experts?'

Her eyes fell shrewdly upon me as she pursed those horrible lips. Even though she didn't trust me she obviously couldn't resist telling me her opinion on the matter. 'You know, from the base – Brawdy, I mean, across the bay. Those Americans.'

'What do you suppose they're doing across there?'

She raised her head into the yellow light, face hardening. 'Scientists, I suppose. They stay here in the Havens from time to time. Up there.' She had turned her head towards the window and was staring at the Haven Hotel at the top of Skyview Hill. 'God knows why! Place hasn't seen a decent run of guests in years, and no wonder! Dusty beer bottles, threadbare curtains. And you know what? Nothing's felt right in this village since that bitch's family moved here.'

'Araceli Romero?' I asked, surprised.

'You know her?' The woman's eyebrows pulled up.

'No,' I said. 'I grew up around here.' It was the truth, but somehow it felt like a lie.

'Ah, well no harm telling you then. She's cut from the same cloth as her mother, if you ask me,' the woman said. 'There's a reason they buried the old cow in the corner of the churchyard with a skull on the gravestone. She was a recluse – odd woman – that's all I'm saying. And her daughter's the same.'

'Araceli?'

The woman nodded. 'Never comes down from up there, never mixes with the village.'

'Do the villagers ever go up there?' I asked. I vaguely remembered Araceli's mother; as children we were convinced she was a witch.

'People aren't welcome up there, that's the point. If they are –' she added matter-of-factly – 'they're the wrong sort of people.'

'Right, well anyway . . . ' I responded politely, 'if you could tell me where I could find Frank Frobisher?'

'Probably still sniffing around that school, I shouldn't wonder.' Pushing up a hinged section in the shop counter, she heaved past me and stopped in front of a grimy window. She pointed into the gloom. 'Come out of here, pass the Ram Inn, up the hill over to Broad Haven. School's on your right. You won't miss it.'

Of course I already knew how to find the school, and I thought it highly unlikely that Frank would be there.

'Thanks.'

I was about to be on my way when something she said earlier surfaced and snagged at my curiosity. 'You said another visitor asked about Frobisher. Who?'

'Some fella, middle-aged. Some sort of psychologist; said he was down here doing research for some book. Looked like a wanderer to me.' She shook her head disapprovingly and the shop counter slammed in a puff of dust. 'Another stranger. Like you.'

'You're sure you can't recall his name?'

'Dr something . . .' After a long moment she nodded her head in the affirmative. 'Yes, that was it. Dr Caxton.'

*

A gust of wind swept the surface of St Brides Bay. There was nothing I would have liked more than the warm indoors, but I was curious to see the school as soon as possible.

Keeping my head low and squinting into the drizzle, I made my way along the narrow road to the school gates, still wondering what I would say to my grandfather if I happened to bump into him. The playground was deserted, and beneath a red and rusting climbing frame crumpled leaves swirled. Notwithstanding the depressing weather, I couldn't help but think that the kids who went to school here were pretty damn lucky. So much open space! I had been lucky too, though this hadn't been my school; by the time I was living at Ravenstone Farm, I was walking two miles each day to catch the bus to Haverfordwest. I felt a sad smile on my lips, scanned my surroundings in quiet appreciation: the small sports field flanking the tarmacked recreational area, the folds of land beyond, breaking into crests of fields.

'Yes? Can I help you?'

The grey-haired woman emerging from the main school building had her arms folded defensively across her chest.

Why is everyone here so guarded?

I strode over to her and said cheerfully, 'Robert Wilding. Hello.' The chances of catching Frobisher here were slim, so I asked for the headmaster instead.

I don't know what I was expecting – words of welcome, a smile, a handshake at least – but at first she said nothing, merely looking me up and down through her spectacles.

'Wilding?' she asked pointedly.

'Yes, from the office of Paul Bestford, MP.' I gave her a reassuring smile.

She met it with a disdainful look, as if amazed that someone my age could be working in the House of Commons. Then she nodded and said, 'Come with me.'

Already feeling deeply unwelcome, I followed her down a bright corridor lined with wooden benches and pegs for hanging coats, passing the assembly hall and heading towards a door plastered with children's paintings.

From the instant I entered the classroom, with its scratched desks spotted with ink and its diminutive ladder-back chairs, I felt like Gulliver in Lilliput.

'Where are the children?' I asked.

'School's closed today on account of the storm. I'm Delyth Cale, classroom assistant. Wait here, please.'

She disappeared for a minute and returned with an older gentleman who looked every bit the headmaster. A tall man with a narrow studious face. 'Howell Cooper, hello.'

His handshake was firm, too firm. And although he greeted me with a confident smile, I did not feel the same confidence when I looked through his horn-rimmed spectacles and into his eyes. They were hard eyes, scheming and quick. I think it was those eyes that prevented me explaining my childhood connection to the area. Remembering why I'd come to the school in the first place, I explained my interest in recent events.

I thought of telling him that I'd quit Parliament – remembering how many of the locals didn't see eye to eye with Bestford – but I didn't think Cooper looked the sort of headmaster who would take kindly to a stranger admitting to calling at his school under false pretences. 'I'd be glad to know the details of the sighting and to help – if I can.'

'Help?' Cooper let the word hang between us as he reached into an open drawer and withdrew a half-empty packet of cigarettes. He gestured at me to sit with him at the imposing desk at the top of the classroom. With the scratch of a match, his cigarette was glowing and he was inhaling deeply.

'Do you know,' he said eventually, 'how long I have worked in this school?'

His dark moustache and side-parted grey hair made him difficult to age. Seeing my hesitation, he said, 'Thirty-two years, Mr Wilding. I must have been near your own age when I became a teacher.' Those hard eyes swivelled over my shoulder. 'And in all that time I thought I'd seen it all, heard it all, learned the ways of children.'

He shook his head and straightened against the back of his chair. 'Well, I'll tell you this: I've learned enough. Enough to know when a child is lying.'

His gaze fastened on me, and with unmistakable solemnity, he said, 'Mr Wilding, I hope you have an open mind.'

– 15 –

Broad Haven Primary School, Marine Lane, 2 p.m.

The story was as remarkable and unusual as any I had encountered. Cooper had been in his study preparing a letter concerning the forthcoming parents' evening. From the playground he heard familiar sounds: squeals and laughter and playful taunts. The *thump* of a booted football, the rhythmic *thwack* of a skipping rope. Then, nothing. He knew most of the school was on a trip to the local caves, but even so thirteen kids can make a lot of noise. And now there was none. He hadn't heard the bell ring. Why were the children suddenly so quiet? He checked his watch – there were still ten minutes of lunch break remaining.

Rising from his desk, he went to the window, peering out into the drizzle. And felt panic surge through him.

'It's like all your worst nightmares coming true at once,' he told me. 'I couldn't believe what I was seeing.'

The playground was empty.

'You didn't imagine the kids had come inside to play?'

'I would have heard them! I stood here in my office staring out over the playground for perhaps ten seconds or more, before the door behind me burst open and in stumbled little Tessa, bawling her eyes out. "Sir, sir –" she was crying "– please, you must come and see. Now!"

'I thought there had been an accident or something. I crouched down, over there by the door, gripped her shoulders and looked her straight in the eye and asked her what was wrong. But she just kept crying and pulling at my arm and begging me to go and see. Well, what else could I do?

'She led me out around the back of the main school building, facing the hill, and that's when I saw twelve of the boys, running towards me, hysterical. I held my hands up and told them to stop, to get in line. But they bolted right past me. I found them in the classroom, Mr Wilding. Cowering at their desks, crying.'

He hesitated then, frowned, and I saw I had a way to go before winning his trust.

'Tell me the rest, sir. Discretion is my forte.'

After a few moments he nodded, rose and led me to the nearest window. 'It seems one of the boys spotted something moving in the field up there near a telegraph pole.' He was pointing to a gap in the hedge between the school and an adjoining field which rose steeply. 'The boys had some difficuly getting nearer because of a stream on the other side. But they all claimed to have a good view of the . . . object.'

'Why weren't these kids on the school trip?'

'Oh, various reasons,' he said hastily. 'Now when the children described the object, I couldn't accept it. Wouldn't accept it. So I separated each child and asked them to draw what they had seen.'

'Very sensible,' I said. 'And the results varied hugely, I suppose?'

'On the contrary.' The headmaster's eyes sharpened, and after a brief moment he reached for a large paper folder, opened it and drew out the pictures, presenting them in a line on the tops of a row of desks.

For a moment I could hardly believe what I was looking at. My surroundings – the classroom, the moan of the wind outside, even Mr Cooper – seemed to withdraw. Thirteen drawings. Each near identical.

'Tell me, Mr Wilding,' said the headmaster, 'what does that look like to you?'

I studied every drawing, transfixed by their similarities. In every one something silver and cigar-shaped was resting on the ground. There were some variations, but in most of the pictures the object had a central dome with a light on top.

That the children had seen something I had little doubt, but what was it? I knew what it *appeared* to be but couldn't accept that. There had to be a better explanation, a rational explanation, and if I was to find out what it was, I needed to see the landing site myself.

'Do you think you can show me the place where they saw it?' I asked the headmaster.

He looked momentarily startled then adopted a more composed expression. 'Really, Mr Wilding, I hardly think now is a good time.'

'Now's the perfect time!' I cut in, peering out into the wet weather. 'If that craft left anything behind – tread marks, imprints, *anything* – it needs to be protected.'

But Mr Cooper was shaking his head. 'We must keep this as quiet as we can, Mr Wilding. There's been some concern over the potential threat to the public from these UFOs. Father O'Riorden has called a public meeting for tomorrow night. It's not easy running a school at the best of times, but in the last few days we've been besieged by journalists, television crews. If you took this information back with you and news got out in London that . . . Well, it would be a circus and make my job impossible. No more, you understand!'

Memories flashed: Room 800 and the boxes of files deep beneath the Hotel Metropole, the speedboat powering its way towards Parliament, Selina in her hospital bed. I imagined her here now, what she'd say to me: *You must find out what they saw.*

'This is bigger than you,' I said to Mr Cooper. 'Perhaps bigger than all of us.'

I said goodbye. As I strode across the playground Delyth Cale caught up with me, full of concern. 'I really wish you hadn't upset him; he's struggling to hold things together. I worry about him. He's been so distant these last few weeks. They make such demands on him.'

'You mean the children?'

She looked bewildered at the question but nodded without any hesitation.

I stopped as we reached the end of the tarmac and looked her straight in the eye. 'Where were you when it happened?'

I heard her take a deep sigh.

'Were you in the playground? Did you see it?

An expectant silence opened between us and I saw undisclosed thoughts crowding her eyes. 'Tell me, please.'

'I know that spot well,' she replied finally. I noticed that she didn't look at the place in question directly, but rather flicked glances at it from the corners of her eyes. 'I walk there frequently. There's a sewage works up there . . .'

'Then perhaps they saw a tanker or some other industrial vehicle?'

She just looked at me, raising her chin. I tried to decipher the expression on her face. Reluctance? No, more than that. She looked frightened. 'You saw it, didn't you?' I asked.

'You must understand that I have to live in this village,' she said in a low, taut voice. 'You can just walk away, while the rest of us suffer.'

'Suffer? It's not as bad as all that, surely?'

She glanced at the sky, then shot me a cold glare. 'You're not going to give up, are you?' Finally she nodded and said quietly, 'Very well. I was talking to one of the chefs in the kitchen and came out of the school by the side door, there.' She pointed back at the building. 'I was facing the field, and I saw the children who hadn't gone on the school trip huddled in a group, up at the top of the hill. Then something shiny caught my eye.' She took a breath and I watched her eyes scan the field. Whatever she had seen, she was seeing it again now. 'It was a large object, oval shaped, with a slight dome. The colour of metal. The whole thing was sharply defined. There were ridges on its surface.' Her eyes were bulging now, and her head was shaking as if the gesture could deny this recollection. 'It was just sitting there in the rain. And then it glided away, into the trees.'

'That's it?' I pressed her.

She nodded quickly. But although she maintained eye contact I could see she was trying hard not to blink.

'Were there any people around? Controlling it, or nearby? Please, whatever you tell me, I promise it will go no further.'

'I saw *something*,' she said reluctantly. 'A strange figure with a blacked-out face. Dressed in silver.'

'How long was it in view?'

'Seconds. It appeared rather suddenly from behind the trees, then climbed into the machine through an opening in its side.'

I scanned the marshy little field, most of which was hidden by banks of fog.

'Please, Mr Wilding, leave it. For all our sakes.'

A fence and a rapidly flowing stream would prevent me from accessing the field with ease, but I wasn't about to let them stop me. I gave her once last glance, then climbed over the fence and peered into the wet gloom.

In five minutes I had made it to the top of the field and the telegraph pole next to which the children had seen the silver object appear.

I looked around the slope for any sign that something had been there, but there was nothing. No tracks, no prints of tyres. Directly behind me was a hedgerow, beyond which lay a narrow road. Mounting the stile in the hedge, I immediately saw the sewage works that Mrs Cale had mentioned. I crossed the road and headed towards them. There was no one about, so I rattled the gates until a man in overalls appeared.

'Did you have a tanker down in that field?' I asked him through the fence.

'Why would we have a tanker down there?' He laughed and shook his head at the idea.

No reason. And anyway the children who saw the anomalous object were mostly from farming backgrounds. They would have recognized a tanker, surely?

'I know why you're asking,' the workman continued. 'I saw the news. If you ask me, those kids are having a game.'

I thanked him and returned to the field, squelching through the glutinous sludge. Even if a tanker had been able to get in there, there was no way it would have got out again.

I was about to return to the school in the valley below when something caught my eye. I craned my neck for a better look, squinting against the freezing drizzle at the telegraph pole. The metal support beam at the top of the pole was bent, almost as if something had . . .

Crashed into it.

The thought had barely occurred to me before another boom, like the crash I had heard the night before, shook the heavens, unleashing pelting rain upon me. I turned. At the doorway to the school the headmaster was standing with his hands clasped behind his back.

Watching.

– 16 –

By the time I had made my way back to Little Haven, the Atlantic mist was spreading hungrily into the village and its huddled maze of pastel cottages.

I parked on the seafront, where the sea thudded in and sprayed up against the sea wall. The postmistress was crossing the road and she granted me a weak smile, tinged blue. *Lips like dead slugs*, I thought again. That smile didn't fool me. Not for a second. Already the strangeness was reverberating around this small community, and the villagers, conservative and God-fearing, could hardly conceal their suspicion of outsiders. I had been gone so long I might as well have been a stranger.

Did the past whisper to the locals as it whispered to me? Did they share my apprehension about this place? Probably, even if they did choose to make their homes here. Maybe they'd convinced themselves that every coastal village felt like this. And maybe they were right. But I doubted it. There were a great many sinister places around the Havens, abandoned forts and lone caverns, coves flanking the wild and unpredictable sea. Even in summer, when sunlit clouds gleamed and shadows grew long, these villages could feel dangerous.

For me that danger had been there since the freezing

currents had flooded the Havens in December '63. I'd never forget. Couldn't forget. A blackness once more fell over me. In my mind I was eleven years old, staring vacantly at the funeral cards on Grandfather's mantelpiece.

I flinched as another pulse of swell crashed in and the water sprayed up.

Hastily I decided to seek refuge in the Ram Inn, partly because I was hoping to find Frobisher, mostly because I wanted to escape the snapping cold. Two elderly men near the fire exchanged sharp glances the instant I closed the door on the chill afternoon air, and as I perched shivering at the bar a muffled silence filled the room.

'Afternoon, gentlemen.' I attempted a smile around the room.

They didn't smile back, just hunched further over their pints.

The landlord looked flushed and weary as he wiped the polished oak bar. He was a thin man with a wasted face and shiny bald head. Behind him an upside-down horseshoe hung on the wall, flanked by several grainy black-and-white photos of what appeared to be flying saucers.

'What'll it be?' the landlord asked.

I hadn't ordered my Guinness before a ragged boom shook the building. Bottles rattled and somewhere a glass smashed. I jumped down off my stool.

'What the hell was that?'

It had come from the sky, a startling roar of . . . something. Yet the landlord, to my amazement, seemed quite unconcerned. So did the middle-aged chap sitting a few stools away from me, staring down at a newspaper.

'That was the worst one in a while,' the man said without looking up. 'We're calling it the sky quake.' He nodded, turned the page of his paper and continued. 'Some sort of sonic boom, if you ask me. Another in a long list of military experiments they're not telling us about.'

Dark hair with just a few grey hairs beginning to show. He was a well built man no older than forty-five. I went and sat next to him. His pint glass was almost empty.

'You want another?' I asked.

'Sure.' He looked up and stuck out his hand. 'Frank Frobisher.' *Success!* 'From the *Western Telegraph*?'

He nodded, smiling as if pleased to be recognized. 'You must be Robert Wilding. We spoke on the phone. So you couldn't keep away, eh? And where's our MP? Not interested in what's been going on down here, eh? In "the Happenings".' He nodded at the blurry photographs on the wall behind the bar. I thought they looked like hubcaps. By the grin on Frobisher's face I'm pretty sure he thought the same, but his tone implied criticism of my former boss that I suspected was widespread in the constituency.

'I suppose you could say I'm here on Bestford's behalf,' I lied.

Frobisher was instantly alert. 'So there's *official* interest now?'

I hesitated, mind racing, and decided to backtrack before I said something I regretted. I gave the journalist what I hoped was my most sincere expression. 'No, no. Nothing that grand. I take a . . . personal interest. I grew up here.'

Admitting this to Frobisher made me feel nauseous. I had hoped to tell as few people as possible about my connections with the area. I felt as if just talking about them might bring the bad wolf of memory to my door.

He looked at me for a moment with a curious expression, then nodded and lifted his pint. 'So, you coming to the public meeting tomorrow?'

Just try to keep me away. I shrugged, feigning nonchalance. 'Perhaps. Where is it?'

'School hall,' Frobisher said, still looking at me. 'You should come. Just don't stay here too long. This place –' he shook his head – 'it's the bloody graveyard of ambition.'

'You ever think about leaving?'

'Me?' He shifted on his stool, his eyebrows lifting. 'Where would I go?'

'I don't know – Cardiff, Bristol, London?'

'Nah.' He dipped his head. 'Too late for me. You need a bloody degree these days to be anyone on Fleet Street. What have I got? Twenty-four years on the local paper. Twenty-four years of town meetings, funerals, weddings and fetes.' He smiled with a hint of sadness. 'I've enjoyed it – big fish in a small pond and all that – but what about you? Enjoy London?'

I thought about that. What was enjoyable about never having enough time to finish my work, always fighting with tourists for space on the Tube, never having enough money to keep up with the other researchers? 'Sure, it's fine.' I paused. 'When the place isn't on high security alert.'

He understood immediately. 'Hell of a thing. Could have been a lot worse too. Were you in Parliament when it happened?'

I blinked and the memories leaped up onto the black screen of my closed eyes. 'Yeah, I was there.'

'You reckon they'll catch who did it?'

'They will,' I said, although after my discussion with the admiral I privately felt it was unlikely. If my long-time mentor's assessment of the attack on Parliament was correct – if the Americans were responsible – that was a line of inquiry that would lead nowhere. *The NSA, the CIA. Don't think they're not capable of it.* But I still wasn't convinced. Extraordinary claims required extraordinary evidence.

Suddenly, the reason why I was there – why I had sought out

Frank Frobisher – came back to me in a rush. 'Mr Frobisher,' I began, choosing my words carefully, 'Lieutenant Colonel Corso was a witness at the recent parliamentary inquiry. You were trying to reach him recently at his hotel in London. Can I ask why?

'Sure. With everything that's been going on around here, I wanted to know why American soldiers were meeting the staff of our local MP.'

'You mean Selina Searle?'

He nodded. 'They met in this very pub.'

'What's odd about that?' I asked. 'The Americans are a vital part of the local economy. You'd expect them to talk to the local MP's staff, wouldn't you?'

'But Colonel Corso wasn't based here in Wales. He was based at Croughton. That's over two hundred miles away. So what was he doing down here?'

I had asked myself the very same thing. I kept my mouth shut.

Frobisher smiled. 'It's always worth asking questions, that's my opinion. And anyway there's a lot of suspicion about the American facility – about the work they're doing up there . . .' He allowed the words to hang between us.

I rushed to fill the silence. 'You think that's what people have been seeing in the sky? American aircraft?'

'It's possible.' He lowered his voice. 'You know the airspace above Brawdy has been completely restricted since the Americans moved in?' I didn't know that. 'No one's allowed near,' he added. 'Which is why I've tried. Many times.'

'Seen anything strange?'

'The runway lights flash on, an aircraft leaves the ground. Seconds later the base is in darkness again. Complete blackout.

You don't see much – just flickers of activity at night, if you're lucky. I've been out to the base three times now. Twice I've seen something, almost as though they've been expecting me. Tuesday and Friday nights. Around ten thirty.'

This was a lot of information for a stranger to offer me; so much that I had to wonder if he was trying to influence me. I'd met too many journalists not to be wise to their crafty ways.

'Did you ask Selina about her meeting with Corso?'

'Oh yeah, I asked, but like everyone else she didn't want to talk. Listen.' He cast a furtive glance towards the men by the fire. 'What do you think is really going on down here?'

I smiled. I liked Frobisher, but I sure as hell wasn't ready to tip off a journalist that nuclear weapons were stored nearby. Not until I had the facts.

'I'm interested in something you said on the phone – the single mother you interviewed, the woman who runs the Haven Hotel.'

'Araceli Romero?'

I nodded. 'You told me on the phone that she was threatened by someone.'

He nodded, pulling a frown. 'She told me about a globe of light that had chased her car – terrified her and her little one half to death – then, when I phoned her a few days later to follow up, she clammed up. She's a strange one,' he added flatly. 'Bit of a recluse, like her mother.'

'What happened to her mother?'

'Died some years back. Left Araceli with a shitload of debt.'

'What about her father?'

'Dunno, some aristocrat. Not been seen in decades.'

'So she's all alone up there?'

'She and her little girl.'

I hesitated, remembering the overgrown driveway that led up to the rambling Haven Hotel.

Frobisher looked me straight in the eye. 'Shit, you're not thinking of staying there?'

'I was hoping I might.'

His eyes widened. 'Why the hell would you want to stay *there*? Bad atmosphere. You know they say it was built on ley lines? They say it's haunted.'

'"They say".' I smiled.

Behind the bar the landlord – eavesdropping – caught my eye then returned his attention to the pint glass he was wiping. He was making me feel uneasy.

'When I was young people used to gossip about Araceli's mother. Do you know what they used to say?'

'Yeah. She lived up there for thirty years and rarely came down into the village. The stories about that woman used to scare me,' I added. 'My parents would drive me to this pub every Friday, after my father has finished work on base, and I'd hear people gossiping about the mad woman on the hill. We'd sit just over there.' I nodded towards the fire, where I could see the ghosts of my parents in memory. 'Just stories . . .'

'They still live around here, your parents?'

I told him then of their mystifying deaths.

'God, I'm sorry,' Frobisher said. I saw that he meant it. 'Too many died that night. But what were they doing up the cliffs?'

'Wish I knew.'

'And what did you do afterwards?'

'Went to live with my grandfather.' I drained my pint and leaned forward. My moment had come. 'Mr Frobisher, is it true that you and Randall Llewellyn Pritchard were the first to visit the landing site at the school?'

Understanding broke over Frobisher's pleasant face. 'Wait, *Randall* is your grandfather?'

I nodded.

'OK. Now I see why you're interested in all this. Sorry. I should have made the connection. I knew Randall had a grandson who worked for Bestford. Sure, I went with him to the school. He was pretty insistent, said there was no way the children were making it up, thought if we were lucky we'd find evidence of what had been there. Nothing. It's as if whatever it was had never been there.'

'I understand my grandfather told you that he had predicted this wave of recent sightings. How is that possible?'

Frobisher frowned again. 'More likely he made an educated guess. There have always been strange goings-on in the Havens. I'm not saying your grandfather is right ... ' His eyes fell to the newspaper once more and he said quietly, 'But I do believe this whole area – Little Haven, Broad Haven, St Brides Bay – is ... haunted. You see, we've had everything – UFOs, ghosts, strange weather – you name it. There's a tale that in 1884 some labourers near Ravenstone Farm were rounding up cattle when they heard a terrific whirring noise from above and looked up to see a blazing object plummeting into the sea near Stack Rocks. They say the water glowed for days afterwards, that the men went blind. And mad. I know we were talking about the Americans, the aircraft, but surely that can't explain everything that's going on.'

'It's just local superstition.'

Frobisher shrugged. 'If you'd asked me twenty years ago, I'd have sounded as sceptical as you. But recently?' He narrowed his eyes.

My gaze drifted to the window and across the horizon beyond. 'Listen. Coastguards, harbour police, tanker crews – '

'What of them?'

'When I was a child only trawlers and lobster boats disturbed these waters.'

'So?'

I turned to face him, 'Well think about it. There are just so many more people about these days – all trained observers. It's their duty to report anything they see, especially if it's unusual. An odd craft, an erratic light . . . ' I was remembering the newspaper stories about dancing lights. 'There would be more official reports.'

He furrowed his brow. 'The liaison officer at RAF Brawdy asked our editor to keep a lid on them.'

'You think that will hold?' I was surprised. Such instructions to the press were usually made with extreme restraint, though more common since the Cold War had heated up.

'With the public meeting tomorrow?' He shook his head. 'I don't see how it can. There'll be busloads of sky watchers here within days. And the history of disappearances and so on will only add more fuel to the fire.'

'Disappearances?' I leaned forward.

'Yes, not just the Jacksons. Years back some fella went out watching for birds on Stack Rocks.' He shook his head hopelessly. 'Never found.'

'When was this?'

'Before my time. Way, way back. It's an eerie place, Stack Rocks Island, with that creepy old fort. Who does it belong to, do you know?'

I processed the question in silence. It had stirred something within me, a latent fear. Of something just beneath the surface of my memory. Whatever it was, I couldn't reach it. So instead I told him what I thought about the local sightings.

'We're witnessing the anxieties of the Cold War manifest-ing in different ways,' I said, my theory forming as I spoke. I gestured at the photographs behind the bar. 'Threats from the sky? Flying saucers fit very nicely with that.'

But Frobisher wasn't interested. 'Some think the whole area is cursed,' he said distantly. 'That is was used for rituals, cere-monies. That sort of thing.'

I gave him a polite but disbelieving smile.

'And then there's the Jacksons, last summer. Look what hap-pened to them.'

'Everybody keeps mentioning them. Exactly what *did* happen to them?'

Frobisher dropped his eyes. Then he told me.

Frobisher spoke to the landlord of the Ram Inn and ensured that the room allocated to me that evening was not only com-fortable but came with a sea view – and a discount! That suited me just fine; with no job I'd be broke soon enough. I couldn't carry on questioning the people of the Havens for ever.

As I showered and shaved I told myself that I wouldn't be staying long, that as soon as I got back to London I would start looking for a new job. Not politics. Journalism, maybe. Still, even with that positive thought in my head, I knew sleep would be slow coming. But I needed rest. I needed to be on best form for the public meeting the next day. So involved was Randall in the sightings, he was bound to make an appearance and advance wild theories. I felt my heart racing at the thought and with an effort turned my mind to other things.

Picking up the phone next to the bed, I decided to try another, more direct route of inquiry to what was going on. I dialled the operator.

'RAF Brawdy, please.'

'One moment, sir.'

RAF Brawdy was a NATO base. With so much strange activity in the area, they had to have some sort of public inquiry line.

As I waited to be connected, I mentally rehearsed the questions I would put, bluntly and directly. Had anything unusual been detected on radar? Had any jets been scrambled to intercept these craft? Could supersonic flights explain the booms that were shaking people's houses? Who knows, I might get lucky and get an answer or two.

Eventually, I was connected to a Group Captain Brian Stamper. I introduced myself and stated what I wanted to know.

'I'm not at liberty to go into detail on this matter,' he told me firmly.

'But you only fly conventional aircraft from Brawdy?' I pressed.

'That's correct. We do receive some visitors. But our own aircraft are the very well-known Hunter and the Meteor.'

'But they couldn't cause the "sky quake"?'

He paused. 'No. And we certainly don't have any military aircraft that could explain such a thing. In any case, it sounds nothing like a sonic boom.'

'Then you've heard it too?'

Another pause. 'Yes. I'm familiar with the noise to which you are referring.'

'Do your aircraft carry red and blue lights?'

'Most aircraft do.'

'Because, you see, I'm trying to work out if local people are mistaking your aircraft for something else —'

'It may be so. But certainly we do very little night flying.'

'Then what do you think people are seeing?'

'Well, I would say ninety-nine point nine per cent of sightings can be explained away as tricks of the light.' He sounded irritated now.

'That leaves zero point one per cent unaccounted for.'

There was a long pause. Then came a startling admission: 'Well, I'm sure we do have some strange things in our skies, but I'm not prepared to go beyond that.'

'You must have top line on the matter. Come on, Group Captain, I know the way this works. These reports have been incessant. You've even asked locals not to talk about it.'

The line went quiet for a few seconds. 'My understanding,' the Group Captain said slowly, 'is that what goes on seems to be . . . paranormal. That's all.'

The line clicked dead.

From the window I could look out across the spray and the rocks. The sun had long lost its grip on the day. The fog had lifted but now the shadows were lengthening. I surveyed the tiny hamlet, listening to the foamy rush of water and thinking that the spectre of uncertainty now hung over this village. *You see, we've had everything – UFOs, ghosts, strange weather . . .* My eyes travelled from the valley where the school lazed in its mystery to the skulking shape of the Haven Hotel with its tall black windows and broken battlements, out past the bobbing boats tethered in the cove, and across to the far end of St Brides Bay.

From here Stack Rocks appeared less threatening and comfortably smaller than from Ravenstone Farm. I could see the fort that crowned the peak and feel only a ripple of anxiety.

Something caught my attention. I strained to see and then opened the window, keeping my eyes on the fort. What was it? A light? Something moving? *There's a tale that in 1884 some labourers near Ravenstone Farm were rounding up cattle when they heard a* terrific whirring noise from above and looked up to see a blazing object plummeting into the sea near Stack Rocks. I closed the window and drew the curtains. *They say the water glowed for days afterwards, that the men went blind. And mad.*

I went to bed. I did not sleep well.

RASH OF UFO SIGHTINGS CONTINUES

Two policemen from the heart of the 'Broad Haven Triangle' agree that many people who are seeing unidentified flying objects (UFOs) are indeed spotting actual aircraft, but question whether UFOs are extraterrestrial spaceships under the control of nonhuman creatures.

'People are not hallucinating,' said Detective Constable Hewitt from Haverfordwest. 'It's also clear that they're seeing things for which standard, run-of-the-mill explanations do not suffice. But just because they see something strange in the skies does not mean that the something strange is a spaceship of extraterrestrial origin. That just doesn't follow.'

The rash of UFO sightings began in west Wales at Christmas when a hotelier driving home late at night witnessed a glowing ball of light that pursued her car. There have been hundreds of other sightings in the area, with a group of children seeing an object on the ground close to their school, which they reported to the police.

Coastguards at St Brides Bay have also logged reports of amber-coloured lights flitting just above the water at night. The lifeboat at Little Haven has been launched to investigate lights at sea three times in as many weeks.

'At first we thought they were distress flares,' said Coastguard Ian Chesterton. 'But when we checked the area there was nothing there.

– 17 –

Friday 11 February 1977, Little Haven, 9 a.m.

My second morning in the Havens.

I thought about calling the admiral in London to let him know I'd arrived but quickly abandoned the idea. He would be keen for an update on my progress, but the truth was I hadn't learned very much about the Happenings. Suppose the admiral asked about my grandfather or why I hadn't yet called on him at Ravenstone Farm?

And then there was the bizarre deluge of rain – *fish* – that had welcomed me back to the Havens. I didn't want to tell anyone about that, not until I had made sense of it myself.

I'd be lying if I didn't admit to feeling freaked out. I kept thinking of the wet thudding sound the fish had made on the car roof as they dropped from the sky. That and the police officer's peculiar warning: *Take care in the Havens.*

I was standing at the start of the stone jetty reaching out into the bay known as Giant's Point. From here I could see the beginning of the narrow path that began at the bottom of the rocky gully and ran up to the cliffs – the route the Jacksons had taken on the morning of their disappearance. Frobisher's telling of the tale was still fresh in my mind, and I decided that I needed to see where it had happened for myself. After all, it could be connected to the sightings and everything else that was going on in the community.

Talbenny Caravan Park, where the Jacksons had last been seen, wasn't far from here – two miles at most. I knew it well because my school bus had stopped just outside its entrance by the rickety signpost that pointed the way to Ravenstone Farm. Ms Hewison, who ran the caravan park, kept four golden retrievers, and they would bark as you walked past the hedge that separated her house from the main road. If she still kept dogs, they might have barked at the Jacksons on the morning they set off on their walk.

'Did you know Mr and Mrs Jackson?' I had asked Frobisher.

'Nope. But I saw them as I was coming out of the post office. They were on the slipway looking at the fishing boats near the shore and pointing at the fort on top of the Stack Rocks.' Then, he told me, they had set off up along the steep footpath, with fields sloping up to their left and the ocean on their right, unaware that whatever time they had left was limited.

Many hours later someone finally telephoned the police.

I stopped on the cliff path. The freezing wind lashed my face as I took in the view. Out to sea banks of clouds were building, threatening trouble. *Did they stand where I am now?* I wondered.

'Sergeant Blakemore did his best to reassure the family that most missing people turn up without harm, eventually,' Frobisher had continued. 'He seemed unconcerned initially, told not them not to panic, to wait a while. He said the couple were known to go on long walks, sometimes at night. And it was quite possible they had got lost on their walk. Never mind the fact that the missing couple had been visiting these parts for ten years and knew the area well. Next morning their son rang the station demanding something be done.'

According to Frobisher, the telephone call that changed everything came four days later, at precisely three o'clock. By then there had still been no sign of the couple, but some ramblers had seen something unusual on the cliff top that day.

'Flies, a whole swarm of them! Sergeant Blakemore demanded to know where. I saw him that morning to take a statement for my article, and his face was white. Something about the report had spooked him, that's for sure. I asked him about it afterwards, off the record. He said it was the mention of the place.'

Immediately opposite Stack Rocks.

Frobisher said it took very little time for Sergeant Blakemore and a PC to navigate the twisting roads serving the inland area from the coast of St Brides Bay. At 15.29 their car rolled to a halt at the end of a bumpy, narrow dirt track. From here the men progressed on foot, pulled by their sniffer dogs past the farmhouse – my grandfather Randall's house – and over the fields behind it, sloping down to the cliffs.

Ahead of them, leading to the cliff edge, was an animal run that might have been made by foxes or badgers. Cutting through the tangled branches and ferns, Sergeant Blakemore advanced cautiously. Then he stopped, sniffed the air, listened to the waves slapping against the rocks. Below him the cliff plummeted to a sparkling ocean. Unlike the PC, Sergeant Blakemore was well acquainted with the smell of death. And he smelt it then: a pungent bouquet, sickening, drawing him towards a thick cluster of bushes and hazel trees some twenty yards away.

Slowly Sergeant Blakemore advanced. 'He had to beat his own path through the long grass,' Frobisher told me. 'Do you know what he found, Rob?'

I shook my head.

'Broken saplings jammed into the ground, woven together with overhanging branches.'

That sounded like a hide to me: a man-made screen. I had learned about the technique at one of Bestford's committee sessions. Sticks were placed so bent-over branches and ferns that still had roots would continue to grow and screen whatever was beneath them.

At the Ram Inn Frobisher had nodded, finished his pint. 'That's exactly what it was. They pulled the screen aside and both men went jelly-legged at what they saw. Blakemore said PC Wheal threw up.' Mr Jackson had been ripped apart by three shotgun blasts, each fired at point-blank range. The first had completely taken off his right leg; the second, which had come from behind, had exploded through his chest, sending chunks of his right lung far into the long grass. But the final shot was the one that did for him, blowing away the central part of his head and brain.

'And his wife?

'Face down in the dirt, hands tied. Fucking mess, Rob, I'll tell you. Blakemore let me see the pictures. Her hair mottled with blood, the side of her face and head completely opened up; just a jagged bony hole with lumps of brain spilling out. Blood fucking everywhere. It had spread out in a dark pool that had hardened, like a big black plate. The worse thing was her husband's eyes . . . Animals must have got to them – rats, birds, maggots? I don't know . . . Whoever did it had fired from a dis- tance of inches, certainly no more than a few feet,' Frobisher added.

'But who would do such a thing?'

'It's baffling. No obvious motive. They seem to have been

picked at random. Police knocked on doors, tried to trace people they had met. Even checked the church visitor books. Didn't find a thing.'

'Then someone was waiting for them up there? A robbery perhaps?'

'Nope, nothing stolen. Their camera was still in their rucksack. Some candles too.'

Not necessarily an odd thing to find, except it turned out that the candles were black and foul smelling. But Frobisher just shrugged that off. 'They used to go walking a lot at night.'

'Then they'd have used a torch, surely? Not candles.'

'Beats me. Blakemore too. Anyway, keep all this to yourself, but he's had some bloody strange reports these last few weeks: frogmen sighted just off the coast during the day and at night. The local diving club say it's nothing to do with them. Seems a strange coincidence.' The reporter had shrugged. 'Might be related, I suppose, might be nothing.'

I thought about this conversation as I took the path back into the village. It was freezing this close to the Atlantic. I thought about the Jacksons' son, Steve, who had apparently spent weeks searching for clues, combing through foxgloves and late bluebells on the cliffs, beating bushes and wandering the fields around the abandoned airfield at Talbenny, just inland from where his parents' bodies were discovered. I knew that area well. I had played there as a child, when my soft hands were fond of uncovering secret hideaways in hedgerows and earthen banks thrown up long ago. Frobisher thought it likely the killer knew the area – that in all likelihood the leafy hedgerows would conceal him.

I rounded the corner by the post office and stopped. The

Haven Hotel sat perched on the cliffs watching over the ocean.
Huge and rambling. The sight of it made my mind jump from
one bad memory to another. I walked on. I understood now,
as I made my way to the school for the public meeting, why
Frobisher had described the Havens as haunted. Who was
responsible for the Jacksons' murder? An outsider? A local?
Was it related to the lights in the sky? Although the killer might
have vanished, the stain he had left behind in the Havens never
would.

Yet even this was not the most disturbing aspect of the whole
thing.

That was to come.

– 18 –

Broad Haven Primary School, 12 noon

The assembly hall at the primary school swelled with anxious voices. Father O'Riorden stood at the front. He was an imposing man in his late sixties, and something of a character with his long white hair and old-fashioned biretta. He gestured for quiet as I took a seat in the front row, next to the headmaster, whose face was ashen.

Father O'Riorden gave a small smile, giving the impression of a patient, contemplative man. 'Ladies and gentlemen, the parish council has convened this meeting to reassure everyone that you have nothing at all to fear from the "flying saucers" reported in the newspapers. We will get to the bottom of these sightings and we will solve the question of what appeared in the fields behind this school!'

There must have been at least a hundred people crammed inside. Teachers and parents lined every wall, and there were many more from the village milling around outside, supervised by the local police. I noticed, right at the back, a bespectacled man in a long raincoat. He was just taking a seat close to the pillow-faced postmistress, the one with the sluggish blue lips. She was watching him intently.

'Let's begin.' It was the headmaster, Howell Cooper. His expression tightened as he adjusted his horn-rimmed spectacles and spoke in a commanding classroom voice that quickly drew all eyes to him. 'Tell me. How many of you have direct experience of the Happenings?'

For a long moment no one spoke. Then someone raised a hand. Soon somewhere close to a quarter of the people in the room had a hand in the air. One belonged to a plump elderly woman with puffy eyes and a short bob of grey hair.

'Please, Mary,' Howell Cooper said, 'tell us what you saw.'

She stared as if not sure how to begin.

'Come on, come on,' the headmaster said. He wasn't encouraging her; he was instructing her, and I didn't like the expression on his face.

The woman swallowed then nodded. 'Two weeks ago, I was driving home from the social club in Talbenny to Little Haven with my friend Pam. Just as we got to the top of the hill we saw a cluster of lights, about five, with perhaps another seven below them. Hanging there in the sky, still. Then, over the brow of the hill, going down towards the village, the engine cut out. The car stopped. On a downhill slope. By itself. No brakes. Then the lights went off!' She dropped her voice. 'We were stuck there for a minute, maybe two. Then the lights shot off across towards Stack Rocks at an incredible speed. And were gone. The lights of the car came on, and we restarted it and got home. My husband was waiting up. Worried. We were late. The fifteen-minute journey had taken almost two hours. We'd lost time. It just doesn't make sense.'

Hearing these words, I remembered my own strange encounter on the road into the village.

Next it was the turn of Trevor Marsh, a blond man somewhere in his twenties. He remained completely baffled by an event that had occurred while driving along a quiet country road between Brawdy and Talbenny earlier that year.

'There was an orange light hovering over Norridge Wood, which I took to be the navigation light of a helicopter. In the blink of an eye the light was over me, some thirty feet off the ground. I looked up and saw this huge circular object, flashing with light, with amazing colours flowing around the outside. Gigantic. And it sounded like a turbine engine!'

I looked again at the man in the raincoat. His face was focused, his eyes wide with interest as he produced a notebook from his inside pocket. The postmistress was still watching him. Was this the visiting psychologist she had told me about – Dr Caxton?

I turned in my seat. 'Perhaps it *was* a turbine engine?' I suggested. 'The noise of an aircraft from the base?'

'No,' he shouted at me across the hall. 'Would a turbine engine do this?'

There was a swell of anxious muttering as he pulled up his sleeve and raised his bare arm. It was covered in a patchy purple rash.

'My doctor can't explain this rash. He can't explain the nausea, vomiting, diarrhoea or weight loss! But I'm sure as hell I can explain it,' he yelled. 'It was that thing from the sky! Ever since we saw it we've had all sorts of weird things happen to us at home – kitchen drawers opening and closing on their own, doors unlocking. And our phone's gone crazy!'

'Me too,' someone else shouted, local garage owner Norman Davies. 'My wife and I saw a large orange ball hovering right over Stack Rocks!'

'Bloody hell, I saw something just like that!' someone else called out.

'Calm down, everyone! At the moment there is absolutely no reason to think that we are in any danger,' said Father O'Riorden. 'The RAF has assured the council –'

'Where is the RAF? Why aren't they here then?' someone interrupted. A voice I recognized immediately.

All heads turned to the man who had spoken, and the hall grew completely silent.

'Frank Frobisher, with the *Western Telegraph*,' he said. 'Father, it is my considered opinion that the military do know more than they are telling us about these sightings – that they may not have our best interests at heart.'

'Isn't that a little paranoid?

Frobisher frowned. 'It's strange that *you* of all people –'

'Sorry?'

'That you of all people mistake curiosity as paranoia.' He lowered his voice. 'Father O'Riorden, it's people like you who made me want to be a journalist in the first place.'

That caught my attention. Was there was something in O'Riorden's past that had invited Frobisher's barbed comment? Something shameful? No, that was unlikely. Surely the Havens were too close-knit a community to be unaware of anything of that nature.

Frobisher was silent a moment longer, then turned back to the crowd. 'Look, I cannot take the safety of our community on faith alone. I need facts. The American facility at Brawdy is just ten miles from here. So when the children reported the object in the field behind this school, I called the base.'

'I doubt they were much help,' Father O'Riorden said. 'It's an oceanographic research station. Nothing more.'

Frobisher cocked his head. 'If you'll forgive my scepticism, Father, the base answered my telephone call with, "US Naval Facility Brawdy, this is not a secure line." Why the hell are they worried about secure lines if it's just an oceanographic research station?'

A murmur of reflection from the crowd.

Frobisher began pacing back and forth at the front of the hall as the wind moaned about the school.

'Now let's be honest: do any of us really know what the military is doing here?' he asked. 'These rumblings we've been hearing, what are they? Sonic booms? Explosions under the sea? Drilling? I also spoke to a young man in the military police over at RAF Brawdy. And he told me that he had been told that if there was a chance of bringing any of them down, they were to open fire, but they were all warned not to tell anyone about this.

'Now, you've all heard what the children have said,' the journalist continued. 'Something very bloody strange came out of the skies last week and landed in the field behind this school. And until someone can tell us what it is, the parish council should do the only sensible thing and close the school.'

More murmurs.

The journalist studied us, nodding his head. 'We have no idea what we're dealing with here. What if the kids saw some sort of secret government exercise gone wrong? What if that object didn't land, but crashed? The fact is that we don't know the first thing about these phenomena.' He hesitated. 'More importantly, we don't know anything about their capabilities, what they might do to us.'

'You're saying they could be dangerous?' a young mother demanded.

Another reaction from the audience.

'I've read reports from all over the world,' Frobisher said. 'Other machines of the same description can give off blinding light, crippling rays and sometimes beams that immobilize people. Now, these incidents are rare, but even so – '

'Excuse me, but I have something to say.'

The weight of the crowd's gaze was hardly reassuring as I stood up, but Father O'Riorden gave an encouraging smile and gestured me to speak.

At that moment I felt closer to my mother's mission than ever. I wondered if anyone in the hall dreamed that their community could be a strike target for the Russians, that tactical nuclear weapons were likely stored just a few miles away. But the last thing these people needed now was to panic. If secret American aircraft – or other dangerous experiments – were to blame it was vital I attempted to prevent panic from setting in. Nothing was more certain to exacerbate the risk of an international incident with the Soviets.

'Um, hello, everyone. I don't think many of you know me, but this used to be my home, and I hate seeing everyone so distressed at something that is bound to have a sensible explanation.'

Silence.

God, I really was an awful public speaker! Always had been. I could hear that my Welsh accent, which had rubbed off a little in London, had deepened, and I cringed when I admitted I had worked for Paul Bestford. No one trusted politicians, especially ones with ruddy faces who rarely showed up in their constituencies, but they needed to know who I was. They needed to know they could trust me. 'We need to keep this in perspective. The last thing we want are more TV camera crews and reporters here. I've learned a bit about the advancement of military technology. Super-speed aircraft.'

More silence. Expectant eyes on me.

But how could I tell them about what was really motivating me now: about the attack on Parliament, Selina and the peculiar drawing passed to her by Colonel Corso.

'I can visit the American facility, and I am reasonably certain, given my background, I can convince them to agree to a meeting. Let me find out more before we give in to panic and speculation.'

Father O'Riorden let out a long breath. 'I think that sounds eminently sensible, Mr Wilding.'

I looked at Frank Frobisher, then into the headmaster's pinched face and said in a calm voice, 'There's got to be a rational explanation for these events, and I'm determined to find out what that is. In the meantime, shutting the school is unnecessary. It will only create panic.'

Mr Cooper paused for just a moment too long. And I knew that I had failed. 'If these phenomena are indeed harmful to our health, until we can explain what our children saw and can guarantee their safety, I can see no other option.' He nodded decisively. 'Close the school. Nobody is safe.'

– 19 –

The assembly hall erupted. 'We must organize a sky watch,' someone was shouting. Ethel Dunwoody, the postmistress. 'We must know the truth. Investigate for ourselves, set up an observation point with cameras.'

'Perfect!' said the headmaster. He had pounced on the suggestion as if he had been praying for it. 'It's the only way to keep our town safe. When?'

'How about Tuesday night?'

The suggestion came from the landlord of the Ram Inn and was met with a murmur of agreement.

Why Tuesday? That's five days from now. Was it a special day? Were sightings of UFOs more likely on a Tuesday? Or was it simply an arbitrary date plucked from the confusion? I opened my mouth to ask, only to hear the headmaster answer my question first.

'Tuesday's the night of the lunar eclipse, isn't it? The eyes of the nation will be on the skies.'

There were cheers and cries of dissent. I could barely make out who was saying what until the door into the hall banged open behind us with startling force.

Everyone stared.

The man advancing towards the front of the hall was swinging a substantial handbell loudly and with purpose. I felt a sickening drop in my stomach. It was my grandfather.

Wearing a stained and shabby long coat, Randall possessed the dark gritty presence of a warrior. He was carrying something slung over his left shoulder, something I couldn't quite make out.

'Mr Pritchard?' Father O'Riorden hesitated. 'Please.'

But Randall, face twisted, mouth tight, only swung the bell harder, and as the clanging reverberated around the hall some of the younger children pressed their hands to their ears. My grandfather paced to the front of the hall, swinging the bell with all the passion of an aggravated headmaster at the end of the lunch hour. It was embarrassing and startling to see my only surviving relative behaving so outlandishly, but also oddly arresting. Every eye was on him.

'Be sober-minded, be watchful,' he shouted, and wheeled on the crowd raising his chin defiantly. 'It says so in the Lord's book! Oh yes, my friends, your adversary the devil prowls like a lion, seeking someone to devour. The Lawless One will arrive with all power, signs and lying wonders. You all speak of finding truth, but when you see it, you may wish you had never looked.'

A sea of suspicious eyes watched him. Whispers rose. I shook my head to regain clarity and focused. Then saw the scar on his left cheek, the scar like a crooked smile.

I was relieved he hadn't spotted me yet, but I *had* worked out what was slung over his left shoulder – a tattered brown sack. Those nearest shrank away from it, covering their noses with their sleeves. That sack was full of something, shapes impossible to make out. Until he held the sack aloft and dumped its contents onto the parquet floor with a repulsive wet *thud*.

I recognized the stench of death immediately and gagged. How many dead rabbits were there? Easily five, maybe six.

A woman shrieked.

'He's mad!' someone shouted. And, as if in agreement, a few people at the back stood and began to walk out, some shaking their heads, some looking back nervously.

To his credit the headmaster was first to intervene. 'Randall!' he roared, stepping towards my grandfather, eyes furious, arms outstretched.

Randall only raised his hand. 'Listen to what I have to say! Then I'll go.'

He stooped, grabbed one of the dead rabbits and held it up for us all to see.

'Please,' Father O'Riorden said, 'you're frightening the children.'

'That's the point!' Randall's voice scraped as his glance swept the room. His nostrils flared, one finger pointed. 'The lights in the sky, the strange sounds, the mysterious objects on the ground are all supposed to be frightening. They are supposed to make us doubt our sanity. They intend to bring us down!'

My horrified eyes fell on the rabbit carcasses, then went to the one in Randall's gnarled hand. The creature's head wasn't right somehow.

'The things from the sky cloak themselves in deception,' Randall shouted. 'They preserve their identity through invisibility and mendacity. And they are responsible for this!'

I could not tear my eyes from the rabbit hanging limp in Randall's grip, the bright white bone on display. And then I realized.

'They're mutilated,' I heard myself say as I tumbled back, sickeningly, into my childhood.

I think the worst sorts of memories are those we suppress. If we're fortunate, they remain buried. But sometimes those memories can rise like cadavers clawing their way up through the earth – as mine did when I saw those mutilated animals.

Thirteen years old at Ravenstone Farm. I had gone to bed after Sunday lunch, not feeling well, and woke late in the afternoon, abruptly. I lay on my bed, still in the grip of sleep, watching the wind sweep fresh snow across the yard and listening to the sea beyond the fields. Listening, also, to something banging downstairs, over and over.

The kitchen door? Yes. Open, swinging back and forth in the wind. Grandfather must have forgotten to lock it.

But he *always* locked it.

Questions became doubt. Then fear. I dressed quickly. Downstairs snow drifted into the kitchen and the stinging wind drew me outside. It didn't matter that the ground was thick with snow as I set off down the gloomy rutted track towards the fields. Why? To prove I wasn't just a child? To tell him, in my own way, that I would never obey him, that in this way he could never replace my parents? Maybe. But as I hurried on past the cattle sheds, the low-hanging trees, hearing the crunch of my footsteps in the packed snow, I sensed a disquieting power in the air drawing me on, inside my head the restless beat of a thought: *He left the door open.*

And where was Grandfather? No sign of him in the yard, or anywhere.

I thought I heard Jasper barking. 'Jasper!' I called. I pictured him trapped somewhere, whining and shivering and alone.

What was that? On the far side of the last field, nearest the coastal path, I had caught a glimpse of something glinting. Perhaps a boat out at sea?

By the time I had crossed the field, the light had gone. I stood alone on the cliff edge in the rushing cold, and I knew that it wasn't by chance that I was standing here. Something had brought me there. Something purposeful.

The sea between the coastal path and Stack Rocks was rough, and from the waves a mournful melody sang to me. Somehow I just knew: it was this exact stretch of water that had claimed my parents.

Another bark. Hope sprang within me and I ran. 'Jasper!'

I was already halfway into the next field – the one from which I was most strictly prohibited – when I saw the standing stones arranged in a circle. Thirteen in total. Grandfather had never mentioned them.

Something made me turn. Not a noise. Not a movement. Just a palpable sense of something other. And I saw with dreadful clarity the wiry shape of a man in the drifting snow. I knew it wasn't a farmer. I knew too the rumours about this stretch of coast. Burial mounds, earthworks, ghosts, smugglers and secret tunnels.

I pulled my coat around me and took a step back. The figure was too far away for me to discern its features, even though it seemed to be facing me head on now – watching me. The shape of a brimmed hat coated with snow was clear, but little else. Only the points of light where his eyes should have been – like tiny flickering flames – and the grim certainty that I was in the presence of something sinister. Malevolent.

Fear made me cover my eyes for one heartbeat, two, three. I peeped between my fingers. The figure was gone.

It wasn't safe out here. I had to go back. But not without Jasper. He was out here somewhere; I'd heard him bark. I was sure that if I searched, I would find him. I didn't. The snow was too thick. Sobbing and scared I ran towards the house, hoping Jasper had made it back, that I'd imagined his barking and the diabolical figure in the snow.

Back at the farmhouse Grandfather was waiting.

He pounced on me as I entered the kitchen, dug his fingers into my arm so hard they left a bruise. I would *never* again defy him, he insisted. For the sake of my *soul*, I would kneel with him in prayer.

Confusion turned to terror as he dragged me into his study. To pray.

Jasper didn't return home. The next day, and the next, I went back to the lower fields in secret. Checked over and over, just to be sure I hadn't missed any vital clues. Nothing. Only on the third day, when the snow was beginning to melt, did I find my best friend. The morning was blazing white, and a bite in the air warned of trouble as I approached the coastal path. There was a strange odour like stinking sulphur. I took a few more steps.

At first I thought the shape protruding through the melt was a fallen branch. It wasn't. The snow wasn't white, either. It was pink. I walked faster until I reached the thing, forced myself to look down.

Not a branch, a leg. Jasper's leg: stiff, matted fur.

I dug him up. I dug him up with my bare hands. The flesh on his neck and head had been entirely sliced away, exposing clean white bone. Where his eyes had been, there were just two black holes. His tail and one ear were missing. And a small hole in the centre of his head showed – I learned afterwards – where the brain had been completely removed. No teeth marks. No clue.

A surge of nausea rose in my throat. Then I heard the crows. Perched like sentinels on the branch of a nearby tree and eyeing Jasper's carcass. Normally they would pick over the dead, but perhaps these scavengers knew better than to interfere with the work of something outside nature.

Fear replaced grief. I ran until my legs were burning towards the relative safety of Ravenstone Farm, stalked by the memory of the sinister dark figure in the brimmed hat whose eyes had flickered like fire.

'For God's sake, restrain him!' someone shouted, and I was pulled back from the memory of that horrendous day to the meeting at the school. Suddenly one of the parents near the front of the hall was lunging towards the man I hadn't seen for ten years.

Wait!' I held up a hand against the stunned crowd. My gaze went again to the rabbit hanging from Randall's gnarled fist. 'Just wait.'

Part of me was thinking of some way to deny what I was now seeing; most of me was thinking of what I was going to say to Randall when he recognized me.

'He's right,' Randall said, looking my way. 'Examine the rabb . . .'

He looked at me with clear intensity, his expression unreadable.

'Hello, boy.' His voice was like dry leaves, a voice belonging to another time. The years had put vast cobwebs of lines around his eyes, but although his face was thinner he was still powerfully built for a man of his age. 'You . . . you should not have come.'

I felt all colour drain from my face. All I could think was, *The kitchen door . . . the man in the snow.*

Ravenstone Farm, me, Randall.

I thought back over the hundreds of times I had checked windows and doors, the number of pills I must have swallowed just to keep control of my nerves, and felt only hatred for the man who was supposed to have cared for me. No wonder I had turned out this way.

I had to force myself to go nearer to him. I felt like I was walking through fog.

The windows in the school hall were creaking under the rising wind as I knelt and examined the carcasses, feeling Randall's hard gaze pressing against my back.

'I forgot,' I whispered as I reached out, daring to touch one of the rabbits.

'Forgot?' echoed the headmaster, looking on.

My heart was weighing heavily in my chest. How could I have forgotten Jasper?

A voice in my head replied, *Except you forgot more than Jasper, didn't you, Rob?*

'Those rabbits were killed by predators, surely?' Father O'Riorden said.

'No!' Randall snapped, and I turned and looked into his craggy face. His grey eyes were steely and knowing. He addressed the room: 'You don't need me to tell you that predators don't drain their prey entirely of blood only to leave the carcasses mostly intact. They don't extract the brain through holes made with almost surgical precision. *Something* is haunting our village. Stalking our community. Something ancient and dangerous. But you must not hunt them, seek them. You must not invite them in, or else there will be a judgement!' He paused. 'Please, I am here to warn you against probing these visitations any further. For your own sakes.'

You may as well raise a red flag to a bull. Telling people not to investigate is as good as telling them they should.

A flash of red caught my eye. At the side of the hall, towards the back, was a girl with long dark hair and pale skin wearing a crimson coat. She was rocking ever so slightly from side to side.

'We shouldn't fool ourselves that the landing at the school was a one-off event,' Randall raved on. 'The Havens have a strange and long history of unusual sightings. Ten years ago the lifeboat was called out to sea to investigate glowing red lights near Stack Rocks. Many years before that, stones rained on the roof of the Haven Hotel.'

The hall was silent, regarding this unkempt but commanding man warily.

In my head Admiral Hill Bartlett's voice repeated, *Artificial objects under intelligent control moving at quite fantastic speeds.*

'I've seen plenty of dead animals,' said Frobisher at last, 'but this . . . this is savagery. You think this is the work of . . . aliens? From another planet?'

'No, I do not.'

'Well, if not aliens then what?'

Randall's face darkened. 'Evil. Deception. Complicated diversions intended to cover up some other activity. These poor animals have served a purpose.' He glanced at me, and I felt my skin crawl into gooseflesh. 'What do you think, boy?'

He seemed to be implying that the events were the work of some supernatural force – some demonic power. None of his words suggested any connection with the military. And yet I knew that his predictions were what had brought me here in the first place. Now, as I looked into his eyes, his grim determination filled me with dread. That determination was the reason the audience was staring at him transfixed. Except the children.

They were motionless, their expressions bordering on empty. Much more of this and it was only a matter of time before he worked this small community into a frenzy.

I shook my head and said finally, 'I'm here in an official capacity. I'm sure we can work this all out if we stand together and stay calm, rational. Just give me time to speak with the authorities. With the children too.'

Absolutely not,' Cooper said. 'All access to the children will be controlled by me and Father O'Riorden, and only in agreement with their parents.'

'Robert, you must not get involved,' Randall protested.

Before I could utter another word the little girl in the red coat snapped her head in the headmaster's direction. Her face was scared, bewildered, her eyes wide. There was something wrong with her, the way her head was tilting to the side, eyes rolling in her head.

Randall, distracted, was shaking his head with the conviction of a fanatic. 'These children are under attack, and you, Headmaster, have an opportunity to avert the chaos that is coming – but only if you listen to me.'

I could feel my anger rising. This community didn't need more mystery, it needed answers.

Suddenly Randall was at a window, pointing a finger at the glass. Curious eyes followed. And there was a stunned silence. I glanced at my watch, the one my father had given me. It had stopped. A low droning sound that set my teeth on edge filled the air. The children in the hall burst into tears. Randall's eyes, full of alarm, met mine just before the lights flickered and dimmed. Blinked off.

Even now I can't explain how the girl in the red coat crossed the hall and came to stand next to me. It happened in a second.

But when the lights flickered back on, there she was: to my right perhaps two feet away. She was motionless except for her delicate fingers, which were twisting at her sides.

I could feel the weight of Father O'Riorden's curiosity as I took a step towards her, tilting my head. I recognized her, the long dark hair framing a gentle pale face.

Then a new voice: 'Get away from my daughter!'

A young woman with a cloud of dark hair burst from the audience. Her shoes clipped the wood with panicked force as she strode towards me.

'Did you hear me? Get away from her!'

I recognized her too: slender and dark with a beautifully curved mouth and strong features. Araceli Romero. And the child was her daughter Tessa. I recognized them from the story in the paper.

A powerful rumble from above, not the sky quake this time but a crash of thunder so loud the entire hall shook. People leaped to their feet, some hurried for the doors. Tessa let out a piercing scream. She stared right at me, and her eyes were like black glass.

'May the Lord protect us from the cunning serpent of deceit,' said Randall. He crossed himself, stepping towards Tessa. 'Protect us from our sins, keep us safe in this, our moment of need.'

Another child screamed.

And another.

The man I thought might be Dr Caxton was on his feet and heading for the doors.

Randall turned to Araceli. 'Come,' he ordered. 'We have to get out of here. Now!'

All around the hall adults were shouting with alarm.

And then chanting. Not just Tessa. All the children: '*Kcab gnimoc era ew rof. Seiks eht hctaw dna rehtag!*'

Welsh? No, but almost.

Tessa began trembling violently. It was enough to spur Araceli into action. She grabbed her daughter by the shoulders and shook her. 'Tessa, darling, what's wrong with you?'

The child's legs unhinged, and she slumped forward.

Randall stooped, caught her.'You're not safe here,' he said, looking at me intently, pained almost.

I tried to read what was in his eyes beyond grim determination. Secrets.

Admiral Lord Hill Bartlett had been right. Grandfather was the key. He knew something. And whatever it was, I had to know it too.

The menacing, metallic droning intensified, the air around us pulsing with vibrations.

'Stop it!' I yelled. 'Whatever you're doing, just stop it!'

'You forgot, boy,' he shouted over the din. 'You ran away and you forgot. But now you're remembering. You should never have come back. It's coming. Evil is coming.'

II

The Broad Haven Triangle

'They worshipped, so they said, the Great Old Ones who lived ages before there were any men, and who came to the young world out of the sky.'

H. P. Lovecraft, *The Call of Cthulhu*

Dearest Julia,

With every passing day my interest in this mystifying community deepens, all because of the Happenings. No single word so instantly provokes a hardening in the residents' attitudes; some become curiously muted, others implacably hostile. Meanwhile, the local newspaper spins ever more outlandish stories about flying saucers.

And there are all sorts of crackpot theories: craft from outer space, visitors from the future, even inter-dimensional beings. The most outlandish theories are floated by demonologists, who think UFOs are fabrications created by evil forces to deceive us mortals. The higher echelons of the Nazi party believed just that, and were involved in occult practices to summon demons from hell and Satan himself – 'the prince of the power of the air'.

Truly these mysterious phenomena present a vexing problem, for how can one account for the fact that so many credible, educated and cultured witnesses claim to have seen something in the sky (or on the ground) that millions of other people insist do not exist? But facts must speak for themselves, and the facts in this case are compelling. I have enclosed the most recent accounts for your entertainment – these will form the basis of my book.

Now my love, just in case you are worried that I am temporarily taking leave of my senses, let me reassure you that I do have a theory. At a public meeting today I was dismayed to witness a startling display of paranoia, superstition and overreaction, which leads me to think that people who are raised in an environment where strange perceptions are considered routine can grow up predisposed to accept the existence of angels, aliens and UFOs. This condition has a name – contagion.

Are the mysterious flying objects objectively true? Unlikely. Are they true to those who live here, at the heart of the Broad Haven Triangle? I very much think so.

But now of course for the hardest part of my endeavour – I must prove it!

All my love,

Caxton

– 20 –

Haven Hotel, Skyview Hill, Little Haven

Araceli Romero was standing against the panelled bar in the main dining room of the Haven Hotel, running an agitated hand through her cloud of black hair. Randall had his back to me. After inspecting some unfinished paintings propped against the wall – seascapes, mainly – he had positioned himself next to a high Gothic window on the opposite side of the dusty dimly lit room. There was an unpleasant chalky smell in the air, and the building was creaking on its foundations under the force of the wind. Upstairs the floorboards creaked too, with footsteps. Araceli had said that if Tessa wasn't tired, she'd often pace the corridors until sleep came.

'Do you know what's wrong with her?' I asked.

'Who the hell are you? Why are you so interested in us?'

When we returned here after Tessa's episode down at the school I was looking forward to the opportunity to question Araceli about the events in the paper – the 'flying football' that had chased her car, and, afterwards, the man who had visited her and warned her not to talk. Most of all I wanted to know whether Selina had been to the hotel. And why.

Araceli was glaring at me. 'Well?'

'I'm investigating the military and their operations in the Havens.'

Her eyebrows drew together. 'Why should I trust you?'

I didn't want to tell her about my parents: my father's job and my mother's campaign against nuclear weapons; the injuries sustained during the protest at RAF Croughton. Because that meant telling her about my connection with nuclear weapons. 'I'm a local boy. I grew up here, and what's happening worries me greatly.'

Araceli bit her lip, her slender body rigid. Then she turned to the bar and poured what remained of a bottle of red wine into a glass that looked cloudy with age. She rubbed at her temples and then looked sadly at an oil painting on the floor. It was of a lighthouse standing in the wild waters of St Brides Bay. A curious painting, I thought, because it reminded me of something. And because there was no lighthouse in St Brides Bay.

'Yours?' I asked, pointing.

'Yes, but you didn't come up here to admire my art.' She gave me a hard look.

I shook my head and said, 'I'm looking for evidence. If the military can explain what the children saw, then –'

'It was the bloody military who told me to keep quiet!' She scowled at me, then at the curve of Randall's back.

At its farthest point the Haven Hotel was so close to the cliff edge I was apprehensive of going too near the window; of looking down onto crashing waves, onto the cliffs near Ravenstone Farm, onto Stack Rocks rising out of the sea.

Araceli said to me, 'Don't think I don't know what's going on here. You've come because of what I saw.'

'Wrong,' Randall said. He turned from the arched window, facing us both across the shadow-haunted restaurant. 'The boy is not here because of you. He is here because of me.'

I met his eyes for three, perhaps five, seconds, until his weighty gaze forced me to drop my attention to the worn carpet.

'It's that drunk Bestford, isn't it? He sent you to find out what's happening here. Hmm? Wants to find out how I know all I do.'

I said nothing.

And you have the audacity to ask for *our* trust.' He let out a harsh and disparaging laugh. 'You? A politician!'

'Don't call me that.'

'But that's why you left, isn't it – to "make a difference"?' he sneered. 'I imagine that Mr Bestford is worried he has approved one too many military bases in the vicinity of our little community – yes? And now he wants my expertise.'

'Your expertise?' I turned towards Araceli and said, 'This man is not your friend. He cannot help you or your daughter.'

'And you can?'

I nodded and told her a direct lie: 'I am sure I can.'

Araceli did something I wasn't expecting. She laughed in a shrill, almost hysterical way. Then she said in a reproachful tone, 'You know, I did ask for help. I came to your MP's office for help. Over and over. What I wanted most was corroboration, do you see?'

I did. She had needed to know these bizarre events weren't just happening to her.

'Eventually, a young woman came to see me.'

'Selina?'

Araceli nodded. 'And guess what? She couldn't help me either. Nothing has changed.'

'If it's any consolation, I couldn't stand it any more in Parliament,' I said flatly. 'I resigned.'

Randall's head snapped up. I could see he wanted to know more but couldn't bring himself to ask. His eyes were calculating, his mind working through possibilities.

'Why?' Araceli asked.

I wanted to tell her, but how could I? There was just too much to share. What was actually going on – what I understood of it, anyway – sounded wild, like most conspiracy theories. And not only did I think they wouldn't believe it, I wasn't sure I believed it. But I needed to be credible if I was to win Araceli's trust and complete the admiral's mission: find out what Randall knew and avert an international incident with the Soviets.

'I am sorry for the way you've been treated,' I continued. 'Genuinely, no one deserves to be treated with such disdain in the light of such –' I searched for the word '– fantastic events. The government knows that what you have seen in the sky is real, and they have done since the '50s,' I added, remembering the strongroom of documents buried beneath the streets of Westminster. 'But they also know that these phenomena originate on this planet, that most sightings are explainable, and those which are not are almost certainly state-of-the-art spy planes which are deployed routinely and deliberately to test the air defences of hostile nations. At airfields all over Britain fighter planes are kept ready to intercept, and if necessary engage, any unidentified flying object within combat range. That is why the subject is regarded as sensitive, and that is why you received such a cold response from the authorities.'

Her eyes were wide and wondering. I reached out to touch her hand in reassurance. What I wanted to tell her more than anything was that I felt an odd connection with her, as if we had shared something once, something deeply important. I had felt this since the morning in London when Selina had shown me her photograph in the newspaper.

Randall turned his back on us, staring out towards the raging sea. 'These phenomena are easily underestimated,' he said.

I felt a flare of anger. Just because there was a mystery here, it didn't mean that Randall had free licence to intimidate people with scare stories like he had done with me.

'More lies?' I asked. 'More scaremongering?' I looked at Araceli. 'This is what he does. All he's ever done.'

Araceli looked me straight in the eye. 'So, you're saying there's a rational explanation?'

I nodded.

She shifted her gaze to Randall. 'And you?'

'Manifestations of a supernatural force.'

Araceli looked again at me, and this time I read something else in her eyes. Optimism perhaps? 'Suppose you're the one who's right,' she said quickly, 'and these UFOs are secret aircraft, how do you know so much?'

I was relieved to hear the hostility had gone out of her voice.

'Because I was briefed. At the highest level.'

'Who briefed you?' Randall demanded. 'Tell me.'

'I no longer have to do as you say.'

I turned towards Araceli and said quietly, 'Let's talk rationally, OK? Please, won't you tell me what's happened to you and your little girl and I'll explain what I can.'

– 21 –

We sat at a dining table, Araceli and I. She poured me a drink, and I thanked her politely. I pretended not to notice the dust on the tablecloth. I pretended not to notice the floorboards above us creaking again.

She was pretty, I noted as I took a sip of the wine and waited for her to speak. Not beautiful, but striking. Tall for a woman and slim, but not a waif – she looked strong. She glanced at the painting again – the lighthouse that seemed so oddly familiar – then at Randall, still stationed at the towering Gothic window, and I saw her swallow. Then she began.

'Just after Christmas, after the light came – the light that chased us in the car – Tessa was so terrified she was trembling. The doctor had to give her a sedative. But afterwards she changed, became so remote. Disconnected. She wasn't sleeping and could barely take one step outside the front door. After a week I was able to take her down to the school, but the teachers made me come and collect her at lunchtime. They said she . . . frightened the other children.'

The strange chant the children had made in the meeting came back to me: *Kcab gnimoc era ew rof.*

Araceli ran a hand through her hair. 'Don't you see? I just

want my baby girl again. And I want an explanation from whoever is responsible. The weird light that chased our car did this,
but the Happenings in these villages began long before that.'

I stared into her distraught, pretty face and felt something.
That nagging familiarity again that made no sense.

'Tell me how your family came by this place.'

She saw my eyes roaming the depressing dining room, and a
look close to embarrassment broke across her features. 'Mother
used to say that the hotel found her. She moved here from Italy.
It's been in my father's family for generations.'

'He doesn't live nearby?'

She dropped her eyes. 'When my parents separated he
moved away; his job took him overseas. Mother tried to make
a business of it.'

'And now it's just the two of you? You and Tess? Alone.'

'We manage fine,' she said, looking me straight in the eye.
She anticipated my next question. 'Tessa's father was a soldier,
American.'

'And where's he now?

'He left.' There was a weary sadness in her eyes, a loneliness
that struck a chord in me.

'Wait,' Araceli said abruptly and tilted her head to the side,
listening.

At the towering window Randall straightened. Upstairs, the
footsteps had ceased. Tessa had gone to bed at last. But Araceli
didn't seem ready to relax.

'Sometimes Tessa listens at the doors,' she whispered, 'or
wanders around the hotel, looking for her.'

'Her?'

Araceli held up a hand. 'Shh!' She approached the door that
led into the musty hallway and pressed her ear to the wood,

before unlatching the door and peering out. 'No, it's all right,' she said at last.

I offered her a smile, though inwardly alarm bells were ringing. I was beginning to wonder if Araceli was afraid of her daughter. Or something in the hotel.

I glanced at Randall. He was watching me. I wondered why he'd gone so silent.

Araceli had returned to her seat and now seemed eager to talk. 'I took over the running of the place when Mum died seven years ago.'

I already knew that Araceli had grown up in the Havens. Maybe that was why her face resonated with me so strongly. It wasn't just that I had seen her in the newspaper; it was something else. 'What school were you at?'

'I was taught at home. My mother didn't want me mixing with other children . . .' She smiled awkwardly as if that could lessen the peculiarity of her mother's wishes.

'I wanted to increase the number of rooms, get the place going again. The east wing particularly.' Her self-conscious look told me she was embarrassed by her failure. 'You saw the scaffolding, I suppose?'

I offered a smile, nodding.

'The roof is unstable – it leaks.'

I was surprised the entire building didn't leak. 'It's a colossal amount of work for just you.'

Her weary eyes travelled over the empty chairs and dusty tables. 'I wanted to make the hotel viable in the winter months – set up a supper club, you know. But, well –' she shook her head '– these days people tend to stay away. You've heard the stories, I suppose? About my mother?'

'No,' I said flatly, hoping the lie didn't show.

'There's no need to be polite. If you're local then you'll have heard,' she said. 'When my father left he didn't leave us with much.'

I looked away and saw that Randall had fixed her with a cold stare.

'The history of the house itself doesn't help. Apparently it's haunted by a white lady.'

'Like every old hotel on a cliff,' I said with a smile.

She dropped her voice and said seriously, 'Do you suppose bad places can attract bad things? Bad people?'

'Absolutely,' Randall answered grittily.

'Military aircraft or not, it's clear there's something very wrong in the Havens,' Araceli said slowly. 'Something rotten here. I can't explain it. I'm not sure you'll find anyone who can.'

I brought the conversation back: 'So, you had a bright light chase your car. Your daughter saw the craft at the school. Anything else?'

'A few days before Christmas I saw a light circling the woods at the back of the hotel.'

'What time was this?'

'The early hours of the morning. I felt the light before I saw it. There was a tremble in the air. I had a look from my bedroom window, and there it was, in the air, a blue light like a blow-lamp, just circling over and over. It hurt my eyes just to look at it. I thought at first it might be a helicopter, but there was no sound at all. Then it just blinked out – almost like a lighthouse.'

'You mean, it was pulsing?'

She nodded, and again I remembered the lighthouse from my dreams. The sensation of waiting and watching.

'Well, perhaps it was some sort of beacon?' I said, smiling reassuringly. 'The lighthouse at Dale?'

She shook her head. 'I waited a whole hour to see whether it would come back. The hotel was in darkness. The lights weren't working. We'd lost all power.'

'That seems to happen a lot around here,' I said.

She nodded. 'I know you said that there's an explanation . . . but in that moment I felt . . . I'm trying to tell you these . . . things are not from here.'

She hadn't said 'from outer space' but I had the definite sense that was what she meant.

'There's something else. But first . . . I don't want anything I tell you to go any further, OK? People will think I'm mad.'

I promised to treat whatever she said in confidence, and I meant it.

She sighed. 'OK. The light didn't just disappear. It landed. In the field out the back.'

'Was it rather like an egg?' Randall asked.

'Here, give me a pen and I'll draw it for you.'

I handed her the pen I kept in my inner jacket pocket and watched, intrigued, as she took a paper napkin from the table and shakily sketched the shape of an object like an upturned frying pan.

'Here, you see, this is how it was.'

'So it was just sitting there on the ground?' Randall queried.

'Yes, like the craft down at the school. And nearby, between the object and the gate at the far end of the field, there were these . . . figures, moving.' She clamped her hand over her mouth for a few seconds. 'I thought someone was trying to break in. I keep some chickens down there, you see. So I had another look through the binoculars. And, well . . .'

'Tell us about the figures,' Randall said in a coaxing voice. I could tell he was intrigued.

It was a few moments before she was able to continue, but when she did, she spoke slowly. 'All this time, as I was watching them, the windows were vibrating. Even my teeth seemed to vibrate. I felt this terrible pressure in my head and shoulders. And those monstrous figures, I couldn't take my eyes off them. They were huge!'

'Giants,' Randall said softly. His eye caught mine and I felt a shiver of memory pass over me.

'They were shining – I mean, their clothes were shining. It was like a ripple effect. Shimmering. Some sort of suit that covered them from head to toe. And their arms were long, too long. One of them was stooped over. I thought it was measuring something.'

'Did you see their faces?' I asked.

'There were no faces! Nothing. Just a black space.'

That made me think of the sketch that Selina had given Colonel Conrad Corso and the menacing figure he claimed had appeared on the night of the protest at RAF Croughton back in 1963.

Their faces are made of shadows.

Somewhere in the Haven Hotel pipes creaked. Outside a gust of wind moaned.

I shivered. 'Right, well, let's keep in mind why we're all here,' I said at last. 'To find out what people have been seeing, what landed at the school. What landed behind your hotel then flew away.'

'Except it didn't fly away, did it?' Randall's eyes narrowed. 'Be precise, boy! What actually happened?'

'It disappeared,' said Araceli. 'Vanished on the spot.'

'Exactly!' he said, snapping his gnarled fingers. 'It. Just. Disappeared. UFOs do the same thing. They vanish and reappear somewhere else in the sky without ever crossing the intermediate space.'

'What's your point?' I asked.

Randall's voice was thoughtful. 'These phenomena bend our minds. What if they can bend space and time as well? What if these phenomena don't so much fly into our world as slip into it?'

'Inter-dimensional?' Araceli ventured, and when Randall nodded, her eyes opened in surprise.

This was too far-fetched for me. I had to get Araceli to stop listening to my grandfather's wild theories. He was derailing the whole interview. Already I could feel a strong connection to this woman. I wanted to know her. I wanted to find out who she was. And to do that, I knew I needed to show more of myself. Offering my most reassuring smile, I said, 'I've lost someone, someone very close to me. The state they left her in –' I shook my head '– she might as well be dead.'

'What happened?'

I spoke very slowly about the sequence of meetings that had led me back to the Havens. I didn't mentioned the admiral in front of Randall, but my story was easy to tell without that detail given that they had both seen the explosion on the Thames in the news.

'So you see I need to know what happened to my friend. I believe she may have stumbled onto something of military significance to the US, something they don't want anyone investigating. And I believe you might have done too.' I paused before asking, 'What did Selina ask you?'

But before anyone could say anything, there came a huge rumbling explosion that rattled the windows and the bottles behind the bar.

'There! You hear it?' cried Randall.

Of course we had. The sound wasn't only beyond the glass, in the crowding darkness; it trembled in the walls of the old building. In the floorboards.

'It's *them*,' Randal hissed.

'Yes, it's them,' I said defiantly. 'The Americans. That was a sonic boom.' I wheeled to face Araceli, remembering what Frobisher had told me about night-time activities at Brawdy. 'The base is only ten miles from here.'

'Yes, but – '

'If we're quick, if we leave now, we may see some activity on the runway.'

'I can't leave Tessa.'

I nodded. Of course she wouldn't leave her daughter.

Randall's determined eyes were riveted on me as I made for the door. 'There's absolutely no point! They won't allow you anywhere near.'

'There you go again,' I almost shouted. 'Well I lived on that base, remember? I know how close you can get. Come with me?'

Randall's stare faltered for a second. If he thought I was extending an olive branch, he was wrong; I hadn't forgotten that he was a piece of this puzzle. Maybe if I got him on his own, he would tell me what he knew.

'Come on,' I said.

He frowned. 'They've got a lookout tower now. Heat sensors in the ground. We'd need to take the utmost care.'

Suddenly I was remembering burning rubber again. A pulsing yellow beam from a distant lighthouse. I hadn't even realized my eyes were clamped shut until I opened them again.

'You all right?' I heard Araceli say.

I tried to focus on her lips. 'Yes . . . umm, yes, thank you.'

But that wasn't really true because the hazy memory was still there. *Somewhere . . . we went somewhere.*

She raised her eyebrows in concern. 'For a moment you reminded me of Tessa. The way she blanks out.'

I shook my head. 'No, I'm fine.'

I thought of the way Tessa had screamed in the school hall and those words she'd chanted that made no sense at all.

Randall was shaking his head. 'If this village knew what I knew –'

'What *you* know. You seem to talk about it an awful lot but never explain anything! Does it make you feel important? Does it give you some sort of weird kick to know more than the rest of us?'

He gave me a black stare, his jaw working.

'Well suppose I'm right,' I continued. 'Suppose that the electrical interference in the village is due to some sort of experiment they're conducting up –'

'I heard something once, from some guests,' Araceli interrupted. 'About Brawdy. They were Americans who worked at the base. Two men and a woman. They only stayed with me for a week at a time, twice last year. They said they worked for some telecommunications company. Nice people, kept themselves to themselves. I liked them because they always telephoned to let me know what time they'd be back, so I could start dinner.' She shook her head. 'One night they phoned to say they were delayed, that they would be very late and not to wait up. But I did wait up. Tessa wouldn't settle and the radio was all fuzzy again with static. There was a rumble in the sky. Every window in the hotel rattled, and I could see across the bay that something was happening at Brawdy – lights flashing.'

'Your guests came back?' I asked, and Araceli nodded slowly.

'It must have been about two in the morning when I let them in. I expected them to go straight to bed, but the woman was sobbing. I got her a drink and asked if she was all right, but the men seemed to want to shut her up. I stole a moment with her on the stairs on her way up to bed, asked her what was wrong.'

'What did she say?'

'Her face was deathly pale,' Araceli answered. 'She whispered to me, "Nobody knows how close we came tonight . . . We almost destroyed the world."'

I felt my face tighten. That was all I had needed to hear.

'Robert!' Randall called after me, but I was already pacing into the gloomy hall. I looked around and found myself face to face with a mannequin attired in a full suit of armour.

The telephone was on a rickety old table that was supposed to pass for a reception desk. As I dialled the number I still had for Frobisher, my eyes alighted on the room keys dangling from their hooks. One was missing. Room 12. Araceli had not mentioned that there were guests staying. In fact, hadn't she said on the phone that she was closed for the season?

At that instant the line connected. 'Robert! How are you? Are they all right?'

'In a manner of speaking. Listen . . .' I told him what I intended to do.

'Security up there is tight. If you're spotted at the main gate, they'll arrest you.'

'Then I won't be spotted.'

I asked him what I wanted to know, then hung up and dialled the number for the admiral at his office in Whitehall. The message I left for his private secretary was short: 'Robert is on his way to Brawdy.' If the worst did happen, at least I had taken precautions.

Then I returned to the dining room, where Randall and Araceli were waiting in silence.

'Frobisher says if we're going to go, then now is the best chance we have of seeing something.'

'I have one question,' Araceli told me, 'that's all. And I want you to answer honestly.'

'All right.'

'Is there anything else? Anything you haven't told us?'

She waited. So did Randall. I could feel his gaze on me. I didn't know whether I could trust either of them – I pretty much knew I couldn't trust my grandfather – but some of my mother's passion surfaced then and compelled me to admit what I had learned back in London. As long as they told no one, it wasn't going to jeopardize the admiral's mission, and at this point I had no idea what lay ahead.

'Nuclear weapons?' I heard Araceli draw breath. 'Oh, dear God.'

'You need to get the hell away from this village,' Randall said. 'Both of you! You're fools if you stay.'

'Let's go.'

− 22 −

The road was wide and smooth – a new road alongside a wide stretch of fields on one side and St Brides Bay on the other. A road sign flashed by: BRAWDY 3 MILES. It had long grown dark, and that suited me just fine. What was it Dad used to say? That the most interesting things on military bases always happened at night.

'What do you honestly hope to see?' Randall asked.

'Maybe nothing. Maybe something.'

He frowned. 'You're as arrogant as your father.'

I pressed down on the accelerator, and the speedometer needle crept towards sixty. On the car radio a news reporter was announcing exactly what I hadn't wanted to hear.

'The Pembrokeshire cliffs nearest Stack Rocks Fort. Bleak and unforgiving and long associated with legends of witchcraft, sorcery and Celtic curses. And now, following a decision by the village's parish council to close its primary school, where a flying saucer allegedly landed last week, the people of the Havens are collectively turning their eyes to the heavens in a group sky watch for "the sky spectres" that have haunted their village. The sky watch is to be led by Headmaster Howell Cooper right here at Giant's Point in Little Haven, this Tuesday night, coinciding with the most anticipated event in astronomy this year – the lunar eclipse.'

I looked over at Randall, who was frowning into the windshield.

'From eight o'clock this Tuesday evening observers could be treated to the rare sight of a blood moon, a rare celestial event in which light from the sun, having passed through the earth's atmosphere, causes the moon to take on a red, or blood-like appearance.

'There is something very . . . unsettling about this part of Pembrokeshire,' the journalist continued. You could hear the wind snapping around him. 'These wild and mysterious cliffs were a favourite destination of the infamous occultist Aleister Crowley. It's here that many people have reported strange lights in the sky. And it was near here that an English couple were brutally murdered.

'Local man Randall Llewellyn Pritchard has warned against the sky watch, believing that the strange sounds and sights in the Havens are dangerous and should be left alone.' A pause. 'I must confess, standing on this lonely spot looking out over the sea, I am beginning to wonder myself –'

'Turn that bloody thing off.'

We sat in silence for most of the journey, the way people do when they have argued and neither quite knows how to begin the conversation again. It was a silence that spanned ten long years. I was thinking about the hotelier's extraordinary story.

'You trust Araceli?' I asked.

'Why would she lie?'

'That's what I'm trying to work out. Her life does seem quite empty,' I said carefully. 'Uneventful. Some might say boring. The same is true of the Havens. These sightings bring thrills, excitement.'

Randall was still frowning, but at me now. 'You think she's doing it for attention? You believe the giant silver figures she saw were local pranksters, dressed up?'

'What do you think is affecting Tessa?'

Randall was silent.

He definitely knew more than he was willing to say. 'How much have you told Araceli about your –' I paused '– interests?' I asked.

'You think *I'm* responsible for her beliefs?' He sounded offended. 'You think I've led the witness?'

Yes, I wanted to shout. Instead I said, 'We crave patterns and reasons and answers, no matter how badly they rebel against our logic. Araceli is searching.' I paused. 'Perhaps you've been feeding her the wrong answers?'

He said nothing. Had I gone too far? Keeping my gaze on the road, I asked another question: 'How did you do it?'

No answer.

'How did you predict the sightings?'

No reply.

'I'm waiting.'

'Do not talk to me about waiting.' His tone was bitterly hollow.

Remembering the admiral's suspicions, I tried again. 'Some people think the Americans are testing secret aircraft in the area, that the Russians are concerned. Taking action. You know they have spies all over the country, just waiting and –'

He gave me a look so sharp it would cut diamonds. 'You think I'm a spy?' He laughed doubtfully. 'Well, well, I must have gone up in your estimation.'

Maybe he was telling the truth. But I couldn't afford to rely on him. Partly because by then my neurosis was running on auto-pilot, but mostly because I hadn't forgotten about the nuclear weapons under wraps nearby and how much was at stake. Even if I determined what was behind the Happenings there was no guarantee I would avert the international incident the admiral had said was hanging over the Havens like a shadow.

In the distance waves crashed against the cliffs. Above the sky bore down on us, heavy and black. I decided to probe a little further.

'It's possible that the lights people have seen are due to ships at sea,' I said.

'Possible.'

'And the weather we've been having, these storms? Strange lightning, perhaps?'

'Perhaps . . .'

'And as for the school, the headmaster's a believer. The children are impressionable. He's clearly feeding them.'

'Clearly.' He glared at me to reinforce his sarcasm. He shook his head. 'Robert, what makes you so determined not to believe?'

I remembered all the crap about giants in the ground that he had poured into my ears when I was a boy. Warnings like that can affect a youngster in the wrong way. They can make you sceptical, make you always demand proof. 'What makes *you* so certain?'

He straightened against the passenger seat. 'I've investigated these sightings in all parts of the country and in many parts of the world. Did you know that in France and Spain there are seventy-two caves with drawings from 13,000 BC showing a variety of oval and disc-shaped objects? Granite carvings in a mountain cave in China's Hunan Province showing helmeted humanoids with large torsos standing upon cylindrical-shaped objects in the sky?'

I didn't know this. Even if true, I didn't see what it proved.

'The only UFOs that people are seeing are secret military aircraft,' I said with confidence. 'And I'll prove it. Tonight.'

We were a short distance inshore now. Up ahead was the turning to the quarry from which the megalithic builders of Stonehenge had taken sandstone blocks to replace the many Carn Alw stones lost during transportation from the Preseli Mountains to Stonehenge.

'All these years,' Randall said, his voice low, 'I thought I might have heard *something*. I waited. When your graduation came, I thought I might have received an invitation, or . . . something. Perhaps a letter . . .'

I found these words surprising from a man I had thought incapable of emotion. Except towards animals of course. Jasper's mutilation was the only time I had ever seen him cry. Is that why he had become a recluse? To avoid having to show concern for people?

'Did you hear what I said, Robert?'

I evaded his question by pulling over. 'I need to check which way we're going.'

'But you already know the way!'

'Just let me check the map, all right?'

I had lost my temper. Randall looked bemused. He lowered his voice. 'Robert, the base doesn't appear on any maps.'

I cut the engine. For a moment there was no sound. Then from above came the squall of a seagull.

'What is it? What's wrong?'

I closed my eyes. 'I used to come here with Mum,' I said distantly, feeling Randall watching me. 'Do you ever think about them?'

A long pause. 'There isn't a day when I don't think about your mother.'

'What about Dad? Didn't he matter?'

Randall seemed not to hear me; he just said, 'Your mother didn't deserve what happened the night of the flood. Neither did you.'

'It wasn't Dad's fault.'

'Oh, you think so?'

A ghost memory of my parents surfaced, the two of them arguing on the morning my mother went to the protests at Croughton, my father shouting at her not to go. *You're putting me in an impossible situation!* Dad had yelled.

Two weeks later – the night of the Great Flood – they were dead.

'Listen, if you know something, then why don't you just *tell* me,' I said. 'What were they doing at the farm that night? On the coastal path?'

His face grew serious again. 'Your mother made him take her out.'

'But why?'

'She'd grown sick of his lies.'

'What lies? Jesus! What are you talking about?'

No answer.

'This is important, Goddamn it. This is who I am!'

'And who is that exactly, boy? Obsessive and paranoid, these are weaknesses that leave you vulnerable.'

'Vulnerable to what?'

'You must trust me. You must put on the whole armour of God to stand against the devil. There are certain things about your past and yourself it is better not to know.'

'Like my parents and how they died?'

'Yes.'

My fear turned to anger. 'You're a sad little man,' I said. 'Does your superior knowledge make you feel significant, powerful? You've made yourself an expert, preaching warnings to a paranoid village.'

'Because I knew what would happen.'

'If you knew, why didn't you stop it?'

'I tried!'

'Then explain it to me!'

He bit his lip. 'Wait, you think *I'm* doing this?' he said suddenly, studying my face.

'You do seem to know a lot about them!' I spat back.

Randall looked at me for a long moment. There was something powerful in that silence. Gripping. Eventually, he said, 'Let's go. Do what you came to do.'

The turning to the base was on a high coastal road that led away from the village of Brawdy, and a high metal fence with a sign stating that photography was prohibited signalled that we had arrived at our destination.

The car headlights picked out another sign:

WARNING

THIS IS A RESTRICTED MILITARY INSTALLATION

NO TRESPASSING

USE OF DEADLY FORCE AUTHORIZED

I killed the ignition, slammed the car door and headed into the darkness.

– 23 –

RAF Brawdy, St Davids, Pembrokeshire

Five minutes later I was on the single-track dirt road that led to Brawdy's main gate. Alone. Randall had refused to leave the car. The sky was the deepest shade of purple and the stars were sparkling. Suns far distant, light years away, but they had never looked so close as they did to me at that moment out in west Wales.

I focused on the brightest point of light and visualized my mother's face. I'd forgotten about Ravenstone Farm and its mysteries and spent three exhausting years in Parliament fighting her war. Why? It wasn't as if I was obligated. Yet I felt obligated. I felt guilty. Why should I feel guilty? Why?

Unless, I reasoned, *there really is more to all this that I don't remember*. The morning of the day they died Mum and Dad hadn't just argued about his military work. They had argued about me.

I walked steadily, straining into the winter darkness and keeping to the edge of the road. Glancing at my watch, I saw it was almost ten o'clock. Only half an hour before Frobisher said things usually got interesting out here.

I was chilled to the marrow as I approached the base

perimeter fence. I cursed myself for not buying a warmer jacket, then remembered with dismay that I couldn't really afford one now anyway. Through the fence, across the flat and barren land, I could see the shapes of the base – huts, hangars and towers arranged in rows around the enormous runway.

The base was sleeping. But I could remember it from childhood: the way the ground rumbled under the roar of the jets coming into land, the airmen swarming onto the runway. And Mum, tight-lipped, increasingly unhappy, pleading with Dad. Not pleading. Begging.

I groped for my torch, then thought better of it.

I looked up into the inky Welsh sky. No sign of any aircraft activity. I remembered Frobisher's warning: *The airspace above Brawdy has been completely restricted since the Americans moved in. No one's allowed near.*

A figure in uniform emerged from the guardhouse.

I dived for the ground and lay face down in a ditch by the roadside, twigs and stones scratching my face. After what seemed like an eternity, I dared to raise my head. The soldier was back in the guardhouse.

I had to get past. I got to my feet and, staying close to the perimeter fence, walked quickly to the end of the road, so that I was now to the left of the guardhouse and outside its direct line of sight. Straight ahead was a narrow road, and at the end of that another security post, which guarded the entrance to the US facility. Crouching in the shadows, I scanned the contours of the facility: the huge lookout tower rising from the ground, a two-storey building crowned with rotating radar dishes. I was close enough now. I waited, tense but excited. Far away, on the opposite side of the fence, I heard men's voices. The sound of something heavy rolling back.

The control tower blinked, and the runway lights flashed on. They were too bright for me to see anything through the glare, but soon, I was sure, would come the sound of thrumming engines or beating propellers.

Nothing.

Then the runway lights blinked out and I was left in near-total darkness. Frobisher had been telling me the truth; something was amiss here, something probably connected with the nuclear warheads hidden on base.

I turned to find a better vantage point. And froze. There was a humming in the air. The same sensation I had encountered on the road into Broad Haven when it had rained black fish. I saw a light. Brilliant orange, rising slowly from the ground. Higher and higher it went. Then stopped. And hung there in the sky over the base, like a bulb suspended from an invisible cord.

No sound of any engines, just a low vibration.

It's just not possible.

It then accelerated so fast that within a second it had travelled right across the sky and was hanging over St Brides Bay.

Behind me I heard voices just as another light appeared, this one not from below but above. It swooped down out of the clouds like a fiery falcon – circled, rose and dived. The other light, emitting sparkles like rays from a diamond, joined it, and together they revolved swiftly in an aerial waltz, turning sharply, skimming and darting, reversing course. A dazzling display. No aircraft could perform such manoeuvres – no *known* aircraft. The G forces must have been astonishing, and even if these were state-of-the-art secret aircraft, I struggled to see how any human pilot could survive them.

Suddenly the lights pulled apart and plunged so rapidly I braced myself for an explosion.

But they vanished.

I caught my breath, too stunned to move. *Did I actually see that?*

'Hey, you!'

I spun round. Two men were running at me. Soldiers.

– 24 –

I ran. Tripped and stumbled and splashed through ditches.

Suddenly, about two yards to my left, an arm appeared from out of the fence and beckoned urgently. 'Come with me,' a voice said. 'Quickly!'

The arm disappeared back through the fence and I realized there was an opening here. I scraped through, feeling the soggy ground beneath my feet on the opposite side, and allowed the stranger to help me. He took my arm and guided me through the darkness onto firmer territory.

'Now for God's sake, run!' he said. 'This way.'

My heart was slamming as I struggled through the field and came to another fence. Barbed wire. He pulled up a section and crawled under. I stood peering at him as he glanced wildly about. He was wearing jeans, clumpy trainers and an ill-fitting black leather jacket that had known better days. I saw now he was young, much younger than me.

I looked back and thought I could see the distant lights of the runway, deep inside the base. Some secret aircraft preparing to take off, maybe? And then I heard the soldiers' voices.

'Is that yours?' said my rescuer, but I was busy squeezing under the fence, and only when I was standing at the edge of the road, catching my breath, did I see what the lad was looking at, some twenty yards away.

'Yes, my car.'

The passenger-side door was opening, and a hunched form in a long coat was climbing out. Randall.

'Let's go!' I shouted and pushed him back inside.

Minutes later the three of us were speeding away along the coastal road.

'You saw them, didn't you?' I was glaring into the rear-view mirror at the teenager in the back seat. 'Tell me you saw them.'

He grinned. 'Sure. Why else do you think I was out there?'

'Saw what?' Randall wanted to know.

'You're kidding me!' I said, exasperated. 'How could you *not* have seen them?'

'Robert, who the hell is this?'

'Martin Marshall,' came the response. 'Keep driving!'

I was feeling light-headed, would rather have pulled over, but I accelerated harder, my heart still beating furiously at the thought of us being pursued. Maybe arrested.

'Do you live in the Havens, boy?'

'No,' Martin answered, still catching his breath. 'But my uncle does.' He grinned at me, looking relieved now. 'I thought you were a bloody soldier. You should have seen your face.' He laughed.

He actually thought this was funny!

'What were you doing out there? At the base?'

'You been drinking, boy?' Grandfather interrupted.

Martin shook his head.

'Liar! I can smell it on you.'

'One pint,' he admitted. 'All right, two. But that doesn't change what we saw.' The lightness in his voice faltered.

I glanced across at Randall and in a strained voice said, 'Probably . . . some sort of . . . state-of-the-art aircraft. Unmanned. It had to be . . .'

'Welcome to the Holy Grail for conspiracy theorists,' Martin said from the back. 'They've been flying spy planes in and out of here for eight years. But that's not what we saw.'

Randall didn't wait to hear the rest. 'Pull over!'

As I did, my memory was replaying the scene: the soldiers' voices, the sound of something rolling back, the runway lights flashing on, the globe of light swooping and dancing with its partner, the speed, the way they had vanished . . . It had been an incredible sight. Otherworldly. Could I really have seen a . . .

'UFO,' Randall said grittily as we got out of the car. 'It was flying and you couldn't identify it.'

'That doesn't make it an alien spacecraft.'

'I didn't say it did,' he replied irritably. 'Evasive motion ability, indicating the possibility of being manually operated, or by electronic or remote control; extreme manoeuvrability and ability to hover; the ability to disappear at high speed or through complete disintegration. All features referenced in the CIA's *Air Intelligence Guide for Flying Saucer Aircraft*.'

'How the hell do you know all this?' I asked, just as he averted his gaze.

An odd dark look had fallen onto Randall's face that made me almost as curious as it did nervous. My grandfather was beginning to sound like an expert or obsessed or both.

I wondered exactly how much he *did* know. Which was an unsettling question.

Martin Marshall, who had gone to relieve himself behind a nearby wall, emerged and came to join us. I had parked the car and it occurred to me then that I hadn't been here since

I was a child. It was a dramatic location on the eastern cliffs of St Brides Bay, with sand dunes on all sides that eventually merged with the beach. In the distance, behind the castle, were woods. They made me think of the woods behind the Haven Hotel. Something bad had happened in those woods once. The wind through the trees made wheezing noises that hinted at it, but I could only remember snatches of a conversation with my father; it had involved something to do with a lighthouse.

Somewhere . . . We went somewhere . . .

'Come closer,' Randall said, peering carefully at Martin.

I studied our companion in the poor light and briefly registered a lean face and fair hair.

'Closer.'

Randall's leathery face was immobile as he kept the young man fixed in his gaze, and then he abruptly extended an open hand in my direction and said, 'Torch.'

Reluctantly I fished it from my pocket and dropped it into his hand. I didn't want to be here. The air was sticky and heavy with the scent of rot and wet branches and leaves. A fine spray was blowing in off the sea and I was damp and cold. My socks and trouser legs were wet and I was covered in mud.

'Your face?' said Randall in a concerned voice, and now, as the harsh torchlight flickered across Martin's expression, I saw with some alarm that the boy's eyes were inflamed and swollen almost shut. There were blisters on his face and head. And just above his right ear a small patch of hair was missing.

'What the hell happened to you?' I blurted out.

He looked at me. 'Saw the same as you, that's all.'

The teenager turned and produced a battered box of cigarettes from inside his leather jacket. There was the scratch of a match as he crouched down behind a bank of sand, knees close to his chin.

'When you're a child,' he began when his cigarette had burned halfway to the filter, 'you hear stories about monsters in the night, and you forget them. You've heard of the bogey-man? Well, I've met him.' He hesitated and looked up at me. 'Those children at the school are telling the truth. What they saw wasn't from this planet. I know it.'

And so, in the shadow of a ruined castle, we heard Martin Marshall's story. It began, as did so many stories of the area, with a strange light in the sky, and by the time he was done I could feel a worm of fear twisting in my gut.

– 25 –

In November – four months earlier – Martin was with his girl-friend in his car, parked in a lay-by that flanked the road leading to RAF Brawdy. The pair argued. Though Martin didn't tell us what about, I had a strong sense from the way he averted his eyes guiltily that it had something to do with sex. Perhaps he'd gone further than she was willing, perhaps he'd raised his voice when she refused him, but whatever the reason for her getting out of the car and striding off into the night, Martin was left alone with only the radio for company.

'I sat there for a while listening to Johnny Rotten,' he told us. 'Had a cigarette, you know, to calm myself down.'

But he didn't stay calm for long. Something disturbed him. It showed its presence firstly though distorting the radio signal, grinding it into a grainy static, and then through pulsing vibrations that made the hairs on his arm prick up.

Martin told us that when he opened the car door and looked about him, he wasn't afraid. Just interested. He certainly didn't believe in ghosts. As the dark trees creaked around him, he began to wonder if his girlfriend was OK. Would she find her way home all right? These were the questions, he told us, that drew him back towards the car. He got in and drove off.

'I stopped next to a gate overlooking the fields, near the spot where I found you tonight. I got out and leaned on the gate to see the lights of the base. That was when I realized there was something blocking my view.'

'You mean,' Randall said, 'that something was on the ground in the field, obstructing your view?'

'Exactly. Well, I lit a cigarette and watched for a few minutes.'

'Can you describe it?' Randall asked. 'What shape was it?'

'Well, it was like a dome,' Martin said slowly. 'I could just see the top of it on the horizon, and it had a faint light around the outside.'

'Around the periphery – the edge?'

'Yeah, that's right.'

'It must have been rather large.'

He nodded. 'It took up a good bit of the field, like a small house.'

'I see. So you were leaning against the gate and watching this thing. Then what?'

'I heard a branch snap. That was when I realized I wasn't alone.' Those last three words came out in slow, measured lengths. 'I didn't see it at first. I heard it. Something in the bushes behind me, rustling. It was some sort of being . . . A silver figure.'

'A soldier?' I ventured.

Martin shook his head firmly. 'It was standing behind the gate. So bloody tall. Not human, more . . . humanoid.'

Humanoid. That word made me think of old horror films and the aliens from *Star Trek*.

'This figure, what was it wearing?'

He shrugged. 'Hard to say. Something glittery, you know? And I could sort of see through it.'

Randall's mouth had curled down into a grimace. 'What then?'

'My feet had turned to concrete boots,' he answered. 'I just stood there, staring at this thing, and it looked back at me. No, I can't really say it was looking, because there weren't any eyes, you know?'

'I don't,' I said.

'Well, it was like it had a helmet. Square. And there was this thing in the mouth, like divers have. Breathing apparatus.'

The boy's face was taut, dead white, and his hand was trembling. That might have been from the cold but I didn't think so.

There are giants, Robert. Giants in the ground.

When Selina and I had first discussed the Broad Haven Triangle I had laughed and had expected her to laugh with me. But I didn't feel like laughing now. There were just so many stories, surely they couldn't all be lies?

'What happened then, Martin?' I asked.

'It came nearer, right up to me, and I swung a punch.'

'That was rather brave,' Randall said.

'Would have hit it too, only it just sort of blinked out. Disappeared! And appeared next to the fence that surrounds the secret American base. And then . . .' He shook his head. 'I know how this is going to sound . . . but I swear it's true . . . It drifted straight through the fence. Like a ghost.'

Drifted through the fence? Wasn't that exactly what had happened at RAF Croughton in 1963, the night of the protests?

'After that,' Martin said in a listless voice, 'all hell broke loose on the base. An explosion. The ground shook. Men bellowing at each other. And then a siren.'

'Robert?' Randall asked. 'You all right?'

'Yeah.' I pulled in a ragged breath. 'Go on, Martin.'

'I found my girlfriend down the road. She had to drive me home. The state I was in.'

'Did she believe you?' I asked.

'Only when I drew it for her. I sat down and smoked about twenty fags and I got a pen and paper and drew that figure.' His eyes went distant again, and he shook his head from side to side. 'Some sort of fucking monster.' He rubbed at his swollen eyelids. 'The next day three men came to my house. Hats, no eyebrows. Men dressed all in black.'

Men dressed all in black? I tried reaching for the memory, but it was blurry.

'After that a woman came – called Selina – said she wanted to help. But she lied!' he said, suddenly excited. 'She took my drawing of the . . . the *thing*, away. All she wanted was information – about what I saw, and that couple who were murdered on the cliffs. Wanted me to go and see her at that hotel in Broad Haven.' He began backing away from us.

I held up a hand. 'Now calm down. All we want to do is h – '

'There's no time, don't you see? What if they come back?' Martin's face was twisted, his eyes glittering furiously. 'I think about doing things sometimes,' he added in a whisper. 'Hurting people. Hurting myself.'

Randall glanced at me and our eyes met.

'I think it would be a good idea for you to stay away from the base from now on,' Randall said gently, but Martin was shaking his head. Before we could say another word, he turned and ran away into the shadows of the ruin.

'There goes a haunted man,' Randall said huskily. From under his fierce eyebrows he gave me a worried stare. 'Robert, do you believe in evil?'

'Of course.'

'What about the devil?'

'No.'

'I'm not talking about a little red man with a fork. I mean the force of evil that is ancient and for ever, the cosmic powers in this present darkness, the spiritual forces of evil in the heavenly places.'

In anger and confusion I turned away as a gust of freezing sea air struck my face. His mention of evil had affected me in a way I didn't understand, pricking the back of my mind, and my legs had a strange, loose feeling.

'I have to go back to the Haven Hotel,' I said.

'Fine, I'll come with you.'

'No.'

He watched me. There was no anger in his face, only deep concern. 'We are but children in the wilderness. Robert, my boy, for the love of God, leave the village. Go now.'

I heard him and I didn't. All his talk of the devil had opened a pit in my mind, and all sorts of troubled thoughts were pouring into it.

Martin's words: *All she wanted was information – about what I saw, and that couple who were murdered on the cliffs. Wanted me to go and see her at that hotel in Broad Haven.*

I stopped, looked briefly across the bay to the Haven Hotel on the cliff edge. What had Selina found there? I voiced the thought, and Randall nodded as if this was no more than he expected. 'You think there's a connection between Selina, the hotel and the Jackson murders?'

'That,' I said, 'is one of the things I intend to find out.'

FROM *THE MIND POSSESSED: A PERSONAL INVESTIGATION INTO THE BROAD HAVEN TRIANGLE*

BY DR R. CAXTON (CLEMENTINE PRESS, 1980) P.28

That winter silver-suited humanoids appeared all over the Havens. My first thought was that a prankster was at work. Was it coincidence that a local company manufactured fire-fighting clothing in the form of a three-piece silver suit? Even though the company was quick to reassure me that they weren't missing any suits, it was still possible that someone local had access to one.

There was however another more intriguing theory to explain the origin of these extraordinary beings. Perhaps they were fantasies of the mind originating from folklore? I certainly couldn't discount that idea. The ancient Celts believed in all sorts of manifestations – gods, light elves, dark elves, men, the dead, dwarves and giants. Indeed, the deity called Grimnismal was also known as Grimr, the Hooded or Masked One. Or Hjalmberi, the Helmet Bearer. We cannot overlook the fact that the giant silver figures witnessed in the Havens were also masked, or faceless; and of course, they appeared to be wearing helmets . . .

– 26 –

Haven Hotel, Skyview Hill, Little Haven

The hotel was in darkness; the power must have been out again. As I picked my way up the meandering driveway, my thoughts slipped from Martin Marshall's description of the faceless humanoid to Selina's covert investigation in the Havens. I didn't know what I feared, only that I had to know how far Selina's investigation had gone, what she had learned. A military experiment gone astray. A clever hoax. Or something . . . what? Supernatural?

As soon as I knew more, I would phone the admiral and update him. What I didn't want to do was ask him for help, or show I needed it. He had trusted me enough to set me this task, and I had no intention of letting him down.

I mounted the steps to the arched Gothic doorway and knocked. Waited. When I looked up into the evening sky punched with stars I thought, *No, there aren't any spiritual forces of evil up there*. Then an irrational but no less disconcerting thought pushed in: *What if the sky is conscious? What if it's watching you right now?*

From behind the door came the rough sound of a bolt shooting back. Then Araceli appeared, standing there with a weary expression. 'Robert, it's late.' She saw the state of me, her eyes running from the scratches on my face down to my mud-covered jeans. 'God! What happened?'

'You told me Selina asked you questions. You didn't tell me she stayed here.'

Araceli blinked once. 'I don't generally give out the names of my guests.'

That felt like an evasive response. 'Can you show me the room she had?'

'I don't remember.'

I studied Araceli's face in the poor light. Her eyes were even puffier than before, and there was a red mark on the left side of her face.

I fished in my pocket for the pencil drawing I had brought from London. An enormous figure which broad shoulders, square head and a blacked-out face. 'Look at this.'

Before taking the paper she produced a torch from her cardigan pocket and clicked it on. She shone the beam on the drawing and I watched a frown crease her brow, watched her hands begin to tremble slightly.

'Selina gave me this drawing. It came to her from Martin Marshall, a young man living near Brawdy,' I said. 'A giant silver figure he saw drift right through the facility's security fence. Selina interviewed him. She knew this had happened before, at RAF Croughton in 1963. I believe she was targeted, in London, for what she knew.'

'Targeted by whom?'

I shook my head. 'Please, I need to see her old room. In case she left something behind.'

'No, I would have noticed.'

'Well, let's make sure, shall we?'

As she hesitated I remembered the missing key I had noticed earlier behind the reception desk. Remembered the hotel was closed for the season.

'It's Room 12, isn't it?'

'All right,' Araceli said finally, 'but you'll have to be quiet. Tessa is sleeping.'

I stepped into the gloomy hallway and registered the same chalky unpleasant smell as before. From the corner the suit of armour watched me. As I followed her up the creaking stairs I wondered how on earth she managed up here alone.

We reached a wooden door marked with a splintered crack and Araceli stopped. She focused the beam of her torch on my chest. 'Does Randall know you're here?'

'He knows,' I said. 'I'm not sure he approves. It's like he doesn't want me anywhere near here.'

She looked away for a moment, looked blank.

'Araceli?'

'Robert, I want you to promise me that whatever you find, whatever information you share with Randall, you'll tell me, won't you?'

I hesitated.

'Promise me!' There was no mistaking the warning in her tone. 'Randall is hiding something from us. But he knows his stuff, and it's important we're all on the same page.'

The episode had left me flustered but keen to explore, so I agreed and looked on as she took a key from her pocket and opened the door. Araceli didn't bother to try the light switch, but swung the torch around. Two beds with floral sheets, dusty pink lampshades, threadbare yellow curtains. I crossed to the window, pressed my fingertips against the cold glass, ran my fingers across the sill.

I lingered for a moment, looking out through the darkness, through my reflection, to a speck of light out to sea in the direction of Stack Rocks.

The room smelt of mildew and mothballs.

'Can I take the torch, please?'

Araceli handed it to me and crossed her arms as I checked the drawers of the bedside cabinet.

Empty.

'How long did she stay?'

'Three nights.'

'And was she the only guest?'

'Yes.'

'Why this room in particular?'

Araceli shrugged, unconcerned. 'She asked for it.'

I considered this. 'You're telling me everything,' I asked. 'Right?'

'I'm sorry,' was all she said, and when I saw her slumped shoulders I wanted to take my question back, make it kinder. More, I wanted to . . . hold her.

'I'm sorry for wasting your time,' I said. 'Let's go.' But then, 'Wait.'

I had glimpsed in the bobbing torchlight a heavy-looking iron grille above the open fireplace. It was probably just an air vent. We would go, but first I had to look behind that grille. I couldn't reach without standing on something. I picked up the bedside cabinet, took it across the room to the fireplace and stood on top of it. It was stable enough. My hand reached for the grille, pulled it out.

'Pass me the torch, please.'

Araceli handed it up to me.

I felt nothing at first. Just cold, damp bricks. And cobwebs.

But wait. I sucked in a breath as my hand touched something firm at the back of the cavity.

'What is it?' Araceli asked.

A notebook . . . was that a notebook?

– 27 –

I turned to the first page. It was Selina's handwriting. No doubt about that.

Why would she hide it here? Why not bring it back to London?

A simple heading confirmed all of my suspicions about Selina's secret work: 'The Broad Haven Triangle.'

'Please, don't read it in here,' Araceli said suddenly. 'I hate this room.' She was at the door, rubbing her arms and eying the battered leather notebook, which was like a deadweight in my hands. 'Bring it downstairs.'

I don't know why I whispered my reply, but I did. 'Wait, please, just a moment.' I sat down on the bed nearest the window. Something was keeping me in this room, a terrible, black fear . . . I pressed my wrists against my eyes, wanting to blot out the image that was surfacing. An image of the future: Selina's coffin sinking into a yawning grave.

'Robert? You've gone white. What is it?'

My head was pulsing, and although my eyes were still closed, the image of Selina's coffin was so clear, as if I could see it floating before me on a movie screen. Everything else – the room, Araceli – had receded, but that dreadful image remained perfectly vivid. Not a fantasy, I thought. This is real, this is happening, right now, or it's going to soon.

Somewhere in the bowels of hotel I heard a floorboard creak. Or a door swing on its hinges. My eyes snapped open. 'I'm sorry,' was all I could say, feeling a total idiot. But the scene I had witnessed just a moment ago had come with startling abruptness.

We left the room together. My knees trembled all the way down to the ground floor.

On impulse I phoned the hospital in London where Selina was being treated. My strange vision had put the fear of God into me. Selina was still critical, they told me – but alive.

Thank God, thank God.

Araceli led me into the bar area, where she encouraged me to sit and rest. She chose the table furthest from the bay window and pulled up two high-backed wooden chairs. I was glad to sit down. I felt physically ill. More than that, I felt convinced that my vision would come true. I was anxious to switch attention away from me to the reason I had returned to the hotel that evening, thinking about Martin Marshall's troubling recollection of the men who had visited him after his encounter with the humanoid.

'Araceli, the men who came here after your sighting, do you remember anything about them?'

'Not really.'

'Think, please think. Cast your mind back and focus. Try for me.'

I could see she was trying. Her eyes had closed tightly as if to press the hidden recollection out. It was coming, slowly. I saw the memory forming on her lips. 'Their eyes . . .' she said distantly. 'I couldn't look away.' There was a long pause. At last she said, 'Dear God,' in a voice so low it took me by surprise. Then, 'No eyebrows – Robert, they had no eyebrows! And their faces were pointed. Their skin was hairless, so smooth. Like a woman's skin.'

A memory – a momentary flicker of a spindly man with gleaming teeth and flawless skin. His hair was as white as snow, and he was staring down at me.

I dropped a comforting hand on Araceli's arm. Something passed between us then – the long gaze we exchanged for five, perhaps ten, seconds confirmed there was a bond between us. That we had shared something. What? I had no idea yet, but the nagging sense of déjà vu was almost overwhelming.

Perhaps didn't just forget these men. She was made to forget.

'Do you think they were from the military?' I asked.

'No, no way.'

'Some government agency?'

Again she shook her head, and with a hoarse shaky quality in her voice said, 'No, you don't understand. Wherever they were from, they were . . . not . . .'

I sensed that she couldn't say what she wanted to, so I said it for her. 'You mean not from our world?'

She nodded slowly.

'But how can you be – '

'Listen to me!' she hissed, her eyes flitting between me and the window, which overlooked the gravel drive. 'They parked just out there – an enormous silver car, very shiny and polished. I couldn't place it; it looked new *and* old. Honest to God, I've never seen a car like that.' A terrible understanding crept across her face. 'I was here, in the bar, and I never heard a thing, don't you see? Nothing! No engine, not even the sound of tyres on the gravel. The first thing I knew of their arrival was them knocking on the door. Three times. Loud thuds.' She paused, looked at me. 'What is it? Robert, what's wrong?'

I wet my lips, shook away a dark memory. 'Nothing. Go on.'

'There were just two seats in the car. I would swear to that. Two. But there were three men.'

Black suits that didn't fit properly. Wide-brimmed hats, hair as white as snow, protruding eyes: these are the descriptions that would stay with me.

The Black-Suited Men.

Messengers of deception.

'Something was strange in their movements. Stilted. The man in the middle was holding a map and had such a dull, strange way of speaking, like he was reciting words. He said, "We have come to talk to you about your flying saucer sighting. But we can't stop today. We will call another time."'

She shook her head, stunned either by the detail of the memory or the fact that she had forgotten. 'So bloody weird, Robert. Why would they come to see me if they couldn't stop? I think they wanted me to see them. They wanted to intimidate me.'

'Did they ask you any questions about your sightings?'

'Actually,' she said, frowning, 'they asked something that made no sense: "Will you give yourself?"'

That didn't sound good and I asked cautiously – hardly wanting to hear the answer – whether she remembered anything else.

She nodded. 'I closed the door, and by the time I came back in here, I saw through that window that the car had, well, gone! Just an empty space, as though it, just . . .'

'Vanished.'

She looked at me uncertainly. 'Do you think I'm crazy?'

'What do you think?' I asked, summoning a reassuring smile. My eyes moved to Selina's open journal on the table and back to Araceli. 'Together we can beat this, whatever this is. But you must trust me, OK?' It came out with more confidence than I felt.

I thought for a moment her face would close up tight, like it had done during our first meeting, so it was a relief when she raised her chin and returned my smile. I couldn't help but admire how brave she had been to endure all this and how calm she still was. That urge to hold her . . .

'Why do you want to help us?'

'Because you're alone here, and no one should have no one.' I gave an honest shrug. 'And because I feel I owe it to you.'

Just then the telephone in the hall rang, startling us both. I wondered if it was the admiral, returning my call from earlier that night.

I stood and said, 'Don't worry – I'll go.'

It was Randall. I pictured him alone in his study over at Ravenstone Farm, watched over by St John the Baptist with his up-pointing finger. 'Well? Learn anything new, boy?'

'Nothing I'm willing to share – yet.' I chanced a peek into the bar to check Araceli wasn't reading Selina's journal.

There was a pronounced silence from the other side of the line. 'If you still think the Americans are behind this then we're all in trouble.'

I wasn't sure I did think that. Not any more. The Black-Suited Men who had come to the hotel asking if Araceli was willing to give herself didn't sound like the American military to me. Didn't sound like anything human. Nor did the silver humanoids witnessed outside RAF Croughton and RAF Brawdy and now Araceli's hotel. While I wasn't ready to accept a supernatural explanation, I *was* beginning to wonder if the possibility of extraterrestrial visitations really was so fantastic, and I told Randall so.

'Be not deceived by lying wonders,' he said quickly. 'You shouldn't be in that hotel, or around that woman.'

'Why on earth not?'

A pause. 'It's not a good place to be. Think about that lad this evening.' I heard him turn a page in a book. '"In 1846 it rained real blood in several areas of the world. And all kinds of odd shapes and lights were seen in the sky. Peculiar figures in silver clothing were also sighted across Europe. They were humanlike but large and possessed the ability to pass through walls and disappear."'

When I heard that I wanted to laugh, but I didn't because what Randall said next wasn't a laughing matter.

'Those who witnessed such beings were said to have lost their minds, Robert.' I was about to hang up when he sighed and said, 'All right, listen. If I can't convince you with words, let me show you. Tomorrow. Perhaps then you'll see sense and leave.'

Saturday. 'I'm busy tomorrow.' I'd promised myself I'd look into the history of the area. Its alternative history.

'Day after tomorrow then. Sunday. Four o'clock. I'll collect you from the Ram Inn.'

'Where are we going?'

'To meet someone who might change your perspective.'

'Lock up well.' It was the last piece of advice I'd given Araceli before wishing her goodnight and making my way back to the Ram Inn in Little Haven. The place was silent and deserted and I was glad.

Now, feeling more puzzled than ever, all I could think about was reading Selina's journal.

I was halfway up the stairs when a hostile voice made me turn round.

'Who exactly do you think you are, eh?'

It was Roger Daley, the landlord. He stood in the half-light at the bottom of the stairs.

'What?' I said.

'You've been getting around quite a bit, haven't you?'

'Needs must.' I gave him a polite smile. 'Well, goodnight.'

'A good night?' he said roughly. 'Been a while since we've seen one of those.'

What was this? Why was he so angry? 'Have I done something wrong, Mr Daley? If you want me to pay more for the room, then I'd be happy to.'

'You wanna be careful about associating with that old Bible-basher.'

'Randall?'

'Reckless old bastard. Ought to be locked up. Probably will be.'

'Why do you say that?'

His eyes flicked up. I remember that moment as vividly as Selina's last words to me because his eyes actually changed. Only for a second, but I'd swear to it on my parents' graves. Those eyes blazed an infernal red.

'Quite the commotion at the school meeting today, wasn't it? Couldn't help thinking most of it focused on you and him. And her.'

'You mean Araceli?'

He nodded his shiny bald head. 'We all saw you leave together.'

'We?'

'Those of us who care most about this community.'

Who did he mean? He and the woman from the post office? The classroom assistant Delyth Cale? Howell Cooper the headmaster? Or how about Father O'Riorden?

'Time well spent?' he probed. I was genuinely surprised by his forceful tone. 'Learn much new about the Happenings?'

'Not really,' I lied.

'What about the hotel? Get a good look around?'

'If you don't mind, Mr Daley, I'm exhausted, and – '

'Pritchard is never to set foot in this establishment. Ever. And he – both of you – are to stay the hell away from the kids. Stay away from my nephew. Understand?'

'Your nephew?'

His lips drew back over stained yellow teeth. 'Martin. Poor lad. Reckons the two of you hounded him out at the base tonight.'

'I'm just trying to help.'

He glared at me fiercely. 'You can help by leaving it alone.'

FROM *THE MIND POSSESSED: A PERSONAL INVESTIGATION INTO THE BROAD HAVEN TRIANGLE*

BY DR R. CAXTON (CLEMENTINE PRESS, 1980) P.35

I soon discovered historical evidence that established some basis for the community's enduring belief in supernatural manifestations. In 1190 the monk Gerald of Wales spoke of spirits that are not visible but present all the same. They ripped up clothes and entered houses that were bolted and barred. And in 1927 a husband and wife from the village saw an object fall into St Brides Bay. A boat was dispatched to search for it. Nothing was found.

Almost ten years later the same thing was seen again. This time the local police were involved. Shortly afterwards Chief Inspector Reginald Jones reported that he and a colleague saw something emerge from the sea near Stack Rocks.

In the witness's own words, 'At first I thought we were seeing a ship on fire on the horizon. But then it rose out of the water like a blood-red sun, a good deal larger than a full-sized harvest moon. It remained at sea level, then suddenly took off at a fantastic speed towards the Atlantic. Afterwards, there was a terrible flood.'

Of course, in such a superstitious community events like these were thought to be connected . . .

– 28 –

Saturday 12 February, 1977, Ram Inn, Little Haven, 1 a.m

As I showered, I thought of Araceli and found myself wishing we had been friends when we were younger. It would have helped me knowing there was another young person as lonely as me shut up in the hotel on the hill with no one but her mother for company, the mad woman on the hill.

Mum was involved with the Rotary Club. Local business owners, some of the elders. Araceli had also told me that Mr Daley was a member, but after my confrontation with him on the stairs that was a difficult idea to swallow. *They raised money for good causes.* I wondered vaguely what good causes?

Araceli hadn't invited me to stay but of course I had offered. Why not? There were plenty of vacant rooms. But she had refused, insisted she was fine up there.

I towelled myself dry and went to the window in the bedroom. A light at the top of the Haven Hotel was still on. For a few moments I contemplated phoning just to check she was all right, but would that look too keen? Heaven knows, I didn't want to scare her off. What I really wanted was to keep her close, to understand why she was at the forefront of my considerations, to know why that concern felt so legitimate. And while I couldn't help but interpret that concern as physical attraction, I knew at the core of my being there was a deeper bond here.

I pulled on some underwear and a T-shirt, sat down at the desk facing the window and flicked on the radio.

Selina's notebook wasn't particularly thick, but still it felt weightily important. Two words scrawled on its inside cover sent a thread of worry worming into me: '*Caveat Lector.*' Let the reader beware.

That sort of poetic flourish was typical of Selina. In other circumstances it might even have brought a smile to my lips.

I flicked further into the journal and stopped at a page headed 'Brawdy'.

The secret US facility is small but perfectly placed – remote, low-density population. The Americans seem to be doing much to ingratiate themselves with the locals: collecting clothing, cleaning up beaches, riverbeds and cemeteries. They've even purchased equipment for the local hospitals. But the American presence on British soil continues to attract criticism from the usual sources. Many suspect the facility at Brawdy is part of a regional defence network. The secrecy surrounding the facility has made it the target of several anti-nuclear protests led by the Campaign for the Accountability of American Bases. Bestford needs to be careful in discussing the facility in public.

I looked up from the text. The radio was murmuring a song. I turned up the volume. Barry White was singing about his first, last and everything. Coincidentally one of Selina's favourites. I forced myself to flick further into the journal. I knew what I was looking for, was certain it would be here. It was. 'The parallels between the sightings here and the incident at RAF Croughton are undeniable now. Colonel Corso has agreed to speak to me in private before he gives evidence to the inquiry. He needs to hear what I learned yesterday.'

As I turned the page, somewhere in the recesses of my mind hidden connections were threading together. Then my eyes fell on the hurriedly scrawled heading 'Interview with Martin Marshall'. 'Perhaps it was because he wasn't feeling well; the boy looked weak, washed-out. His slow responses suggest the flu – or something. He also had hearing problems, difficulty remembering things.'

The notebook proceeded to tell the same story I had heard that evening from Martin, but it also detailed the sense of darkness and hopelessness that had overwhelmed him after his encounter.

> *I wondered whether he might be on drugs or lying, but if he was acting, this boy deserves an Oscar! And as for substance abuse, it's possible that he was delusional, I suppose, but it's clear to me that something happened on the base that night. Some sort of commotion – an explosion. People in the closest village heard it.*
>
> *Martin has made a sketch of the figure he witnessed. My plan is to show it to Colonel Corso and perhaps encourage the two of them to meet. But Martin was hostile. He said he would never forget the figure. 'Its face was made of shadows.'*

Six pages from the back I found more notes referencing the man who was supposed to be our star witness, Lieutenant Colonel Corso.

This is far worse than I feared. According to Colonel Corso there exists a highly secret report associated with the UFO sightings – associated with someone called Jack Parsons. This report fell into the hands of a group of people who call themselves the Parsons Elite. Who are they? I have no idea. The report warns that UFOs – whatever they are – are dangerous. Deadly. But who wrote this report? Who leaked it?

I looked up, feeling the colour drain from my face. I silenced the radio, feeling my heart rate pick up. Something made me turn round. Feeling no longer alone.

I checked the window and then went to the door to check it was properly shut. Rattled the door handle three times then ran my fingers along the edge of the door, checking it was flush against the frame. It was. I knelt and peered through the keyhole to make sure there was no one outside in the corridor. There wasn't. The only thing of interest in the corridor was a malfunctioning light that flickered and blinked at me, as if to say, *You're crazy, Robert. You know that? Crazy!*

I squeezed my wrists against my eyes and said out loud, 'This has got to stop. Soon you won't know what's real and what's not.'

When I finally made it into bed, I flicked off the light and the swell of the sea brought me back to the present. I lay there in the pitch black picturing Araceli's haunted face. Was it possible? Aliens in this remote, unimportant corner of the world? Except it wasn't unimportant. Not to the Soviets. From behind the Iron Curtain, predators were eyeing this little corner of the world.

I tried to distance myself from these thoughts, but it was useless. Nagging doubts kept my gaze riveted on the door handle as cold uncertainty crept in. Some things I couldn't doubt, like the lights I had witnessed cartwheeling in the sky over Brawdy. They were real, and everything about that aerial display was unnatural: the impossible speeds, the sharp turns, the breathtaking acceleration no human pilot would ever survive.

I started to shake. Paranoia was affecting my judgement, and I had responsibilities – to Araceli and her daughter, who were vulnerable, to Selina, and to the admiral, who had sent me here to solve this mystery. Didn't they deserve someone who was equal to the task?

My thoughts returned to Frobisher's tale about the glowing object that had crashed into the sea centuries ago; to the Jacksons, who had died while walking on the cliffs; to the mutilated animals; to the silver-suited figures stalking the countryside. And to the Black-Suited Men with skin like wax and eyes like fire and ice.

FROM *THE MIND POSSESSED: A PERSONAL INVESTIGATION INTO THE BROAD HAVEN TRIANGLE*

BY DR R. CAXTON (CLEMENTINE PRESS, 1980), P.50

That winter the Havens slept beneath glaring stars. In farm-houses and hotels, on the sea and in the fields and on deserted country roads the darkest imaginings were coming true. By the weekend that preceded the sky watch, the twice-daily buses from Haverfordwest had emptied; the fishermen from Milford Haven who for decades had come to St Brides Bay for their catch kept instead to their own patch. Even the Saturday after-noon excursion from the home for the elderly in Pembroke Dock turned its back on Broad Haven's finest fish and chip shop. Something had gone wrong in this part of Pembrokeshire. Outsiders couldn't tell you what, exactly, or why – only that they believed with conviction that the Havens had turned bad.

– 29 –

Saturday 12 February 1977, four days
until the sky watch . . .

By half past eight the sun had passed the horizon and was
glimmering weakly on St Brides Bay. Over breakfast at the
window table in the Nest Bistro I watched the cockle women
in their shawls heading for the sands. When I had finished and
stepped outside, a grizzly fisherman unmooring his bobbing
vessel raised a courteous but wary hand in my direction, and I
played my part, waving back confidently.

I didn't trust him. After the previous night's confrontation
with the landlord I wasn't sure who to trust. Except perhaps
Araceli and Frobisher. And the admiral? An hour or two earlier
I had written him a short note telling him about the sinister
people in the village – my suspicions that they might be connected, somehow, with the unusual sightings. I wrote too about
the incredible light display above RAF Brawdy and Selina's notes
referencing a secret report associated with someone called Jack
Parsons.

The gulls were shrieking overhead. The wind gusted. I felt
so lonely here, so cut off.

As I passed the post office, I saw Ethel Dunwoody's bloated distrustful face peering out at me from the window. I remembered how the ROTARY pin she had been wearing had caught my eye, and that made me wonder who else was a member.

If there was one thing I had learned from my committee work in Parliament, it was that small groups of people with influence have a funny way of pursuing the agendas that matter most to them. Idly I wondered what had mattered most to the members of the Havens Rotary Club, and to Araceli's late mother. Someone would know, but I would have to ask around and hope I got lucky; people in the Havens weren't exactly forthcoming.

'The Rotary Club?' My informant was a middle-aged man coming out of the Nest Bistro. He looked around as if to check no one was listening then dropped his voice to a confidential tone. 'To be honest, they're a bit odd. I reckon they think they're like the Masons or something. Self-important bunch the lot of 'em, but I suppose they have some influence.'

'Know much about their charitable work?'

'Well I think they raised some money for the lifeboat.'

I was beginning to think I would get nowhere until a young woman stretching after her run along the beach suggested it might help me to check out the information board outside the village hall.

The noticeboard was covered with coloured leaflets promoting the sort of occasions you'd expect in a remote community like the Havens: parish council meetings, book clubs, after-school private tuition and dog-walking services. There was still one leaflet promoting the eventful public meeting at the school. Someone had defaced it with a crude drawing of an extraterrestrial. It looked exactly as you would expect – right out of the movies, with a tiny slit for a mouth, almond-shaped eyes and a large pear-shaped head. An alien face.

Funny, I thought. Except it wasn't. Because none of the menacing humanoids seen in the area looked anything like this picture. Those figures had no faces. Those figures were broad and seven feet tall, with silver clothing that rustled when they walked and shimmered in the moonlight. Those figures could vanish in an instant, walk through fences and traumatize a young man's mind.

This thought was troubling enough but it wasn't what made the shiver run up my back. That came a few moments later when I spotted what was I looking for, hidden away in the bottom right corner of the noticeboard. A single card. Tiny writing. 'The Havens Rotary Club thanks you for your support. This year we will continue to support the lifeboat appeal, as well as new equipment for the school. Work continues on the Stack Rocks Fort renovation project to create a visitors' centre but remains in its very early stages. We would like to remind anyone thinking of visiting the rocks that landing there is difficult and that the fort is in an extremely dilapidated, dangerous condition. All donations gratefully received. Our next meeting is on 2 April at . . .'

Stack Rocks again. This was what it was really like, knowing that your worst suspicions weren't paranoid imaginings – however much one hoped they were – but real. Stack Rocks Fort was connected to the Happenings – somehow – and so were the individuals who called themselves the Havens Rotary Club. I knew that as certainly as I now knew who controlled access to the fort. I knew something else too. Araceli would tell me more. I'd make certain of it.

I decided to go into the post office for a newspaper, and when I pushed open the door and entered the dusty interior found a few of the village women mid-gossip.

'Mary Dee had a strange phone call the other night. No one there, she said, just heavy breathing. When I got a call I reported it to the telephone company. Our number's unlisted, so it must have been a fault on the line.'

Another woman chipped in, 'Well, we had a man call at the house asking questions for the council – so he said. Tanned, looked foreign to me. Wanted to know about Isaac and what he saw at the school.'

My ears pricked up. That didn't sound like the council to me.

'Isaac's not feeling too well today, are you, dear?' I heard his mother say. 'Good job the school is closed.'

Isaac was a rotund eleven-year-old. At least nine stone. He was standing next to his mother at the counter as I laid down my morning paper for payment.

Hey, weren't *you* interested in all that?' the postmistress said, turning to me. Ethel Dunwoody's voice was unmistakably hostile, so much so that I decided immediately it would be unwise to tell her too much or to ask about her involvement with the Rotary Club. 'You find what you were looking for?' she added.

'I think so,' I muttered, trying not to look at her lapel pin.

Isaac's mother stood staring at me. 'You were at the town meeting.'

I nodded, smiled. 'I couldn't help overhearing you just now. Can I ask what's wrong with your son?'

'What's it to you?' she asked with sudden hostility.

It wasn't the response I was hoping for.

'Well, I've met others who have seen these strange craft in

the air and close to the ground. I'm interested to know whether there are any physical effects.' I glanced down at Isaac. Not a handsome child: his dark hair was too long, his skin a sun-starved white. And his stillness was unsettling. He hadn't moved. Hadn't even blinked. 'What I mean is, have you noticed any changes in Isaac's behaviour? It's natural for a youngster to be unnerved seeing something so out of the ordinary.'

She seemed to read the insinuation in my question, but with Isaac standing right next to her said nothing. The kid's eyes had a glassy sheen I didn't care for at all.

'You some sort of expert?'

'Not exactly.' I paused, then turned to the boy. 'Isaac?' I asked lightly.

He turned to look at me wordlessly. I took a step back. It wasn't just that he looked ill; he was *changed*. His face was . . . older, his skin almost grey.

'Oh goodness,' the postmistress remarked, 'the poor love really doesn't look well.' She almost sounded pleased.

I asked, 'Isaac, when you and the other children saw that object, did any of your teachers see it too? Maybe when you and your friends ran in to get the headmaster?'

He shook his head, and I saw that the glassy sheen in his eyes had vanished. Then he said, 'If sir hadn't let us out of class early, we probably wouldn't have seen it at all.'

That got my attention. Howell Cooper had never mentioned anything about letting the children out early.

'And why did he do that?' I asked.

'Because the priest came,' the child said innocently.

'Father O'Riorden?'

Isaac nodded. 'Sir said they had to talk in private.'

His mother gave me a questioning look.

'What else did Mr Cooper say, Isaac? After you saw the silver object?' I was trying to sound unconcerned.

'Sir said we should rest and that we should keep our minds open because that's when we hear them best.'

'Hear who, Isaac ?'

'The voices. The voices from the sky.'

'Do *you* hear them, Isaac? What do they say?'

'That we must be ready. That we must watch the skies.'

'Oh, not this again!' his mother said curtly, sounding more nervous than exasperated.

'Daddy's heard the voices too,' the child cut in. 'Daddy's not well.'

The postmistress brushed her hands down her apron. 'Well, must get on. Lots to do!'

My spotlight of suspicion dropped on Father O'Riorden. Why was the priest at the school at the same time as the sighting?

'Father O'Riorden, what can you tell me about him?' I asked Ethel Dunwoody.

But the postmistress just shook her head.

'Right, well. Take Isaac straight home,' I said, turning to his mother, who was leading the boy towards the post office door. 'Watch him carefully, OK? He's had a terrible shock.'

She nodded.

A terrible shock. Just like Martin Marshall and little Tessa. And, like them, Isaac's behaviour, even his appearance, was changing in subtle ways. *Perhaps that's what happens when you observe these UFOs up close. Perhaps they change you. Not for the better*.

'We did try taking advice from Mr Pritchard,' Isaac's mother disclosed. 'He wasn't much help.' She didn't just look worried now; she looked distressed. 'You don't think it's anything . . . sinister, do you?'

'I'm sure it's not,' I replied, offering a smile.

But as the shop bell jangled and the door shut behind them, I had to pretend I hadn't seen the missing patch of hair on the back of Isaac's head.

– 30 –

Broad Haven Church, Marine Road

Father O'Riorden hadn't seen me.

I watched him from behind the churchyard gate. He was alone in the cemetery, a dominating figure with his domed pate and white hair, watching over the village as though it were a sleeping child. I tracked his gaze over the maze of pastel cottages below. Little Haven didn't feel awake that morning – even as the clock tower struck eleven – as though it was hesitating to accept the day had begun. I thought I saw the same hesitation in the priest's sagging face, a sort of weariness.

I had looked into O'Riorden's background and now had questions. I wanted to know what he had been doing at the school the day of the sighting, why he was so unpopular in the Havens and more about his association with the headmaster.

Although Mr Daley at the Ram Inn hadn't much wanted to discuss the priest, I encountered no such problem with Frank Frobisher when I caught him in the bar enjoying his morning coffee. Not only did I show him Martin Marshall's drawing of the giant figure, but I questioned him about Father O'Riorden. After hearing what the journalist had to say about the priest's interests, his politics and his writings, I'd come straight to the churchyard.

I unlatched the gate and Father O'Riorden looked up sharply.

'What do you know about Howell Cooper?'

O'Riorden smiled warmly and in his rich voice said, 'Not even a hello?'

I pushed on. 'The day of the sighting he let the kids out into the playground early. Why?'

Father O'Riorden gave an unconcerned shrug. 'Oh well, I suppose he wanted a break. It wasn't a normal school day. All the other children were on an excursion.'

'Why were you there? You never mentioned that before.'

'We had business to discuss. School assemblies, the Easter concert, some charitable work.'

I wasn't convinced. 'Howell, is he a religious man?'

The priest looked at me uneasily. 'Well, he writes local history, comes in once in a while to look over the church records: births, deaths, baptisms. Why are you asking?'

Still suspicious, I told him about my conversation in the post office and that I'd tried to find Cooper, first at the school, then at home in Marine Close, without success.

A small smile surfaced on the priest's face, one that said, *You are as paranoid as your grandfather*, and then his expression subsided into puzzlement again. 'You mean the sky watch business? Howell is conscientious, that's all. The kids are his first priority. He never forgets a name, never gets them mixed up. Maybe he is a bit superstitious for his own good, but he means well.'

I wasn't quite convinced. I felt there was something he wasn't telling me. 'Father, you saw the way the children behaved at the public meeting.'

'Yes. I saw the way *everyone* behaved,' the priest answered, throwing a glance at the sky. His gaze dropped to the sea. 'It's sad,' he added in a flat voice, 'but when it comes to self-delusion there are no age limits. Forgive me, but I find all of this rather too far-fetched.'

I didn't want to follow him into the church. It was only my determination to find the truth and my concern for the children that led me into the cool, dark gloom. The instant I saw the altar and an image of Christ bleeding on the cross I felt uncomfortable. Unwelcome. I couldn't explain why, but I hadn't really felt at ease in religious buildings since I had gone to live with Randall.

'Father, I'm determined to get to the bottom of this.'

Then something against the north wall of the church caught my attention, an ancient-looking document with faded writing, protected by an expensive-looking glass cabinet. 'What is this?'

'Our own piece of local history,' he said, following me to the cabinet. 'Discovered back in the seventeenth century. The Rotary Club had it translated, I believe, by the British Museum.'

But it wasn't the text that had caught my attention.

ᛏᚼ∑Δиᛢi∑иᛏ◊и∑ ᛑ∆Я∑ᛢ◊iи

'What are these symbols?'

Father O Riorden shrugged. 'Their meaning has never been ascertained. But the text itself is rather clearer. See for yourself.'

I leaned closer to read it:

Gha D'rcest Cthasska, Gha D'rcest Cthassiss.
          In the name of the Father, Son and of the Holy Ghost
Amen X X X and in the name of the Lord Jesus Christ I

will delive Elizabeth Loyd from all witchcraft and from all
evil spirites and from all evil men or women or wizardes
or hardness of heart Amen X X X

Witchcraft and evil. Two words I hadn't expected to read on
the wall of a church. I glanced across at Father O Riorden. 'An
incantation from the seventeenth century purported to have
been used to exorcize a young woman.'

Exorcize. That word made me flinch. I remembered St John
the Baptist looking down at me from the wall, his finger pointing skyward.

'What about these words?' I pointed. *Gha D'rcest Cthasska, Gha
D'rcest Cthassiss.*

'It's gibberish,' Father O'Riorden said dismissively. 'More
superstition.'

'Even so, would you mind if I copied this down?'

He didn't look pleased at the idea but he didn't stop me
either. One day soon I would be very, very glad of that.

I tried to make sense of the unsettling déjà vu that was
coming over me, strange enough for me to want to read the rest
of the incantation. It went on in a mixture of Roman Catholic
Latin and cabbalistic words of power like Tetragrammaton, the
name of God. At the bottom were two rows of planetary symbols. The sun, the moon and Venus were obvious.

I will trust in the Lord Jesus Christ my Redeemer and
Saviour from all evil spirites and from all other assaltes
of the Devil and that he will delive Elizabeth Loyd from
all witchcraft and from all evil spirites by the same power
as he did cause the blind to see, the lame to walke and
that thou findest with unclean spirites to be in thire one

mindes amen X X X as weeth Jehovah Amen. The witches compassed her abought but in the name of the lord i will destroy them Amen

'Strikes me as a very odd thing to find in a Christian Church,' I declared.

'Oh, not really. Historical accounts of exorcisms are common, especially those involving moon children.'

'Huh?'

'The idea of the moon child is that a perfect soul can be created – captured – at an early age through a process of demonization. According to legend, blood sacrifices and human sacrifices were required. The moon child, it was thought, would rise to be mightier than all the kings on earth.'

'And this woman –' I glanced again at the incantation.

'– Elizabeth Loyd, she was a moon child?'

Father O' Riorden gave a wry smile. 'According to legend, yes. 'He shook his head emphatically. 'But this is a myth, Mr Wilding. Just like your UFOs.'

'Father, I understand your scepticism. Until recently I was exactly the same way. But I've seen the evidence with my own eyes: *something* changed those kids, something is in the village, watching people. There are strange men visiting witnesses, asking questions about the children. And I want an explanation.'

'What sort of explanation would you like?' he asked. 'Spacecraft from another solar system?'

'Maybe,' I whispered. 'Father, if those kids saw what they think they saw – intelligent beings sharing our existence – that would change everything we assume or know to be true. There's no more significant revelation, no single more important truth.'

'You speak about truth as though it can be dug out of the

ground, tested and examined. My truths are protected with faith.'

'You know, there are people who think flying saucers appeared in the Bible,' I said, remembering Randall's whisperings from childhood.

Father O'Riorden folded his arms across his expansive chest and looked at me steadily. 'I cannot accept that. If the earth were to be visited by extraterrestrials from a galaxy far, far away, such an event would redefine man's place in the universe. So why doesn't the Bible and God, in his infinite wisdom, mention such a momentous occasion?'

'Ezekiel 1: "Out of the sky came a wheel within a wheel."'

A tense silence opened between us.

'A wheel within a wheel, Father,' I said again. 'What does that sound like to you?'

The priest levelled his gaze at me. 'I appreciate your concern, young man. But I'm doing all I can to reassure this community, to protect the villagers from sensationalism.'

'You mean protect them from Randall?'

'His faith is grossly misplaced.'

O'Riorden seemed not to want to look at me. Was he afraid that the phenomena in the village would call into question his god? Or did the root of his unease lie deeper? Watching his face harden as he looked past me towards the row of symbols on the wall, I began to wonder whether that was the problem – not that he feared losing his faith, but that he had already lost it.

'You have to remember,' he said eventually, 'that this whole area is rich in legend and folklore.' His eyes, I noticed, were still fixed on the strange symbols.

'Father, tell me, how often did the headmaster come here to check records of baptisms? What was the nature of his interest?'

Silence

'Did he ever ask you about these symbols? Make copies of them?'

More silence. But on his face I could see defiance turning to anger and the sudden wildness in his eyes made me step back. 'You think the people of this community don't know what lurks beneath the surface here? They are afraid to face it!'

It was not what he said that made me worry but how he said it. His voice had become louder and unmistakably afraid, as if I was on the verge of extracting from him a long suppressed and dangerous secret.

I would have pressed him but I was too shocked to speak.

'I know you are struggling,' he said finally. The priest lowered his head, eyes closed. 'But we are all struggling. Go with God.'

– 31 –

Outside the church I wandered down to the deserted seafront, wondering whether the admiral had received my note mentioning Selina's research and her reference to someone called Jack Parsons. I might have kept thinking about this if not for a distraction. My gaze swept half a mile out to sea and settled upon Stack Rocks Island and the circular fort that crowned its highest point.

I knew the fort had been abandoned for over a hundred years. So why did I now feel as though it sensed me here? I had to force myself to look away. When I did, I saw something else that made my spirits sink: a granite plaque affixed to the sea wall.

Fifty-nine people had died at this spot fourteen years earlier. After the storm surge the sea wall had been built. Bestford campaigned for it. It wasn't an argument he had to struggle with. Outrage had erupted in the village. There had been other floods, but none that had arrived so suddenly as this. Why hadn't there been proper defences? More than one hundred people gathered to hear Bestford unveil the plaque erected in memory of those who had perished. Me? I stayed away that day. The pain was still too raw.

I checked my watch. Midday. I had until tomorrow afternoon before meeting Randall at the pub, when I would tell him what I'd heard and seen in the post office. I didn't want to spend the day barricaded in my room, so I walked to Giant's Point, an incredible place to look out along the coastline. I thought about searching for the headmaster again at the school. Just because Father O'Riorden thought Howell Cooper was harmless didn't mean the man didn't have a part in this.

If sir hadn't let us out of class early, we probably wouldn't have seen it at all.

I turned to walk back the way I had come and got only as far as the steps which led up to the coastal path that I knew so well. This wasn't just the last path the murdered Jacksons had ever walked; it was the path to my past. To Ravenstone Farm.

A rickety white sign pointed the way to Talbenny.

What the hell, I thought. And took the path.

After a couple of hundred yards I climbed a stile and kept going, with the fields sloping up to my left and the seagulls swooping over St Brides Bay to my right. Almost an hour later, I knew I was close, that if I kept going I would soon catch sight of Randall's house perched on the cliffs.

I should go back, I thought.

Suddenly I saw a figure coming towards me from across the adjoining field. I couldn't see his face at first, just filthy baggy trousers and a long coat flapping in the morning wind. He was carrying a wooden post and for a second I thought it was Randall, but this person was walking with the ease of a younger man. He raised his hand. It was a few seconds before I realised his identity.

'Robert? Bloody hell, it's been years!'

'Hello, Gethin.' I clasped his rough hand. He was a grizzly

man of around fifty, strong and sturdily built with a grey beard that made him look much older.

'Great to see you again,' I lied.

Randall had always kept relations with Gethin Yates ostensibly cordial out of simple necessity. Gethin was his neighbour, and a farmer, and that was an end to the subject, no matter how little regard he really had for the man, who was a gossip and a braggart. You never knew when you might find yourself in need of a neighbour on a farm. Especially somewhere as isolated as this.

'Randall mentioned you were back.' Then he paused awkwardly. I had expected him to immediately launch into a detailed interrogation of my life or an exaggerated account of how thriving his herd and business was. Yet he was just standing here. Waiting for a response.

'Well, I'm not staying long.'

The look on his face mirrored the dismal weather. 'What brings you back now?'

I considered how much to divulge. Gethin would know about the UFO sightings and might offer helpful information on Randall's involvement. I still didn't know how the old man had predicted the sightings or knew so much about the phenomena. On the other hand, Gethin was hardly known for his discretion, so I decided to ask about the Jacksons. 'I heard about that poor couple who went missing up here. Awful thing . . .?'

He studied me for a moment and frowned. He opened his mouth to say something, then closed it the way people do when they have no idea what to say to the bereaved.

'That was a long time ago, anyway,' I said. 'And this is work.'

'Well, it's all been pretty well covered in the newspapers.' Gethin paused, squinting against the sea wind. 'I'd have thought you would have spoken to Randall about this? He told the police everything he knows.'

'I beg your pardon?'

'Well, it's all right now, isn't it? Now they've ruled him out of any involvement.'

What sort of bloody involvement? My mind raced. Was this why Selina had urged me to stay close to this case, why she had asked me what sort of man my grandfather was? I didn't want to betray my ignorance, and while I was sure that Gethin would be happy to inform me of anything besmirching Randall's reputation, I was equally sure that he would let it be known about the village that I had been asking questions about Randall behind his back. That would have obvious consequences once it got back to Randall.

I would have to pursue the possibility that Randall was more deeply involved than I had believed. But not now, not with Gethin.

'Of course, of course,' I bluffed, nodding as if this was old news, then did my best to swerve the conversation away from Randall. 'What are you doing down here?'

I thought this was moving to safer ground, but it appeared that I had miscalculated. Gethin's expression stiffened. 'Fixing the fence,' he said, hefting the wooden post. 'Don't want anything getting in.'

'Foxes?'

A mirthless grin crossed his face momentarily, really no more than a flexing of the lips. 'Ha. Foxes. Yeah, sure, always got to keep the foxes out, don't you? Leaving holes in fences is just sloppy farming, you know that, Robert. Asking for trouble. Anything could get in.'

His gaze floated above my head, out to sea and then back

inland. His attention snapped back as he became aware of me watching, and he fixed me with a hard stare. 'You know, Robert, you really shouldn't come up here alone. Not at the moment. With all that's been happening here recently.'

'You mean the Jackson murders.'

'Them. And the ... sightings, you know.' His expression wavered between tentative embarrassment and slight defiance.

I thought back suddenly to the freezing morning here on the cliffs when Randall had raved about forces of darkness, his eyes glittering furiously as he denounced my father as a monster. It was Gethin who had appeared on the coastal path and waved at us. Gethin was the last person I would have expected to voice opinions that echoed Randall's. I was sure that some of the less charitable rumours which had circulated about Randall owed their existence to the speculations of his nearest neighbour.

'Surely you've heard about the Happenings?'

I hesitated. I didn't want to show too much of my own interest in the sightings or reveal the real reason I was here when there was already talk in the village.

'Oh, come on, Gethin, you're not taken in by all this mumbo-jumbo, are you?' I couched my inquiry amiably, forcing out a little chuckle that by no means reflected my feelings.

'Mumbo-jumbo?' He wasn't laughing. 'I wouldn't call it that exactly.'

'Then what would you call it?'

'I wouldn't call it anything if I could help it, Robert,' he answered coldly, holding up his hand to forestall the objection forming on my lips. 'And neither should you, if you had half the sense you were born with. Isn't wise to talk about these things too much, nor openly. Names have power, you know! Names *invite them in*, you understand? Have you been gone so long and so far you forgot where you came from? Scoff if you want to, Robert. After all, you're the one with the fancy education. But I promise you – you go around talking about things you got no business knowing and putting names to such things as you shouldn't, and you'll live to regret it. Perhaps we all will.'

Was my mind playing tricks on me, projecting monsters into every shadow, or had a distinct edge of menace crept into Gethin's voice? It had risen in volume, certainly. And half an octave for that matter. I knew he could be a bit of a pain in the neck, but surely he wasn't actually threatening me? Was he?

He shouldered the fence post and without further comment strode briskly off towards a gap in the fence. 'Wait,' I called out, turning and trotting after him, cursing myself for a fool even as I ran. How had I failed to recognize that look? Of course Gethin wasn't trying to threaten me; that strange light in his eyes wasn't menace – it was fear. No wonder he was babbling nonsense; the man was terrified. I had to find out who had got to him, and how.

I caught up with him after a dozen paces, but he would not slow his pace, nor would he look at me. He just kept marching towards that gap in the fence, staring fixedly ahead. 'Gethin, please,' I appealed to his reason. 'I need to know who's been speaking to you.'

But his palm flicked up defensively, fending me off.

'This is important, Gethin. It's a matter of national security, you understand?'

This seemed to produce an effect. He stopped in his tracks with a grunt, still a dozen yards shy of the fence, and flung the post down on the ground.

'You want to know what's going on? Try looking right under your own nose! You read about the mutilations?'

'Mutilations?'

He nodded and his eyes sharpened. I was remembering the rabbits Randall had brought to the public meeting. That must be what he must be referring to.

'You read the paper this morning? Fifteen dogs hung in the woods down near the primary school. Throats cut, all the skin removed. Some sort of ritual, the police are saying.'

'When was this?'

'It was done yesterday, around the same time as that meeting in the school.'

'So what do you think it means?' I asked.

For a moment our eyes met. I could feel he wanted to impart something important, and in that moment he reminded me a great deal of Randall.

'People around here talk as though these UFOs are the ones visiting us, you know, just dropping in, observing us.' He shook his head. 'But what if it's not that way. What if it's us calling them?'

'Sorry, but are you suggesting that someone is summoning these phenomena?

He nodded.

Part of me wanted to laugh, if only to release the tension, but I couldn't, and I'm glad. Because if I had laughed then I wouldn't have heard amusement or even ridicule. I would have heard hysteria breaking in a wave that threatened to wash my sanity away.

Both of us looked out onto the slate-grey sullen sea towards Stack Rocks.

Both of us were silent.

– 32 –

Ram Inn, Little Haven

'I want to ask you something extremely important.'

Frobisher tossed his newspaper aside and warmed his hands before the dancing flames in the hearth of the inn. 'Hello again. Fire away.'

'Why didn't you tell me the police had interviewed Randall about the Jacksons?'

He shrugged. 'Assumed you'd know already. Pritchard was one of the first questioned. He didn't exactly give them a warm welcome. They searched his barn, the whole farm. Then they held him.'

'As a suspect?' I looked at him with strained composure. Randall had said nothing. 'Right. Well, after that he was cleared, yes?'

Frobisher just looked at me.

I was filled with a wave of nausea 'You mean he's still a suspect?'

Frobisher nodded. 'Well, Ravenstone Farm is the nearest property to where the Jacksons were found. You should talk to your grandfather, Rob.'

'I intend to. He's coming here. Tomorrow afternoon.'

Frobisher checked his watch then drained his pint. 'Good luck. I gotta get going.'

'Who are you meeting?'

'Father O'Riorden. Going to see if I can get him involved with the sky watch on Tuesday. Drum up some more support.'

'Frank, I really think that whipping up public hysteria like this is not a good idea.'

Frobisher scowled. 'What's the harm? It sells newspapers and the holiday cottages are filling up fast. Everyone's a winner.' He looked down at his discarded newspaper. 'Anyway, this lunar eclipse is going to pull in the crowds regardless. You ever seen a blood moon before, Rob?'

'No. A blood moon? This is too weird,' I said to Frobisher. 'Too much of a coincidence. The same night?'

'Sure,' he said, grinning. 'Good story, right?'

But I didn't think there was anything good about it. 'Frank, what does Father O'Riorden believe about the sightings? I went to see him but I just couldn't figure out – '

'That's always been a mystery.'

'Has Father O'Riorden interviewed the children?' I asked then, remembering Isaac Jones's unsettling behaviour in the post office. 'Or their parents?'

'Nope. All access to the children is being controlled by Howell Cooper.'

That made me sit up. 'What do you know about the school then, about Howell Cooper in particular?'

'What is it, Robert? You seem edgy.'

'It's just that the headmaster was very keen to shut the school, to encourage the sky watch.'

Frobisher hesitated, frowning. When he spoke again his voice carried a note of warning. 'If I were you, I would think very carefully before throwing around accusations. I don't need to tell you, of all people, that this community rallies around those who keep it safe.'

'What about the Parsons Elite?' I asked. 'That phrase mean anything to you?'

'Nope.'

He left then, clearly fed up with my questions. I waited for a while longer and then got up to go. As I stood, my legs suddenly unhinged. I gasped, gripped the table for support, and the periphery of my vision exploded with colour. Not only could I not stand, I couldn't see. It was as though I had snapped out of my reality and into another.

Somewhere in my mind a machine beeped, somewhere else a voice said, *Hurry, she's slipping away*. A moment later I felt the same black fear that had possessed me in Selina's old room at the Haven Hotel. Not a fear, the certainty that I would never see her again.

What the hell is happening to me? My perspective had shifted like in a dream. I was no longer watching the scene; I was part of it – in Selina's hospital room, in her body, watching the doctors and nurses crowding around, feeling her pain, her fear. Seeing nothing but bleak darkness as she passed out of this world.

Selina!

I couldn't speak; I could only tilt my head back and dare to allow a final image to slide into my mind: her coffin sinking into the ground, fistfuls of earth dropping on top.

My eyes snapped wide open, a voice in my head saying that there was only one word to describe the vision I had just experienced, a word that frightened me to half to death.

Premonition.

– 33 –

Sunday 13 February 1977, two days until the sky watch . . .

I was in my room at the Ram Inn. After the episode downstairs I really didn't want to be alone, but I couldn't face seeing Randall either so I'd rearranged our meeting for Monday. My thoughts returned to Selina's notebook, which I'd left in the drawer next to my bed.

I was looking for a pattern, any sign of reason or intelligence behind the fantastic events I was uncovering. I couldn't shake my suspicion that Father O'Riorden had been holding back on me, that some dark secret was buried the heart of the Havens, perhaps a secret connected with its military history. I flicked to the last page of the notebook, a page I had already read many times.

According to Colonel Corso there exists a highly secret report associated with the UFO sightings – someone called Jack Parsons. This report fell into the hands of a group of people who call themselves the Parsons Elite. Who are they? I have no idea. The report warns that UFOs – whatever they are – are dangerous. Deadly. But who wrote this report? Who leaked it?

I read the entry twice, three times, threw the notebook onto the bed and said, 'Fuck this!' then dialled the number of my old office in Parliament.

With no one to manage his office any more, I was surprised Bestford answered at all, and even more surprised that he was sober, given the state I had left him in.

'Robert? Thank God you called. Where are you?'

'The Havens. Wait. Why were you expecting me to call?'

A brief silence. A long silence.

'She went into surgery Saturday afternoon. The damage to her brain was worse than they had anticipated. I'm sorry, Robert . . .'

He trailed off. I said nothing. Stunned. And then the shock dissolved into something worse, a sort of disgusted bitterness at whoever, or whatever, was responsible.

Deep inside me was an intuitive understanding that I had come to a crossroads. One route led out of the Havens, back to London. The other route led not just to the truth behind the Happenings but a deeper truth about myself. The feeling of foreboding was almost overwhelming.

'Please, say something, Robert.'

What I felt when I heard his hoarse voice wasn't anger, as I had expected, but a peculiar relief – relief that he was still there, my only link to the world I had left behind. More importantly, my only link to a best friend it turned out I had hardly known.

'She was tired of fighting, Robert. Her blood pressure started to rise and she slipped away.'

I know. I felt it. I saw it.

'Robert? You there?'

I felt a sting of sympathy for my old boss as his voice cracked. That probably explains why I allowed our conversation to spin out as I sat on the edge of the bed listening to him ramble. He talked about Parliament. He talked about tensions with the Soviet Union. He talked about the Queen's Silver Jubilee. The only thing he didn't talk about was how his drinking problem was going. It wasn't that I didn't like to ask; I just didn't care as much as I once had. In the background Big Ben chimed the hour as Bestford shared with me that there had been a spate of alarming UFO sightings over Russia. Luminous bodies over many towns emitting rays of light. 'They think it's us or the Americans. Now the prime minister is considering an order to shoot down anything similar that appears in our skies.'

'That sounds escalatory to me,' I said.

'My thoughts exactly.'

There was an awkward pause which Bestford rushed to fill. 'I was afraid, I was a coward. And you were right,' he added. 'The committee, the inquiry, they were absolutely the questions we should have been asking. Colonel Corso was a link to a mystery unfurling in our own constituency.'

'I don't think it's about the committee inquiry any more, Paul.' I glanced down at Selina's notebook. 'What's happening here goes far, far deeper. Selina's inquiries were extensive, and they didn't stop with the UFO sightings.'

'I know. I turned a blind eye to the fact that they were storing nuclear weapons at Brawdy. But there was nothing I could do.'

'What did Selina's work turn up?'

A long pause. Then Bestford said, 'Robert, you don't sound too well.'

'I'm fine, really. Tell me.'

'OK.' I heard a heavy sigh over the line. 'Selina was afraid something was wrong in the village. With the people. She thought the constituency was under surveillance. She thought that priest might be a spy.'

I remembered what the admiral had said about the Soviets monitoring the area.

'We know that Father O'Riorden has communist sympathies; perhaps he is more involved that we realize. After all, who better to employ? a priest has a unique form of access to communities and their people.'

Perhaps that was true, but it wasn't what was worrying me the most. 'What else did Selina tell you, Paul?'

'She thought she might have discovered something about the Jackson murders.'

'Did she mention any names?' Silence. 'She thought Randall might be mixed up in it, didn't she?'

'How did you know that?'

'Someone told me,' I said, struggling to suppress my anger. I couldn't believe Bestford had held this back from me along with everything else.

'Listen. I wanted to tell you, Robert. I almost did before you left. But I was afraid how you'd react.'

'You should have been more bothered about lying to someone who has never shown you anything but loyalty,' I said bitterly. 'What else did Selina tell you that you kept from me?'

'Selina may have been right about O'Riorden but she became too paranoid. She thought there were forces in the village that meant to do her harm, thought she was under surveillance.' Bestford's voice sounded heavy, almost mournful.

'Well, perhaps she was right,' I said, remembering the powerboat explosion, the panic, the flames. 'Perhaps someone did mean to harm her. Harm both of you.'

'Not that again,' Bestford said, annoyed, though there was a trace of something else in his voice. Doubt? Fear? 'Robert, what happened in Parliament was an accident.'

But I didn't think he really sounded convinced, not any more. As I scanned the tantalizing passages in Selina's open notebook, I certainly wasn't. 'She knew about a confidential report on the sort of things people have been seeing down here.'

'Doesn't mean anything to me.'

'She also mentions a name. Jack Parsons.'

Silence spun out between us.

At last Bestford said, reluctantly I thought, 'Jack Whiteside Parsons was an American genius. A scientist so esteemed they even named a crater on the far side of the moon in his honour.'

'And what was his connection with the Havens?'

'Are you familiar with a post-war project known as Operation Backfire?'

Perhaps as a former employee of the chair of the Defence Select Committee I should have been. 'Remind me.'

'Our dirty secret. The British government, along with the Americans, protected some Nazi scientists in exchange for access to German rocket technology. As part of the arrangement the Americans threw in the expertise of their very best. Parsons was a rocket scientist and former naval intelligence officer who helped lead NASA into deep space.'

'And he came here? To Pembrokeshire?'

'Yes. To the missile testing range at Apperporth. Less than a mile from Broad Haven.' Another in the long list of local military establishments. 'The missile launches at Apperporth were overseen – '

'By Parsons.'

'Correct,' Bestford said. 'Though his involvement in all this was necessarily classified above top secret. You see, Parson's work with rockets wasn't the only way in which he attempted to shape the future of humanity. By the end of the war many in the military-industrial complex in Britain and America regarded him as something of a mad scientist.'

'Why, Paul? What did he do?'

'Parsons was a student of Aleister Crowley. I'd be surprised if that name means anything to you. Am I wrong?'

He was. Hadn't I read something in the newspaper or heard something on the radio about Aleister Crowley? His name made me think fleetingly of black masses, the number 666 and satanic images from horror movies. It also made me think of something Randall and said about animal mutilations, but I didn't want to say so.

'Robert, you there?'

I snapped back. 'Go on.'

'Following Crowley's teachings, Parsons came to believe in the reality of magic as a force that could be explained through quantum physics. He experimented with the occult.'

'He *was* mad,' I said, though I was far from sure.

'No doubt. But Parsons devoted more and more of his time to witchcraft, convinced that he could summon powerful spirits.'

Now I remembered the symbols and the incantation I had seen at the church.

'He even reported paranormal events in his home, phenomena he believed were a direct product of his rituals: poltergeist activity, disembodied voices, even apparitions.'

I could tell Bestford was sceptical from the way he lightened his voice. It was the same tone he adopted whenever political opponents tried convincing him of their views.

'What happened to Jack Parsons?' I asked.

'Died in an explosion at home. The files on his death are

still classified, but there is every reason to believe that before he visited Wales he was working on some very peculiar experiments in the California desert.'

'What sort of experiments?'

'Secret experiments conceived by Crowley. The available records refer to "a project to advance humanity". That's what Selina discovered, Robert. That is what she imparted to me. And that is all I know. I swear.'

My mind spun. Selina here in the Havens, stepping ever nearer the end of her life. Not knowing what was behind the strange sightings. Selina interviewing the locals, witnesses like Martin Marshall, and establishing connections with similar events at RAF Croughton in 1963. Selina asking questions about the American facility and the Jacksons, the sort of questions that stirred up local tensions, according to Frank Frobisher, but she hadn't let that stop her. There was a reason Bestford had always left constituency business to Selina. She was more tenacious than the best journalists I knew, and when she wanted to get to the bottom of something she didn't stop digging.

'Robert, I do know your nerves can be bad. When you're stressed. If Selina's death risks making you unwell, if you need something to set your mind on – '

'I need to finish what she started here, Paul. And not for your sake. Not for Selina's either.'

It was the right answer. The only answer. Partly because at that instant I cared about everyone in the village I had once called home. I cared like I had never cared before. I had never felt so determined to help them, and I was confident I could. But I also cared about my recent premonitions and buried memories, the ugly ones that seemed intent on clawing their way back up the longer I stayed here.

'Paul, is it possible that Jack Parsons conducted occult experiments here in Pembrokeshire?'

'I doubt it.' A pause. 'But anything's possible.'

After Bestford hung up, I cleaned myself up, then checked the door, then checked the window, then checked the door, then got undressed, then checked the window, the door, and finally got into bed, though I knew I wouldn't sleep. The only thing preventing me from calling Araceli to see if she was OK was knowing I might wake Tessa. Still, the urge to call was punishingly strong as I lay there, gazing up at the cliff and the dark shape of the Haven Hotel.

There must be a rational explanation for all this. That was the thought in my head, which I knew the admiral would tell me if he were here, but it was becoming increasingly difficult to believe. I had been a sceptic for so long, but I was running out of explanations for what was happening in the Havens. Could it be that some of it, even all of it, was real? The UFOs, the silver-suited humanoids, the Black-Suited Men . . . Day-by-day events and people were forcing me to edge closer to belief in . . . what?

I had been sent here to investigate the sightings and prove that the Americans were responsible. After all the stories, all the twisted tales Randall had subjected me to, I'd vowed never to listen to such nonsense again – there was always a rational reason if you looked hard enough. But despite the many strong personal reasons I had for succeeding in that mission, what I had uncovered was leading me to an altogether different conclusion.

The children aren't normal. People here are changing. Their minds are changing.

I wanted to push away the thoughts, but I couldn't. Was the sighting at the school part of a bigger plan? Some sort of subtle programming process maybe?

No, Robert. That's crazy. Because if that were true, it would mean that the UFOs are linked to some sort of controlling force, some psychic force. And that's mad.

What was it Bestford used to say? All evidence is for it, but all reason is against it?

Then what? Spectres of our own worst fears. Yes. The shimmering silver giant was a teenager's science fiction image; the intimidating men from the government issuing threatening warnings were lonely impersonators. And as for the facility on the cliffs – an oceanographic research centre . . .

I rolled on my side. I could just make out the dark windows on the top floor of the Haven Hotel. A light blinked on. I wondered what Araceli was doing.

A noise at the window. I sat bolt upright. *You're fine. Nothing can get in.*

A stone bounced across the floor. I leaped out of bed, startled. And yes, afraid. It was a black pebble, warm to touch. My heart began to pound. Where the hell had it come from?

The roof rattled. Then shook with the force of what sounded like hailstones. More pebbles? My mind was razor sharp. Which is why it was hard to doubt my own eyes, to deny what was now taking form at the locked bedroom door. An awful shape. Dark, like a shadow with dense substance.

My breaths came in short, quick gasps. I could run. Take Selina's journal from the drawer and go. But something was keeping me in that room. Something had come for me, wanted me to stay.

So I did.

God help me, I did.

Against every rational instinct, my mind started recalling the instructions uttered by Randall all those years ago:

Don't study them.

Don't invite them in.

Too late for that. I froze. It wasn't fear that paralysed me, though I was now desperately afraid – it was a force, a low vibration I recognized from childhood. An intense green light flooded the room. And in that moment of sheer terror I thought clearly: *This is the shadow of an ancient evil.*

Concentrate, Robert.

Two possibilities – equally terrifying. Either something really was in the room with me, or I was imagining the spectre. And if I was imagining it, then that was a sure sign I was heading the way of the mental hospital.

It's not real . . .

But if not a hallucination, then what?

There was another possibility of course. An almost unthinkable possibility.

'A memory,' I heard myself whisper, and the combination of those words and the threatening apparition before me forged an instant connection with a long-buried recollection. Something so awful I had suppressed it.

'Show me,' I whispered to my own unconscious.

The room tilted, time swivelled. And in a white flashback I glimpsed the jagged image of my parents arguing. Dad becoming violent, his eyes desperate. 'It's got to be done!' he yelled as Mum, tearful, backed away, shaking her head.

The memory folded into another. It was shortly before they died. I was in bed at our house on base, watching my bedroom door creep open, watching a figure slip in. My father.

'You must come with me, son.' His voice was very stern, and even though I trusted him, I pulled the bedclothes up to my chin.

Then I was back in the present, back in the Ram Inn. Alone.

'My God,' I said aloud, picturing my father's face. 'We really did go somewhere. What did you do to me, Father?'

– 34 –

Monday 14 February 1977, one day until the sky watch . . .

'Sleep well?'

Randall's smile was razor sharp with sarcasm as I slammed shut the creaky passenger door of his Hillman Hunter. The car stank of damp, and the dog hair on my seat was already clinging to my jeans.

'I can't believe you've still got this car.'

'I can't believe you think that's important. You heard about what they found up on the cliffs?'

I nodded. Workmen had unearthed components of ten car bombs and a collection of timers on the coastal path. Speculation was rife among the drinkers at the Ram with theories ranging from arms smugglers to terrorism, although most people thought the American military had something to do with it.

'It's just another sign of the rot setting in,' he said, tossing the morning newspaper into my lap. 'There have been more animal deaths too, more mutilations. And they'll continue as we approach the sky watch.'

Jesus. Can this really be happening?

I couldn't remember my dreams from that night. Could only

remember what I had seen – the ghost of a memory – before bed. Morning had brought with it a redoubled conviction: I had to see this through. I wanted the truth.

It was late morning now, and great bruise-coloured clouds hung low over St Brides Bay. There was a rough clanging noise as Randall started the engine, and as we pulled away from the Ram Inn I wondered whether to ask him about the Jackson murders. But he was still on the subject of that day's news: 'Animal mutilations have been reported for centuries. In ancient Rome farmers spoke of demons attacking their livestock.'

'Demons?'

He held up a hand. 'In 1874 sheep were found oddly slaughtered in Ireland and Wales. And last year more than ten thousand mutilated cattle were discovered across the mid-western United States.'

'With no explanation?' I asked.

'Oh, many! But what good's an explanation if it doesn't make sense, eh?' He paused, keeping his eyes on the road. 'In Latin American cultures strange animal killings are blamed on the *chupacabra* – that's Spanish for "goat sucker" – a small grey creature, big head, bulging black eyes. In the United States the dominant suspects are visitors from another planet.' He smiled. 'It's been that way since 1967, when a pony was found dead on a farm in Alamosa County, Colorado.'

'And what was so interesting about that pony?'

'Its abdomen, skull and spinal cavities were completely hollowed out.'

Suddenly I was eleven again, digging Jasper out of the ground with my bare hands; staring with stunned tearful eyes at the place on his neck and head where the flesh had been completely stripped away. My stomach could hardly stand to hear Randall prattle on about similar mutilations. At the same time I saw something on his face that made me curious. His eyes were wide and dark, knowledgeable, I suppose. And if I'm honest, they didn't look so crazy to me now. Not crazy at all.

'The woman living on the farm claimed that a large object had passed over the ranch on the night of the mutilation. It soon became a common belief that aliens were responsible for these killings.'

'But you don't believe that?'

He looked at me like I was stupid. 'I believe the mutilations are connected with the UFOs. But I do not believe the UFOs are invaders from other worlds. My study of the subject indicates that flying discs and their entities have been reported for a long, long time. Would extraterrestrials really persist in visiting our planet for thousands of years and never make their presence widely known?'

It was a fair point. 'So what do you think it means?'

'The mutilated rabbits I presented at the school didn't just follow the universal pattern,' he answered, swerving the car into a narrow country lane. 'I found something else in their systems – high doses of atropine. I tested them myself; it was easy enough.' He saw my puzzled expression and added, 'It's a tranquillizing drug.'

'Who administered it? For what purpose?'

'The carcasses are deliberately left to create fear.'

'Left by whom?'

'Surely you've realized by now?' Randall pinned me with his eyes. 'We're dealing with a cult.'

'I've heard of sacrificial rituals in Afro-Caribbean religions,' I muttered, glancing out of the window. The car rounded a bend and from here I could see miles of rough fields sloping this way and that, dropping sharply towards the cliffs. 'But here in the Havens?'

Then, suddenly, *What if it's the Rotary Club?*

The idea seemed to come from out of nowhere. Except it hadn't, not entirely. Where it had come from was something a local had told me when I asked him about the club's work: *I reckon they think they're like the Masons or something. Self-important bunch the lot of 'em, but I suppose they have some influence.* I wondered fleetingly what the admiral would make of that. *He'd think it was time to send me for some psychotherapy.*

I asked Randall to slow down.

'We've people to see,' he protested, swerving the battered Hillman Hunter onto a single-track dirt road. 'As I told you, boy, if I can't convince you to leave this place with words, I'll have to show you.'

We pulled up outside a well-maintained house. The plaque next to the front door said we had arrived at Rose Cottage.

'Who . . .' I began, but the front door was opening and I recognized the distressed-looking woman standing there, though she seemed considerably paler than when we had met in the post office.

'Come along, Robert,' said Randall as if I were a kid again and he my guardian.

We got out of the car.

'Good to see you again.' Isaac's mother granted me a meek smile and I knew just looking at her that matters were about to get worse; the woman's face was a mask of worry. 'Come in, please.'

The cottage had a still, uncomfortable atmosphere. We were shown through into a room with a low-beamed ceiling, stained

cream carpet and cheap-looking furniture. Here a tall bespectacled gentleman in a smart cardigan was waiting. He was pale
and thin with curly grey hair beginning to recede. I recognized
him immediately from the town hall.

'Dr Caxton,' he said, standing and putting out a hand.

Randall took the hand.

'The doctor is a psychologist visiting from London,' Mrs Jones
said.

'Parapsychologist,' Dr Caxton corrected her with a pleasant
but intense expression. I smiled at him. Two things struck me
about this man. First, he was thorough and careful. Second, his
mind was acute. 'I've been staying in the area,' he continued
smoothly. 'Mrs Jones asked me to check over young Isaac, as
well as have a look at her husband.'

'Neither Dylan nor young Issac have been at all themselves
recently,' Mrs Jones said. She kept a wary eye on Randall as he
took a chair next to the fireplace. I sat with Mrs Jones on a long
sofa beneath the bay window.

Dr Caxton was the only one who remained standing.

'I've spoken to Randall about this, after what happened at
the school,' Mrs Jones said to me. 'He suggested it would be
helpful for me to repeat the story for your benefit.'

'Yes, I want to hear it,' I said firmly.

Now she began to look scared. 'My husband is a keen diver,
a fit man. Usually. His health has deteriorated rapidly in
recent weeks, and his personality has . . . He's become distant,
aggressive.'

'They're both extremely unwell,' continued Dr Caxton. 'Isaac
is sleeping now. And his father –'

'Is wide awake,' said a frail voice.

All heads turned.

A tall, gaunt man had entered the room. I saw from his unsteady gait that he was unwell, but nothing prepared me for what followed.

Nothing.

– 35 –

Dylan Jones's shock of white hair looked thin and dry. His face was narrow and drawn, cheeks sunken, and he hadn't shaved for days. There was an inflamed lesion on the right side of his neck and a red boil above his left eye.

'Don't stare, please.'

He tottered into the room, taking the chair nearest the door, and his wife eyed him warily. I suppose we all did.

'Well. Shall we get on with it?' he said. 'You came here because you want to know more about –'

'Your sighting. Yes,' Randall said. 'And the diving . . . incident.'

I didn't think this man looked capable of diving; he hardly looked capable of standing. He started from the beginning. Around Christmas time he had woken early, shortly before 3 a.m., because of a strange orange light in the bedroom.

'My wife and son were at my sister-in-law's, so I was alone. The light was coming from outside and it was pulsating off the walls. So I got out of bed, looked out the window and saw this silvery object in the sky, high above the houses opposite. It was like a very large Easter egg – maybe six feet in diameter – swinging back and forth, like a pendulum.'

'Did you hear any noise?' I asked.

'None, apart from the window. It was shaking, vibrating. Then I saw the man. Well, I say "man". It had the shape of a man but was much too tall, too wide. Do you know what it reminded me of? That figure off the telly – the Michelin Man.'

Randall nodded. 'There have been other sightings. Where was it standing? In the road?'

Dylan shook his head. 'No, no. It was in the sky. Floating over the house opposite.'

'Floating? Now come on. You can't be . . .' I stopped myself as Randall scowled at me. 'Go on, please.'

Dylan gave a slight shiver. 'It just bloody floated there with its arms and legs outstretched, like a free-fall parachute jumper.'

I sat very still, struggling to picture this. 'You mean it was hovering face down?'

Dylan nodded. 'And all this time the egg thing was moving back and forth, until it and the figure glided away sideways, over the roofs of the houses, and went out of view. The dog was going completely mad, barking and barking. I just wish there was some sort of proof,' Dylan said, eyeing Dr Caxton. 'Without firm proof you begin to doubt yourself.' He gave me an uncertain glance. 'Know what I mean?'

I nodded. I knew exactly what he meant.

Dr Caxton, who had taken a seat next to me and Mrs Jones, was now opening a notepad. 'You mustn't worry about that, Mr Jones. A fruitless exercise. Simply trying to understand how the experience affected you is likely to – '

'Understand?' Dylan interrupted, touching the inflamed skin on his neck. 'How do I understand this? Life used to be clear and understandable. Now I go to bed at night afraid of what might come out of the sky. Afraid that I'm becoming delusional!'

Again this resonated with me.

'Have you ever taken an interest in UFOs?' Randall asked.

'Not before Isaac and his friends saw that thing at the school, no.'

Randall checked his notes. 'According to your wife you did experience another unexplained event, while you were diving in St Brides Bay? That's right, isn't it? A few days after the school sighting?'

Dylan nodded and looked doubtfully around the room until his eyes fixed on the window and its all-too-clear view of Stack Rocks. When he spoke next he was slurring and his voice sounded forced. 'I was on a dive out there. Not the safest spot in the bay, I admit. The north side of Stack Rocks Island has deep gullies, underwater caves and fissures with strong currents coursing through them, but I've twenty years' diving experience in these waters. I thought I'd seen it all, but that day I was about to swim to the surface when I was startled by a bright flash of light under the water.'

Dr Caxton leaned forward, scribbling in his notepad.

'I know how it sounds, but the water was glowing! I'm telling you now, it was as if something was down there with me. An object.'

We all looked at each other, except for Randall, whose gaze was now focused on the three humps of Stack Rocks framed in the cottage window. Meanwhile, Frobisher's comments to me on my first day in the village were surfacing: *There's a tale that in 1884 some labourers . . . saw a blazing object plummeting into the sea near Stack Rocks. They say the water glowed for days afterwards, that the men went blind. And mad.*

'What did it look like?' I asked.

'I didn't see it so I don't know, but I felt it in the water with me. It felt like it was . . . alive.'

Dr Caxton cleared his throat. 'Mr Jones, are you aware of any strange stories about these rocks – legends and so forth – that may have influenced your reaction to what you saw?'

Dylan shrugged, glanced at his wife. 'Sure, all sorts of stories, I suppose. They say Stack Rocks and that old fort belong to that hotel, the big one on the cliffs, you know? That nobody goes there except – '

'Araceli Romero owns Stack Rocks?' I interrupted.

'So they say.' Dylan's gaze had drifted to the window again. 'Her father was a recluse, like her mother. Before he left the Havens some of the locals would see the lights on up there in the bar, late at night when the place was shut up, and a string of cars on the drive. There were rumours. Nothing proved but word got around. People heard singing up there, chanting. Some speculated it was something to do with a conspiracy of dark forces.'

A cult? That's what is sounded like to me. But how it could be connected to this man's experiences, his physical symptoms, was far from clear. Yet.

'Do you think that your incident underwater is in any way connected with the figure you saw?' asked Dr Caxton.

Dylan's sallow face hardened with grim conviction. He nodded.

'And how did you feel during both of these experiences?'

'Disorientated, frightened. My head was filled with thoughts that weren't my own.'

'What do you mean by that?'

He wet his lips before answering. 'When I was under the water there was a moment when I thought I could have stayed there and let my air run out.' He looked at his wife, who was hunched over and shaking her head, her eyes glistening. 'You understand? I'd lost all control and every desire to live. I wanted to die.'

There was an awkward pause. 'And now? Do you still think about harming yourself?'

Dylan nodded and said, 'All the time.'

'Dylan, no!' his wife said, her voice rising. She stood up and said to Dr Caxton, 'For God's sake, make him see sense. There must be an explanation!'

'If there is, I'd certainly like to hear it,' Randall said. His tone was doubtful, and I shot him a warning look to suggest that it would be unwise for him to annoy Dr Caxton or the Joneses.

'I'm sorry,' Randall muttered. 'I have an unfortunate habit of interrupting.'

'You're an experienced diver, Mr Jones,' Dr Caxton went on. He removed his spectacles and turned to face the gaunt Welshman. 'I assume you're familiar with the rapture of the deep – narcosis?'

'You think I imagined all this? Hallucinated?'

'Diving any deeper than thirty metres can be hazardous for the mind. At its most dangerous, narcosis results in the impairment of judgement – the loss of decision-making ability and focus. There can be visual or auditory disturbances. And the syndrome can cause extreme anxiety, depression or paranoia.'

'That must be it,' Mrs Jones said, going to her husband's side. 'That's what happened, dear.'

'After what happened in the water, I started getting these bouts of fatigue. I would be walking the dog or working in the garden when I would get cold and start to shake. Isaac's been the same since that thing at the school. He gets so exhausted and crawls into bed trembling.'

Dr Caxton turned then and gave Randall a direct stare. 'I

understand from what the locals say that you predicted the sightings in a very public manner,' he said. 'Do you not think, Mr Pritchard, that you planted the seed?'

He certainly did, I thought. But what nobody is talking about is how.

'I am afraid I made an error,' Randall conceded. 'By warning people I only increased their interest – the opposite of what I intended.'

Dr Caxton nodded. It was a gesture of understanding, not criticism. 'What happened at the school was the catalyst, and from that stories of unusual happenings have spread through the community, each more dramatic than the last. An ingrained lack of faith in the authorities allows people to accept these stories more easily than they would otherwise.'

I thought as he spoke that Dr Caxton was clearly an intelligent man, but as he warmed to his theme Randall glowered at him.

'What about all *I've* seen?' he demanded.

'The more you look for something, the more likely you are to expect to find it,' Dr Caxton said, giving a slight shrug. 'Whether they've seen something or not, everyone in the village seems to agree on certain "facts" about these UFOs – that they make roof tiles rattle, car radios go fuzzy. The greater the expectation that such events will happen, the less reliable the witness's memory. A light in the sky quickly becomes a flying saucer. A ripple in Loch Ness rolls and rolls until it becomes a monster. I know it is difficult to accept but, trust me, in a restricted area the effects can be most dramatic. *Folie à deux*,' he said. 'Madness shared by two.'

This was interesting – was it the explanation? Were the giant figures in silver suits, like the ones seen by Araceli and

Martin Marshall and now Dylan, a perfect example of shared delusions?

When I first saw the drawing made by Martin Marshall my first impression had been of an astronaut because the entity's appearance fitted very well with images from NASA missions. Almost too well. Had Araceli, Martin and Dylan seen 'aliens' simply because that's the context they understood such beings in? Possibly. If Dr Caxton was right, then in another era they might just as easily have interpreted those figures as God or angels of light. It sounded plausible but it didn't account for the fact that they still had seen *something*. Also, the man we had come to see, Dylan Jones, looked desperately unwell, and I wasn't at all convinced that some form of mass hallucination could do that. More specifically, speculating was fine but not at the expense of action: I didn't want anyone else to get hurt, particularly Araceli or Tessa.

Randall was clearly of the same mind. 'What about Dylan's physical symptoms? Those aren't imagined.'

'No, of course not,' Dr Caxton said. 'But physical changes may be psychologically induced. In Celtic folklore it is an old and widespread belief that sickness was caused by elves. In the Middle Ages there was a condition known as *alfabruni* – elf burn. Now then. People who study UFOs don't talk about elf disease,' he said, nodding at Randall. 'Nowadays we might interpret this man's lesions and boils as radiation burn. They will lessen in time.'

Randall just shook his head in stubborn disagreement. Mrs Jones, however, seemed relieved by what she had heard. Dylan still seemed less than convinced.

'I'm telling you, Dr Caxton. Something wants control of my mind. There is something out there, crossing over from another world into ours.' He touched his neck wound again. 'Whatever it is, it's alive, it's dangerous and it brings dread upon me.'

I wanted to be completely satisfied by Dr Caxton's explanation, which appealed to my belief that there was always a logical explanation to outlandish events – but I had to admit feeling a little doubtful as we left the Joneses' house. More than a little doubtful, actually. Not only was I still struggling with my flashbacks from the previous night – the memory of my father coming into my room, taking me somewhere – I was also thinking of Araceli. I pictured her on her own in that dilapidated hotel, cleaning glasses, making beds and not even thinking about me.

Now, bidding goodbye to Mr Jones, taking one last look at the seriously ill man who had witnessed nightmarish visions, I drew a comparison between him and the woman whose picture had enticed me here. And I knew very well that this situation was getting worse.

Randall had mentioned a cult which he believed was connected with the Happenings and the killing and mutilation of animals in the area. If the Haven Hotel and Araceli's family was in any way connected to that cult, as Dylan Jones had implied, then that worried me. But what worried me more was the knowledge that a satanist – Jack Parsons, a protégé of the self-proclaimed wickedest man on earth – had lived and operated in this area shortly after the war. Parsons, whose name appeared over and over in Selina's reports. It wasn't much to go on, but it told me that Parsons was a figure of interest and probably therefore a figure of influence. As influential as the greatest stage hypnotist capable of making you feel as though you're a passenger in your own body.

Perhaps Dylan Jones was just suffering from hallucinations. Perhaps he was suffering from depression, was suicidal. That seemed possible. But of course there were doubts.

'I brought you there because I wanted you to see what state Dylan was in. I did not expect Dr Caxton to be there,' Randall said, restlessly nodding. 'And yet, as we both know, science cannot explain everything. Dylan had a close encounter; so did his son. And now unearthly forces are distorting his reality, just as easily as they manipulate space and time and physical matter and minds like his little boy's.'

Just at that moment Dr Caxton came out of the house. He stood rigid in the slanting, sharp rain. 'Poor man. His mind has created a fantasy.'

Randall shook his head. I was eager to return to the village because if Randall was correct – if any of this was connected to a cult engaged in ritualistic slaughter – then I wanted to know, and to make sure that the community was safe.

I turned to leave, squinting against the rain.

'What the hell is that?' I asked. There was a mark on the roof of the house opposite.

It was the impression of a figure. A very large figure.

Giants, Robert . . .

Randall and Dr Caxton followed me as I strode swiftly into the middle of the road to examine the roof more closely. The stain had to be at least eight feet long. It stretched from where the guttering collected the rain to a few feet below the chimney stack.

Randall was already marching back to Rose Cottage to see if Mrs Jones had a ladder.

When he returned with the ladder, Dylan came to the door and looked across at the stain on the roof.

'You haven't noticed this before?'

He shook his head. 'You're going up?'

'Why not?' Randall said. Then looked at me.

I didn't look down as I climbed. I was trying to think of an excuse in case whoever lived here came home. I had to be quick. It began to rain harder.

'See anything?' Randall called from below.

I pulled myself up, gripping the guttering, and scanned the roof tiles.

The area that had stood out to me below was visible now, and the truth sank in slowly as the rain fell. *This is crazy. This defies every law of physics.* The mark on the roof wasn't a stain. It was a dry patch.

− 36 −

'Completely dry!' Randall took charge as Dr Caxton and I followed him back into Rose Cottage. 'So we're dealing with a close encounter of the second kind. The sighting of a UFO with associated physical effects – an object summoned here.'

What if it's us calling them? Gethin's question came back to me.

I had wanted to believe that our old neighbour was a superstitious fool; now I really wasn't sure. Of anything. I kept trying to make sense of it all and kept drawing a blank. How could the UFO sightings, or their physical effects, have anything to do with a cult in the local community?

Unless Gethin had been right: we weren't being visited, we were being *listened* to; someone in the community, or a group of people, was summoning these phenomena. But who and why? This was the question I put to Randall in the hall of Rose Cottage, and although it was one I expected him to rebuff, he answered it decisively.

'These phenomena are extremely powerful, boy. Whoever controls the skies controls the world.'

That sounded mildly convincing, but when the words came out his eyes slid past me, and that told me that maybe, probably, he was holding something back. Protecting himself perhaps, or protecting me.

'And I'll not hear much more of your specious explanations and facile attempts to demean these poor people's experiences,' Randall thundered, his eyes flashing defiance. The atmosphere in the hallway was tense and uncomfortable as his gaze jumped to a well-supplied bookcase in the Joneses' living room. 'Got any maps of the area?'

Mrs Jones found an Ordnance Survey map and handed it to Randall, who spread it open over the dining-room table. After examining it for a minute or so he took a red pen from his jacket pocket and marked the map. 'I'd like to show you all something I have discovered – the reason I came here with Robert,' he said. 'There is a method behind these sightings – a pattern, an intelligence.'

We all leaned over and looked down at the map. He had marked various locations.

'Ley lines,' Randall said. 'Straight lines linking sites and objects of prehistoric antiquity – burial chambers, hill forts and temples. See how this line connects underground caves, standing stone circles, wells and earthworks? In ancient folklore these points, where two ley lines cross, are known as nodal connections, ley markers. Supposedly strange things can happen at these points – dizziness, disorientation, visions, and even – '

'The appearance of UFOs?' I asked.

Randall shot me a glance. 'Exactly right, Robert. Monumental sites like the fort at Stack Rocks are believed to be ancient centres of power that incorporate ley lines and earth energies.'

Dr Caxton was shaking his head. 'You're making a connection between UFOs and lines connecting the paths of prehistory? You're trying to explain one mystery with another.' And it was unclear to me how this had anything to do with the cult that Randall had mentioned and implicated in the strange happenings. Yet, unlike Dr Caxton, I was at least prepared to hear Randall out in the hope of learning something new here.

Randall pointed to a long red line. 'This very house sits on a ley line. It terminates here.' He pointed to Stack Rocks. 'And Stack Rocks intersects every significant site in our investigations.' He circled the primary school and the Haven Hotel.

'But what's so significant about Stack Rocks?' I asked. 'Or the Haven Hotel?'

Randall's face darkened. 'There are some who believe ley nodes may be the doorways to other worlds and times running parallel to our own. The ancient Celts believed that the worlds of spirit and man were separated by a veil that grew thin at certain periods of the year and in certain places. Perhaps that time is now.'

'Why now?' I said.

An idea ignited in Randall's eyes and he glanced hopefully at Mrs Jones. 'How's your boy? Can we see him?'

She returned minutes later, guiding the rotund eleven-year-old into the room, carefully, deliberately, as if the child was blind. We all heard his rough breathing. Trying not to look at his missing hair – there was more than one patch now – I said, 'Hello again, Isaac.'

The boy didn't speak, didn't move. His mother tried her best to summon up a smile while looking fearfully at her son.

'Come on, Izzy. You remember meeting Robert at the post office. Say hello.'

Isaac puckered up his face and shrugged.

'Izzy, these nice gentlemen are here to help.'

'Can you tell us again about school?' I asked. 'About your headmaster?'

'Shut up, shut up, shut up!' Isaac yelled.

After a moment his mother glanced away and shook her head. 'You see what I mean? He's changed. I think that –'

Isaac whipped round and bit his mother's arm.

I didn't know what was worse: Mrs Jones's cry of pain, the blood that was drip drip dripping onto the carpet or the blood smeared around her son's mouth. At the same time I began to hear strange sounds that no one else seemed to register, fierce guttural moanings.

'Quickly, we need to bandage it,' Dr Caxton said. He had gone towards Mrs Jones. 'I'll get a towel.' He left the room.

Abruptly Isaac threw his head back and growled. I swear, the boy actually growled. The skin prickled across the back of my neck and I saw something on Randall's face that I hadn't seen since I was a boy. It was a look of pure fear. Isaac was watching me like his life depended on it. Just me. I felt in that moment as if I had stopped breathing. The room had receded into silence. I could feel the boy's fury while the moaning, agonized cries intensified around me. And at the same time I suddenly knew Isaac hadn't intended to shock us; he was ashamed and frightened and couldn't help it.

I thought suddenly of the evening I had first laid eyes on Randall's farm, the rusty swing outside my window, creaking through the night and the sense of feeling utterly alone.

'What's *wrong* with you!?' Mrs Jones screamed. It took me a second to realize she was addressing her husband. 'For Christ's sake, I need you!'

Dylan didn't move.

Isaac's eyelids fluttered and the overhead light bulb exploded with a *pop*. He scrambled away into the hall and up the stairs, leaving us stunned.

Somewhere upstairs a door slammed.

Mrs Jones sat numbly, resting her bleeding arm on her skirt, which produced a spreading stain. She was trembling all over.

Dr Caxton returned with a towel for her arm and glanced at her husband, who was staring out of the window at the sea – or at the Stack Rocks. Suddenly I remembered that the Havens Rotary Club planned to restore it, turn it into a visitors' centre ... Something floated up in my mind. Something that made me freeze. The symbols at the church, the ancient incantation protected by the expensive-looking glass cabinet. Father O'Riorden had told me, *The Rotary Club had it translated*.

'Mr Wilding, are you all right?'

How could I have missed it?

'Mr Wilding?' Dr Caxton said again.

'The Rotary Club!' I shouted. Startled glances. 'Mrs Jones, do you know anything about their work?'

'Yes, a little, but I don't see wh –'

'The headmaster, Howell Cooper. Is he a member?'

'Why is that important?' Dr Caxton asked. He looked confused; everyone did. Except Randall, who just gave a curt nod.

'Is he a member?' I demanded again of Mrs Jones.

'Yes. Yes, I think he is. Why?'

I thought about the headmaster visiting Father O'Riorden. I thought about the ancient prayer for exorcism on the wall in the church, which the priest said the Rotary Club had had translated. And I thought again of Gethin Yates on the cliff path telling me he thought the UFOs had been summoned.

'I have a growing suspicion that the Rotary Club is somehow behind all this.' It sounded mad, so I hurried to explain about the Stack Rocks Fort 'renovation' and reminded them that many of the sightings had occurred near or above that tiny island in St Brides Bay. Then I looked at Randall, whose expression had become grave.

'And I think my grandfather is right. Your husband and your son are sick because of the UFOs . . .' I trailed off.

Isaac's mother looked me in the eyes. 'And you suspect the headmaster because he let the children out early, the day they saw it?'

I nodded. I didn't want to tell her about the symbols at the church, not until I knew what they meant. 'They wouldn't have seen it otherwise.'

'Isaac . . . he's been saying that the craft at the school was communicating with him and his friends.' She was still nursing her arm. 'Isaac says he *felt* it. Evil. Danger. Bad feelings. These words come up again and again.' She explained that her son was increasingly kept awake at night by a message which 'pops into his head'. 'He says it's about something that's going to happen. That the world is going to end.'

Randall's face was crumpled with concern. He looked at the frightened couple and said, 'There are worse things you could do now than pray.'

'We're not at all religious,' Mrs Jones said shakily. 'Never even had Isaac baptized.'

Dr Caxton looked up suddenly.

'What is it?' Randall asked.

'Something one of the locals said, down in the village – a very odd comment, really. They said that there "weren't enough baptisms in the area".' He tilted his head to the side, musing on the memory. 'Not important.'

'It could be,' I said steadily. 'Very important.' A dizzying memory swirled of my conversation with Father O'Riorden about Howell Cooper: *He comes in once in a while to look over the church records: births, deaths, baptisms.*

'Were the other children who saw the craft baptized? Was Tessa?'

'Robert, what's wrong?' Randall was staring at me.

I told him.

His nostrils flared, either from surprise or anger. 'It's clear that the children are the key to this. The headmaster must be found and questioned. And we need the addresses of every child witness from the school.'

'What's the urgency?' broke in Dr Caxton.

'Just help with those addresses. If I'm right,' Randall said, 'it's not just these children and their families who are in terrible danger. We all are.'

FROM *THE MIND POSSESSED: A PERSONAL INVESTIGATION INTO THE BROAD HAVEN TRIANGLE*

BY DR R. CAXTON (CLEMENTINE PRESS, 1980) P.56

After the scandals caused by the Society for Psychical Research's poor quality control in certain high-profile investigations, anyone operating in this field is compelled to act in accordance with the highest professional standards, and this was very much at the front of my mind during my discreet inquiry in the Havens.

It wasn't an easy task. The locals were rather closed off, and not just in their suspicions of the English.

I was fortunate to stay with a relative during my time in the Havens; I certainly had no wish to stay at the local inn, of which my enduring memory is of a bleached goat's skull hanging beside the bar. The horned goat, of course, is a symbol of the occult, intended to mock the image of Jesus as the lamb who died for Man's sins, after a reference in the Bible to the obedient sheep being separated from the unruly, non-believing goats.

In retrospect, I came to the Havens determined to prove that there was a prosaic explanation for everything. Who or what was behind the UFO and humanoid sightings? I had no idea. But aliens? A technologically advanced civilization visiting this remote corner of the British Isles? To contemplate such an absurd notion made the rational part of me yearn to know the truth.

If I had recognized the clues earlier, I doubt I would have looked so hard.

− 37 −

Evening of Monday 14 February 1977, thirty-six hours
until the sky watch . . .

I couldn't exorcize the terrible thought running through my
mind: perhaps Howell Cooper was mixed up in some sort of
cult – the Parsons Elite? Perhaps the Rotary Club was a cover
for that cult. Perhaps Selina had discovered something about
it and was now . . .

'You know the way?' Randall asked. He was in the driver's
seat with me beside him.

'Up ahead, take a right.'

The car swerved into another winding lane. We were coming
into Little Haven and the light was draining from the afternoon.
I thought about Dr Caxton, who had surprisingly agreed to help
us. He would visit Father O'Riorden and find out where each of
the schoolchildren who saw the UFO could be found.

Randall and I had our own sights trained on the headmaster.

The wind had got up and was screaming around the village
as we drove past the Nest Bistro and pulled into Marine Close.
Howell Cooper's house was directly ahead, I remembered. His
car was in the drive but the curtains were drawn. I rang the

doorbell. Waited. Then knocked, pulling my coat around me against the rising gale.

A middle-aged woman finally answered the door. Her hair was a tangled mess and she was wearing a red towelling robe. 'Yes?'

'Mrs Cooper?'

She nodded at Randall, looking dazed.

'I wonder if you could help us, please? I'm sorry to bother you, but I'm looking for your husband.'

'Howell?' She shook her head hopelessly and I felt a jagged jolt of shock. 'Howell is dead.'

'What! How? When?' I gasped out.

'You'll have to . . . excuse me.' She swallowed back tears. 'Such a shock. You see, he took his own life,' she managed to say. 'They found him last night.'

'I'm . . . God, I'm so sorry! Where did this happen?'

'On the coastal path.' She shook her head.

'And the police have confirmed it was suicide?' Randall asked.

'He was . . . I'm sorry. He was hanging from a tree. No note. No explanation.'

And I had no words.

An eerie twilight had crept across the day by the time we got back to Little Haven. Randall stopped the car near the slipway, next to the beginning of Giant's Point, and stared past me at the door into the Ram Inn. There was a look on his face that could have been sadness. Or hope.

'We've both had a great shock. Fancy a pint, boy?'

I almost said yes, but the answer stuck in my throat. An old memory, surfacing. Someone knocking at Ravenstone Farm. Randall standing before me, his shotgun raised and pointing at the front door.

'Well, what do you say?'

I felt conflicted because a part of me needed a drink. The rest of me hated Randall for whatever obscure knowledge about these events, and my own past, he was still concealing.

'Thank you but I need some time alone,' I said eventually. 'I need to process what's happening.'

Randall accepted my rebuff immediately, which made me feel guilty. Shitty, actually. For someone who had lost so much I suppose it was pretty staggering that I should push away my only remaining relative. My only consolation was knowing that he had once done the same to me.

I was also thinking about the admiral. I needed his advice. During the crazy events of the last few days I had almost forgotten why I was there in the first place. Now my original brief surfaced in my mind – find out about the sightings and how they might be linked to military operations – but it seemed distant and almost childlike in its simplicity. So very much had happened since I first came to the Havens.

'Robert.' Randall broke in on my thoughts. 'I said I would convince you that there's something terrible afoot. Did I succeed? You saw the state of Dylan Jones. You've seen how they operate, how insidious they are, how dangerous they can be.'

'But why didn't you tell me before? How can I trust anything you say?' I said sharply. Instantly he straightened in his seat. Thinking back to my dream, I remembered again the day my parents died, the way they had argued. In the darkest part of my mind a question was forming. 'You hide so many things. For example, there's something about Mum and Dad you never told me, isn't there?'

Silence.

'You keep telling me I shouldn't have come back. You called Dad a monster.'

Then Randall did look me in the eye.

I swallowed. 'And what about the Jacksons. Why didn't you say you were a suspect?'

'When I said you should leave for your own sake, I meant it, boy. But I must remain here and do what I can for the village. The children.'

'I just don't know what to think any more. I have to go.'

'Robert, wait.' He shook his head from side to side as the car door on my side swung open. 'If you are determined to stay, you must try to let me help you.'

I didn't say yes. I didn't say no either.

As his battered old Hillman drove away, out of habit I glanced up at the Haven Hotel brooding on the cliff. The place was in darkness, whereas all the other lights in the village were on. Another power cut. But why only there?

Frobisher, the admiral – everyone had said that Randall had initially provoked the hysteria. But that wasn't quite true, I mused. After all, the very first sightings had actually involved Araceli. And Tessa. And now I had learned of their possible connection to Stack Rocks. Too much of this revolved around them.

I decided to return to my room and call her to check whether she was OK and to ask if there was any change in Tessa's condition, but I'd barely taken a step inside the inn when the landlord informed me that Araceli had called three times that afternoon and left messages. I tried calling from the phone in the bar. No reply.

I went immediately up to my room, opened the door and froze. Someone had been in there. It wasn't imagination or paranoia, no way. Paranoia hadn't emptied my drawers all over the floor. Gone were my notepads and bundles of newspaper clippings. My head throbbed as anxiety snaked through me. Outside an enormous silver car was parked across the street, empty. My eyes swept the deserted street for any signs of life and found none. But I could hear the engine running.

I ran for the door, wrestled with the lock and then plunged downstairs, through the bar and out into the narrow road. The car was gone.

Back inside the Ram, Roger Daley was drying a glass and eyeing me. I thought about asking him to call the police, to report the break-in and . . . what? A car?

The landlord put down the glass. 'Are you all right, Mr Wilding?' His tone suggested he knew the answer was no. And the hint of a smile forming on his lips suggested this pleased him very much indeed.

'Fine,' I told him.

I'm fine, I'm fine, I'm fine, I told myself with each step up the stairs.

And suddenly the landlord was behind me at the bottom of the stairs. I knew it before I even turned round. His expression was distressing because it was so strange, not just angry but full of rage and quiet malevolence. For a moment I thought his eyes flashed red again, and my heart raced. Daley laughed, revealing his stained yellow teeth. Then he gave me an obscene leer and his voice sounded in my head. I literally heard what he was thinking: *Robert Wilding, your time is running out.*

Back in my room – door locked, window fastened – the phone rang. It didn't matter how many times I answered it, there was no one at the other end, just distorted mechanical beeping sounds. I was about to unplug it from the wall when

I had a different idea. I dialled the MoD. When an operator answered, I said, 'Lord Hill Bartlett's office, please.'

A moment later I heard a secretary's voice: 'The Admiral of the Fleet's office.'

'I want to speak to him.'

'I'm sorry, the admiral is not avail—'

'Tell him it's Robert Wilding and I'm in trouble.'

'Just a moment, please.' There was a brief pause before the secretary buzzed me through and my mentor came on the line.

'Someone knows what I'm doing here,' I said to the admiral. Then I told him about the break-in.

I heard him cough before he answered. 'You think they were after your notes?'

'Not just mine. Selina's notes. They're all gone.' There was a further bout of coughing. He sounded dreadful. 'Admiral, are you—'

'Never mind about me. Go on.'

'She wrote about something called the Parsons Report. I sent you a note. Do you know anything about this document?'

'I had hoped to spare you this, old chap.' There was a brief silence. I wondered if he was thinking or stifling another spasm of coughing. 'We've known about the Parsons Report for some time now.'

'We?'

'The National Security Council.'

I didn't tell him then how furious I was at hearing he had kept this from me, but only because I couldn't find the words to express that anger. 'Tell me now, Admiral. What is it?'

'The Parsons Report was written during the '60s by a British citizen, an expert with an intense interest in UFO phenomena. It warned of the threat that flying saucers pose to this country and indeed the world. Our intelligence suggests it was leaked to those at the very top of the British Establishment.'

'Who?' I whispered into the phone. 'The prime minister?'

'MPs, peers of the realm, top officials, certain factions of the military.'

I glanced out of the window up at the Haven Hotel. The light in Araceli's bedroom had blinked on. 'Admiral, is this really why you sent me here? To find this report.'

'Not at all. But clearly someone else wants it now. The Soviets perhaps.'

That made me think of the peculiar silver car I had seen parked outside.

He produced another hacking cough that sounded so painful I actually winced. 'Your grandfather may have the Parsons Report. I want you to find it, old chap.'

I was not a religious man but I offered up a silent prayer then, a prayer that Randall had nothing to do with the animal mutilations or with Jack Parsons, the rocket scientist and occultist who had come to west Wales after the war. *He died in an explosion at home. The files on his death are still classified.*

I thought of Randall and his suggestion that a cult was at work in the Havens. A secretive, tightly knit group of people. That description could fit the whole community. It could also describe a body like the Rotary Club with members like Howell Cooper and Roger Daley. Couldn't it? I thought so. And that suspicion conjured up icy fingertips that stroked my neck.

I told the admiral what I was thinking. 'Parsons was an occultist, dabbled in rocket technology. Experiments. Right here in the Havens. But now the headmaster's dead and I think there's a group of people here up to something sinister. I need to know if Parsons had anything to do with this group – if he might have been the first member.'

It was a very tenuous possibility at this point, but if true it could explain why there was a cult in the Havens, where it had come from and even what it was up to. But I needed to find some evidence that the link was there.

I took a deep breath. My next request felt like a big deal and I at once felt guilty making it. 'I know you're busy, I know you're unwell, but can you get down here? I don't know if I can do this alone.'

Silence.

'I feel out of my depth. Please come. If you can manage it.'

I felt like I was twelve again, vying for Randall's attention. Except this was different. The admiral understood me in a way that Randall never had.

'What would that achieve, Robert?'

I couldn't say, not immediately, but I felt deeply moved by an obscure foreboding. I remembered why I had returned here, and it felt like so long ago. I had come here to investigate the weapons at the RAF base and to try to make some sense of my parents' deaths. That had been overshadowed by the Happenings, and yet I had a terrible sense that it might all be connected.

'Admiral, I feel as though we're building to something here . . . something dreadful. I'm doing the best I can but I still don't know how the military is involved, or even if they are, and things are getting more and more complicated. I would feel better knowing someone here was in charge, was able to go to the places I haven't been able to.'

'All right.'

I breathed a deep sigh of relief. 'Thank you.'

'Where are you?'

'The Ram Inn, Little Haven.'

'I'll see you tomorrow evening.'

As I hung up I thought again about the documents that had been stolen from my room and glanced out of the window at the hotel. I had got distracted by the missing documents and still hadn't returned Araceli's calls. It was clear she was at the centre of this somehow, and I knew that the first step to understanding it all would be to figure out how and why.

I dialled her number immediately.

'Robert, thank God.'

Fear in her voice. I sat bolt upright. 'Araceli, what's wrong?'

'You won't believe what's happened this afternoon. The hotel's a mess. Things aren't right here. Either I'm seeing and hearing things, or – '

'All right, calm down, speak slowly.'

'You'll think I'm crazy.'

'What happened?'

'I was in the bar earlier when I saw something over St Brides Bay. I thought it was a bird, the way it was wheeling through the sky. It was white and catching the light of the sun.'

'Did you get a good look at it?'

'It was some sort of disc. I don't want to say it was a flying saucer, I don't, but that's exactly what it looked like to me.'

'What was it doing?'

'Just hurtling through the sky towards Giant's Point. Then it stopped and hung in the air above Stack Rocks.'

'Now you're scaring me,' I heard myself say.

'I couldn't believe my eyes, Robert.' She drew in a sharp breath. 'The bloody thing nosedived into the side of Stack Rocks!'

'You mean it crashed?'

'Well, sort of, except . . . I expected flames, an explosion – and I know how this is going to sound – but I thought I saw a door open in the rock face.'

'Robert?'

'I'm here.'

'Impossible, right? A door! It opened, and the disc dived into it and vanished.' She was gasping to get the words out. 'I'm beginning to think I'm losing my mind. There can't be a door in the rock, can there?'

You should know. 'Is it true Stack Rocks Island belongs to your family?'

She hesitated. 'It came with the estate.'

'And now the locals, the Rotary Club, want to do up the abandoned fort on the island?'

'You think that's important?'

My mind went back to the conversations of that afternoon. 'I don't know what to make of this, Araceli. I'm coming over. Sit tight.'

I ended the call. The telephone rang again immediately. I lifted the receiver.

'Hello?'

The line crackled and buzzed.

'Hello, Mr Wilding.'

My breath caught. The voice had a stilted metallic quality, as if I wasn't speaking to a person but a . . .

'Will you give yourself too, Mr Wilding?'

My skin prickled. 'Will I what? Who is this?'

'Are you enjoying yourself, Mr Wilding? We are enjoying watching you ever so much.'

I was so furious, so scared, that I wanted to throw the phone down, smash it against the wall.

'Tell me who you are!'

'Robert, you will come to us. We are legion. And we are coming. Coming back.'

The line clicked dead.

− 38 −

Haven Hotel, Skyview Hill, Little Haven

I stumbled out of the car, ran to the great front door and pounded on it. 'Araceli?'

I tried ringing the bell. No reply, no sign of life.

I looked around me wildly. The moon was hidden behind a bank of cloud. I felt like I was drowning in the dark.

Will you give yourself too, Mr Wilding?

I couldn't get that voice on the telephone out of my head. 'Araceli!'

A sound from within, bolts drawing back. The door opened. She looked dreadful. Her face was dead white, her eyes red and swollen. I gave in to the urge and pulled her to me. She let me hold her.

'Since I saw that thing earlier, this place has gone mad,' she whimpered. 'It's out of control. I don't know how much more I can take.'

I looked past her and started with surprise. For a few seconds I was speechless. There were fresh paintings on the floor – paintings that had not been there when I had last visited – six or seven of them propped against the wall.

'When did you find the time to do these?' I asked.

A strange look crossed her face as if she was reaching for an answer but couldn't find one.

That lighthouse again – Stack Rocks clearly recognizable – projecting its sickly beam of yellow light across a turbulent sea. There was something about the image that filled me with an intolerable, uncertain dread. There was no lighthouse on Stack Rocks, and yet it was in every one of her pictures. It was purely a figment of her imagination. Or a memory of something else. Hidden.

'I can't explain why,' she said falteringly, 'but the lighthouse is important. I'm sure. The lighthouse is vital, Robert. To you and to me.'

Somewhere . . . we went somewhere.

We turned to go inside and the stench from the hall hit me. Jesus, what is that?' I asked, too shocked to feel nauseous. 'Sulphur?'

Her head shook with bewilderment. 'It's everywhere!'

I let go of her and went into the hall. Followed my nose. The odour grew stronger with each step, drawing me past the suit of armour towards a wooden door.

'Where does this lead?'

'The cellar.'

Suddenly Randall's voice was in my head again. The sightings occur on historical points, ley lines. Frequently there is an underground connection. And Frobisher's comment: *You know they say it was built on ley lines.*

'Can I go down there?' I asked, shivering and rubbing my arms.

When we had located a torch and the key to the cellar door, she led me down into the dusty dark, both of us clasping our hands over our noses and mouths.

At first there was just old furniture and boxes of foul-smelling candles piled in a corner. 'Why do you have so many of these?'

'Mother always worried about the lights going out,' she said in a curt tone that suggested this wasn't something she wanted to discuss.

I reached into a box of candles anyway and pulled some out. They were black. The Jacksons. They were found with black candles.

'Did the Jacksons come here?' I asked. 'Did they stay here before their murder? Is that why Selina asked for that particular room?'

Araceli blinked, then nodded, her eyes rolling back to look reluctantly about. Her face turned towards the wall.

'Why the hell didn't you tell me, Araceli?'

Silence.

'Wait. What the hell is this?' I had noticed something on the rough stone and peered hard at it. 'There's something here in chalk.'

A symbol, a five-pointed star, pointing down. Beneath it a chiselled inscription.

> *Bydd giât y cythraul*
> *yn agor a bydd y frwydr*
> *o bridd yn dechrau*

'That's always been there. I don't know what it means,' Araceli said. 'Can you read it?'

I had never learned Welsh. So I had Araceli hold the torch as I scribbled it down. Then I saw a row of symbols to the right of the inscription. They looked familiar. I copied them down too.

Otherwise, the cellar was empty. No clue as to where the smell was coming from.

'Now, please, let's go,' Araceli said.

When we were back in the hall, I demanded she tell me about the Jacksons.

'I told the police everything I know, OK?'

It was very far from OK. 'What were they up to? They were local, so why stay here?'

'They'd been coming here for years. Long-time friends of my parents. All that time we've had . . . disturbances here. Objects disappearing, reappearing. It got worse recently.' She told me what had happened since she had seen the disc dive into the rocks. Doors opened and closed on their own, lights in empty rooms, unexplained banging, objects moving and furniture being overturned.

First UFOs, now poltergeists? It was too much. Still, there was no doubting Araceli's distress or the awful atmosphere that permeated the hotel's hall.

'How's Tessa?'

'I had to put her to bed. Her hair's falling out, and her eyes are red and swollen with conjunctivitis.'

I thought back to my conversation with Randall and Dr Caxton. 'Araceli, tell me. Was Tessa baptized?'

'Is that important?'

'I don't yet know how, but yes, I think it could be.'

Araceli shook her head warily. There were other emotions in her eyes. Guilt? Suspicion? Alarm?

'Right, let's get her and leave. You can't stay here tonight.'

As I said this, I wasn't just thinking about Araceli and her daughter; I was remembering the bizarre phone call at the inn, the metallic taunting voice.

We got as far as the stairs when the lights blinked on.

'Power's back,' said Araceli, sounding relieved but only a little, I thought. The scent of sulphur was definitely growing stronger again on the first-floor landing, and by the time we reached Tessa's bedroom door, it was almost overpowering. I was about to mention it again when a scream ripped through the hotel.

Tessa.

'The door, it's locked!' Araceli shouted.

The scream came again from behind the door as Araceli fumbled with the lock.

'Hurry, hurry!' I said, my hands on hers, trying to help.

The lock clicked. And as the bedroom door swung inward my stomach gave a sickening lurch. The room was empty.

Tessa? *Tessa?*'

Araceli's eyes were wild with panic as she hurtled around the room, throwing open the wardrobe and diving to the floor to look under the bed.

'We'll find her.' But even as I said it, scanning the dolls that lay scattered on the floor, I was seized with uncertainty. How could a child get out of a locked room?

'My God,' Araceli whispered.

Her eyes were fixed not on the French windows but something beyond – a white nightdress fluttering in the wind.

Tessa was outside.

I grabbed the handle. 'It won't open!'

'It doesn't open! How the hell did she get out there?'

I hurled a chair at the windows. The glass smashed, spraying out onto the flat roof beyond and crunching under my shoes as I stepped out.

The roof was spongy underfoot, cracked and blackened, a raindrop away from collapse.

'Tessa,' I said, reaching out a hand, 'Come to me. Come away from the edge.'

But the girl seemed not to hear. Her back to me, she was walking with purpose across that roof with an awful stop-motion slowness.

She's going to throw herself off the roof. The thought hit me so clearly I didn't pause to doubt it.

I knew what was beyond the edge of this roof. A sheer drop off the cliff.

I took a step. The roof creaked under my weight.

'Tessa, sweetie, just don't move,' I called, amazed at how calm I sounded.

Another step. Another.

Araceli screamed again.

The wind pulled at me.

Tessa was at the edge now. Still. Arms raised. Head tilting back. One foot stepping out into nothing . . .

My hand found the back of her nightdress, grabbed it and yanked her back against me. She was rigid for a moment and then melted into me, and I clasped her in my arms. Held her tight. Felt the relief rush from my hands, up my arms and into me.

I glanced down long enough to glimpse the sea smashing into the rocks and then crept back across the roof to Araceli's outstretched arms. She ripped her daughter from me, staggered back inside and collapsed to the floor.

Tessa lay limp in her mother's lap, eyes closed. But there was a pulse. Strong and regular.

'Sleeping,' I told Araceli. 'She's sleeping.'

Tears were streaming down Araceli's face and her body was shuddering. She looked up at me with pleading eyes and I cupped her cheek with my hand. I wanted to reassure her. To tell her the child had simply been sleepwalking. That she must have opened the window somehow. But lying wouldn't erase the terror from this mother's eyes.

'You need help,' I told her.

We needed help.

III

Sky Watch

'What does all this stuff about flying saucers amount to?
What can it mean? What is the truth?'

Prime Minister Winston Churchill, 28 July 1952

FROM *THE MIND POSSESSED:*
A PERSONAL INVESTIGATION INTO
THE BROAD HAVEN TRIANGLE

BY DR R. CAXTON (CLEMENTINE PRESS, 1980) P.100

The hours that led to the sky watch, that tragic event, were packed with events that skewed my interpretation of what it means to be human, indeed what it means to be me. They were hours that cast the longest shadow of doubt across my science, and they were hours I would give anything to forget.

Perhaps it's because I knew that strange things seen in the sky were once interpreted as religious signs and wonders that I came away from the Joneses' house hoping for a rational explanation for the shocking behaviour exhibited by young Isaac, but hope was all I could do as I drove away from Rose Cottage.

Deep down I knew that Randall Llewellyn Pritchard was right. There had been too many UFO reports at ancient sites and along ley lines, too many sightings that coincided with natural disasters. And too many witnesses with horrific physical side-effects.

The UFO experiences in the Broad Haven Triangle were not the result of local superstition and folklore. It wasn't folklore that made Isaac bite his mother's arm, and it wasn't folklore that induced Tessa Romero to try to throw herself off the roof of the Haven Hotel. Both events were symptomatic of an occult condition known as demonomania, an affliction that drives individuals to harm themselves or others, a weakening of the soul that can lead to possession.

Was this a real condition? I'd always assumed most cases had psychological explanations. But now? Increasingly I felt I had to do more to help Randall and his grandson. I had to check all of the children. Were they also exhibiting symptoms of demonomania? If so, God help them.

– 39 –

Monday 14 February 1977, twenty-four hours until the sky watch . . .

It was gone nine o'clock.

As the road uncoiled from the biting blackness I became aware of the blood pulsing behind my eyes. I was scared and with good reason. Because we were close now and I had nothing but bad feelings for Ravenstone Farm.

So what makes you think Araceli and Tessa will be safe here? Perhaps it will be different for them, I wondered. Hoped. Because my decision to bring them here came purely from the desire to alleviate their fear. To make them safe. And yet it was hardly the work of some noble saviour. Rather, I felt I had lost my grip on the world – my best friend dead, my job forgotten, my sanity . . .? Some part of me knew that returning to Ravenstone Farm wasn't just a way of helping Araceli and Tessa, it was a last, desperate attempt to help myself.

I knew my grandfather thought that the Happenings were real and related to a religious cult operating in the village – members of the Rotary Club, by my guess. I also knew that whatever they were doing was creating a force so menacing, so powerful that it could influence people's behaviour. Perhaps even control them. But how far could I trust Randall? After our conversations about my parents and about the Jacksons, it was clear he was still keeping many things hidden.

Trees arched together overhead. As we approached the farm down the narrow rutted track I heard the scrape of branches on the car doors and roof and pictured myself coming here for the first time, all those years ago, in the back seat of Randall's truck, huddled under a blanket, frightened and grief-stricken, watching the crucifix dangling from his rear-view mirror.

I brought the car to a stop, killed the engine.

'Welcome to the end of the world,' I said. We were three hundred miles from London. Araceli looked at me silently. I looked back for a moment, until my gaze drifted and settled on the house to which I had hoped never to return.

'You're sure it's OK for us to be here, Robert?'

'Sure. Just give me a moment.' Just keeping my voice steady was an effort, and she must have noticed me trembling – her eyes were wide and wondering as she touched my hand. The contact gave me gooseflesh. I was filled with a sudden longing to abandon this responsibility I felt for Araceli, for Tessa, but resisted. I made myself get out of the car and look around me.

The place stank of manure, but that wasn't the first thing I noticed. Randall had never taken much pride in the upkeep of the place. But whereas such details were hazy in my memory, the emotions that swept through me were not: a powerful mixture of grief mixed with anger and fear made me lean for support on the front of the car.

'This place still feels unnatural,' I whispered to myself. And it did. It felt like nowhere else on earth. A slight but undeniable disturbance suffused the air, an electric charge that prickled the skin and filled me with the deepest conviction that at Ravenstone Farm the fabric of the world was so thin you could believe it touched another.

Araceli was staring at me through the windscreen, and from the back seat of the car so was Tessa. The child's face was still tear-stained and exhausted.

'Give me a minute,' I muttered.

I could hear my breathing – rough and dry – as I walked towards the farmhouse. Squat and sullen. A monument to everything I hated in life. I focused on the small window with iron bars just above the porch. The glass was rattling in the sea wind. The wave of memory that rolled through me was so intense I couldn't help but shiver, and in jagged white flashes I remembered what had happened to me here: Randall forcing me to kneel and pray on the hard floor of his study; Randall training his shotgun on the front door as the thuds had shaken the house. But what had happened after that?

No, a voice in my head said. *We forget because we must.*

The car alarm went off. I jumped and spun round.

'We didn't touch anything!' Araceli shouted as she helped Tessa out of the back. Her face was panicked. 'You've got the keys!'

She was right; I could feel them in the pocket of my jeans.

The car's headlights burst into life, projecting two powerful beams at the farmhouse. I turned to look. A black space had replaced where the front door had been. And framed within it was Randall, unshaven and in his dressing gown.

He surveyed the scene before him: the shrieking car, the flashing headlamps, Araceli holding a sobbing Tessa in her arms, backing away from the car. Finally, he looked at me.

'Welcome home, boy.'

FROM *THE MIND POSSESSED:*
A PERSONAL INVESTIGATION INTO
THE BROAD HAVEN TRIANGLE

BY DR R. CAXTON (CLEMENTINE PRESS, 1980) P.120

Randall Llewellyn Pritchard was born and raised in Egryn, a scattered hamlet on the coast of Merionethshire between Barmouth and Harlech in north Wales. As far as I can tell, his early life was spent at the bleak farmhouse owned by his mother, Mrs Pauline Pritchard, a religious mystic who had endured many personal tragedies, most notably the death of three infants in childbirth. In 1904, the year of Randall's birth, Mrs Pritchard was at the heart of a religious revival that was bringing whole congregations to their knees.

In the opinion of this psychologist the spectacular incidents surrounding Mrs Pritchard's mission make up one of the most astonishing accounts of paranormal events in British history. At the dilapidated roadside chapel in Egryn the Welsh Seeress (as she became known) would lead scores of people to Christ, making reference to signs in the heavens, telling how she had seen each night a fire rise before her from the marshy shore, a rapidly vibrating light, 'as though full of eyes'.

According to one report from the time, 'The chapel became bathed in mysterious light. After the meeting a professional gentleman returning homeward suddenly saw a gigantic figure rising over a hedgerow, with right arm extended over the road.

Then a ball of fire appeared above, a long white ray descended and pierced the figure, which vanished . . .'

We now know that it wasn't just lights that Randall's mother saw, but visions of the devil. In the years following the manifestations – Randall's formative years – Mrs Pritchard became distant and ranted incessantly about a battle with Satan for human souls. By the time Randall was fifteen his mother had stopped speaking to him, stopped speaking to anyone. And by the time Randall was eighteen, she had been locked in an asylum.

We now know, of course, that Randall would grow up to embrace his mother's fascination with religion and the occult and would become the focus of intense media speculation and mass hysteria when the Broad Haven manifestations reached their climax.

– 40 –

Monday 14 February 1977, Ravenstone Farm

'My God, what's wrong with the lights?' Araceli asked as the bulbs blinked on and off in the kitchen. Tessa was shaking and pale-faced on her lap at the imposing kitchen table.

You'd better get used to it, I was thinking. *Because anything electrical or mechanical has a habit of going wrong at Ravenstone Farm.*

I put my hand on Araceli's shoulder and gave it a reassuring squeeze. After what had happened at the hotel, I knew the monsters weren't just in my head any more. They were in the village, in the sky and in the sea. Even in the phone lines.

Randall had gone out to inspect my car. He came in, shaking his head and frowning. 'Nothing wrong with it as far as I can see.' He looked down at Araceli coldly.

'It's all right,' she managed to say, stroking her daughter's hair. 'We're OK, aren't we, Tess?'

The child nodded, yet her skin was the colour of gone-off milk and oddly shiny.

The kettle whined as it came to the boil. 'Coffee?' Randall asked.

Araceli nodded wearily and Randall got to work.

'There's a bed upstairs for the child, if you like.'

'Absolutely not!' Araceli answered. 'She isn't leaving my sight.'

Randall handed her a mug, all the time keeping an uneasy gaze on Tessa, who was not just withdrawn now but sullen. 'Do you remember your dreams, Tessa?' he asked suddenly, surprisingly gentle.

She hesitated, then nodded.

'And do you like dreaming?'

'No,' she replied.

'Can you tell me what you see in your dreams, Tessa?'

'The bad men.'

'Tell me,' Randall said, taking a seat at the table opposite mother and daughter. 'When did you first see these bad men?'

'The night before the football.'

Araceli was watching Randall intently from under her lashes. 'She means the light that chased our car. Before the thing at the school.'

'There was a man in my bedroom,' Tessa said. Then, with a little more prompting from Randall, 'A big black shape. I knew he was bad. I hid under the blankets, and when I looked again he was gone.'

'She had to sleep in with me,' Araceli said.

Randall asked for a further description but Tessa only pursed her lips and shook her head.

'You'll remember what I told you, boy: the Black-Suited Men are the messengers of deception, the harbingers of death.' He glanced at Araceli and added, 'There are secrets buried in houses all over the Havens.'

For a further ten minutes Randall asked us both more questions and listened in silent fascination as we told him about the unexplained knockings and poundings at the hotel and Tessa's misadventure.

'How on earth did you get onto the roof?' Randall asked the girl.

She shook her head.

Then Randall began reciting from the Bible: '"Let there not be found among you anyone who immolates his son or daughter in the fire, not a fortune-teller, soothsayer, charmer, diviner, or caster of spells, nor one who consults ghosts and spirits or seeks oracles from the dead."'

'I don't know what you mean. We haven't done anything like that!' Araceli insisted. 'We're not consulting with the dead. Why would we do such a thing?'

Randall looked suspicious.

Araceli shook her head vigorously. 'It's true!"

'Have you or your daughter brought any unusual items into the hotel recently? Gifts perhaps?'

'No.'

'Any unusual guests stayed with you?'

'No.'

'Do you know anyone who might want to hurt you?'

'No.'

'And you say there was a distinct smell of sulphur?'

Araceli and I nodded without speaking, and I watched Randall's gaze travel from the young mother and her daughter to the window and the night beyond. 'Isn't it extraordinary,' he said, 'how many so-called poltergeist infestations have succeeded or coincided with spates of intense UFO activity?'

I had no idea whether this was true or even why it was important, but Araceli leaned forward and said hopefully, 'Other people experience these things?'

'Many other people,' Randall answered. 'And foul odours like sulphur are common at seances and in haunted locations. They are also extremely common at UFO landing sites.'

He's right, I thought. The coincidences are undeniable. The spontaneous movement of objects at the Haven Hotel. And here, at Ravenstone Farm, when I was a boy, the picture on the wall that had turned upside down in Randall's study. My mind raced and I decided to confront him on an earlier comment.

'What did you mean – secrets all over the village?'

'Did you explore the cellar at the Haven Hotel?' Randall asked.

How did he know?

'You saw the inscription.'

I had it written on a scrap of paper in my pocket. I took it out and tried reading it aloud then asked, 'What the hell does it mean?'

'Ask her,' Randall said sternly. His gaze, clear and penetrating, focused on Araceli, and she looked up sharply.

'She said she doesn't know,' I countered. But then I looked in her eyes and saw they were furtive.

'I don't want to say it.'

'No, young lady. I bet you don't.'

But eventually she got the words out. She didn't need to translate, I quickly realized; she knew the words by heart.

I wrote them down.

The battle on earth will commence with signs in the heavens.
The Demon's Gate will open.
Darkness will rule for eternity.

− 41 −

The wind was moaning about the farmhouse. Even from the kitchen I could hear the rusty old swing at the front creaking as it kicked back and forth.

'You said you didn't know what the inscription meant,' I said to Araceli. My accusing tone was deliberate. I was hurt to think she was holding back on me again, especially after what we had just been through together. 'Who chiselled it into the wall?'

Silence.

Frustrated by her refusal to answer me, I got up from the table and stalked into my grandfather's study.

I needed some time to think. I would call Dr Caxton, I decided. Like me he was a sceptic at heart. He was obviously here to learn the same things as I was, and would be able to apply a scientific mind to the problem. And maybe, when the admiral arrived, we could all work together. As it stood, I wasn't sure how many more lies and superstitions I could take before I went completely mad.

Inside Randall's study the air was as perfectly still and stale as I remembered, but the room seemed much smaller. There was the picture that had turned on its nail. Now it was in its proper position, thank God, the androgynous St John the Baptist with his enigmatic smile, taunting me, still pointing into the sky. I couldn't take my eyes off that finger. *The truth is up there*, it said.

Only the walls had changed. Whereas before they had been lined with overstocked bookshelves, now they were covered, floor to ceiling, with newspaper clippings, fuzzy photographs of flying saucers and drawings of bulky, wide-shouldered, helmeted figures with black spaces where their faces should have been. There were maps of west Wales too. Clusters of red pins marked the locations of the reported sightings that formed the Broad Haven Triangle.

I dialled Dr Caxton's number and released a sigh of relief when he answered.

'Hello, Robert. You sound terrible.'

I updated him on recent events. 'I know you are an expert in paranormal psychology and sightings. I also know you are a sceptic, but I don't know what to believe any more, and I really think we need as much help as we can get. How soon can you get over here?' I gave him my location.

'I'll be there as soon as I can.' He sounded perturbed. 'I wanted to speak to you and your grandfather in any case. I have some new information concerning the children.'

'You got the addresses?'

'No. Something else.' He left a pronounced pause that quickened my blood. 'I owe Randall an apology. Something very dangerous is most definitely taking place here.'

'Why the change of heart?'

'I've discovered something deeply troubling.'

'What is it?'

'Not over the phone. I'll tell you when I get there.'

The call over, I steeled myself to return to the kitchen to question Araceli. I needed to know what she was hiding. But as I headed for the door, I knew I had one person left to speak to. The admiral. Perhaps he was still in his Westminster office.

I dialled the first three numbers quickly, facing a wall plastered with newspaper clippings I had once considered sensational, scanning the headlines. I held the telephone against my ear, thinking, *Please answer, please answer*.

'Admiral of the Fleet.'

'There was something I didn't tell you. Something I only suspected before but now I know.' I said immediately. 'It's not the Americans.'

'Robert? What's wrong, old chap? It's late.' His voice sounded terribly hoarse. He coughed, then said, 'Did you find the Parsons Report?' I told him I hadn't. 'Then what has happened?'

'Too many things,' I said, hardly knowing where to start. 'Seriously weird things. My gaze roamed the forest of red pins protruding from the map on the wall. 'Admiral, what I have learned . . . These UFOs, they seem to come and go as they please. They buzz planes and cars. They terrify and they never make a mistake. They never crash. And there's no consistent appearance – many shapes and sizes, with no obvious power source. Everything about their behaviour suggests to me that they are trying to confuse us. No, not confuse us. Deceive us.'

'Robert – '

'They can be seen or not seen, even by radar. Admiral, it's almost as if they operate outside our laws of science.'

He coughed again, long and hard this time.

'Also, they're definitely not harmless. They have substance,' I said, scanning the pictures and articles on the study wall. 'They can inflict what look to me like radiation burns. They can stop cars.'

'Old chap?'

'I'm here.'

'I'm worried about you. You sound . . . strained.'

He means mad.

'I'm fine,' I lied.

Then came a bout of fierce coughing. I knew then that there was something awful rattling around in his chest, and I was pretty damn sure it wasn't any sort of cold.

'Robert, it's important you don't lose perspective now.' It was clear he was still thinking that this was something to do with the Americans and the Soviets. 'Exactly how much does Randall know about all this?' he continued.

I glanced at the desk, at the piles of letters, documents, tape recordings and dog-eared books. 'I don't know. It's hard to tell but . . . more than he's saying.'

Another hacking cough. 'Robert, remember why you went down there in the first place. You *must* make him tell you what he knows.'

I thought about the enormous floating figure that had appeared opposite Dylan Jones's cottage, I saw Isaac biting his mother's arm, and I knew something was hiding in the folds of these experiences, some sort of controlling force. I could feel it pressing against the back of my mind, as if it was struggling to take a part of me.

'We're not just talking about UFO sightings,' I said firmly. 'When people see these craft, the entities controlling them . . . I don't know, it's like they suffer intimate intrusions into their minds. Their souls.'

This time there was no coughing, no words either. Just a long silence.

'Admiral, why did you send me here if you won't believe what I've found?'

'Find out what Randall Llewellyn Pritchard knows,' the admiral said in response. He sounded like he had lost all confidence in me. 'I'll aim to be at Brawdy from midday tomorrow.'

I replaced the handset and looked down at Randall's desk. Tried the top drawer. Locked. The others. Locked. There was no key in sight. My gaze roamed from the desk to the walls. Clippings. Map. Picture over the mantelpiece hanging upside down.

Hanging upside down!

I felt a sudden burst of adrenaline that quickened the blood, my eyes going in and out of focus. *I'm supposed to notice it.*

Cautiously I reached up, gripped the painting and lifted it off the wall. Nothing. Just a faint mark where it had been. But wait – taped to the back of the painting was a small key.

Feeling my heartbeat quicken, I removed the key, hung the painting back in position and tried the top drawer of the desk. It slid out. And I looked down at the truth.

— 42 —

The small booklet in the drawer wasn't thick, thirty-five pages at most, but it certainly looked old. The title, positioned in the centre of the cover page, was in block capital letters:

'SKY SPECTRES'
THE PARSONS REPORT
SELECTED CIRCULATION

I opened the booklet and scanned down to the introduction: 'This report is being brought to the attention of a considerable number of very responsible and influential people. Its subject is of the greatest possible importance to every human being on this planet.' And on the next page: 'UFOs are essentially a religious matter rather than a military threat from outer space. The problem of the UFO phenomenon is that of a non-human paranormal kind. It isn't just anti-Christian, it is demonic, in nature and intent.'

I winced at that passage, and wave after wave of anxiety pulsed through me. What would it take, I wondered, to become convinced? I wasn't religious, but at the same time my determination to know the truth, to find some frame of reference for everything that was happening, was overwhelming and forcing me to revaluate what I thought about UFOs.

Demonic? Was this report how Randall knew so much about the UFOs? How had he got his hands on it? Were they looking for it? Was it the reason they had ransacked my room at the Ram Inn? Who were *they*? The Parsons Elite maybe?

I turned the page and another passage stood out:

What we are witnessing are modern manifestations and interpretations of archaic legends found in all major religions. The most pertinent being the struggle for the souls of humanity, the battle between good and evil, God and Satan. But the rules of the game have changed. Religious symbols and imagery have been replaced by sky spectres – flying saucers and their pilots. And they are working against the Peace of Christ.

Beneath this was a tantalizing extract from the Bible, Ephesians 6: 12: 'Our wrestling is not against flesh and blood: but against . . . the spirits of wickedness in the high places.'

'Boy?' Randall called from the kitchen.

'Yes, yes.' I dropped the report into the top drawer, locked it quickly and returned the key.

'What were you doing?' he said as I entered the kitchen.

'Calling Caxton. He said he's got something he needs to tell us.'

I was surprised to see Randall donning his overcoat, collar pulled up. He saw my questioning expression and said gruffly, 'Going to check on the animals.'

The kitchen door banged shut behind him and I locked it immediately. I felt Araceli watching me but she said nothing.

Through the barred window over the sink I watched Randall

by moonlight, huddled against the freezing coastal wind, a lone figure in the night.

Araceli gave me an exhausted smile and ran a hand through her cloud of black hair. I thought she looked beautiful, but I was beginning to realize that she wasn't all she seemed either. *Why did you feign ignorance about the inscription we found in your cellar?* I wondered, and then I knew, just as I had known she was withholding information concerning Selina.

'Something wrong, Robert?'

I stared at her in blank astonishment.

'What is it? You've gone white!'

'The room in your hotel, Selina's room – that was your mother's old bedroom, wasn't it.' The thought had slipped in as if from nowhere.

Already Araceli's face was changing in a way that made me uncomfortable. She looked at her daughter. 'I'm not supposed to talk about this, Robert.'

'Why did your mother ever want to live in that hotel?'

'I told you. She was keen to run it as a business.'

'Really?'

'Yes. My father – I *told* you – he moved away and – '

'Left you both with nothing. Yes, you said. And the people in the village told me your mother was mixed up with black magic. Witchcraft.'

'Oh now, come on, Robert.'

I thought of the black candles we had seen in the cellar of the Haven Hotel.

'How many times did the Jacksons stay at your hotel?'

'I don't know exactly. They visited my mother.'

'And my colleague Selina knew this? She asked you about them?'

'Yes.'

'I thought I'd have earned your trust by now, after what happened this evening.'

She just looked at me tiredly.

'They had maps and cameras. They went walking at night. The Jacksons were looking for UFOs.' I couldn't be sure of that and yet I was. 'Correct?'

'It's possible,' Araceli said. 'Yes.'

A thought leaped into my head. 'Araceli, did they know about the inscription in the cellar? Did they ever ask to see it?'

She looked at me, and I looked back at her; neither of us broke the connection.

'I'm right?' I asked. 'That's why they always came back. Because of the inscription in the cellar. It meant something to them, like it meant something to your moth – '

'No, enough! I've heard this shit all my life. I don't need to hear it from you too!'

I thought about Selina's notebook and imagined I was holding it now as if it proved my case. 'My colleague discovered the existence of something called the Parsons Report, warning the government about the dangers of these phenomena.'

'Really? Well I know nothing about that.'

'Selina traced the origins of that document right here to the Havens. For some reason the Havens have had an extraordinarily long association with UFOs and other phenomena – whatever they are. Now Selina is dead because of a deliberate attack carried out by someone who wanted her silenced.'

'And you know this for sure?'

Yes, I thought fiercely.

She shook her head, tense and angry. 'There are easier ways to get rid of people, Robert.'

'Are there?'

'Ask him!' Araceli snapped. I followed her gaze to the kitchen window, out into the night. Randall had turned on the outside lights. The enormous concrete yard was bathed in a harsh glow.

I was torn. Go back to the study and read the Parsons Report or follow Randall?

'If you want answers,' Araceli said. 'Talk to him.'

− 43 −

The wind was screaming across the cliff tops as I took the route I remembered so well. I imagined Jasper trotting along beside me, loveable and alive – tongue out, tail beating.

It was only ten thirty, but the evening was inky black with just the huddled lights of Broad Haven twinkling across St Brides Bay. If the sky watch went ahead as planned tomorrow night for the lunar eclipse, I was willing to bet there would many more lights around the beach – campfires, torches, headlights.

My hands were stinging from the cold, and the night felt dead and black. I went slowly into that darkness, keeping close to the rutted path I must have walked hundreds of times as a boy.

I tried focusing on the stinging smell of cow manure but all that came to mind were the faces of the dead: my parents, Selina, the Jacksons – murdered just a few fields away on the coastal path. Anyone could be out here, watching me now. I did all I could not to imagine the gigantic silver humanoids with black spaces for faces and spindly Black-Suited Men with eyes like fire and ice.

With the Atlantic wind at my back, I took another step, looked anxiously about me. Nothing. Nobody.

What was that?

I froze. I had heard something behind me in the tomb-like blackness. It sounded like footsteps. Something moving. An animal perhaps? I listened intently. Nothing.

The Watchers were judged by God and bound for seventy generations. Randall's voice echoed in my mind, a story told to me years ago, something about legions of devils in the earth.

A long way off a fox howled, and a shiver ran down my spine. I tried not to think about the Parsons Report or the occultist Jack Parsons and quickened my pace.

Randall's milking shed was a huge concrete and asbestos building that had always reminded me of an aircraft hangar. Inside everywhere was corrugated metal bolted together, and there was the stench of manure. I found Randall standing in one of the first internal enclosures watching over a cow pacing around in agitation.

'She's going into labour, boy,' he said.

I stood awkwardly beside him, watching the animal panting. It was always a long and anxious process, but Randall must have done it hundreds of times before. He looked out across the paddocks that contained the other hundred or so cows and said, 'I just hope the rest of them are all right. Milk yield is down some 40 per cent. They won't even enter the lower fields.' He gave me a grim look. 'I found footprints down there. Gigantic, at least fifteen inches long, with a smooth surface and a prominent rounded heel. Circular burn marks too. Now every time I get the herd to the gates they turn and stampede in the opposite direction. Perhaps they can see something we can't.'

I felt my uneasiness grow. 'I feel like that sometimes,' I said, remembering how I had known of Selina's death before it had happened. 'Like I'm aware of things I shouldn't be.'

He looked straight at me, raising an eyebrow. 'I was afraid of this. You're remembering. It's easier to forget when the past is hundreds of miles away and your focus each day is protecting the country. Serving government. But here, at the eye of the storm, the memories are closer, less easily suppressed.'

'This place makes it worse,' I admitted. 'The farm never felt right to me.'

'Aye, your mother used to say the same thing.' He smiled fleetingly.

A picture rose in my mind: Randall dragging me into his study to pray. Had he done the same to Mum? Was that why she had stayed away?

'What won't you tell me?' I demanded.

'How much do you remember?' he countered.

'I remember Mum and Dad arguing. I remember it was something about me. I remember him taking me somewhere late at night, and a lighthouse.' I squeezed my eyes tightly shut. 'Afterwards, you brought me here. I remember the cross in the sky and Jasper. I remember you making me pray. I remember someone hammering on the door, you pointing your shotgun.'

His eyes met mine, and the memory travelled between us.

'I was trying to protect you.'

'From who? What?'

A haziness entered his expression. He blinked and it cleared. 'Tomorrow isn't the first sky watch; there was one planned for that night too. The people outside the farm were locals but members of a nasty association with a global reach. People like them have existed in this village for centuries. Members of a cult.'

A cult now calling itself the Parsons Elite.

'Did they come for you,' I asked, 'or for me?'

Or did they come for the Parsons Report?

'The less you know about it, the better – you'll just have to trust me on that.' He nodded towards the farmhouse, where Araceli was waiting, and sighed. 'Her mother was a member of the cult, her father too, I believe. Evil places attract evil people. That's why they bought the place. It drew them as it drew the Jacksons. That couple weren't innocent either; they had blood on their hands, no doubt. Whoever finished them off did the world a favour.'

'Please don't tell me you –'

'Killed them? Course not. But I imagine you've already heard differently down in the village. Who told you about all that?'

'Frobisher.'

'Oh, really? I thought it might have been that filthy communist priest . . .' He cracked his knuckles. 'You don't trust a man who thinks Marxism is the future. That Russia is a land where dreams come true.'

'How do you know he does?'

'It wasn't coincidence he arrived in this village when they upgraded the runways over at Brawdy. He's different.'

'And being different makes him suspicious?'

'Don't apologize for him. You can't reconcile Christianity and communism. I look at that regime – its stinking corruption – and I see the devil. Father O'Riorden looks and sees the kingdom of heaven. Paradise! But it's not a paradise. It's shrewd and godless and cruel, with labour camps and show trials.' He shook his head. 'Who'd have thought that after the last world war we'd find ourselves living again on the brink of annihilation? In a land of nightmares.'

His passion was undeniable. Listening to his voice I was

struck by the memory of my mother denouncing nuclear weapons as *a reckless threat to world peace*. My father – being a military man – hated her for that.

'Assume you're right,' I said. 'Assume there is a cult at work here in Little Haven. Why did they come to the farm? We're out in the middle of nowhere.'

He was still holding back as if a truthful answer would inflict upon me irreparable harm, and that made me even more nervous.

'This farm and its immediate surroundings – Stack Rocks, the abandoned airfield up the road at Talbenny – these areas are of intense interest to this group.'

'Why? And what makes you an expert?'

'You forget I served in the air force during the war.'

It suddenly dawned on me that he was referring to a specific military site in the area. But which one? The number of airfields abandoned by the RAF and converted to agriculture was almost as great as the plethora of shipwrecks in St Brides Bay. Randall could have been stationed at any of these, but there really was only one plausible candidate.

'RAF Ravenstone?'

He nodded. 'Nothing but isolated ruined structures now, less than half a mile from here. That substantial brick building near the turning for Dale? That was the operations block, part of a radar station where we tracked enemy aircraft.'

'You were a radar operator?'

Randall nodded. 'We had targets on radar that moved like nothing you've ever seen, but when you looked with the naked eye, they weren't there. Unexplainable echoes. Some people refer to them as "angels". I know them as sky spectres.'

My stomach jumped. That was the phrase from the Parsons Report, the document hidden in his study, the document that someone wanted – badly.

'Definitely not German aircraft?'

'Do you think a German aircraft could reach twenty-eight thousand miles per hour, come to a dead stop, then disappear?'

I was silent. Stunned.

'That was my reaction,' Randall said heavily. 'We considered scrambling some planes before we realized they didn't stand a chance in hell of keeping up. But I didn't forget it. The target disappeared over St Brides Bay immediately above Stack Rocks. That's when I decided to buy this farm. It's the nearest property. And I imagine that's why the atmosphere here always feels so . . . alien. '

'What about Grandmother?'

He smiled distantly. 'Of course she died before you were born, but she left me when I bought this place. I became obsessed. I wanted to know everything I could about the sky spectres. And as soon as I began my studies, I was monitored.'

'By whom?'

'I never knew their names. Slender, dressed all in black. The telephone rang at all times, hissed and buzzed. Someone's idea of a joke, I thought at first. I was wrong about that.' He looked at me for a long moment. 'What's important is that you help me ensure that this sky watch tomorrow does *not* happen. You've seen what happens when people experience these things up close, the way they change. Imagine that happening en masse.'

I was imagining it, and it worried me enormously. At the same time I was thinking of Isaac Jones and his desperately ill father.

I was about to ask Randall if he was the author of the secret report I had left in his desk drawer when the cow we were watching groaned.

'Help me with her,' Randall said.

'She's out!' Randall cried. His face radiated genuine happiness, pure relief.

For just over an hour we had worked side by side to deliver the calf. An exhausting tense experience, but a release because I had allowed myself to forget, just for a while, Araceli sitting in the farmhouse, Dr Caxton on his way and all the horrors of the farm and the village.

Randall was still smiling, his eyes on mine.

A question occurred to me, one I had pondered hundreds of times in the last ten years. Only now, with the mother licking her newborn calf at our feet, did I find the courage to ask it. 'Why did you never cry? After Mum and Dad's accident?'

His smile faded but his tone remained warm. 'You never *saw* me cry. I had to be strong for us both.'

The memory of that time – the night of the Great Flood – caught in my throat. I looked away, suddenly angry. How could my parents have been so bloody stupid, so reckless, to go out on a night like that, to leave me?

Randall's next question was careful. 'Do you recall our sessions together?'

I shook my head, waited for more.

'Those were bad times. You were in a terrible way. Hysterical, kicking over furniture, writhing on the floor.'

I stared at him. I thought this had to be bullshit.

'You were a violent child, boy. But I brought you through the worst of it,' he said gently.

My limbs had gone cold. I remembered anger, rage. Was that why I had been kept away from the funeral?

'On one occasion you lashed out at the other children in school.'

I didn't like what I was hearing, not a bit. But it sounded . . . right. The more he spoke, the more I thought perhaps I could reach fragments of memory that confirmed what he was saying: the stale scent of his study, my head tilted back as I sat in a deep armchair, his hypnotic voice.

'I had to keep you safe, Robert. It was my duty.'

My mind filled with wisps of black memories, long buried . . . and there it was, the door handle turning, the dark profile I knew now was my father, creeping into my room. Taking me away.

Then Randall's husky voice in the gloom – the voice of a reasonable man bartering with someone who didn't know where reality begins and ends – was back in my ear. 'If you decide to stay, if I can't change your mind, then it's important you face this darkness, boy.'

'Listen to yourself!' I shouted so suddenly he gave a start. The cow groaned. 'Is it any wonder I'm so confused? Growing up with you and your secrets, I was a nervous wreck. I still am!'

I lost control. An awful jumble of half-formed, half-choked-back words spilled from my mouth before embarrassment took the place of anger. I crouched down in the milking shed, hanging my head so he couldn't see my tears.

His heavy hand dropped on my shoulder. It provided unexpected reassurance. 'Robert.' I was momentarily shaken by the empathy in his tone. For the first time he really sounded like a parent. 'Let's try again, shall we? If you're to face your fear you must understand it. Why are you afraid? Why must you constantly lock doors? Why did you never return to the farm?'

'Because of what might happen,' I heard myself say. My eyes closed and the memories crowded in.

'Why? What do you fear?'

'That they can see me.'

'Who, boy?'

And suddenly the words were out. 'Them,' I heard myself answer. 'The Watchers.'

− 44 −

Monday, Ravenstone Farm, 11.30 p.m.

I closed my eyes and saw the Black-Suited Men at the farmhouse door fourteen years ago. This memory wasn't a momentary flicker; this was a lasting and harrowing image. Their hair was as white as snow, their lips so red they might have been covered with blood. I didn't need to ask Randall what they were. The answer was already floating up: *messengers of deception, harbingers of death.*

When Randall had first uttered those words, when I was a boy, I had thought he was mad. I didn't think that now. What I thought now was, *Why had they come? When are they coming back?*

These questions must have shown on my face but they never made it from my mouth. I was too stunned to speak.

'The Lawless One will arrive with all power, signs and lying wonders,' Randall said in a low voice. 'He promotes false miracles. What we call flying saucers are really images from hell. The sky spectres, the Black-Suited Men, the silver giants – the world naively thinks of these phenomena as aliens.' He shook his head. 'They are here to deceive us. Demonic manifestations.

Fallen angels.' He nodded grimly. 'The Bible refers to them as the Watchers.'

I had so many questions but the only one I could manage was, 'Will they come again?'

'I fear so. They have been summoned by the cult at work in this village.'

'When will they come? Tonight, tomorrow?'

'They will keep coming until they get what they want.'

'Which is what?

He gave me a hard look. 'Our souls.'

From overhead came a loud crack of thunder. As the rain began to fall, Randall helped me to my feet and studied my face for a long time. I studied his and wondered again about the jagged scar on his face. That scar was easily his most compelling feature and, looking at it, I sensed there was so much more to learn about him, so much more he might tell me if I only knew the right questions to ask. 'We ought to get back inside,' he said, 'check on the girls.'

'Yes,' I said distantly. I was still thinking about what he had said as he slammed the gate to the cattle shed shut and shot the bolt: *You were a violent child, boy. But I brought you through the worst of it.*

Nerves still jumping, I followed him across the yard to the farmhouse. The outside lights blinked out behind us and we covered the distance in less than a minute. I was glad to get out of the rain and the freezing sideswipes of the coastal wind. I needed rest. The phone was ringing. There was no sign of Araceli or Tessa in the kitchen – I thought they must have finally gone upstairs to sleep. Grandfather went into his study to take the call. I headed for the stairs, but his words stopped me short.

'Could you say that again? They're not my cows, Gethin . . . Yes, I'm bloody sure.'

I stepped back to watch him from the hall.

'An hour? No, impossible. I've just been with them . . . Yes, a bloody minute ago.' Randall saw me in the doorway. 'It's Gethin over at Broadmoor Farm,' he said, covering the mouthpiece. 'He reckons my cows are on his land, right now, making a hell of a mess. All of them.'

'He's having you on,' I said with a note of derision. 'Or he's mistaken.'

'Well, he reckons they've been there for over an hour. He's been phoning.'

Of course it was impossible. Not only had I watched Randall secure the milking shed just now, he'd triple-checked the bolt as well as lashed it with twine to be extra sure. There had to be another explanation.

'Wait here,' I said.

The freezing night air struck me as I plunged out of the front door again, running now, until the yard lights blinked on. Then I walked slowly. Suppose, just suppose, someone was watching me from beyond the trees that screened the farmyard from the fields. The same someone, perhaps, who had done that terrible thing to Jasper. I wouldn't see them in the darkness through the glare of the lights. If they ran at me, I wouldn't stand a chance.

There was no one. Yet some presence was with me. Nerves sloshed in the pit of my stomach as I approached the cowshed gate. My gaze fell on the bolt. It was still shot and lashed with twine. One-hundred-per-cent secure.

I leaned over the gate and into the darkness, flicked on the light switch.

Vanished off the face of the earth.

All of them.

But that wasn't quite true, because if our nearest neighbour was to be believed the herd was a mile away, scattering grain everywhere and trampling all over Broadmoor Farm.

Randall was still holding the phone in his hand when I re-entered the farmhouse. When I told him his cattle were gone he looked both confused and afraid. 'I . . . I really don't know how this happened, Gethin,' he said, 'but I'm coming to get them. Now. I'll herd them back myself.'

It would have been churlish of Gethin to insist on that, considering the lateness of the hour, so it was a relief to hear that he was willing to wait until morning.

Randall thanked him, sounding dazed, and dropped the phone into its cradle.

When Dr Caxton arrived, around midnight, I greeted him warmly and with genuine relief. Despite our differences, I felt I was at risk of losing perspective on everything that had happened and was eager to hear his opinion on the cattle as well as whatever new information he had gleaned.

'I'm not going to deny it's extremely strange,' he said, taking a stool in the kitchen. 'Some sort of intruder driving the cows off would seem the likeliest explanation, but still . . .'

There was no route the cows could have taken to reach Broadmoor Farm other than the lane out of Ravenstone Farm which ran immediately adjacent to the house. If one hundred and forty-two cows had passed the house, we would certainly have heard them. And even if we hadn't, they could never have covered that distance so quickly.

'They moved a mile in a matter of minutes,' I said.

The psychologist shook his head. 'That's impossible.'

'But how did they get there?' Randall asked, rapping his hand on the table. 'They can't possibly have crossed any of the fields because of the electric fences.'

Dr Caxton had brought with him a small leather bag from which he removed a thick bundle of notes. 'How are Araceli and the little one faring?'

'They're upstairs asleep,' I answered. I had gone to check on them after Randall had got off the phone.

Randall was sitting at the head of the kitchen table, his penetrating eyes fixed on our visitor. 'Remind me of your qualifications,' he said, and Caxton straightened at the sharpness in his tone.

'Ah, well, it might interest you to know that I am related to one of the greatest psychical researchers ever to have lived.' He listed his father's greatest cases and Randall seemed to know immediately to whom he was referring.

'The man was a charlatan. A fraud.'

'Perhaps,' Dr Caxton said, keeping his voice level. 'But in many respects he was a diligent researcher and a committed investigator. Ruthlessly sceptical.'

'The acorn never falls far from the tree, does it?'

We didn't have time to squabble like this. 'You said on the telephone you had something important to tell us?' I reminded the doctor.

He nodded. 'I did as I said I would and visited some of the children from the school.' His face turned dark. 'They're in a bad, bad way. Crying, shaking, mumbling about "the Summoning" . . . One of the children, Dafydd Pugh, poor thing, was completely distraught. Couldn't speak, wouldn't eat.' He went quiet for a moment, as if selecting the order in which to tell us the important facts. 'We were in the lounge and his mother had made him a sandwich which was on a plate on the coffee table. I saw the plate move. No, not move. It flipped right off the table! And I swear no one was near it.'

I realized then that the psychologist had been building his courage to tell us this, that his scepticism was protection against phenomena he simply could not explain.

Dr Caxton cleared his throat. 'I'm not sure the conclusion I might draw would have any form of scientific validity, but I believe the witnesses are either attracting poltergeist phenomena, or – '

'Or the sky spectres are inducing psychic abilities in the children,' Randall broke in. 'Just as they induce physical symptoms and psychosis in adults. This is how the Watchers operate. They induce terror and then feed off that terror.'

For once I was taking him seriously – the events involving the cattle shed were too strange to ignore. What if a power existed that could project itself in whatever form it wanted? And what if that power could exert influence over the minds of people who saw it? Make them do things against their will?

I thought of the sky watch planned for tomorrow night and understood why Randall wanted so badly to prevent it.

'I am worried,' Dr Caxton said cautiously, 'that we are dealing with something . . . diabolical. As far as I have been able to ascertain, none of the children who observed the UFO at the primary school was baptized. Not one. Whereas every child who attended the school trip, *was* baptized. Now, I'm all for coincidences, but that's rather remarkable, wouldn't you say?'

A flash on the horizon.

We leaped to the kitchen window.

There was something in the sky, an orange streak, arcing away from the lower fields up and out across St Brides Bay.

FROM *THE MIND POSSESSED:*
A PERSONAL INVESTIGATION INTO
THE BROAD HAVEN TRIANGLE

BY DR R. CAXTON (CLEMENTINE PRESS, 1980) P.110

My wife, Julia, often asks me what I dream about. This might surprise me because dreams are so rarely interesting to anyone except the person who has them, as I am fond of telling my students whenever they ask me to interpret their dreams. But when Julia asks, it's different. Because Julia knows that for too long I only dreamed about one thing. That terrible Tuesday. The night of the sky watch in the Havens.

The hours that led to that event were packed with things that skewed my interpretation of what it means to be human, indeed what it means to be me. They were hours that cast the longest shadow of doubt across my science and they were hours I would give anything to forget.

After I had inspected Randall Pritchard's cattle shed for myself, I decided to return to the village. The rain was driving down as if someone wanted to cleanse the Havens of all their trouble. Wherever I went in the Havens, whoever I spoke to, I could feel heaviness in the air. An expectant dread.

'You know, Doctor, ever since those kids at the school saw that damn thing, this place hasn't been right.' I heard that a lot. Only the sky watchers seemed content, in spite of the rain. As I drove around the Havens I noticed a surprising number of people with maps and backpacks, and cars loaded with camping gear. By mid-morning there must have been over a dozen cars parked around the slipway, which should have been kept clear for the lifeboat. Some were here for the lunar eclipse; most were here to look for UFOs.

They had come like moths to the flame and seemed to have no idea of how dangerous these phenomena were. I drove around the bay and parked on the stone jetty known as Giant's Point. The sea was crashing in on both sides.

'Out there,' a local woman told me, pointing. 'That place is in my nightmares, at the heart of them.'

She was staring out to sea at Stack Rocks, the fort crouched sullenly on its peak.

– 45 –

Tuesday 15 February 1977, 9.30 a.m., eleven hours until the sky watch . . .

Randall had dozed in his study, then left early for Broadmoor Farm to round up his cows.

I hadn't slept well. All night the rain had been drumming harder and harder on the roof. By now the fields surrounding the farmhouse were nothing but mud and ice. The nightmare hadn't helped either. It came back to me as I scrambled some eggs on the hotplate of the Aga. In the dream I saw myself surrounded by ancient trees, saw the lighthouse in the distance. Except this time there was something else – a group of hooded strangers. Watching me.

As I downed some coffee and struggled to finish my eggs, I wondered again what it meant. The dream had never been clear but previously it had always been mixed with memories: Dad's motorcycle, Randall's facial scar, the child I had been before coming to live here at Ravenstone Farm. I dropped my plate in the sink, looking out over the fields and St Brides Bay and thinking about what Randall had told me about my childhood.

A violent child?

So much I had forgotten.

I crept into his study. The Parsons Report would be where I had left it. I had a suspicion he didn't want me, or anyone, anywhere near it. All the same I felt a deep and welling desire to read it, a feeling that was like going for a medical test you knew deep down was very likely to come back with a dreaded, life-changing result. Although I had never been religious, I had always wondered about the source of Randall's fervour, whether his interest in UFOs and religion ended with him or went back generations. Either way, the Parsons Report echoed his warnings, warnings that I had thought so long to be the product of his religious fanaticism.

I retrieved the key to his desk and unlocked the drawer. There was no chance of being disturbed. Randall was at Broadmoor Farm; Dr Caxton had left early. Araceli and Tessa were still asleep. I slid open the drawer.

The Parsons Report was gone.

Back in the kitchen my mind was still trying to catch up with everything that had happened. The headmaster had known something about the Happenings and had killed himself. The Jacksons had also known something. I thought about heading over to Broadmoor to help Randall, but before I had a chance to put my coat on the telephone jangled in the study. Frobisher was on the line, and I had never heard a man sound so frightened.

'Where the hell were you? I waited on the beach like you said.'

'What are you talking about?'

'Last night! You called and told me to meet you this morning. Seven thirty sharp, you said.'

That stunned me into silence.

'Remember we talked about your grandfather, and you said you had found a document to show me?'

The line crackled and hissed. Whoever was behind these phone calls wanted me to know that they knew my every move. They wanted to intimidate me. And they were succeeding.

'Frank, we never spoke.'

'So what's in this report?'

The fear that had clutched my stomach the night before returned now, made me clutch the phone with mounting alarm. 'It's a document that was circulated among an elite group of the Establishment – military, politicians, the Church. It talks about UFOs as signs. Religious signs. And now it's gone. It could be the key to all of this.'

'I'm worried, Wilding. My phone's been going crazy all morning.' Even as he told me this, heavy static was drowning out his voice.

'What do you mean?'

'This morning it was a little girl. She said, "Events in the Havens will worsen with the Summoning. There will be a war that marks the coming of the beast." I mean, what the hell is that supposed to mean? What's the Summoning?'

The rain drummed down harder.

'Frank, were you planning on attending the sky watch tonight?'

'Not with all this rain. Much more of this and they'll call it off.'

No. The Watchers are too clever for that. The village will have its lunar eclipse.

'Frank, come here, to Randall's farm. Please. Come as quickly as you can.'

– 46 –

Tuesday 15 February 1977, 10.30 a.m., ten hours until the sky watch . . .

'I found circular burn marks in the lower fields,' Randall said conversationally, pulling off his overcoat. Araceli and Tessa were with me in the kitchen. 'And more footprints near the cattle shed and the house.'

He handed me some Polaroid shots showing sets of prints. They looked as though they had been made by enormous ripple-soled boots.

'The force that has targeted us,' Randall said in a hushed voice, 'is getting nearer. I want everyone inside the farmhouse for the rest of the day – and the night.'

Shortly afterwards Dr Caxton arrived back from the village. 'Who's for a cup of tea?' he asked, trying to lighten the mood. Tessa hummed quietly to herself in the corner of the kitchen. Araceli and Randall sat at the vast table looking deeply troubled as I told them about what Frobisher had said on the phone.

Araceli gave Dr Caxton a direct stare. 'Something bad is going to happen, isn't it?'

'I fear so, young lady.'

I glanced up. Part of me thought he was mistaken; most of me knew he wasn't.

After lunch I called RAF Brawdy and asked for the admiral. He should have arrived by then.

'You made it, thank God!'

'Yes.' His voice sounded terribly hoarse and he was coughing fitfully. Painfully. 'Did you find the Parsons Report.'

I told him I had. I also told him that now it was missing.

'Can you drive over and meet me?'

'There's no time,' I said. 'Something terrible is going to happen. Tonight.'

He thinks I've lost it, I thought as he gave a sympathetic sigh on the other end of the line, but my sense of expectation was so strong that I was all but paralysed.

'Admiral, the sky watch – '

'How are your nerves?' He sounded genuinely concerned. I imagined he was wondering what had happened to his ever-reliable source on the Defence Select Committee. At last he said, 'So be it.'

I gripped the phone tighter. 'Admiral, if one of these . . . sky spectres – UFOs – appears in front of so many people at the same time, it could have disastrous consequences.'

'If you're telling me you anticipate further sightings, I will inform NATO that we anticipate a breach of our air defences by a prototype foreign jet and give strict instructions not to scramble any interceptors.'

'Except they're not jets,' I said a little too quickly.

The admiral drew another ragged breath. 'What are they then, Robert?'

Here it was, the question I knew how to answer. But who

was I fooling? Getting the words out wasn't going to be as easy. The strength left my legs and I had to sit down.

Randall was right. Long ago he had told me that there were Watchers, ancient beings who wanted to open the minds of men and flood them with horror. After all I had learned, I could only conclude that the UFOs were directly related to the entities and occult manifestations involved in seances and poltergeist events. They came from another reality, a world interpenetrating and interlocking with our own.

'Robert?' The admiral sounded pained; he probably was.

'The UFOs are spiritual deceptions that have been summoned by a cult, the Parsons Elite, to induce fear and panic,' I declared. At once I felt a weight lift. 'Randall has a term for them – sky spectres. Paranormal manifestations that precede a catastrophe.'

Silence.

'You think I'm crazy, don't you?'

The silence spun out, and when the admiral spoke again it was in a calm and patient voice that made me feel diminished.

'Robert, of course I don't think you're insane. But it is clear that you're under a great deal of stress.'

'Admiral –'

'I should never have sent you here. I'm sorry. What you need now is to rest and –'

'I need you to listen to what I'm saying!' I said, then went on.

With every word I heard the weight of the admiral's concern and a sense of his own responsibility building in his every sigh and breath. When I had finished telling him about the cows he said in a low voice, 'Do you realize how that sounds? An entire herd spirited away?'

'Admiral, you must warn the prime minister.'

'Warn him that demonic sky spectres are manifesting off the Welsh coast?' I could almost see him shaking his head. 'Be reasonable.'

Perhaps I really have lost it, said a voice in my head.

'Come on, old chap.' The admiral continued, his tone soothing. 'We'll get you back to London tomorrow. You can come back with me in the morning. Today you rest.'

Except I couldn't rest. Because from the window I had seen the one thing I had prayed wouldn't happen.

The rain had stopped.

Q: Clearly you have been through a terrible ordeal. It falls to us to ascertain the nature of that ordeal.

A. If you wish.

Q. Ms Garwood, you have a part-time job at the Ram Inn?

A. I did.

Q. So you moved away?

A. There's nothing left.

Q. Do you remember the atmosphere in the village before the sky watch commenced?

A: You don't forget something like that.

Q: Describe it for us, please.

A. Well, I remember looking down from my window in the inn. Where the road skirts the cove there must have been a hundred or more down there, checking the sky like fishermen do before a storm. The seafront was brimming with people with their heads tipped back, and there must have been ten or twelve small boats out in the bay, anchored and waiting. I looked past the slipway and out onto the bay at the *Austin Burnet* on the water, her deck full of crew and their wives and kids. They had flasks of coffee and picnic hampers with sandwiches. Everyone, whether they were standing by their cars, outside the inn on the seafront or on the *Austin Burnet*, was holding a camera or had binoculars around their neck. *Time wasters*, I thought. *Nothing's gonna happen. I hope it rains on the lot of them.*

Q. Do you regret that thought now, Ms Garwood?

A. What do you think?

– 47 –

Tuesday 15 February 1977, 12.30 p.m., eight hours until the sky watch . . .

That afternoon passed more slowly than any in my childhood summers, when I would play outside the main gates at RAF Brawdy. Around mid-afternoon I went out into the fields – fighting through the mud – and looked across the bay at the crowds on the shore and the boats under the oppressive sky. I tried telling myself they were foolish, that nothing would happen. I felt the lie and didn't linger, returning quickly to the farmhouse, where Araceli was standing in Randall's study wearing a black jumper and a blue skirt.

It caught at me, how familiar she looked, as she glanced at me then turned back to studying the newspaper articles pinned to the wall. Her expression was more wary than warm, and I thought she looked distracted and drained.

'I can tell Randall doesn't want us here.'

'Why do you say that?' I asked.

'Oh, come on. He looks agitated whenever he's in the room with us.' She sat down at the desk and her attention switched to one of the skeletal trees opposite the farmhouse. 'I had the most terrible nightmare last night. I tried telling Randall about it before he went out. He cut me off.'

'What nightmare? Can you describe it for me?'

She pondered this, brow furrowed, eyes distant.

'It's been the same nightmare, off and on, for years,' she answered finally. 'It's dark. I'm been dragged along the ground. There's an awful pain in my leg and a light shining above me through the forest.'

At the mention of her leg I noticed for the first time a jagged scar running down her knee. It was faded, clearly old.

'How did you get that?'

She looked down, and I felt an odd tingling on my neck. I suddenly felt more worried for her than ever before. At that instant Tessa appeared at the study door. Araceli looked up sharply and the child pierced me with an accusing gaze.

'He's been thinking a lot about you – about us,' Tessa said to her mother, pointing at me. 'He's been wondering why we are alone, where Daddy went.'

'Is that right, Robert?'

The intensity of Araceli's tone made it hard to deny. But how the hell had Tessa known what I had been thinking?

'Because Mummy says I'm clever,' Tessa answered.

My throat went dry. I thought I'd got used to strange surprises, but I was still shocked that the child appeared to have heard my thought. She had a look on her face that was . . . pleased? An unsettling smile played on her lips.

Araceli stood, moved past me into the hall. She said to her daughter, 'After tonight we're getting out of here.'

Did she mean the farm or the Havens? Both?

'You could have left the area long before now,' I said.

'What makes you think I've had a choice?' she replied, striding away.

'The light in your nightmares,' I called after her. 'What does it look like?'

She paused at the door to the kitchen. Her words came with an immeasurable sadness that stole the breath from my mouth. 'It pulses. Like the beam of a lighthouse.'

Frobisher pulled up outside Ravenstone Farm just as the dusk was sucking all the colour from the day. It was around five in the evening, and the burly journalist looked disturbed; as he approached the house he kept looking back over his shoulder.

'I was followed,' he said, stepping into the narrow hall. 'Three men in a bloody huge silver car.'

'Where is it now?' I asked, peering into the scarlet evening.

'I lost it at the crossroads. Listen, who the hell are these men?'

I heard my voice become confiding as I listed the attributes I had come to associate with these shadowy figures. 'They arrive in badly fitting clothes and their vehicles look futuristic. They ask the most bizarre questions, sometimes posing as officials.'

'You're staying, right?' Araceli said to Frobisher. I hadn't heard her come downstairs. She looked relieved to see someone else in the house. So did Dr Caxton, who followed closely behind. Only Grandfather, who was at the Aga in the kitchen, looked suspicious.

'Of course I'll stay,' Frobisher said. 'But I'm not sure I can offer much comfort.'

In the kitchen we watched Frobisher take out a Dictaphone and place it on the table. When he pressed Play, children's voices – cracked and distorted – filled the room.

'*Kcab gnimoc era ew rof. Seiks eht hctaw dna rehtag.*'

The children at the town meeting. Chanting.

'It's gibberish,' Dr Caxton said.

'Until you slow it down,' Frobisher said, 'and play it backwards.'

He changed the tape, pressed Play, and the voices from the tape recorder stilled us all.

'Gather and watch the skies. For we are coming back.'

For several moments we said nothing.

I had begun to feel foolish for ever having doubted Randall's warnings. I watched him raise his hand to touch the scar on his face. It was an involuntary reaction and curious.

'How the hell could the kids speak backwards?' Araceli asked. 'In unison?'

'These children are imbued with psychic abilities because of what they saw at the school,' said Randall.

Gather and watch the skies.

Although it was definitely the children chanting, the message hadn't come from them. I was certain of that. The words had found their way through from something else, to reach the people of the village, to draw them into doing something we needed to prevent.

Randall's glance flickered to mother and daughter. 'Take Tessa upstairs, please.'

Araceli did what she was asked. When she returned alone a few moments later she met my eyes, and again I felt that unsettling sensation that we shared something unique.

'Possession,' Randall said with grim conviction. 'When the demonic truly take control of a person, observable phenomena may occur – '

Araceli twisted in her chair, eying Randall with alarm, as Frobisher slapped his hand on the kitchen table.

'Randall, really!?'

'After all we've seen, don't doubt it, don't you bloody dare!' Randall's temper flared. 'In biblical times they were known as fallen angels. Now the newspapers call them aliens. Their real name is the Watchers.'

'Under the circumstances,' Dr Caxton said, 'after all we've seen, after all we've experienced . . . I'm sorry, but I'm not sure I can deny such an explanation any longer.'

Randall nodded, patting his Bible.

'Assume you're right,' Frobisher said. 'Why wait until now to tell us this?'

It was a good question, and from the guarded expression on Randall's face I knew there had to be a good answer. He just wasn't prepared to divulge it. Yet.

'So what do we do?' Frobisher asked. 'I thought you were the great expert, Randall. If you're so knowledgeable, then why not just reason with these Watchers? They must *want* something. What do they need?'

'How many people are gathered for the sky watch?'

'I don't know,' Frobisher replied. 'Earlier today a hundred maybe. There'll be many more by now.'

'If the sky spectres appear en masse, they'll take their souls. Every last one. When the Watchers are seen, disaster surely follows. They have been awakened by a cult,' Randall said darkly. 'As part of an ancient ritual called the Summoning.'

'How do you know this?' Dr Caxton asked.

'I know because I've confronted this cult before.' Randall's eyes glinted and locked with mine. 'A long time ago. The Parsons Elite is a satanic brotherhood – a hierarchical order of patriotic, influential men and women whose primary motive is to prepare our world for the End of Days – the arrival of the Angel of the Bottomless Pitt, the Lawless One.'

So he had known it all along.

'I assure you, the Parsons Elite exists,' Grandfather said. His words came out with grim defiance.

I felt squeezed, diminished, by the burden of my own secret knowledge. *Could Randall belong to this cult? Had the Jacksons belonged to this cult? The headmaster also?*

Something thumped in the room above us in my old bedroom, where Tessa was sleeping. The light bulb flickered.

Thoughts flew at me then, thoughts I wanted to bat away, but Grandfather's words had opened a door at the back of my mind that had been closed (By me or by him?) a long time ago. What flooded in were memories, snatches of conversation and images which finally, horribly, made sense. *I saw something when I was young. It affected me, and Grandfather helped me forget.* I found myself thinking of the Great Flood – the night my parents died – and the Jacksons, whom Selina had traced to the Haven Hotel.

'The battle on earth will commence with signs in the heavens ... The Demon's Gate will open. Darkness will rule for eternity.' I said the words out loud and everyone stared.

'It's a prophecy,' Randall said at last. 'Worshipped by the Parsons Elite.'

'So what do we *do*?' Frobisher demanded again.

'We have faith,' Grandfather said simply.

'That's it?' Frobisher looked about ready to explode.

That was the moment I decided to tell them about the incantation I had found at the church and the curious symbols I had copied down. I was thankful I hadn't left the paper on which they were written in my room at the Ram Inn, where it would have vanished with the rest of my notes.

I showed them.

₮ⱡ∑ΔᴎçǀΣᴎ₮◊ᴎ∑ Ↄ ΔЯ∑ς◊iᴎ

Araceli didn't look. Not directly. Dr Caxton looked very carefully indeed, however, tracing the outline of each symbol with a cautious finger.

'Do you recognize these?' I asked.

'Oh yes, indeed,' he said in a quiet voice, and when he raised his head the alarm in his eyes provoked a scraping sensation in my gut. 'These are sigils from the magical traditions of antiquity. I've seen something similar in the texts held at the Library of Magical Literature at Senate House in London.'

'Texts about what?' I asked.

'Exorcism,' Dr Caxton breathed.

'I should have told you, boy,' said Grandfather. 'I just didn't want you getting too close. Whatever happens now, whatever you may see, don't look at it, do not be fooled by lying wonders. Your greatest protection is in faith.'

But faith in what?

There was a screeching noise that made us all tense.

'What the hell?' Frobisher reached into his inside pocket, producing his Dictaphone. 'It's turned itself on,' Frobisher shouted. His eyes were wide and incredulous. 'I didn't touch it! Honestly.'

The voices of the children chanting in unison spooled out, louder than before. Unnaturally loud for such a small device: *'Kcab gnimoc era ew rof. Seiks eht hctaw dna rehtag.'*

The tape recorder burst into flames and Frobisher threw up his arms. The device clattered to the ground, smoking.

'There is a war raging,' Randall declared, 'between the forces of good and evil, between order and chaos. And the battleground is right here in the Havens.'

His eyes jumped from the smouldering tape recorder on the flagged floor to the ceiling that separated us from the room in which Tessa was asleep. His face hardened with decision. 'There is somewhere I need to be,' he said quickly, pulling on his shabby overcoat as though it was a suit of armour and he was preparing to go into battle.

His resolution, his passion – he reminded me so much of my mother in that moment that I wanted to tell him I was sorry. Sorry for ever doubting him.

Then he dropped a heavy hand on my shoulder, squeezed tight, let go and marched out into the yard.

'Grandfather, stop. Wait!'

He stopped just in front of his battered Hillman Hunter and turned to me. 'Robert, my boy,' he said, 'your mother would be so proud.'

Something in his tone frightened me. As if this was the last time we would speak.

'You don't have to go.'

'But I do. I made a promise a long time ago to a power higher than man. And one day, maybe soon, I'll have to face that power.'

'Please tell me where you're going?' I knew it wasn't to warn the villagers. He had already tried to do that.

'It's better you don't know. You can't know.' He paused, flashing a glance over my shoulder back at the farmhouse. 'Do not trust that woman, boy.'

'What? But why not?'

'All alone in that rambling hotel. Her life makes absolutely no sense.'

I thought of her parents. The fact that she never mentioned her father was troubling because if her mother really had been mixed up in the occult, what about him? Where was he and why had he left her here alone?

Randall saw these thoughts on my face and nodded. 'Protect the child.'

'How?'

'Remember,' he said, touching a calloused hand to my cheek, 'you can hold them back with faith. Faith can nullify evil, can form a psychic barrier.'

He got into his car. The door slammed, the engine started, and the Hillman Hunter crunched away over the half-frozen puddles. I followed it with my eyes up the narrow lane.

When I turned back towards the house, the others were on the doorstep.

FROM THE OFFICIAL TESTIMONY OF
EMMA WHEAL, TAKEN BEFORE THE NATIONAL
SECURITY COUNCIL IN CONNECTION WITH
THE EVENTS OF TUESDAY 15 FEBRUARY 1977
IN THE HAVENS, WEST WALES

Q. Ms Wheal, do you still live in Little Haven?

A. No.

Q. Where do you live now?

A. Milford Haven. Little Haven was always a ghost town, especially in winter, but after what happened, well, very few people wanted to stay around, you know. Businesses closed up. The post office went, so did the Nest Bistro. I was glad to leave. No place for a young person.

Q. Were you at home on the night of 15 February at midnight?

A. I was working late in the Ram Inn. I was paid double-time that night, it was so busy.

Q. What was so special about that night?

A. The sky watch. There were camera crews and tourists and everything. Every holiday cottage in the village was booked because of the blood moon. You know, the lunar eclipse.

Q. And you rented out your home, Albert's Cottage on Wesley Road?

A. Yeah, well, people were paying a lot. It's only three hundred yards from the seafront, you see.

Q. And who did you rent it to?

A. A pair of UFO spotters. They were everywhere. Even the Talbenny Caravan Park was full, and that's completely dead in winter.

Q. All right. Let's discuss the events of the night of 15 February. What was the general mood in the pub before the sky watch began?

A. Well, excitement, I suppose. A lot of people were taking it seriously, but some weren't. They were laughing and joking and saying they were going to be taken, you know, by aliens. That was around seven o'clock. We had the radio on loud in the bar; they were reporting live from the front. That was where people would have the best view of the sky. At Giant's Point.

Q. And what did you think of people's behaviour?

A. Well, it wasn't normal, but at the same time you couldn't help going along with it. Everyone seemed convinced that something was going to happen, with all the stories in the papers, you know, and everyone wanted to go out along Giant's Point to see. I'd never believed the stories or taken an interest, but if it wasn't for me working and having to lock up, I probably would have gone too.

Q. What happened then? Later, at 8.30?

A. We were listening to the radio, and we could hear everyone at Giant's Point cheering and whooping, and . . . well, that was when things began to get really strange.

– 48 –

8.30 p.m.

And so we come to the worst of it.

I was in the front room of Ravenstone Farm, and Dr Caxton was snoozing in the armchair nearest the fire with his hands interlocked across his chest. He had been asleep for about an hour, and during that time not a word has passed between Araceli and me, sitting side by side on Grandfather's tattered old sofa. I don't know what thoughts were keeping her silent, but as for me, my head was full of satanic cults and demons from the deep. Frobisher, still unsettled by his exploding Dictaphone, was preparing coffee in the kitchen

I thought of the incantation at the church that I'd copied down: '*Gha D'rcest Cthasska, Gha D'rcest Cthassiss.*'

The sense that these words were important, that I might need them, still hadn't left me, and that's probably why I had taken the paper on which they were written into Randall's study. And locked it in the desk drawer.

I stared at the barred window and the darkness beyond. Grandfather out there somewhere.

Gather and watch the skies.

He'll come back, I told myself. *He'll take one look at the crowds, realize it's too late, realize he can do nothing and come back.*

'What time does the sky watch begin?' Araceli asked.

My gaze shifted from the flickering television to the small silver clock on the mantelpiece. 'Any time now. We spend the night here. None of us leaves this house until it's over. You should go to bed,' I said, 'get some rest.'

'What if something happens again?' As she spoke Dr Caxton stirred and opened his eyes. 'Besides, I want to hear how they report it on the local news.' She rubbed at her eyes and drew her knees up to her chin.

'You know, tiredness only makes anxiety worse,' I said.

'And you're an expert on anxiety?'

I surprised myself with a laugh. 'I've learned a thing or two.'

'Indeed,' Dr Caxton said. 'Hunger, anger, loneliness and tiredness: all of these states heighten anxiety.' He kept his eyes on me. 'It must be very difficult for you being back in this house, Robert.'

My gaze shifted to the study, just visible across the hall through the doorway, and I thought of the picture hanging over the mantelpiece. My shoulders tensed. I glanced at Araceli. Something in her eyes. Pity? Understanding?

Frobisher appeared in the doorway, coffee mug in one hand. He looked agitated. 'I'm going upstairs for a lie-down. I'll check on Tessa while I'm at it.'

Araceli nodded thanks and ran an agitated hand through her hair.

As I watched him go, I dug my fingers into the cushion next to me. 'My friend Selina used to say my face was a mask of worry. I thought I'd grow out of it, but you know what happens with habits – they take hold of you.' I stood and went over to the fire, gazing at my hands as I spread them before the flames. 'I suppose the only thing to do is shake them off.'

'Or prevent them taking hold,' Dr Caxton said. 'The more you indulge your fears, the more they will rule you. You can't control events, Robert. Only how you respond to them. When you see a distracting thought flying at you, name it for what it is. Then step out of its way, cast it away.'

'You make it sound so easy,' I said.

'What if?' Dr Caxton said. 'The most worrying words in the English language, because once a person starts asking that question, it can be very hard to stop. The problem,' he added, leaning forward, 'is that that particular question never allows you a satisfactory answer. Robert, you crave certainty, it's what you need to feel safe, but I promise you this. You'll never lay a hand on it.'

I allowed the words to sink in but almost immediately my head began to swim like it had done at the hotel and at the Ram when I had witnessed – predicted – Selina's death. Dr Caxton must have seen that memory on my face because he promptly asked what was wrong.

'I don't just fear what's happening here; I fear for my sanity.' He listened patiently as I told him about my premonitions, my visions.

'And these visions are new?'

'Yes. Yes, I think so.' It was hard to be sure when so much of my childhood was hidden from me. 'Doctor, what's causing them?'

His tone became peremptory. 'Have you seen a UFO up close, like the children at the school?'

I hadn't. Only the amazing lights cartwheeling over RAF Brawdy. 'But my visions began after that. And since I've been here they've been getting stronger.'

Dr Caxton's expression betrayed not the slightest hesitation or embarrassment. 'If you are psychic, you should endeavour to nurture that ability. Master it before anyone else does.' He smiled. 'Perhaps it will go away, perhaps it will get stronger, but there is no reason to think that you are suffering from pathological hallucinations. OK?'

I felt at once reassured by his tone, which was clear and calm and commanding. Yet I was still confused. 'If I can see the future – if the future already exists – then our actions, ours words, our choices, they all count for nothing.'

Either he had heard such musings before or they vexed him because he simultaneously nodded and frowned. 'Instead of thinking of time as a sequence of events, try picturing it as a series of overlapping and interlocking dimensions, like a deck of cards shuffled with another.'

I tried but came up with a mess.

'That would make your premonition a shadow of one future reality. Our reality. But equally,' he smiled, 'there could be other realities, dimensions in which your friend is still alive.' His academic's eyebrows drew together. 'If there *are* other dimensions, it's certainly conceivable that the human unconscious might glimpse them or even influence them.' He told me then about clairvoyance, psychogenesis and other psychic phenomena, and I was enthralled until an unsettling thought broke in.

'If other dimensions exist it follows that other life forms exist . . .'

His smile faded. 'Your grandfather believes that the entities plaguing this community originate in hell. He thinks they are demons.'

'And you?'

'I don't care where they come from or what they're called.'

His intelligent eyes met mine. 'I care about what they want from us.'

When I opened my eyes, the others were fast asleep, the television flickering its harsh light across Araceli's face. A local news reporter faced the camera; behind him the scene reminded me of Guy Fawkes night: groups of excited youngsters and people with flasks of coffee, binoculars and cameras.

'I'm here in Little Haven, where a group sky watch has been under way for the last forty-five minutes,' the reporter said. The grin on his face was saying, *Stay with me, folks. We all know this is a bit of fun.*

As I shifted in my seat something made me turn my attention towards the window – a slight movement, a flicker of light. No more than that.

I held still, really focusing on the window. Lightning? If so, it would come again. But I couldn't hear thunder.

Your imagination. You're seeing things that don't exist.

There! I definitely wasn't imagining it: a light had flashed in the bottom of the window.

Don't respond, I reminded myself. *The more you indulge your fears, the more they will rule you.* Just a day earlier my response to a strange light would have been totally different. I would have been on my feet, checking and checking, until my paranoia turned to anger at myself and finally guilt. Not this time. I squeezed my eyes shut, yet even as I did the air hummed, vibrating. I opened my eyes again. The urge to wake Araceli or Dr Caxton was almost irrepressible.

How are they sleeping through this? And why are both of them asleep? That didn't seem right to me, didn't seem natural, somehow. Unless something was making them sleep.

The light came again, and again.

Just ignore it. Nothing will happen. Nothing will happen.

But something was happening. There was a heaviness in the air and the flickering light was getting brighter.

My heart was thundering now as I sat upright, frozen, on the edge of the sofa. The ice-white glare shimmered at the bottom of the window. Determined. It wanted my attention. It wanted me to look. I wrenched my gaze away.

Suddenly I found the strength to move again. If there had been any curtains I would have shut out the light by dragging them across, but as there were none I turned to face Dr Caxton. I whispered, 'Wake up.'

His eyes fluttered as he surfaced from sleep. Then he saw it. He leaned forward out of his armchair. 'What on earth . . .?'

I raised a hand. The doctor nodded in understanding, his eyes as wide as saucers.

I tracked his bewildered gaze back to the window. 'What do you think it is?' I whispered. I felt a panicky twist in my gut. 'Can you feel that tremble in the air?'

Dr Caxton nodded. 'I can see it too.'

The window's single pane of glass was trembling. Rattling now. The silvery light on the other side had begun to shift and swirl, slowly, slowly . . . solidifying.

Dr Caxton was staring into the room across the hall. 'Robert! Oh Jesus. Look!'

The Welsh dresser in Grandfather's study was pushed aside and the carpet on the floor was rolled back, light spilling in and flooding the floor.

That was when Araceli woke. She jumped to her feet and stumbled, disorientated, releasing a startled cry. Any nightmare she had been having had fused with waking reality. 'What is it?' she managed to say. She was pointing at the window.

An awful figure was framed there.

The glass rattled even harder and the television hissed snowy static.

The three of us fell silent.

It was huge. Wide shoulders seemed to fill most of the window. It was pressed right up against the glass and at least seven feet tall. 'Spaceman' was the word that came to mind, but at no point did I think this was an alien; rather something or someone that was trying to look like someone's conception of an alien. It wore a one-piece silvery suit similar to the sort of protective gear worn in a nuclear plant. Its arms were disproportionately long, its neck too short, and the head wasn't round, but rose to a peak. I caught myself staring at where its face should have been and knowing I could not look away. There were no features – none at all – just a convex black visor framed by a silver helmet.

This is what Selina was looking for. This is what Martin Marshall saw. This is what appeared at RAF Croughton in 1963. I didn't know why it was there, but a sickening thought occurred to me: *It's come for the child.*

Araceli looked at me with sudden horror.

'Go to Tessa,' I shouted, and she darted for the stairs.

Dr Caxton was paralysed. There was no sign of Frobisher.

I turned back to the window. The figure was still there, motionless, menacing, its whole body emitting a shimmering white light.

One day, Robert, the giants will return. Randall's warning from my childhood rattled in my head. *If Grandfather was here he'd know what to do.* But Grandfather wasn't there. And whatever this entity was, I was certain of one thing: it wanted to get in.

I thought desperately, almost with relief, *Thank God for the bars over the windows*, but then I remembered what had happened at RAF Croughton. If these entities could pass through chain-link fences then bars and glass wouldn't stop them.

My stomach rolled, and I thought I might pass out.

Suddenly, the beat of feet on the stairs. Frobisher burst into the room and immediately staggered back, falling against the wall, arms outstretched as if to push the frightful vision away. 'What the hell is it?' he yelled.

I couldn't speak, couldn't move. Evil was everywhere, corrupting and persuasive.

That glass is going to shatter. Those bars will bend, and that monstrous thing will get in here with us. And some part of me thought that was all right.

'Robert, listen to me.'

Was that Dr Caxton speaking? I thought it might be.

'You remember what your grandfather told us? They can't get in unless they're invited. Don't look at it. Turn your back. Deny it!'

The giant silver figure, standing like a statue, began to glow an eerie red and raised an arm. The temperature had rocketed. My face was burning and the rank smell of sulphur filled the air.

I took a step forward, weakening. I wanted a closer look. I wanted to let it in. The black space where its face should have been was mesmerizing. *It's easy*, a voice in my head said. *Just unlatch the window and push it up.*

'Robert, what are you doing?' It was as if Dr Caxton was calling to me through a dream. 'Get the hell away from the window!'

Suddenly I thought of the incantation that Father O'Riorden had allowed me to copy down, and something in me snapped free. Without a moment's hesitation I bolted from the living room into the study and to the top drawer in Grandfather's desk.

Locked, of course.

The picture above the mantelpiece fell from the wall with a *thump*. A moment later I had retrieved the key from the back of the picture. The lock turned and the desk drawer slid out.

From the front room I could hear nothing but silence now, but when I went into the hall I saw the Watcher again, its broad shoulders, wide chest and one enormous gloved hand extending between the bars and pressed against the rattling window. And I saw Dr Caxton and Frobisher. Their eyes were fastened on the giant like a magnet, their feet taking small steps towards the window.

'Both of you get out!' I yelled into the sitting room. 'Take your eyes off it!'

Then I lurched forward with the same urgency I had experienced on the roof at the hotel. I felt feverish, the way you do when you have a terrible shock, and without thinking I held up the paper on which the incantation was written, thrusting it towards the glimmering Watcher as though it was a weapon. I did it without thinking, as though unseen hands had done it for me, and I screamed the words, '*Gha D'rcest Cthasska, Gha D'rcest Cthassiss.*'

I didn't pray to God but put my faith in the power of the document between my fingers. I called on the power and knowledge within those words, crying aloud my defiance of evil, and before my eyes the enormous Watcher seemed to fade. I struggled to focus on it, uncertain for a few brief seconds whether it was even there at all.

Suddenly there was a blinding white flash, and even as I shielded my eyes with my right arm I knew what was about to happen. When the light dimmed and I looked again, I saw that I was right.

The figure had vanished.

My hands were shaking as I dialled Father O'Riorden's number. When he answered, it wasn't just his panicked voice I could hear. Somewhere in the background were voices and cars. Sirens.

'What's happening?'

People are leaving their houses, heading for the beach. They all look so dazed.'

'Something's influencing them,' I said. 'Something's trying to take control of them. Have you seen Randall?'

'No, why?'

'Father, we need your help.' I shot a glance at the nearest window into the yard. *That Watcher is still out there and it could come back at any moment.* 'Ravenstone Farm. Come now!'

'What do you expect me to do?'

'Pray. We can defeat the Watchers with faith.'

A pause. Then Father O'Riorden said, 'My God, I can see them. In the sky. Thirteen. There are thirteen of them! They . . . they're so beautiful.'

'Don't look at them,' I said, 'not even for a second.'

'You were right, my son. Dear Lord,' he said, his voice a shuddering whisper. The line crackled and went dead. I banged the phone down.

Frobisher had appeared at the study door. His face was naked with shock. 'Rob . . . she's disappeared. She's gone.'

The thought that Tessa had been stolen from our protection made the bottom drop out of my stomach. 'That's impossible. There's no way Tessa could have got out.'

'Not Tessa,' Frobisher said. 'Araceli.'

– 49 –

Despair made me freeze. And that paralysis was hardened by fear, the same fear that was growing in the eyes of the gruff journalist who blocked my way into the hall.

'So what next?' Frobisher asked.

I didn't speak. The only answer was one neither of us wanted to hear.

When the Watchers are seen, disaster surely follows.

Finally I found my voice. 'We have to do something . . . We have to get away from here.'

A shuffling sound made me turn my head towards the door. Dr Caxton stood there with Tessa at his side. Her eyes were sharp with interest, or suspicion.

'Who did you just call on the phone?' the child asked. She didn't seem in the least distressed that her mother had vanished from the house. And that was alarming.

'The police,' I lied. 'Where did your mother go, Tess? What happened to her?'

'I don't know,' she said.

Too calm. She's way too calm.

'So when are they coming?' she asked. Her body was perfectly still, arms rigid at her sides, but her voice had an edge.

'Soon.'

'When are they coming?'

The nearest light bulb popped. It was the bulb fitted in Grandfather's desk lamp, and it didn't just pop, it exploded.

'*He* did it,' Tessa said. Her gaze pierced me.

'We all need to remain calm,' Dr Caxton said, glancing warily at the window. 'It's a little power surge, that's all.'

'That doesn't seem likely,' Frobisher said. 'The other lights are fine.'

'Let's go into the kitchen, where we can keep warm next to the Aga,' Dr Caxton suggested. I promptly agreed, though Tessa was still looking at me doubtfully.

'When are the police coming?' she said again.

All along, from the first encounter – the 'flying football' that had chased Tessa and Araceli in their car on a lonely country road – to the UFO landing at the primary school, the phenomena had targeted this child. And now she wanted something from me. What?

Perhaps Father O'Riorden would have the answer. If he made it here. Grandfather had said we were dealing with demons. Well, weren't Catholic priests empowered to defeat such forces? I had very little time to find out.

'The police station is about the same distance as your mummy's hotel,' I said to Tessa, trying hard not to betray my rising fear. 'They'll be ten minutes. No longer.'

'Do you think I am stupid, Robert Wilding?'

'What?'

'The kitchen?' Dr Caxton said again, his voice tight with tension. 'I really think – '

'Because that's what it feels like to me,' the child said sweetly. 'It sounds like you, Robert Wilding, think I am a gullible little *bitch*.'

Dr Caxton shot me a glance that was alarmed enough for me to read his concern.

'Tell me who you really spoke to on the phone,' Tessa demanded. 'Was it your drunkard boss, Robert?'

The sneer in those words stung me.

'Or did you phone your filthy murdering grandfather?'

'Why don't we put Tessa back to bed,' I said, hearing the strain in my voice.

'Or why don't you tell us what you are up to?' She gave me a razor-sharp smile, keeping her lips together. Then her gaze dropped to the jagged remains of the light bulb.

There was a long moment of silence.

Abruptly, Tessa pinned a stare on Caxton and Frobisher. Their eyes were rolling back in their heads then closing as if they were going to sleep standing up. Suddenly their eyes snapped open in unison. Both men faced me, their faces masks of agitation.

'Why don't you answer her, Robert?' Frobisher said.

'Frank, now wait a moment. Let's go into the kitchen and – '

'I'd like to know too,' Dr Caxton said.

The light above us flickered.

'I was talking to the police.'

'That's what you said,' Frobisher responded. His eyes were sharply scrutinizing. 'I wonder, are you lying? What other lies have you told?'

'I think we all need to sit tight and remain very quiet, all right? For all we know that . . . silver giant is still out there.'

'And for all we know,' Tessa said in a delicate voice, '*you* are on its side.'

I faced the child. It was clear that there was very little of the old Tessa behind those eyes, but I could think of nothing else to do at that moment except try to reason with her . . . or it. 'I've already explained to you, I'm trying to solve this. The Happenings have nothing to do with me.'

'But these events occur when you're around. You can't deny that,' said Frobisher.

'Frank, you're being unreasonable. Something is disturbing your judgement.'

'You're not above suspicion either, Frank,' Dr Caxton said.

'Or you!' Frobisher said, wheeling to face Caxton.

Just then a burst of static made us all jump. All except Tessa.

I turned my head to Grandfather's radio set by the window. It was the old square sort from the '60s, with a protruding rectangular handle, two dials and a slatted front.

'The Met Office has issued a severe weather warning,' said a husky voice from the radio. 'Areas particularly at risk include parts of Pembrokeshire near St Brides Bay in Wales. In other news, Prime Minister Harold Macmillan has declined to comment on rumours of his imminent retirement.'

I pulled the radio's power cord from the wall just as I registered what had been said. I realized my mouth had fallen open. 'Harold Macmillan was prime minister in 1963!'

Frobisher took a step towards me. 'News broadcasts out of time – whatever next?'

'I have no idea how it did that,' I said. 'I swear!'

'This is madness,' Frobisher shouted.

'You're right,' Dr Caxton said. 'Madness is precisely what it is.'

I raised an apprehensive hand. 'Look, we need to stick together. Whatever the hell is out there could come back at any – '

Another burst of sound from the radio. We all stared at the power cord on the floor. Unplugged.

'Officials at the Ministry of Defence as well as the RAF have confirmed that unusual aerial phenomena have been reported in west Wales and that this activity is not attributable to any military operations. Reports are also coming in of strange lights and objects over London which are not visible on radar . . .'

'Whatever you are,' I said to Tessa, 'however you're doing this, just stop.'

A foul odour filled the study. The radio buzzed.

'I don't think you look very well,' Dr Caxton said. It took me a second or two to realize he was talking to me.

Frobisher was nodding at me. 'Doesn't he look shifty?'

'Yes, he looks strained too,' Tessa said in a sweet voice. 'I imagine this *is* a great strain – for such a forgetful man.'

I doubt my heart really missed a beat, but I thought for a moment it did.

We went somewhere. We went somewhere.

'All of you keep away from me!' I said, backing against the wall.

On the radio the newsreader said, 'The sky watchers have gathered. Fire will be produced from heaven in the presence of men.'

Whatever power was controlling the lights was also controlling the radio. And the child, and Frobisher, and Dr Caxton. I had no doubt that together they would make this remote and lonely farmhouse my prison. The safe, certain, knowable world that I had craved for so long couldn't have been any further from my reach now. Fantastic forces and materializations. Grandfather gone. Araceli gone. Tessa, Frobisher, Caxton – *gone*.

'Frank,' I tried again, 'think about what happened to the

other children, the adult witnesses. You too, Dr Caxton. Tessa's mind was susceptible; her defences were down from the day she saw the craft at the school. Your minds are stronger. You both need to stop listening to her. We'll get away from here, warn the base, try to evacuate the village.'

'I think you need to calm down,' Dr Caxton said.

'No! You need to listen to what I'm saying! Very soon everyone gathered at Giant's Point for the sky watch will be victims. And if the military open fire on whatever appears, the whole world could fall victim. It's our duty to help them.'

At the window the wind screamed as if offended, and almost at once the farmhouse roof began clattering. Tessa raised her eyes to the ceiling. 'Stones,' she said flatly.

The barrage intensified, and I thought the roof would surely collapse.

Tessa looked at me and smiled. 'Chuck him outside.'

Both men gave me a long, cold look.

'Don't think about it,' Tessa said. 'Just do it!'

'Listen to me!' My voice rose to fever pitch. 'We know what the Watchers are capable of. Their appearance always precedes disaster. We have a chance now to avert that disaster. If there's evidence in this house drawing them here, we must destroy it.'

'He's lying to us like he lied from the beginning,' Tessa said in a menacing but somehow amiable voice. Her eyes were on mine, narrow and mocking. 'Throw him out. *Now!*'

I bolted for the door into the hall but they were too quick. Time slowed. I saw Dr Caxton lunging, seizing my right arm, felt Frobisher pulling on my left.

I wish I hadn't looked at Tessa's face just then, because I saw the impossible: her features twisting, contorting, hatred turning to pain then back to hatred. And then her face *changed*.

Suddenly I was staring at a child's body with an adult's face. Selina's face.

'No! No, this isn't real! Grandfather, help me,' I shouted, but the stones on the roof just fell harder. I kicked wildly, straining against the two men as they dragged me towards the door.

'It was your fault I died,' Tessa said horribly. Not in her voice at all, but a malign impersonation of my friend's. 'Your fault, Robert. Your sin . . .'

I caught the edge of the desk, tried to hang on.

'And you know what happens to sinners . . .'

Frantically I grabbed the door frame.

'They are rendered powerless and devastated by the will of the Lawless One . . .'

I hit out at Frobisher.

'For he alone lives in unsleeping matter, our king of phenomena . . .'

Dr Caxton pushed me hard, and I went crashing into the closed front door. Frobisher unlocked it.

'No!' I yelled. 'Help me!'

'And he welcomes you to drown in his sea of fire!'

– 50 –

A voice as chilling as the raw darkness all around me struck me as I stumbled out of the farmhouse and glanced wildly about me.

The rain of stones had ceased, but there was a new threat, far worse.

'Hello again, Robert.'

I tensed at the reptilian voice and turned to see a gaunt figure with white skin and high cheekbones.

'I have travelled a long way,' he said from the gateway into the yard.

My stomach dropped. Horrified, I realized I was staring into the same slanted eyes that had so cruelly regarded me one early morning in my childhood. My Black-Suited Man had returned.

'What did we tell you, Robert? People who look for UFOs should be very, very careful.'

His lips drew back into a dreadful grin. He stepped forward. I stepped back; but it was no good. Frobisher and Caxton were behind me. They seized me, pinning my arms.

'No! Please, let me go!'

Their faces were unsettlingly blank, their eyes hazy, windows to a world beyond.

The Black-Suited Man advanced across the yard. Not walking, though; he lifted one foot and began to bring it forward, but then in a stroboscopic blink he flickered and was suddenly closer without moving through the space in between. Behind him trailed a blurred string of ghostly shadow selves, each one simultaneously performing a different part of the motion, like a poorly exposed photograph.

I looked away. *This cannot be happening.* I closed my eyes. Then Tessa called out from behind me, in a voice so imperious it instantly pierced my stupor of denial, 'Yes, do be good dogs and let him go. Cast him out.'

I could hear my heart thumping in my ears like a tribal drum as Caxton and Frobisher pushed me forward.

The Black-Suited Man started glowing.

Don't look in his eyes, Robert.

'Where is Araceli?' I demanded, focusing on his hat – wide-brimmed, black.

'She has the honour of being part of our design.'

'What design?'

'A soul is required. The cycle is complete. Our time has come again, and the final ritual shall be invoked. A Summoning is due.'

'Don't you bloody dare!' I yelled. 'Don't you touch her!'

The Black-Suited Man's shoulders rolled with silent, mocking laughter. He moved closer, would be upon me in another moment.

Suddenly a sound made the Black-Suited Man freeze. His head snapped to the right, sniffing the air like a dog catching a scent.

A car was rolling into the farmyard, washing it in the glow of its headlights. It stopped, a door opened, and a figure emerged.

Father O'Riorden saw me, saw Dr Caxton and Frobisher holding me prisoner, and then he saw the Black-Suited Man. Instantly I recognized the blooming contrition in the priest's eyes.

'Be careful!' I shouted.

Almost immediately the priest held up a large silver cross that dangled against his chest. He held it at arm's length and sighted down his arm at his opponent as if the crucifix were the sights of a rifle. 'Unholy abomination.'

'Your relic is as useless as you are, priest.'

Father O'Riorden's eyes were hard with an authority that went beyond his full robes and white collar. 'I know what you are.'

'Then know us better,' the Black-Suited Man answered, 'for we are legion.'

And from the trees surrounding the yard two identical figures appeared. They didn't walk; they cut jagged trajectories through space, insinuating themselves closer.

'We can appear in any shape we desire and in any place,' the Black-Suited Man said. 'We were present at the dawn of creation.'

'You over-reach yourself, fiend,' Father O'Riorden said. 'Whatever false realities you have projected into these people's minds, your powers are unequal to the grace and providence of Almighty God.'

'The End of Days is upon you,' the men said in perfect unison. 'The Falling.'

'What is the Falling?'

'You will find out. Tonight.'

'Still your lying tongues,' said the priest. 'No one will fall.'

'*Everyone* will fall,' the three men said in synchrony. 'Soon our kind will assume its rightful place in the End of Days.'

Father O'Riorden stood firm at the side of his car. He glanced at me, Dr Caxton and Frobisher. 'I stand here as the agent of a greater power and as these people's protector. As his sword and as their righteous shield. In the name of God the Creator, I will banish you!'

The Black-Suited Man's gaze fixed on the crucifix. 'Your relics are useless without faith. You stopped believing years ago.'

For the first time Father O'Riorden's expression of zealous fury seemed to falter. 'How do you . . .'

'We know everything. Especially your secrets. We like those best.' The first Black-Suited Man sounded more confident than ever. 'Haven't you heard? Knowledge is power . . . and we know all about you, false prophet.'

'No!' There was an edge of desperation in Father O'Riorden's protest.

The Black-Suited Man gave him a chilling smile. 'If your parishioners could only feel your contempt for them, how you resent them.'

'I have not lost my faith in the Lord.'

'But you have lost your faith in humanity, in human institutions.'

The Black-Suited Man's eyes became a lacework of black filaments, as if bloodshot with oil. Then the strands thickened and coalesced, and an inky glaze spread over the whole of his eyes, turning them into slashes in reality, windows onto the void. The eyes of his companions, standing behind and to either side of him, collapsed too into pools of unfathomed darkness, leaving ragged holes in their faces.

The Black-Suited Man thrust his hideous face towards the priest and stretched his lips in a grin of malign triumph. 'It is our right to claim the unbelievers, to winnow the unrighteous and the sinful from the herd of men. We were cast in the role of his instruments of vengeance and wrath before your pitiful race was raised from the clay. You have felt his love? Now you will know his fury – it will pour, scalding, onto you.'

'*What do you want?*' Father O'Riorden screamed.

'To gorge on your soul.'

Panic flared in the priest's eyes, then collapsed into . . . regret?

'Release Robert,' he said.

I felt the hands gripping me slacken instantly.

Frobisher blinked, shook his head as if to clear his vision, saw the Black-Suited Men and his hands clawed at the air. He staggered back, tumbling into the house. Dr Caxton was staring horrified at his hands. His gaze jumped to my face. 'I'm . . . I'm so sorry. What . . . what have I done?' He looked down at Tessa, who had appeared from the house. She smiled at him, smiled at us both. Blinked.

The Black-Suited Man turned his head towards me, slowly, deliberately, and gave me a smile so sharp it sliced through my paralysing fear. I stumbled back, tripped, but somehow kept my balance.

'You will come to us, Robert,' he said with dreadful certainly. 'It's in your blood. Your presence is required for the Summoning. Fire will manifest from heaven in the sight of men.'

'Run, Robert!' Caxton burst out. 'Did you hear what I said? *Run!*'

And I did.

FROM *THE MIND POSSESSED: A PERSONAL INVESTIGATION INTO THE BROAD HAVEN TRIANGLE*

BY DR R. CAXTON (CLEMENTINE PRESS, 1980), P.137

To come to the level of understanding of the demonic forces that I, regrettably, have achieved requires one to throw out the notions of reason and order that underpin the modern scientific paradigm. It is with grim hopelessness that I transcribe this warning, knowing how likely it is to be taken for a lurid work of fiction at best, and at worst the ravings of a lunatic. But the patient and open-minded inquirer should take heed: whether you believe in the bogeyman or not matters little, for it is certain that he believes in you.

I looked for Tessa, but she had vanished. Frobisher was on his knees in the doorway of the farmhouse, and we could only watch as the Black-Suited Man moved towards Father O'Riorden.

The poor man shrank back, scanning from side to side in a desperate search for an escape route, only to register the two other Black-Suited Men, closing in on him in a classic pincer formation. It was appalling, the anguish contorting his face as he realized he was trapped. As the Black-Suited Men continued their slow advance, he managed somehow to stay on his feet and draw himself up to face what hunted him.

My heart was beating hard with panic but I couldn't move. Couldn't do anything. Although I had been released from the state of possession that had made me throw Robert out into the yard and hold him in a vice-like grip, I could now only watch; this was the lesson I had to learn, as my father had learned it: those who hunt ghosts are hunted in turn by them.

Father O'Riorden had made a deal with the devil and that deal had allowed Robert to get away.

'I deny you in the name of Jesus Christ,' the priest roared at the three men. He was clasping the silver crucifix that hung around his neck and brandishing it at the nearest predator.

Something shuddered beneath the ground, and the air between the priest and the Black-Suited Man spasmed, flexing and distorting like a bedsheet blowing in the wind. The unholy creature shrieked and flung up its arms, turning its face away from Father O'Riorden and towards me, and what I saw engraved itself on my mind for ever. A ripple swept over its disproportioned face, and for just a moment I glimpsed the traumatized but indubitably human face of the person this creature used to be. I could have sworn it was the face of the deceased headmaster, Howell Cooper, a sinner's soul reincarnated in this fiendish form.

Then the torrent of energy pouring out of the Black-Suited Man dissipated; space snapped back into its normal shape, and when it did the demon was twenty feet from where he had been, just a tall thin man staring blankly into space. For a moment I felt hope, but then the man's blank eyes became wounds in the world; the transformative wave flowed back, and the demon reasserted control of the flesh.

'That's not going to work,' snarled the Black-Suited Man. He rolled his shoulders and flexed his neck languorously then strode towards O'Riorden, even as the other two were just reaching him. The priest swivelled to face the closer one and opened his mouth to speak, but the third was on him from behind, seizing his neck and ripping the crucifix from his hands. Then each grasped the priest by an arm and pinioned him in a cruciform position.

Every part of the priest's body went rigid apart from his face. My heart clenches even now to remember that expression, so distorted in agony.

'Damn you, hell's spawn,' gasped O'Riorden. The shreds of faith he had been able to recover in his final moments had been too little and far, far too late. Now he would pay with his soul, and he knew it. But still he held on to a kernel of defiance. He struggled not to show his fear. He would not beg. And still, even facing oblivion, Father O'Riorden thought of others. He turned his head and shouted directly at Frank and me, 'Run!'

Although at that instant we were able to move again, neither of us fled. We just looked on in horror. The leader straightened his black hat, then plunged his bony white hand into Father O'Riorden's chest. There was no blood, just a throaty scream as the hand passed as easily as smoke through his clothes, into his body.

When Father O'Riorden uttered his last words, his voice came out in shuddering starts. 'My heart!' he gasped. 'Please, not my heart!'

'Make it still,' one of the Black-Suited Men said.

Threads of light forked from the priest's chest, and I could not remember ever being so cold.

− 51 −

Tuesday 15 February 1977, 10.30 p.m.

Running, chest tightening, breath burning in my throat, along
the rutted path that led towards the lower fields. I went past
the cattle shed's great black shadows and into a field thick with
clots of thistles, stumbled on more giant ruts made by Randall's
tractor. I did not look back.

Although I was afraid, deeply afraid and shocked by what I
had seen, I wasn't running from Ravenstone Farm to get away.
I was running because I desperately wanted the truth, the truth
about the Parsons Elite, the truth about my parents' deaths and
the truth about Araceli and her daughter.

You left her, Robert, my conscience murmured. *You left Tessa
behind.* Though if Randall's theories were right, I'd left behind
a girl that *used* to be Tessa, a girl that could control other people's minds, a girl now possessed by an ancient demonic force
that was responsible for the UFO sightings and the appearance
of the Black-Suited Man − a force unleashed in the Havens by
the scientist and occultist Jack Parsons over thirty years ago.

If I could find the physical source of that force, I might find
Araceli and discover what it was about her, this place and my

family that had drawn these forces. Stop whoever – whatever – was responsible.

The Parsons Elite were at the heart of all this, I was convinced of it now. *But you'll never defeat them*, warned a voice in my head. 'But I must try,' I said aloud.

From behind me came a sound to torture the ears: Father O'Riorden's scream. I stopped. I had to go back, see if he was OK, check on the others. But as I turned, the sky roared and my eye was drawn to movement in Little Haven across the dark expanse of St Brides Bay. Pinpricks of light. Torches. People gathering on the beach. Guilt mixed with terror. My gaze swept the sky for anything unusual. Nothing. Only a low ceiling of dark clouds which would soon sheet rain. But the sky watch was approaching. And then what?

I wanted to scream at the people on the beach to run, to get away. But even if they could have heard me, my warning would go ignored because their attention was elsewhere, just like Grandfather had predicted, on the heavens, with all their 'signs and wonders'. I knew that the Havens were in a desperate situation.

What will happen if you don't stop this? What will happen if sky spectres are summoned en masse with all these people watching?

The admiral's voice sounded in my mind: *The Russians will think it's the Americans and vice versa. With nuclear weapons on our doorstep? You know what could happen!*

My thoughts turned to Araceli. She was the key to all of this. And I felt sure that she needed me.

She could be anywhere. No. Not anywhere. Her location, I felt sure as I scanned St Brides Bay, was Stack Rocks Fort. Didn't everything lead there?

It wasn't coincidence that for centuries UFOs had appeared

around those rocks; it wasn't coincidence that a ley line ran right through them, connecting with Broad Haven Primary School and the Haven Hotel. And it wasn't coincidence, surely, that the island belonged to Araceli's family! At least it didn't feel like coincidence. There was a reason, a good reason, why Randall had warned me to stay away, a reason why the Rotary Club was involved with the fort's renovation.

I ran on. The breath tore in my chest. But I kept going, until finally I reached the cliff path. Here I felt the past all around me. My parents. Were they watching me now?

I decided to take the rickety wooden staircase down to the cove nearest Stack Rocks and find Gethin's fishing boat. It wasn't large but it would get me across to the fort. There was only one problem: Monks Cove was the last place I ever wanted to visit. I had told Frobisher my parents had died on the night of the Great Flood, but I hadn't told him where their bodies were recovered. Monks Cove.

But I had to do this.

I stumbled down the steps onto the shore and into a freezing rock pool. Gasping, I heaved myself out and took a moment to catch my breath. I ran, twisted my ankle on a rock, and nearly fell. My chest felt tight. The adrenaline was really pumping now. And it didn't just make me fast, it made me sharp. For once my nerves were working in my favour.

Scanning the secluded cove, my eyes picked out a dark shape against the night at the far end of the rocky beach. It had to be Gethin's boat. I could reach it easily; the problem would be launching it on my own. Nevertheless, I had to try.

As I crossed the beach, the wind off the Atlantic whipped around me, the salt air and sand scouring my face. An alarming thought hit me as I approached the boat: I was suddenly afraid that I was repeating a course of action my parents had taken ten years earlier on a night just like this. The journey I was about to make might be my last.

So be it, I thought. Final or not, this was a journey to the truth.

FROM *THE MIND POSSESSED: A PERSONAL INVESTIGATION INTO THE BROAD HAVEN TRIANGLE*

BY DR R. CAXTON (CLEMENTINE PRESS, 1980) P.150

They stopped his heart. The priest was murdered in front of us.

Even before Father O'Riorden had dropped lifelessly to his knees, slumping face forward into the mud, Frobisher and I were running for his car, not looking back.

The cold sliced through me, made my hands shake as I struggled to open the car door. I felt certain Randall Llewellyn Pritchard wasn't coming back, and I thought we would probably never see his grandson, Robert Wilding, again. The three shadowy figures were motionless, watching us from beneath the brims of their wide hats.

The engine growled. 'What about Tessa?' Frobisher asked.

My gaze jumped to where Tessa had stood.

'She's gone. Let's get out of here,' I said, and immediately hated myself. How could I not feel guilt? She was just nine years old. But she was not Tessa any more. Something else was in control of her – had taken control of Frobisher and me, made us throw Robert Wilding into the yard. Now we were free, we had to get to the village, help in whatever way we could.

The Black-Suited Men didn't try to stop us, but I could feel their malevolence even as we left them behind and their forms shrank in the rear-view mirror. But then a dazzling red light was behind us, pouring ruddy phosphorescence into the car.

'What the hell is that?' Frobisher yelled, his gaze jumping between the windscreen and the rear-view mirror.

I twisted round in my seat. Powering through the air behind the car, half-filling the rear window, was a shining crimson orb, perhaps twenty feet in diameter, its surface continually flinging out threads of crackling light that whipped and flailed for yards around, before collapsing back to the surface of the sphere, utterly unaffected by the resistance of the air it rushed through.

'Speed up, speed up!' I shouted. 'Don't look at it, Frank!'

The zooming orb looked like a miniature sun seething with flares, but there was no mistaking it for anything remotely natural. Where the light it emitted touched my face, my skin itched and crawled, and I was filled with a mixture of fear and despair that threatened to overwhelm me. There were techniques I had learned from arcane books in my father's library, texts like the *Pnakotic Manuscripts* and the *Diablonomicon*. A trance would amplify my strength of will, but I doubted it would be enough.

The light cut through the darkness, growing ever bigger. Blood red.

With an enormous surge of will I managed to wrench my gaze away and faced forward again, panting.

We had to go faster, but Frobisher had floored the accelerator. The suspension shrieked in protest as the car crashed along the unmade road. How he kept control of the car I'll never know.

Suddenly, mercifully, a plan presented itself to me, appearing fully formed in my mind. If we couldn't outrun the globe, that left only one option. We had to fight.

Luckily Frobisher's attention was riveted to the road, distracting him from what I was about to do.

– 52 –

Monks Cove, St Brides Bay

Just fifteen feet long, the boat was speedy. Made of fibreglass and aluminium it was light too, which had made the task of dragging it into the water easier than it might have been. But the sea was choppy. Even though the boat had a motor, I was exhausted.

I was halfway across the black sea to Stack Rocks when I saw the shape of the ruined fort standing out against the sky. The place looked deserted. Then I saw a faint glimmer of a light, a torch possibly or a flame, in the top casemate, and with renewed courage I pressed on. What was I going to do once I got there? I had no idea. The only thing I was sure of was that going back wasn't an option. No matter how bad things got or what I found out there, I wasn't going to give in.

The sea picked up, waves slapping against the hull. It hit me that these weren't normal waves. Normal waves didn't erupt spontaneously from out of the ocean, and this part of the bay was sheltered from the worst of the winds. Then I saw it: a shining object in the sea no more than fifty feet away. It was cigar-shaped and at least a hundred feet in length, and as it ran silently and without a wake through the water it emitted a powerful blue and white glow.

What the hell is that? A submarine?

A larger wave struck the boat; I lost my balance and plunged into the inky darkness. *I'm in the water with it.* I tried to swim, but the cold just gripped me, reduced my attempts to swim to wild, helpless thrashing. Then came a terrible realization: something was beneath me, rising, *something that would drag me down.* The massive object was almost upon me. The glow had turned from blue to an intense red. *Is this what Dylan Jones saw? Is this what turned him suicidal?*

I was reaching for the boat. In the distance I saw the lights on the seafront, saw a boat moored in the bay. I shouted for help. Useless. I managed to grab the side of the boat. Waves pummelled me from all sides but I somehow held on. I gasped, overwhelmed by the need to get out of the water, and heaved myself up, collapsing into the boat.

I got my breath, raised my head. The object in the water had vanished.

I was certain it wasn't a submarine, not just because there had been no engine noise. I simply knew. Pure knowledge had crept into my head. And even though I couldn't explain how it was happening, I knew my mind was changing in an alarming way. Awakening.

I felt a moment of private triumph before getting control of the boat and turning it back towards Stack Rocks, which soon loomed nearer. I held on as the boat was battered by more rough waters, and just when I thought I could go no further, I saw the jetty.

FROM *THE MIND POSSESSED: A PERSONAL INVESTIGATION INTO THE BROAD HAVEN TRIANGLE*

BY DR R. CAXTON (CLEMENTINE PRESS: 1980) P.156

The light grew even bigger. Redder than rage.

Frobisher kept his foot to the floor. The back end of the car fishtailed wildly as he shot us through a kink in the lane, threatening to roll the car.

'Frank, slow down,' I said, controlling my urge to shout.

A few hundred yards away the lane veered left, and there was no way we could make the turn at this speed. Hedgerows whipped past on either side like the oncoming cars on a motorway, herding us towards disaster.

Still the light followed. One thing might save our sanity: the possibility that all of this was an elaborate deception cooked up by the American military in their base up on the cliffs. An exercise in mind control, perhaps? Of course it wasn't. But if I could convince Frank, if only for a moment, it might make all the difference . . .

'It's OK, Frank,' I lied. 'It's not a UFO.'

'What the hell are you talking about? Do you know what it is?' he demanded, shooting me a suspicious, angry look.

'Yes, it's a prototype remote-controlled aircraft equipped with experimental weaponry.'

He glanced at me again, incredulous now. 'What?' he yelled.

'You knew? Why didn't you say that before? You bastard, Caxton, what the hell are you playing at?'

The car hurtled towards the bend at a suicidal rate. I began to slow my breathing, closed my eyes and focused my thoughts on the memory of my father, a man who had once stared directly into the occult and allowed it to stare into him, a man who had spent countless hours confronting the unknown – challenging it, explaining it. A person I had never known yet had doubted all my adult life.

The symbols Wilding had shown me, the symbols from the church, flashed before my eyes.

The illusion of a cage of shadows within the car vanished in a blink, and the ruby light waned from pulse to pulse. And as the red glare within the car withered and died, so the illumination from the pursuing spectre began to dwindle.

Randall Llewellyn Pritchard was right: the best weapon against them was faith.

'Slow down, Frank. You're hallucinating. Those men at the cottage were soldiers. Special forces. They hypnotized us, made us suggestible.'

'Suggestible,' he echoed vacantly, oblivious to the irony, but as the bend rushed to meet us, he lifted his foot from the accelerator and pressed the brake pedal. The drums squealed, the dirt and gravel beneath the shuddering wheels rasped, and inertia threw us forward into the bruising embrace of our seatbelts.

The car didn't stop, but slowed just enough to take the corner.

Frobisher yanked the wheel down to the left, the back wheels scythed around, skimming sideways over the rough terrain, and I thought for one terrifying instant that we would slam broadside into the bank that bounded the lane. But then he shifted down a gear and stamped on the accelerator, and the front wheels bit into the dirt, hauling the car out of the turn and into the next straight just as the offside brake light kissed the hedgerow, which exploded in a burst of leaves and plastic shards.

Frobisher's terror had subsided, but it had been replaced with anger. At me.

'What the hell are you up to, you shifty bastard?' he growled. 'And what the hell was that bloody thing? How do you know what the military are up to anyway?'

'Er, well, that's . . . I . . . I'm actually a journalist too, Frank,' I stammered.

We weren't in the clear yet, and it was crucial that Frobisher didn't slip back into superstition and believe the truth about the sky spectres before we had reached the village. If I had to destroy his trust in me to guarantee that, it was a price I would pay.

'Investigative. I've been looking into unsupervised air force and navy weapons programmes at Brawdy. Wilding was right. They've been conducting unauthorized weapons tests on civilians, and I intend to hang the bastards out to dry.'

He eyed me suspiciously, then said with unconcealed hostility, 'So why didn't you mention anything about this before? You let me think we were going to die, for God's sake!' He checked the rear-view mirror. 'Where the hell has it gone anyway? And how did they hypnotize us?'

I could tell he wasn't buying it. My brain raced to improvise. 'It was a remote-controlled miniature aircraft, equipped with holographic lasers and a directed ultra-low-frequency infrasound cannon.'

Silence. He gave me a look, straight and sceptical.

Darkness folded around us. Neither of us looked back, neither dared.

– 53 –

Stack Rocks, St Brides Bay, 11.20 p.m.

My teeth were chattering as I hurled the mooring rope, jumped from the boat down onto the jetty and tied the boat up with numb raw hands. I had a torch from the boat – that was something – but I was soaked through, hair plastered to my face, clothes soggy and heavy. And ice cold.

What now? I asked myself, the wind gusting around me. The doors to the fort were at the end of the jetty, but they were secured with industrial-grade padlocks. I had to find another way. To the left of the jetty I could see the mouth of a cave. From certain angles, a plateau of rock concealed the entrance, so much so that from Little Haven it was not visible at all. I headed to the cave and peered into the darkness. Even though fear was pulsing in my chest, my throat, behind my eyes, I clicked on my torch and went inside.

'Hello?' The torch beam ran over glimmering stalagmites, mossy walls and sheets of water that were almost luminescent. 'Anyone there?'

Silence.

I stood in silent wonder at the jagged walls of granite soaring above me. There was no telling how deep into Stack Rocks this cave went.

'Araceli?'

My voice echoed around the cavern and I shivered. Anything could be watching me from the jagged crevices. There was a sudden crash, and I couldn't help but cry out. I pivoted and saw what remained of Gethin's boat on the rocks. The foaming sea was washing it away. It was hard to stay calm. The noise of the sea and wind set in motion another chain of disquieting thoughts: *This cave is going to flood, Rob. It's going to flood and you're going to drown.*

My next few steps were more cautious. I ran my torch over the wall and glimpsed an opening in the rock. I went towards it. I could hear something. It sounded like chanting, a rhythmic drone that drew me through into a smaller space. I ran my hand over the walls and instead of jagged rock felt smooth concrete. Man made. A spiral staircase.

I took the staircase, close enough to the sound now to realize it was definitely a man's voice, speaking in the manner of a priest: 'I call thee, the one without human head, that did appear upon earth from the heavens, that did come by day and go by night, that came in the light and disappeared into the depths of darkness. In your name I dedicate this offering!'

I reached the top and crouched down. I had emerged into a cavernous circular chamber with a domed ceiling that may once have been used to house guns but was now given over to a very different purpose. There was a central stone pillar and the chamber's curved walls were covered in symmetrical markings reminiscent of those I had seen in the cellar at the Haven Hotel. There were also drawings: of signs in the heavens too bizarre to be meteors, beings too large to be human. The floor was stone, littered with silver crucifixes and other objects, and marked with painted symbols around a circle that seemed to shimmer in the faint light coming through four gun casemates looking out across the sea and towards the Havens, which lay in the unnatural glow of something hovering in the sky. In the centre of the circle, before a stone altar, a pentacle had been drawn.

Inside it was Araceli.

She lay writhing beneath a man who stood over her, face obscured by the hood of a white robe, hand etching a shape – an inverted cross – in the air above her head.

'To do my will shall be the whole of the law!' the man cried, and without warning there came a sound to torture the ears: a bleating goat ringing shrilly with the wretched snarls of a prowling dog.

Then there was only a brilliant white light and silence.

When I opened my eyes the light had faded and the man had gone from the room but Araceli remained in the circle, unmoving, dark hair fanned out around her head. Her skin looked grey.

When I reached her side, touched a hand to her cheek, she looked up at me, dazed, and whispered, 'Tessa? Is she OK?'

I didn't want to tell her what I had learned about her daughter, wanted to spare her that. But I had no option now, after everything.

'Araceli, I think Tessa is possessed,' I said, hearing how alien these words sounded but not doubting them for a second.

Her expression didn't change.

'How did you get here?' I asked, looking frantically back over my shoulder then all around me. There was no sign of the figure I had seen. 'How did you get out of the house?'

'When that thing was at the window,' she swallowed, 'I ran

upstairs, held Tessa. The temperature rose. The roof had turned red. I could see through it, like it had turned to glass. I could see the sky, Robert, the stars. There was a red light in the sky. It made me feel drowsy. Then it glowed like a neon lamp, and a ray hit me. And I was here.'

It sounded incredible, but after all that had happened I was ready to believe it.

'That man just now, who was he?'

She turned her head away.

'I'm going to take you away from here,' I said, taking her by the shoulders.

'No, we can't leave,' she said. She felt heavy, lifeless, and instead of looking relieved to see me, she seemed fearful. 'Don't you see? They've brought us here because they need us.'

From the direction of Little Haven there echoed a distant explosion.

'Come on,' I said more urgently now, but she was still resisting. 'Araceli, for God's sake, there must be a way – somehow. If we hurry we can . . .'

I tried pulling her up, but she was a deadweight. 'Let me go!' she moaned. 'Let me go! Let me go!'

A sudden, sickening realization.

They've brought us here.

I stooped over her, looking down into her dark eyes. I'd thought them beautiful before, but now I saw something else, something unnatural. The irises were black.

'You had to come here of your own free will.' There was a flatness to her voice. 'The Demon's Gate will open and we will be at peace.'

I shut my eyes, pulled a deep breath down into my lungs, held it.

'Robert, you will understand,' she whispered. 'When you see him, he will explain.'

'Who?' I demanded.

She didn't answer, just pointed. The robed figure was in the doorway. He had removed his hood.

'Hello, old chap,' he said.

FROM *THE MIND POSSESSED: A PERSONAL INVESTIGATION INTO THE BROAD HAVEN TRIANGLE*

BY DR R. CAXTON (CLEMENTINE PRESS, 1980) P.139

We had to slow down as we reached the village. Parked cars lined the road next to the Ram Inn and the post office and the bridge that crossed the stream flowing down into the cove.

'What the hell?' Frobisher said. His eyes had gone wide with alarm, and when I saw what he was looking at I felt a chill shudder through me.

People crowded the beach. Friends on telephones had arranged to meet. The newspapers had encouraged it. The curious were hungry for answers and, yes, perhaps a little magic. And those desperate to know had found it impossible not to come. But there was something wrong. No one moved. No one spoke.

The parents of the children from Broad Haven Primary School were lined up at the slipway, staring out to sea. In front of them, with their heads tilted up towards the heavens, were their children. And watching this bizarre scene from a short distance away were the elders of the village – Delyth Cale, Ethel Dunwoody and Roger Daley – huddled together. Winding down the window, I could hear the conspirators joined in a dissonant chant.

What I was hearing was the perfect confirmation of what Wilding's grandfather had told us in the kitchen at Ravenstone

Farm. Without thinking, I said to Frobisher, 'We have to stop them!'

Sheer terror made me get out of the car. That was before the roar and flash of light which came out of the sky.

One by one, every light in the village blinked out.

The car's engine failed.

And the elders bowed their heads. 'To do thy will shall be the whole of the law,' one of them said

The others repeated the words, spreading their arms: 'To do thy will shall be the whole of the law.'

Then the rain came in a great hissing rush.

– 54 –

It was Admiral Lord Hill Bartlett.

He had come from London, just as I had asked, but not to help. No. The truth was in his baleful gaze and in his smile, which was as thin as the curved blade in his gloved hand.

'I . . . I don't understand,' I heard myself say eventually, just as Araceli stumbled to join Bartlett. 'You . . . know each other?'

'My father,' she admitted.

'You and Araceli were acquainted in childhood, brought together to witness something honourable. Something life-changing,' he said.

'It's clear to me now,' Araceli said. 'Oh, it was beautiful, Robert. Do you remember?'

Did I? Perhaps enough to realize remembering wouldn't be a good idea. The admiral took a step towards me. 'Our brotherhood is indebted to you,' he said.

Brotherhood? I thought, *This is not happening.*

'I assure you this *is* happening,' the admiral said so quickly it was as if he could hear my thoughts. He didn't just sound unwell, he looked it. Still recognizably the man who had once confided in me, but now inhabiting a dying body. His face was haggard and drawn, his arms scrawny.

He nodded at Araceli. 'Look,' he instructed. 'Look at her!'

I obeyed, and all the stories about her family and the Haven Hotel came rushing back, along with an unwavering conviction I barely had strength to acknowledge: that there was a reason I was obsessed with this woman, a reason I had wanted to help her. A reason so dangerous I had locked it away behind every door in my memory. I tried to summon some strength. The totality of what I was about to learn at Stack Rocks I wasn't sure of, but that process of understanding began with acceptance that I had been duped by the admiral and his daughter. They had lured me here together, ensnared me. I didn't yet know why, but I knew I would learn truths this night.

'If you concentrate, really focus, you'll remember what your grandfather tried so hard to make you forget.'

I brought you through the worst of it.

I stared at the admiral and Araceli, my head shaking in automatic denial. Opened my mouth to reply, before closing it again, because in a white flash of memory I was seeing it again: the Haven Hotel framed against a purple sky, and in the woods behind the hotel a ball of yellow light. Floating. Hypnotic. Silent.

Pulsing.

'I don't remember!' I screamed, stepping back 'I *won't* remember!'

'Ah, there it is,' the admiral said calmly. 'All that anger and rage that has kept you fighting, brought you here.'

'Shut up, *shut up!*' My cry echoed around the dank chamber. 'Whatever he has made you believe,' I said to Araceli, 'whatever sick fantasies he has tricked you into indulging, this man is a liar and a traitor.' My voice was shuddering, my limbs trembling with fury – and with frustration, because Araceli wasn't hearing me. Her body was rigid, her eyes unresponsive.

The admiral snorted, a thick phlegmy sound, and suddenly I saw the truth. His connection to the conspiracy I had unmasked was now undeniable. The admiral, a man who had always savoured power and clamoured for more, had led me out to this island fortress for a reason.

'You wanted to know about Jack Parsons?' the admiral said in his hoarse voice. 'A dangerous visionary who conducted experiments here in the Havens, Parsons believed that the many tales of UFOs and extraterrestrial visitations that had surfaced since the 1940s were actually evidence of the presence of satanic forces engaged in worldwide deceit.' He coughed roughly. 'Oh, Parsons was clever and ambitious. He saw the potential of manipulating these powers.'

'Manipulating how?' I asked, wondering how the admiral could even hope to overpower me. His eyes had become dark hollows, his face was wasted.

'Parsons believed that ancient occult rituals could open portals between the human world and the other side – the Abyss, the Kingdom of Shadows.' His voice was reasonable. 'Just imagine how quickly the world's problems would dissolve, how quickly we would come together, if the world faced a threat from outside our planet? A new world order would be needed. Those who had prepared the way for these powers would take control.'

'People like you,' I said bitterly, and the admiral nodded.

'The Parsons Elite has one goal: to convince the world that extraterrestrial life exists and has been visiting this planet for centuries.'

Remembering Grandfather's prophetic warnings, I said, 'In the last times some will abandon the faith and follow deceiving spirits and things taught by demons.'

The admiral nodded. Satanism offered him the most power, but it had needed an appropriate disguise – evil always does. In this case the lie was clear. He and the Parsons Elite had spun the lie of extraterrestrial life visiting this planet into the hearts and minds of millions. Prepared the way for a grand deception that would breed panic and dread and damn souls to hell.

This was the crux of it, this was the truth.

'In the face of fear, in the face of the unknown, individuals will be silenced; they will scream for leadership. It is as Parsons planned. In the aftermath of the crisis a small group of elite men will take control. In the name of the Dark Father, the Lawless One.'

I said, 'This has nothing to do with me or Araceli.'

'Wrong. You are descendants of the project. Jack Parsons learned, as you did, that these airborne visions of hell can be summoned through ritual prayer, but also that exposure to them at close quarters induces a gradual descent into mental anguish which sometimes results in suicide.'

And here was the truth I'd been blind to until now. Missiles and explosions and fallout weren't the only weapons of conquest. Subtler methods led to the same end. Our minds could be used against us. Thoughts and attitudes subverted.

The admiral said, 'Demonomania is significantly more pronounced in children who are unprotected.'

Those who were not baptized. 'But that would mean the sightings were arranged, the children at the school – '

'Were deliberately exposed,' the admiral finished. 'Correct.'

Araceli released a scream of agony and guilt, collapsing to

her knees. I recalled the emptiness in her daughter's eyes and realized that, like her own child, a demon had long ago reached into her mind, hungry for its ruin, and used her.

'The rituals that summon the sky spectres are derived from work carried out by Jack Parsons and Aleister Crowley, grand masters of the occult, both brilliant men, who first opened a portal to the Kingdom of Shadows in America. When Parsons came here after the war, he achieved the same thing, right here in Stack Rocks Fort.

'It's a tradition our order has worked hard to honour. We identify our thoughts and actions with the images of deities we wish to invoke: flying saucers, faceless humanoids. When children see these phenomena, the change is induced – a state of demonomania. Over time programming takes place. Godly spiritual foundations are shattered, the soul is weakened, the witness possessed, their soul damned to hell.

'Think of us as parents,' he added. I could tell from the tone of his voice that he believed his cause was noble and just. 'The child's wellbeing is our chief concern. Over time every one of the Ten Commandments is violated in the presence of the child, breaking God's will. Leaving us with a shapeless rock to chisel and sculpt as we will.'

'You're sick!' I said. The admiral only nodded, a simple gesture of conviction. He glanced down at Araceli, whose face was buried in her hands. 'Dear Araceli,' the admiral said, and the ghost of a smile touched his lips. 'The name is appropriate, don't you think? It means altar of the skies. And like her mother, Tessa will never hear the Lord's name. The only name she will hear is the name of the Dark Master, who in time will be presented to her as God.'

He wasn't gloating. In a way that would have been easier to

bear, because his deliberate tone was sending dread coursing through me. *He wants me to know all this for a reason. He wants me to understand.*

'I am not frightened,' I said.

'You should be. How's the anxiety?' the admiral asked suddenly. He came right up to me and pressed his cold bony figures against my temples. The sensation of his papery skin against mine made me think of dead leaves, and when I smelt his putrid breath, hot against my face, I felt my gorge rise and pushed him away. 'All your fears, your memories, your worries, these aren't just anxiety, Robert.'

'What are they then?'

Angling his head to one side as his clear eyes looked into me, he said, 'Think of your brain as a radio. All that festering anxiety, churning away, making you a slave to your memories. And all your life you've wondered, haven't you? What's the cause of your private little hell? Your grandfather? The way he treated you, filling your head with his notions?' He dropped his voice. 'No, Robert.'

For a moment those words just hung there. Behind me, far below, I heard the waves pounding the rocks. Denial was clutching my heart. 'Enough,' I muttered, closing my eyes.

'Listen to me!'

He hit my face so hard I tasted blood. I was too shocked to fight back, too numb to move, the way people freeze when they're about to get hit by a train. And the admiral knew I was defenceless, which was the worst part. He was grinning, playing with me.

'Yes, I'm sure that, in your darkest moments, you must have comforted yourself with all sorts of reassurances,' he said, 'convinced yourself that you were overreacting, perhaps . . .

seeing things that weren't there? And it's an interesting question: how does a man halfway to losing his mind ever properly comprehend that it has finally gone?' The playful trill went out of his voice and his face turned to stone. 'Well, let me put you right. You're not mad, old chap. You are . . . *selected*.'

'You brought me here under false pretences?'

'Guided you.'

'From London?'

'From childhood.' His cruel smile emphasized the years of planning that had gone into luring me to this island fortress. 'You are the child of our order.'

'The child?'

He sprang at me and with one hand slammed me back into the pillar in the centre of the room. I'm not sure which was more surprising, his speed or the crack of pain as my head connected with the stone. He was unwell, probably dying, and he was old, which could only mean that he was drawing his power from somewhere else.

'You have a duty to carry out,' he said in a desperate growl, so close that I felt his saliva flecking my cheek.

I was afraid of what he would do to me, but I was also afraid of what he intended me to do to others. I struggled but was still exhausted by my ordeal in the bay.

'Tonight the world goes to war,' the admiral hissed. From outside a malevolent light poured into the chamber. It stabbed my eyes, reflecting off the silver objects on the floor and from the knife that was just inches from my face.

I dug my fingers into his neck, squeezed, and the admiral snarled in pain.

'Araceli, help me!' I shouted.

She ran to my side, stooped and reached for something on

the floor. I couldn't look down, couldn't see what she was doing, but I could hear the chink of metal on stone.

'Do it, girl,' the admiral commanded. '*Do it!*'

A searing pain. My hands spasmed and the admiral wrenched free from my grasp. I looked down at my feet, already knowing what I would see. One ankle was encircled by a heavy band of metal attached to the floor with a chain.

'You're both insane!' I yelled, more at the admiral than Araceli. She had her back to me and was gazing at the casemate that faced the shore where the villagers had gathered and where all hell was about to be let loose.

'The Falling!' the admiral said in a low voice. 'Now it begins!'

Crouching and tilting my head to one side, I saw what the villagers were seeing: fiery balls of light dropping from the heavens, casting deathly reflections on the waters of St Brides Bay.

Thunder roared, mixing with another sound, the wailing of a distant siren.

FROM *THE MIND POSSESSED: A PERSONAL INVESTIGATION INTO THE BROAD HAVEN TRIANGLE*

BY DR R. CAXTON (CLEMENTINE PRESS, 1980) P.180

11. p.m. Outside the Ram Inn, close to the sea wall, the elders were still muttering and swaying, but with greater passion. I could hear them in spite of the rain, which had begun to drive down in torrents, and in spite of the lifeboat station's emergency siren.

'To do thy will shall be the whole of the law.'

Pritchard was correct: there was a secret group in the village that had been waiting for the call of the Watchers in the sky. It was in part thanks to them that the demons had gained a foothold in the minds of the local populace. I was about to tell Frobisher we should leave when I saw his eyes darken and fix on the sky. 'Sweet Jesus,' he whispered.

We watched, tense with fear, as a red fireball dropped from the sky and swooped, stopping over a boat in the bay. Another joined it. Hanging motionless together, they were like a pair of demon's eyes.

I dragged my eyes away. 'Don't look, Frank,' I said, but it was no good. His head was tilted back and he had begun to walk towards the Giant's Point. 'Frank!'

Slowly the people on the beach began to move as one – up the slipway, turning at the post office and walking out along Giant's Point. More than a hundred people. No one broke away;

no one spoke except for the elders in their circle: the teaching assistant, the postmistress, the landlord of the Ram Inn. 'To do my will shall be the whole of the law . . .'

A police car screeched to a halt behind me, its blue lights flashing in the dark, Sergeant Blakemore's pale face behind the windscreen. He got out but then did nothing, just stood there, gaze locked on the lights above the water.

Just then lightning ripped across the sky, and against the dark, on the nearest hill, the Haven Hotel stood out in sharp relief. There was a single light glowing in a ground-floor window. Someone was up there. My brain and body made the decision in unison. I turned into the streaks of rain and headed for the Haven Hotel.

– 55 –

At Stack Rocks Fort the sky boomed and everything shook. Jagged shafts of light flashed through the casemates and the air vibrated. Through the nearest opening I could see the glow of something in the sky reflecting off the sea and, beyond, Little Haven drenched in an eerie flickering light.

'What's happening?' I shouted just as the red globes falling from the sky began to track across the bay.

'They're heading for RAF Brawdy,' the admiral said.

But they weren't just heading for the base; they were heading for its nuclear weapons. Suddenly I could see how everything was connected – what part those weapons were to play in all of this, if the admiral had his way.

'We will watch as a new era begins,' said my former mentor reverently, 'and I become its master.'

'We'll all be destroyed in any explosion,' I said.

'No, I am protected. I am promised a long, long life.'

'What if you're wrong? What if they won't be controlled?' There wasn't a doubt in the admiral's eyes, not even a glimmer. 'You're so certain the Watchers will give you what you want. Immortality? Power?'

He nodded. 'Now I am dying, but they will reward me with everlasting life.'

'You're sure they'll bargain? You've opened a portal to hell. Or somewhere worse.'

'I bring the ancient deities, I am completing Jack Parsons' work.'

'Just listen!' I screamed. 'Jack Parsons failed. He may have raised these powers but he was destroyed. Why should you succeed?'

'Because of the prize I have won for them.'

'And what prize is that?' I asked.

'You.'

All the air was punched from my chest.

'You are our selection. You are the moon child.' His voice was unsettlingly calm. He looked down at the blade in his hands.

'I don't understand,' I murmured.

The admiral came nearer. 'You had to come here of your own free will. That was essential to the ritual. That is why we needed Araceli – to lure you here.'

She looked up at her father. I saw tears shimmering in her eyes. This time they were genuine.

'I'm sorry to say you're going to die tonight, Robert, just like the Jacksons.' He saw the question on my face and nodded. 'When they threatened to expose our plans, they had to be silenced.'

'But they were members of the Parsons Elite?'

He nodded. 'They complained when they realized they weren't to assume positions of power. They needed to be silenced.'

'Like you silenced Howell Cooper, the headmaster?'

The admiral nodded, feigning sadness. 'Poor Howell. His

suicide was a great sadness to the order. You see, old chap, when he realized how he had been used against his will, he objected strenuously. His soul was taken and damned. We had to show him what he had done, hold a mirror to his crimes. Just like your parents.' He looked back towards the mainland. 'They died over there, you know, up on the coastal path, very near where the Jacksons were killed.'

My stomach dropped. For a moment I couldn't speak. I felt faint.

'No . . . My parents died in the Great Flood. Their bodies were washed ashore.'

He looked down at his knife. 'But it was not the water that killed them.'

− 56 −

I felt his disclosure rip through me like white lightning.

'You complete bastard,' I said in a low, trembling voice. 'You manipulative, twisted bastard.'

His thin lips curved into a smile.

'*Tell me!* Tell me who killed them.'

'Oh Robert. All your life combating war, fighting the good fight, striving to complete your mother's good work, never pausing to consider what took her from you in the first place. You were so easily convinced it was the Americans − or the Russians. Look how easily led you are, how blind you were to the truth. Your sins are multiple and they have followed you here.' He listed them on his fingers: 'Self-deceit, stupidity, pretentiousness. No one should be protected from the conse-quences of their own stupidity.'

'What did you do to them?' I managed to ask.

Araceli bowed her head.

'Like your grandfather, your mother understood very well the dangers of dabbling with the occult. And living with a man on a military base intimately associated with the subject, it was something she came to know a lot about.'

I raised my head slowly, defiant but also resigned. Here it

was at last, the truth I had been running from since the day they died.

'Based at Brawdy, it was inevitable your father would read the Parsons Report – your grandfather circulated it at the highest level there.'

'*Randall* circulated the report?'

'But your father showed wisdom, foresight. The potential of that report spoke to him, as it spoke to me.' The admiral smiled. 'I'd wager your grandfather will regret circulating that document for the rest of his days.' He took a step towards me. 'Do you know what your father did? When he realized the limitless power available to him through worshipping the Lawless One? He joined our order, even involved his own family. The ritual of initiation requires the sacrifice of an innocent. A child who is selected for exposure to demonic manifestations. You.'

He paused for a moment, and I felt a sensation of awakening within me. It was similar to the sensation that had accompanied my visions, except it was stronger.

'The exposure left you damaged; you were mentally scarred, anxious, made worse when your parents died. But your grandfather's religion, his devotion to you, gave you some protection. He helped you to forget. But now –' the admiral's tawny eyes gleamed an eerie yellow '– your grandfather is nowhere to be seen, and you have no faith. No hope.'

The sky cracked. I was incapable of speech. My head was whirling.

'Remember that day, old chap? The sun was setting over St Brides Bay. Your mother was away at the Croughton protests. And that night your father asked . . .' *whether I wanted to ride with him on his motorcycle.*

The memory broke in as it had done many times over the

years. The difference now was it had colour and sound: the radio announcer was saying something about Harold Macmillan, and I could taste the sausage and egg that Dad had made me for dinner.

'Do you remember going with him, Robert? Do you remember he . . .' *whispered to me about that place. The women damned as witches, put on trial there and burned. The children who had chased a yellow balloon through the woods in the hotel grounds. A balloon . . .* 'that floated among the branches, back and forth, back and forth . . .' *a balloon, bright and yellow and shining. Like a tiny sun.*

My eyes flashed open and I whispered, 'I remember!'

'But you *didn't* remember, did you?' The admiral's voice was soft, hypnotic. 'You forgot. Because your grandfather was watching. He saw what your father had exposed you to – what he had arranged – and when your parents were dead and gone, he kept you safe. Helped you. And in your ignorance you repaid him with hatred.'

He gazed at me with a half-smile on his dry lips, and the dreaded memories flooded back.

We went somewhere. I'm seeing it again, all of it. Reliving it in my head.

– 57 –

February 1963

Eleven years old.

Mum hasn't returned from RAF Croughton. When she does she'll have forgotten what happened there and how she lost her sight in one eye.

Dad entering my bedroom. I see the whites of his eyes as he tells me to get out of bed, to get dressed.

His heavy bike wobbling underneath me as we get on; the catch of the ignition and the snarl of the engine. We're flying, I think, as his bike rips along the coastal road, Dad leaning over the handlebars, head low.

It's a clear night, oddly warm for a winter's evening.

'This way.'

We leave the motorcycle in the shadows of the Haven Hotel to walk through ancient trees and wet leaves, twigs snapping beneath our feet.

After a short while we enter a clearing. And I freeze. Five figures – hooded and robed – stand before me in a circle.

'Don't be afraid,' Dad whispers. 'Stand in the centre.'

I don't want to. In the middle of the circle are dark silhouettes

I can't make out clearly. Logs perhaps?

I look back at my father with pleading eyes.

'Do as I say, son.'

The robed figures part and beckon me forward, but I only manage a few faltering steps. Something makes me look up. Dangling from the gnarled branches overheard is an assortment of broken wooden crucifixes.

'Dad?' I say, looking around me.

No sign of him but the five hooded figures have become six.

'Get in the circle,' a woman's voice commands.

Though every muscle screams against it, I obey.

I see now that the dark shapes in the circle are not logs but the eviscerated corpses of three black Labradors. The creatures have been blinded; their eyes are nothing but black holes.

My stomach lurches sickeningly and I'm screaming now: 'Mum! *Mum! Help!*'

'Shut up!' Dad barks, and I obey.

One of the dogs is still alive. It whimpers, one paw twitching.

'Sit down on the ground,' says the woman's voice.

She isn't talking to me.

A dark figure advances from the shadows, kneels beside me on the tangled floor. A girl on the verge of adulthood. She looks me in the eye. It's Araceli. Her expression is pained, her hands clasped behind her back.

'It's time,' one of the figures says, and the three figures in front of me break the circle to stand behind me.

I stare ahead into the gaps between the trees, back in the direction from which we came. Towards the sea. Towards Stack Rocks.

Araceli doesn't move.

'Keep looking that way,' Dad instructs, and that's when I

catch the light in the distance, flashing through the spikes of dark trees. 'Don't move.'

His words sweep away any hope of escape. I squint hard, listening to my breathing, focusing on the light. A sickly yellow light.

I think perhaps it's a lighthouse, because that's what it looks like, but I know it's not. It's bright, brighter than Venus. And it's moving.

The hooded figures chant faster, harder: ancient words, evil words charged with power. My impression is that they are causing this light to exist; they are calling it. This thought strips away any vestiges of calm and leaves me with the most awful sensation of helplessness.

'Here they come,' Dad whispers.

From Stack Rocks the light arcs across the sky – it is astonishingly quick – leaving no trail. No sound.

For a moment there is just darkness. Then it is above the trees directly ahead of me, slowly descending. It's an enormous eye, I think, winking at me. It appears to be dripping molten metal, and as it falls it swings with the motion of a pendulum, scattering beams through the trees.

Next to me Araceli begins to cry.

I call out. No response. They've gone, I think. The adults have left us here.

There is a sudden blistering flash, so hot across my face I assume the yellow ball has exploded, but when I open my eyes I see that I am wrong. The light hasn't exploded; it has transformed. I'm staring at a dome-shaped object, some sort of craft. It's at least twenty feet wide and dark grey with a rough surface. It looks mechanical.

I feel my bile rise as a stench overcomes me. It arrives the moment the craft releases two balls – each about four feet wide and covered with spikes. They remind me of sea mines.

They come rolling across the tangled ground. Towards us. One ball connects with Araceli's leg. She screams as its spikes dig in and I watch, transfixed, horrified, as the ball drags her towards the craft.

Araceli's eyes scorch into me and nightmarish images flash in my mind: debauched ceremonies at her father's hotel, men whispering unholy prayers, Araceli, just a teenager, tied down on the floor, animal guts spilled around her. And, watching from the shadows, my father. Araceli screams again.

The other spiked ball rolls towards me.

Suddenly someone grabs me, heaves me up. 'You're coming with me,' Grandfather's voice hisses urgently in my ear. He breaks into a run, stumbles, and we hit the ground with a thud. My head throbs, but I manage to open my eyes.

No sign of Araceli but the domed craft is still visible. So is the spiked ball. It rolls but not towards me; it heads for Grandfather.

'No!' The spike catches him; skin rips.

Then he is on his feet and pulling me up and away, but my head hurts and I am shaking and so he heaves me onto his shoulders and struggles through the maze of trees.

We reach his car, and he bundles me into the back. I stare at him blankly, at the blood, bright and flowing, from his torn-open cheek. The jagged cut looks painful. And I want him to feel the pain. I do not know why, just as I do not know how he had found us or for how long he had been watching.

'I'm going back for her,' he says coarsely. 'Robert, my boy, your father will be punished and I will protect you. You will not remember this night.'

I close my eyes and surrender to his promise.

– 58 –

Stack Rocks Fort, St Brides Bay

Thunder split the sky. Shadows leaped at me from every corner of the dilapidated gun chamber. *Everything Grandfather did was for me*, I thought, and from out of the past my own demons reached with guilty claws.

Grandfather's voice: *You were in a terrible way. Hysterical, kicking over furniture, writhing on the floor. You were a violent child, boy. But I brought you through the worst of it. On one occasion you lashed out at the other children in school.*

'He knew,' I muttered. 'All this time he knew.' *That's why he was wary of me.*

The admiral nodded as I looked at him desperately. The betrayal of the man I trusted and a woman I had come here to help had left me empty. Yet I wanted to feel anger and rage. He had told me my father had sacrificed me and my parents had been murdered. I wanted the rage to flare from me and burn the admiral.

And now Araceli was lighting black candles.

'What does this make me?' I managed to ask.

The admiral met my gaze. There was a horrible intent behind

his eyes that could have been madness or determination. 'The night your father exposed you to the sky spectres, your grandfather intervened, disrupting the process of demonizing you and Araceli. But something, some small residue, remained.'

'What do you mean, "something"?'

'Remember the strange disturbances in and around your home?' the admiral asked. 'Electrical appliances malfunctioning? Odd sounds? The telephone ringing at strange times? The spontaneous movement of objects?'

Only as a boy. I didn't want to give him the satisfaction of being right, so I shook my head. I had always known that I was different to other people and felt guilty for it.

And there was something else. Grandfather had always regarded me warily; I used to think he hated me. But perhaps he was simply protecting himself from whatever abilities the process of demonization had awakened in me.

As I struggled to process this the admiral said, 'Your anxieties – the buried memories – are the after-effect of psychic abilities induced in you as a child after your own sighting of a sky spectre. It's not your own fear, anxiety and guilt that make you the way you are; it's the anxiety and fear and guilt of everyone around you. Your brain is tuned to these neuroses like a radio. Your subconscious awareness of other people's problems has consumed you.' He came right up to me and added, 'You should be thanking me. Without my guidance it might have driven you mad.'

Time halted with this revelation. The moment I inhabited felt like an eternity of loneliness. The admiral's shadow wavered on the decrepit stonework of the chamber. Behind him I could see Little Haven flickering in the glow of an evil light, and as I pictured the sky watchers huddled in the darkness, I realized what was going to happen.

The admiral turned towards Araceli, who was looking out over the sea. 'Do you know,' he said, 'I remember the days when Robert was a bright young thing in the halls of power. Wilding, oh, that rising star, waging his war against the injustice of foreign weapons based in the UK. Battling scientific progress, demanding the abolition of nuclear weapons, calling for the accountability of American bases.'

He gave me a pitying look. 'And look at you now. Trembling before the greatest weapon of all.'

I looked on as the admiral prepared to summon some unspeakable intelligence. 'Begin!' he ordered his daughter, and Araceli began muttering strange sounds that were almost exactly like the ones made by the children at the school. She was possessed, she had to be. God only knew how many times her father and his confederates had exposed her to the sky spectres.

The admiral said, 'What do you feel now, old chap? Rage, despair?'

I didn't need to answer, my emotions were graven on my face.

'Good. That will help.'

Before the altar, the admiral closed his eyes and in a low, controlled voice began murmuring invocations.

For a very short moment everything was quiet.

A: We felt this terrible rumble – that was when Stack Rocks opened up.

Q. Stack Rocks is about half a mile offshore from Little Haven?

A. That's right.

Q. Could you see Stack Rocks from the pub?

A. In daytime, yes.

Q. But this was at night. How did you know the rocks had . . . uh . . . opened up?

A. Well, that's the difficult part.

Q. Just tell the committee what happened in your own words, please, Ms Wheal.

A. A shaft of light came out of the sea, just off the headland next to Giant's Point. Scared the life out of me. It lit up the whole bay. It was like a tower, beaming up.

Q. And this light was coming out of Stack Rocks?

A. Yes. All silver. Then it turned red. So bright.

Q. What time did this occur?

A. About quarter to midnight. That was when people were running around, screaming and shouting, you know.

Q. With excitement?

A. No. I thought we were having some sort of earthquake. And I followed the others outside.

Q. Why did you go outside if you were afraid?

A. The light . . . it drew you. You wanted to walk towards it.

Q. What happened after the light appeared?

A. After? That was when hell opened.

– 59 –

Stack Rocks Fort, St Brides Bay

A concussive column of light – silver then red – burst through the floor, passing up through the centre of the circle which enclosed the pentacle. My face stung with the rushing blast of fiery air.

'He is coming,' the admiral cried, personifying the obscenity that was about to appear.

I was only five feet or so away from the column of flaming light, watching the ripples of heat spiralling out of the floor. Araceli was staring into it, her eyes as wide as planets, and I realized the heat was drying my drenched clothes. To my disgust I found the sensation almost pleasant.

The gun chamber filled with a swirling mist and the putrid stench of sulphur. I didn't want to look at the pentacle, but it drew my gaze as water draws a dowsing rod. The centre of the pentacle was a curtain of shimming radiance, and within that light, gradually taking form, becoming solid, was the shape of . . . something monstrous.

I looked with growing revulsion at the legs – not human legs. They were glimmering silver, as thick as pillars. And some sort of a face was taking shape, a diabolical cluster of interwoven shadows. I watched as gradually the light became brighter until the materialization was complete and towering over me.

'My Lord Taranis,' the admiral cried. 'Welcome to your new domain!'

It looks just like the Watcher at the window, I thought. A silver giant in a shimmering one-piece spacesuit. The mass of shadows where its face should have been had solidified to form a convex black visor, which glowed. The visor flickered with features that were at once recognizable and unfathomable: the face of a cherub, the face of a man, a lion and then an eagle.

It's reaching for my mind, I thought. And what I felt then was an emotion that went far beyond terror. *But why doesn't it advance? Why doesn't it come for me?*

The Watcher was so large, exuded such power, it should easily have breached the circle. But when it tried, it flinched back, as if an invisible barrier was stopping it.

The admiral addressed me: 'Only your sacrifice can unleash the ultimate sky spectre.'

In those breathless seconds I saw what the admiral intended. Not by his actions or any words. I saw it in my mind: panic in the streets of the village, people running, falling over one another as the sky above them burned.

This awful ceremony, the admiral's chanting of blasphemous prayers, his knife, had one purpose: my soul was to be offered to the Watcher, this *thing* that had possessed minds, projected fearsome images into the skies, invoked fear so that it might feed.

'No,' I pleaded, looking desperately into the eyes of the man I had always trusted.

The admiral raised his knife.

– 60 –

Darkness.

Then the distant crashing of the surf against the cliffs.

I was floating on seawater that should have been freezing and turbulent. A presence was watching over me. 'You shouldn't be here, Robert. It's too soon.' My father's voice. Never a man who could show his emotions, but in this nebulous moment that was at once disconnected from the world and part of it, he had returned to me.

I saw the dark water around me break as a bony shape rose from out of the sea.

'Dad?'

He looked diminished and frail, an echo of the sea, nothing like the muscular soldier who had yelled at my mother, demanded she give up her anti-nuclear protests. His teeth were black, the skin of his face split and raw in patches. 'I should have listened to her,' he said in a coarse voice. 'I should have listened to your grandfather too. Son, I am haunted by shame for my mistakes.'

It was him all right. Only it wasn't, couldn't be, because my father was dead.

'Where am I?'

Lying on my back on the still water, I could see the stars above, could hear the suck of the tide, could see the lights of Little Haven on the distant shore. But what was keeping me afloat? Why wasn't I wet or cold or sinking? I didn't care. I was alive. Somehow. But not physically. None of this was real. I was drifting in a space between two worlds.

'I came to ask for your forgiveness. And to guide you.' He looked at me with sorrowful eyes and said, 'There isn't much time.'

The way his form merged with the darkness and the water on which I was somehow floating was particularly unsettling. It made me think of ancient legends of creatures dwelling beneath the sea. And I understood that he wasn't real.

'You must understand how we died and why you are special.'

'Then tell me.'

But I wasn't sure I was ready to hear what I feared the most. I only knew this: I had been wrong to blame Grandfather and I wished I could see him again and tell him so.

'What happened to you and Mum?' I asked through numb lips.

My father's lifeless eyes were swimming with guilt and his once-handsome face was contorted in a way that communicated unspeakable truths. I was afraid, not of him, but of what he would tell me. Though I knew it was necessary for me to hear it. How did the old saying go? *Tell the truth and shame the devil.*

'It was the night of the Great Flood. December 1963. I think you realize there was nothing natural about that event.'

'The sky spectres?'

He nodded sorrowfully. 'They had been summoned. And your brain was coming to life in new, remarkable ways. But your mother –' his eyes dropped '– it was as if all the torments of the world were at work in her body. It was ten months since Croughton, ten months since the protest and the arrests.'

My breath became shallow as I remembered Mum coming back to us afterwards, blind in one eye, her face horribly burned, disorientated. Forgetful. I remembered her nausea, vomiting and weakness. I remembered the painful blisters on her skin.

He nodded and said in a slow voice, 'When I realized she had witnessed a sky spectre, I brought her to Ravenstone Farm. Randall would know what to do. But there was no controlling her. She ran from the house down to the cliffs.'

'What then?'

'Your grandfather had the courage and the faith to confront what I never could. As you will discover, if you go back.' Under the stars in that other place, somewhere beyond the sea, my father looked down on me with an expression I had never seen him wear in life. 'Go back. Warn the world.'

'The world won't believe me.'

Then warn someone who will. You've always fought for justice and peace, but your fears have paralysed you. Rebel now, my boy. Use your one true defence.'

'And what is that?'

'Faith.'

The air became tense and I felt the water beneath me solidifying.

'Certain minds, minds like yours, can tune into the extra-dimensional world. You're doing it now, Robert. Use it. You are not defeated.'

And I wasn't. Not yet.

The ghostly shape of my father receded, merged with the glassy water and the darkness and the distant shore. The stars above me began to spin.

FROM *THE MIND POSSESSED: A PERSONAL INVESTIGATION INTO THE BROAD HAVEN TRIANGLE*

BY DR R. CAXTON (CLEMENTINE PRESS, 1980) P.213

11.50 p.m. Praying that Frobisher would be all right, I reached the black bulk of the Haven Hotel up on the hill just as St Brides Bay turned crimson. I could still hear the village drains gurgling with the sudden downpour; could still see the narrow lanes turning into dark rivers; could still see the slow procession of people heading for the end of Giant's Point.

I came to the great door of the Haven Hotel, surprised it was unlocked, and pushed it open. The smell in the main hall was of wet leaves.

'Randall?' I called, and my heart kicked into overdrive as I realized that anyone – or anything – could be in here with me.

I went into the ground-floor dining room and from the window looked down on to Little Haven. A second later I witnessed the spectacle that has for ever remained burned onto my retinas: out to sea a great column of light was punching out of Stack Rocks, up into the clotted clouds, as if it had exploded right out of hell.

Then I saw a vast shadow break through the clouds and descend towards the sea. It appeared in the sky immediately above Stack Rocks Island, and as it did a low rumbling sound came down from the heavens.

Those who survived that night would all give varying

descriptions of the object, but most agreed it was like no aircraft they'd ever seen. Gigantic, triangular, emerging from rolls of swirling mist. If it had any engines, they weren't making any sound.

An advanced airship, some sort of balloon?

I heard a low bellowing roar and for an instant night turned to day: the craft projected a great red radiance that washed the shore of Little Haven in a shimmering glow. As it did I thought, *We should have evacuated the village.*

The rain was torrential. The river above the school burst its banks. Water cascaded down the steep hill towards Little Haven. Anyone who saw the water and mud and sewage from the plant at the top of the hill come pouring down would have said there was something unnatural about the sight, but the truth is there weren't many people looking. They were on Giant's Point, as still as statues, gazing up.

The school, where all of this strangeness began, was hit first. A pole carrying electric wires was ripped right out of the ground by the torrent. Cables snapped, sparks flew, and under a bellowing wind the pole crashed down onto the school hall.

The school hall exploded. And the water rushed on.

By 11.55 it was sweeping through the village towards the cove. The post office, the pub and the church were flooded, and those people who remained on the seafront were swept away in the surge. A team of investigators later said it was the water in the Ram Inn that seeped through into the electrical system of the restaurant next door that caused the Nest Bistro at 42 Grove Road to explode. Even from the Haven Hotel I felt the shudder as flames leaped from the windows, licking out into the night. Then the roof came off, flipping in the wind, crashing into rivers that had been roads.

In the sky over Stack Rocks the triangular craft was rotating. Its underbelly was the source of the light beam which burst across the sky and held the village, but as I struggled to rip free from the paralysis that kept me there, watching, I couldn't think of it purely as a light beam. More of a death ray.

– 61 –

Awake. Rain was sweeping into the fort, my island prison, and from across the black expanse of sea I heard screams, hundreds of screams – a nightmarish chorus that sounded as though all the horrors of hell were pouring into the Havens. Two realities spinning together. This world and another.

What happens when they clash?

The Watcher was still in the chamber with us, its broad silvery outline flickering in and out as if it was only halfway through the portal or was about to change its appearance. Through the nearest casemate I could see the glow of something in the sky reflecting off the seawater and, beyond, Little Haven drenched in an eerie light. Something told me it wasn't the light of the blood moon.

I've been led here, I've been used as bait.

And the admiral's knife came down.

I rolled, heard the strike of the blade on stone. Heard the admiral's frustrated cry.

He came at me again. I swept my leg into his, flooring him. Scrambled to my feet.

'I came willingly,' I cried, looking down at him. He started coughing so badly I wondered if he would be able to breathe.

'But not for this. I came for justice and peace.' I glanced at Araceli, who was now still and quiet next to the altar. 'I came in the name of this woman's protection.'

'Look at her eyes!' the admiral said, his voice full of rage. 'She can't *hear* you.'

The Watcher flickered again, and this time a sickly green glow traced its shape.

I reached for Araceli with the part of my mind that had been lighting up these past few days, the part of my mind that saw the future and had dismissed the Watcher at the window, but there was nothing. All trace of the woman I had once thought warm, attractive, had burned away.

'Stop this!' A hoarse voice bellowed around the seething space of that chamber.

Who could have come at this crucial moment? Who could have made it across the rough sea at the heart of the storm?

I wheeled around and relief swept through me.

Grandfather. His face was dirty and drawn, his greatcoat muddy and black.

'How the hell did you get here?' I asked.

No answer.

Something bothered me about his appearance, but I couldn't pin it down.

'Randall Llewellyn Pritchard,' the admiral snarled. He was on his feet now and looked both surprised and furious. 'You are a welcome addition to this sabbat.'

'You think I'm afraid?' Grandfather rasped. His head shook as he faltered forward – a weary soldier. 'What else have I to lose? You took my life when you took my daughter.'

'You should be afraid,' the admiral said. 'Actions have conse-quences and must be reconciled with them. Not in the manner of a Christian. Not by turning the other cheek or by making excuses for the offender. Actions that are wrong must be reconciled by the way of the Watchers.'

The admiral came for me then, quick as a dog, seized me and raised his knife.

How is he so strong?

The Watcher was towering before us, its putrid stench in my nostrils.

The admiral addressed it with reverence: 'My Lawless One, Beast of the Apocalypse, Duke of the Thirteenth Gate, accept this man as testament to our loyalty, an original moon child, who came of his own free will. I demand you claim his soul!'

The eyes of the Watcher flashed.

'You demand it?'

Hard and commanding, the voice did not come from anywhere around me, nor press against my ears; it arrived directly in my head.

'Who else?' the admiral said to the Watcher. 'I am your brethren. I have led the others in worship of you. And with obedience and will, it is I who have summoned you here.'

'Why now?'

'To fulfil your plan as it is foretold.'

A distant siren wailed from the shores of Little Haven.

'Just listen! The masses will live in misery, in fear of the skies. They will feel the emancipation of the Lawless One. Take what is offered. Grant to me what is promised.'

Grandfather said grittily, 'You can't control their thoughts.'

'Who is this?' the Watcher demanded. It shifted but again failed to break the circle.

Grandfather seemed to understand. 'It can't break your

mental force,' he muttered to me, before raising his eyes defiantly and addressing the Watcher.

'I've been waiting for you, oh, a long long time.' He shook his head with deliberate purpose. 'Demonic entities masquerading as aliens, using wicked humans to run the new world order. But you need a moon child to do it. Or someone who has sinned.'

The sky roared. Jagged shafts of light penetrated the casemates as the air vibrated.

'I offer knowledge. Secrets,' cried Randall.

'*Speak then. Offer.*'

'First let the moon child go.'

'No!' the admiral shouted. 'My Lord, this man is disruptive and clever. You must destroy him.'

'*I decide who lives who dies.*'

The admiral's grip on me slackened for a moment. I scrambled away to Grandfather's side and immediately noticed the old man's shoulders were shaking.

'You all right, boy?'

'I am now,' I managed.

His eyes met mine. I saw him draw a breath, saw his bottom lip tremble.

'What's happening?'

Grandfather took my hands. There was little strength in his grip, and his calloused hands were icy. 'It's the end, boy. It's falling apart out there.'

'No. You know what to do. We're going to be OK. Aren't we?'

'*You* will be fine. Tell the story. Warn people.' I saw the shimmer of tears in his eyes. 'Signs and lying wonders, boy – that's all they are. Like your doubts and fears that never went away but taught you to fight. This ends now. But before it does, there's something I want you to know.'

'Grandfather, there's no –'

'I love you, boy. I love you dearly. And I always did.'

He turned to face the Watcher and the admiral. Even though the world seemed to shake, I saw a controlled calm come into his face.

'It is I who warned of the sky spectres,' Grandfather announced. 'I am the reason Jack Parsons and the others who revered his work came here to the Havens.'

The Watcher twisted its head towards me.

'An original moon child. He can unleash the powers of hell upon this world if his soul is given unto you,' said Randall.

Apparently revitalized, the admiral came for me again, and I felt his cold knife against my throat. He shouted at Grandfather, 'Choose, Randall! You will die tonight. But if you want your grandson to live, bow down before the Lawless One.'

'Grandfather,' I whispered, 'I have faith in you.'

That was when the Watcher released a horrific sound that reverberated around the gun chamber. But still it didn't break the circle. *Something's holding it back.*

'Your grandfather has failed,' the admiral said to me. I felt his knife draw blood. It was trickling down my neck. 'The sky spectres have been released!' he then declared to the room. 'Seal the portal, swear the Oath of the Abyss.'

Suddenly I understood. I looked far into my own mind and made a decision to release the hate I had felt for Grandfather for so long. To let it go and believe in him totally.

'Bow down in the name of the Lawless One if you want your boy to live.'

Grandfather's eyes were suddenly hard with an emotion I couldn't read. 'He's not my boy,' he said in a flat voice.

I thought I was used to his surprises, but what was this?

'Cut his throat,' said Grandfather.

I stared at him, blinking. He was bluffing, wasn't he?

'Did you hear what I said?' Grandfather said to the admiral.

I tried not to let my uncertainty show, tried not to flinch.

'I said cut his throat!'

This time I did flinch. This time the shock travelled all the way to my lungs.

The admiral nodded to himself. 'The great prophet finally understands.'

'I always understood,' Grandfather said, looking into my eyes, which must have been wide and stunned. 'Since the day he came to live with me. Why do you think I drove him away? A lonely child who drew the emissaries of wickedness to our door. I knew his soul was corrupt.'

'Grandfather, please!' My voice cracked on the last word.

Then an unforgettable disclosure. Unforgettable because it broke me.

'It was I who killed your father, boy. At the cliff edge, after your mother jumped.'

He gave me a look that pierced my soul and broke my heart and made my faith in him bleed out.

'The look on his face when I pushed him . . .' He paused, pulled in a breath. 'You were there, Robert. You saw it all. And I helped you forget.'

'You *made* him forget,' the admiral said.

'As you made your daughter forget, made the headmaster forget what he had done to those poor children at the school.'

The light of hope inside me went out.

'Finish this,' the admiral said to the Watcher. 'Take their souls.'

There was a blinding light, a scream to torture the ears, and Randall dropped to his knees. I wanted to run to him but couldn't move; wanted to call out to him but couldn't speak. His cry competed with the thunder that ripped the sky. Then the life went out of his eyes and Grandfather's body slumped forward. When his face hit the stone floor there was a sharp *snap*, then thick dark blood pooled around his head.

My grandfather was dead.

When I looked up again, I saw that the Watcher had changed: there was no silver suit, no helmet, no convex black visor. Gaunt, misted within a black shadow that fell to the ground, the figure still towered over all of us, and it had acquired a face.

My God, that face.

I was staring at a sharp beak that reminded me of the raven-nosed masks worn by fourteenth-century plague doctors. That beak must have been half a foot long, and curved up into two black holes that might have been eye sockets. Only there were no eyes; just hollows that blazed with a red light – an evil light – that paralysed me.

The Watcher advanced, breaking the circle, and the admiral's grip on me tightened.

In a flash I understood what Grandfather had done. My faith in him had held the Watcher back. Grandfather had broken that faith, so now the Watcher could move, could break its circle. Could attack any one of us – including the admiral.

Throwing all caution to the wind, I forced myself to look again upon that beaked face, those burning sockets. This time I didn't just look at them; I looked *into* them, and I whispered, 'You will not harm me.'

The black candles spluttered.

'What are you doing?' the admiral said. His voice shook with fury. His blade was cut further into my skin. I should have been terrified. But what did I have to lose?

'This man has summoned you prematurely,' I told the Watcher. 'He doesn't react to your presence because he has protected himself. He means to control you.'

The Watcher glowed with crimson light and the admiral released me. He stood frozen in the centre of the chamber.

'Is this the truth?'

'Control is necessary to maintain the new order,' the admiral protested. 'Master, do not doubt me. We will have this world. Fire will rain from the heavens and I will lead them in your name.'

The entire fort shook. The admiral dropped to his knees, face contorted with agony. His knife clattered to the floor.

It came to me in a flash: *The conscious mind can exert control over the material universe.* That's why the admiral had brought me here, why he had wanted to use me.

The Watcher's gaze stabbed the admiral's face.

My old mentor cried out, 'Help me, Robert. Help me!'

And a part of me wanted to – the part that remembered the way he had first taken me under his wing in Parliament. I thought of that freezing morning overlooking Westminster when, on the roof of the House of Commons, he had told me to keep faith – to never give in. Then horrific images surfaced: the committee room in Parliament exploding into flame, Selina's coffin sinking into its grave and finally the awful compassion in Grandfather's face as he sacrificed himself.

My mind drifted: *You can't control events, Robert. Only how you respond to them.*

'You wanted a world of pain and suffering,' I said softly, 'well feel it now.' I only had to concentrate for a second, and the admiral jerked his head back; his hand went to his heart and his eyes bulged. I focused, really concentrated. Everything at that moment felt different. Looked different. I was experiencing a state of heightened awareness I'd known only in dreams. Textures and landscapes, sounds and fragrances, unfurled before me, energy fields and particles – the very fabric of reality.

Certain minds can tune into the extra-dimensional world. You're doing it now, Robert. Use it.

In rapid flashes I glimpsed the future and the past, worlds that are and have never been. And I understood: the normal, solid world was just a facade, an illusion of normality.

I willed him to die. And the admiral collapsed, clawing the air.

'Robert, stop! Stop!'

I thought of Selina. I felt sure the attack on Parliament had been orchestrated by the admiral and had channelled my anger. I was pulling on invisible threads to manifest my will directly on him. From nowhere I heard myself mutter the incantation from the church: '*Gha D'rcest Cthasska, Ha D'rcest Cthassiss.*' As the words fell from my lips, the sigils etched themselves in the air in front of me, rendered in thin strokes of shining silver, as if my tongue was writing on the world with liquid light. Sliding onto the admiral's chest as if projected there, they proliferated, entwining about his entire body like a living tattoo.

He screamed.

Araceli was staggering towards me. There was something human in her eyes again. I felt a link open to her mind, giving me direct access to her subconscious. Ghosts of her emotions buffeted my awareness like a psychic storm, her fear an enveloping chill, her worry for her daughter a stinging lash. But stronger was her reluctance to believe she had done what her father had instructed – deceived me, lured me here – and that she had involved her own daughter in a web of deceit and darkness.

She came close, not even looking at the Watcher, which towered before us, and wrapped her hand around mine. 'Stop now, stop. Your grandfather would never have wanted you to kill him.'

I felt a smile come on my lips, knew she was right, and released the admiral from the mental vice I had seized him in. And was suddenly horrified, disgusted at myself.

The Watcher's arcane voice burst in my head: *'Finish him, finish him.'*

Scalding air washed over me. I could feel the suffering the Watcher had inflicted on this village, how its malign influence had seeped into its consciousness, drawn people here since Jack Parsons' experiments, made men, women and children fearful and corrupted minds. I was in no doubt: the Watcher was the reason people had drowned. It was the reason the locals never walked the cliffs alone, saw strange lights in the sky and told stories about mutilated farm animals. It was the reason my parents were dead.

I would not stoop to its level. I stepped back, relinquished my hold on the admiral and watched as he staggered to his feet, tripped and fell into the circle.

There was a blast of ferocious light. The admiral lifted his head and tried to raise himself. Looking at Araceli at my side, he said, 'My little girl,' then raised his voice. 'Get away from him! Continue our work!'

Blood ran from his ears, from his nose, his eyes. A putrid stench filled the trembling air.

'Oh God,' Araceli said. She started forward.

'My lungs.' The admiral dropped to his elbows. His face was yellowing, his eyes pleading, bulging. 'Araceli, my lungs . . .' A phlegmy racking sound emanated from his chest and blood erupted from his mouth. His whole body lurched as he retched, retched, retched. Blood puddled around him. Blood everywhere.

Araceli stared at him with glazed, horrified eyes.

'No!' he growled desperately. Then his body slumped forward, lifeless.

Araceli dug her fingers into my arm and I felt her shudder, either in grief in guilt or horror.

The Watcher's beaked face stared down at me with nightmarish clarity, and in its eyes I saw Little Haven in flames. *'Give yourself to me. Swear the Oath of the Abyss.'*

A burst of radiant red light came down from the sky, reflected off the sea, flooding the island fort. The earth trembled. Sirens and screams sounded from the village.

'I have a better suggestion. I'll have hope. Faith. In the people of our world.' I fixed my eyes on Grandfather's lifeless body, the jagged scar on his face. 'He thought you were from hell. So did Jack Parsons. And maybe you *are* from hell. Or maybe that's just what you wanted us to believe – like maybe you wanted everyone in this village, everyone in our world, to think that the sky spectres were from outer space.'

The Watcher twisted and shuddered.

Grandfather, Grandfather . . .

'You hear all those people screaming? Well done! You've made them believe. All those little people. The blessed and the damned. Husbands and wives. Brothers and sisters. They're terrified now because you tricked them. And now you're tasting their terror.'

As the fear in the Havens had grown, the Watchers had

grown, and now they wanted the one they had marked with their power fourteen years ago. Me.

I spread my arms wide. 'So what's stopping you? Feed on *my* fear!'

Its beaked face yawned open, releasing a burst of unholy light that drenched me from head to toe, and a raw wind ripped into the fort. And somehow, perhaps because I wasn't afraid any more, I pulled out a formidable voice that convinced me I could win.

'I fought for my country! And my grandfather fought for our country. He foresaw the coming of your sky spectres!'

The Watcher howled. But that wasn't what made me raise my voice. What did that was my fury, my self-belief. My faith in the man who had raised me to be the man I was.

'Do you think you can just use people? Expect them to forget? Do you think secrets as black and depraved as yours can be supressed?' I raised my chin.

I saw its immense form flicker as it howled again and understood that it wasn't my physical strength that enabled me to resist; it was the force within me, planted long ago. Secrets had consequences. I had faced down my fears with faith in myself. I had learned there were worse threats to our world than military weapons.

'I will stop you,' I vowed quietly. 'I deny you in the name of this woman's protection. I deny you in the name of truth.' I closed my eyes, blinked out a trickling tear and pictured my mother. My father too. 'And I deny you in the name of the man who gave us hope. Randall Llewellyn Pritchard!'

The gun chamber shook. Cracks leaped through the floor and up the walls as if the earth itself was splitting open. And the Watcher threw back its head and staggered back, releasing a wrenching sound that went beyond a scream.

'*Give us leave to go. Release us!*'

'I do!' I shouted, remembering the ancient prayer from the church. 'I cast you out!'

There was a thunderous explosion from across the bay, and a flash of white light spliced through the night to Stack Rocks.

I stared at the Havens, where the huddled houses across the sea were now illuminated by flickering flames. A pillar of fire rose from where Broad Haven Primary School had stood.

— 62 —

It was hard to believe the Watcher was gone.

'Araceli!' My voice competed with the bellowing wind, the water crashing below.

The walls and floor were still shaking. *You have to get her out.* At any minute this place would be underwater. But there was no way to escape: the boat had been smashed to pieces. A freezing hand gripped mine. I felt the squeeze of hope in my hand and in my heart.

'There is a way,' she said urgently.

Araceli grabbed a stone and chiseled the metal band off, then led me around the curved edge of the room until the smooth stone floor gave way to a rockier surface. I felt a rush of freezing air. *We're entering a cave – or a tunnel.*

And then I realized what it was about Grandfather's appearance that had nagged at me when he'd burst into the room. He had been dishevelled, bloody – but dry.

'You're sure?' I asked.

'Trust me.'

'Wait.'

Against every impulse I went back, picking my way back to my grandfather. I knelt, touched his rough face and allowed my fingers to trace the scar on his cheek. Which emotion to feel first? There were so many: remorse and fear and anger. The thought of myself as a little boy under his secret protection magnified every emotion and made my parents' legacy complete.

I had grown up, moved away, and left him to grow old alone. And I'd preserved the guilt, kept it inside. Grief welled up inside me then. I couldn't help reflecting on the similarities between loneliness and obsession – emotions that bred sad and destructive and addictive behaviours – the enemies of peace and restfulness – and then I held those thoughts down and pressed a kiss onto Grandfather's forehead.

Peeping out from inside his jacket was a booklet. I wasn't surprised to see it was the Parsons Report. I claimed it, struggled to my feet and made my way back to Araceli.

'We have to go.'

I was right: there was a tunnel. We were passing under the seabed, I felt sure, because above us we could hear the crashing of waves. Our only light my torch, we stumbled through the damp darkness for what felt like for ever. I assumed the tunnel had been dug when the fort was constructed, but it was not well maintained. Araceli was breathing heavily and her face was drawn. But she held my hand tightly. I had asked her where the tunnel led but she was silent, and all I could do was remember Grandfather's dry coat and have faith.

Finally the floor began to slope up and a few minutes later I made out the faint light of an opening ahead. Araceli had slowed, and now instead of her leading me I was pulling her along. As I helped her over the rubble into the space beyond, the reason for her reluctance became clear.

It's the cellar of the Haven hotel. This is how Grandfather got out to the fort. How long had he known it was here?

I saw the old furniture, the boxes of black candles Araceli had claimed her mother kept for power failures, a fragment of the inscription that had marked the location of the tunnel on a brick lying at my feet. My mind raced, making connections: this place had belonged to Araceli's father – the admiral. He had been stationed here during the war when Jack Parsons had conducted his experiments, had read Grandfather's Parsons Report and had joined a deranged cult, then manipulated my father and Araceli and God knows how many others from the village.

Araceli was gasping for air now.

'Come on,' I said, leading her up the stairs. 'Come away.'

I planned to take her to the dining room, to sit her down and find a dusty bottle of brandy to take the edge off the shock. *It's just shock. Just shock. The Watcher is gone.* But there was a man in the hall blocking our way.

– 63 –

Dr Caxton was shockingly pale and struggling to speak. 'You have to see!' he said. 'Come quickly!'

'It's over,' I said, staggering past him with Araceli to the dining room. 'We defeated it.'

Then I saw through the highest window what had petrified the psychologist and a new horror took hold of me.

'My God . . .'

Roads had turned to rivers, trees were ripped up and cottages burning. About fifty or sixty people were huddled down on Giant's Point, gazing at the sky.

I looked at the devastation and thought, *I did this*. All along I was too slow to see the true nature of the phenomenon. Too preoccupied with every threat except the one that mattered most: a demonic influence that painted visions in the sky designed to deceive us.

Dr Caxton's gaze held me. 'You actually *saw* the force that caused this?'

I nodded, the movement feeling slow and dreamlike. The Watcher was a memory now, a nightmare. 'I questioned it, defeated it, cast it out.'

His face looked suddenly panicked. 'What did it say to you, Robert?'

'It vanished, like it couldn't stand to be in my presence.'

'But what did it *say*?' he almost screamed.

My breath caught. I felt my heart racing. 'It pleaded with me for release,' I answered. My voice was a whisper because I knew what was coming next.

The psychologist was looking straight at me as he recited a passage from the Book of Matthew, a passage I'd read less than a week ago, standing in my flat in London, flicking through Selina's Bible: 'The demons begged Jesus, "If you drive us out, send us into the herd of pigs." He said to them, "Go!" So they came out and went into the pigs, and the whole herd rushed down the steep bank into the lake and died in the water.'

Fear gripped Araceli, shocked her into action.

She bolted through the door and out onto the drive. I did all I could to catch up with her but froze when I saw her stumble close to the edge of the cliff. In the far distance, at the end of the jetty reaching out into the bay, I could see the sky watchers lined up at the edge of the water.

'Get away from the edge,' I yelled. 'Araceli, there's no time.' I pulled her away and held her as she shuddered in my arms.

'*No!*' She screamed. '*No, no, no, no!*'

Her cry was lost on the wind, the sky watchers simply too far away to hear. But I'll never stop hearing it.

I held Araceli as we looked down upon Giant's Point, at the men and women and their children. There was no way to stop what we were seeing, nothing we could do to help. Hopelessly I gazed out over the black waves – from Stack Rocks to Monks Cove and back to Giant's Point – as the children jumped one after another. The adults went next. Every one. Finally only a lone child remained. One little girl. Tessa.

She faced us as if she knew we were watching, and I felt the presence of the malignant demon in my mind as the little girl took three paces towards the edge of Giant's Point and raised her arms.

A gesture of despair maybe or a final goodbye.

Afterwards

Emergency services in west Wales report that the number dead in Little Haven stands at 324 with many more reported missing. Investigations into reports of strange lights in the sky are ongoing amid persistent reports by some survivors of a triangular aircraft that appeared in the sky shortly before the terrible flood destroyed much of the community. The nearest military base, RAF Brawdy, has confirmed no aircraft were flying at the time. The Welsh Office has announced an official investigation into the tragedy.

FROM *THE MIND POSSESSED: A PERSONAL INVESTIGATION INTO THE BROAD HAVEN TRIANGLE*

BY DR R. CAXTON (CLEMENTINE PRESS, 1980) P.230

The authorities blame the high rainfall, the saturated soils. They point the finger for the Havens tragedy at natural causes. I know better.

It was, Wilding believed (and I am forced to agree with him), the fault of the Parsons Elite, a malevolent international cult long established in the village with members like the local headmaster. This was founded by a snake at the heart of the British government, Admiral of the Fleet, Lord Hill Bartlett, whose family has for generations owned the Haven Hotel on Skyview Hill. The admiral, like the rocket scientist in whose name the cult was founded, believed that the skin of this world is particularly weak in locations like the Havens and that such points could be ripped open with ritual prayer and sacrificial ritual.

I remember a time, not so long ago, when I would have dismissed such a bizarre claim. Not now.

Today, if you visit the Havens, you will still find those who remember the Happenings, but you won't find many who will talk about the sky watchers who threw themselves from Giant's Point. Like the Stack Rocks Fort, their memories are suspiciously off limits. Perhaps they made themselves forget, as I tried to do. Only my wife and family know how hard I tried to forget – for their sakes and for my own sanity.

But then came a general election. Then came our new prime minister and the extraordinary meeting of the National Security Council.

And that's when a new terror began.

FROM *THE EXTRAORDINARY MEETING OF THE NATIONAL SECURITY COUNCIL*

BY JONATHAN HARRISON, FORMER SPECIAL ADVISER TO THE PRIME MINISTER

Wednesday 22 May 1979, 10 Downing Street, London

'Not one word of this will be made public,' the prime minister said from the middle of the Cabinet table. And with her usual composure she closed the file in front of her and put it aside. But no one attending the extraordinary meeting of the National Security Council at 10 Downing Street believed the matter was closed; not the politicians, not the generals, certainly not me. I said nothing, of course. Only the most reckless civil servants in Whitehall speak their minds.

A man across the table sniffed. The psychologist, a key witness. His face bore the signs of many sleepless nights, and though he was composed, his eyes were narrowed and fixed on Wilding, to his right. I saw the two exchange a look, and then Wilding's eyes slid to the chair to his left: carved mahogany, conspicuously empty.

The prime minister said, 'You have both clearly suffered an ordeal, Mr Wilding, Dr Caxton. But the events you describe, their alleged connection with the attack on Parliament, if true would create unimaginable panic.'

That had to be right. Wilding's theory was that the admiral had been at the root of it all. Perhaps he was right too. Probably he was right. But there was no proof, and I was in little doubt that the prime minister was relieved to know it.

Wilding's countenance was steely as he leaned forward and said, 'It is all true, and the people have a right to know. Don't you see? Admiral Hill Bartlett knew about the attack on Parliament *before* it happened. One of many national disasters he was planning to create fear and panic so that the Parsons Elite could more easily take control. Whoever assisted the admiral must be hunted down and punished.'

'We already know the identity of one accomplice.'

'You mean Araceli Romero?'

'She was complicit in the plan to ensnare you.'

'Her father was responsible! She did her best in the end – did what she could.'

'And how is she faring?'

'Her daughter drowned. How do you think she's faring?'

Mrs Thatcher raised an eyebrow. 'Tell us where Araceli is.'

'You have to tell me why you want her first.'

'Your presumption exceeds your abilities, Mr Wilding,' the prime minister said. 'We need Araceli. As we need you.'

'Forget me; warn the world!'

He said this with feverish passion; it was, after all, his grandfather's dying wish.

The prime minister peered at him over her half-moon spectacles. 'Domestic terror motivated by satanic rituals and lights in the sky? What would you have me do? Tell the world we are surrounded by spirits penetrating our world, that one of Britain's highest-ranking government officials was a . . . satanist?'

Caxton cleared his throat. 'Having witnessed the tragic and premature death of those civilians, I believe the people deserve justice, Prime Minister. Their families deserve the truth.'

'I don't think so. *We* don't think so.' She looked slowly around at her colleagues, all of whom nodded their assent. 'Therefore the official record will show that the limits of government interest in this affair extended only as far as a discreet investigation carried out by the Security Service, who concluded that the sightings were a clever hoax.'

'No, no, this is wrong!' Wilding shouted, his voice full of outrage. 'Bestford will help me get the truth out.' Caxton nodded his agreement.

'Feel free to try,' the prime minister said calmly, handing the Parsons Report to the general on her right. 'But it won't be difficult for us to deny the ramblings of a discredited alcoholic who had to resign his seat in Parliament.' She produced a confident smile. 'You see, Mr Wilding, now that you have so kindly handed over this report, you have no evidence. No proof. And as the admiral's body was never found, your story can quite easily be dismissed as the fantasy of an anxious and deluded mind.'

For a long moment Wilding could find no words to express his astonishment. 'But my grandfather's body was recovered,' he said finally, a little desperately.

'Cause of death unknown. With all due respect, Mr Wilding, you'll have to do rather better than that.'

Wilding sagged back in his chair. A single bead of perspiration was forming on his brow. 'Why did you bring me here?' he said hopelessly.

The prime minister looked around the table. 'Leave us,' she instructed with a wave of her hand. 'Jonathan, you stay.'

One of the ministers scowled at her imperious tone; another paused as if he felt it his duty to remain for what followed, but no one disobeyed.

I thought Dr Caxton and Wilding might relax a little when alone with her, but if anything they only looked more on edge.

Thatcher stood and wandered over to the towering windows overlooking St James's Park. 'Would you like to know what happened at RAF Brawdy while you were at Stack Rocks Fort, the night of the sky watch?' she asked, keeping her back to the room.

Caxton glanced nervously at Wilding, who seemed to be turning the question over in his mind. Was that suspicion in his eyes, or alarm? I wasn't sure.

'There was a craft over the sea . . .' Wilding shook his head at the memory.

The prime minister turned. 'You know pieces of the whole. Mrs Thatcher sat with quiet menace beneath the immense portrait of Sir Robert Walpole, Britain's first prime minister. 'Now before we go any further, Mr Wilding, I have a very pointed question for you. Do you know of any direct connection between Lieutenant Colonel Corso and Araceli Romero?'

Corso, Wilding's original informant.

'No direct connection,' Wilding answered.

Dr Caxton looked baffled.

'But you are familiar with the incident which occurred at RAF Croughton in 1963 and Project Caesar?'

Wilding glared at the prime minister. 'You mean the runway explosion and its cover-up. Yes. Colonel Corso told me everything. But that doesn't matter now.'

'On the contrary, it matters a great deal.' She glanced at the door and said to me, 'Show him in.'

I crossed to the door, opened it and showed in the man waiting outside. The American looked distinctly out of place in the

Cabinet Room, with his bloodshot eyes, greasy hair, unkempt beard and shabby attire.

Wilding was incredulous.

'You . . . you're alive?!'

'I feel half dead,' Lieutenant Colonel Corso muttered.

Thatcher pointed and he took a chair beside Wilding.

'What the hell's going on?' Wilding demanded. 'What is this?''

'This is where you agree to help,' the prime minister said. 'You wanted the truth, Mr Wilding? The truth is that our nation, our world, faces an ancient evil that must be understood. For all our sakes.'

She switched her attention to Corso. 'Colonel, thank you for being here today and for cooperating with this inquiry.'

He nodded.

'Colonel, we have learned that you were in contact with Selina Searle and Robert Wilding shortly before and after the explosion at Parliament in February 1977.'

'That's correct.'

'And that you passed Mr Wilding highly secret information.'

Wilding's face was rigid, but I caught Corso's wince.

'What motivated this action?' demanded Thatcher.

'My knowledge of a conspiracy against the British and American people,' said Corso in a voice that tried to be strong. 'A conspiracy involving an elite satanic cult at the heart of the British Establishment – the Parsons Elite.'

Wilding's head snapped round and he gazed at Corso in disbelief. 'But you never mentioned a cult! That night in St James's Park, you never mentioned – '

'Colonel Corso,' Thatcher broke in, 'in 1963 you were involved in a potentially catastrophic accident at RAF Croughton.'

The American nodded wearily. 'There were UFO sightings on base that night. Afterwards the witnesses were drugged, the whole affair covered up.'

'By whom?'

'Either someone in the US Air Force, or someone in a senior position within the British government.'

Margaret Thatcher nodded. Dr Caxton's whole body was tense. As for Wilding, his face was naked with alarm. It was rapidly becoming clear to him – to all of us – that the prime minister had known the details of his tale perhaps for quite some time.

'In 1963,' she said, 'Admiral Hill Bartlett was director of tactical weapons and policy at the MoD. Do you believe he was involved in the Croughton case?'

'I do.'

She smiled. 'Then please continue. Tell Mr Wilding what he doesn't know.'

Corso clasped his hands together and after a lengthy silence said, 'The perimeter fence of the base was breached by a humanoid entity exactly like that observed in Wales, and at that moment –'

'Electrical malfunction,' Wilding said. 'You told me.'

'At that moment a number of nuclear missiles on base were activated.'

Wilding's eyes became huge.

'The missiles went into launch mode, although something prevented them firing.'

'Something?'

'I couldn't tell you what.'

Even Caxton was alarmed at this; it was clear from the way he was leaning forward, his eyes bulging.

'You should know,' the prime minister said to Wilding, 'that the exact same sequence of events occurred at Brawdy the night you confronted the admiral. It's as if these . . . sky spectres were able to access the codes required to launch the weapons –'

'Nearly unleashing a third world war,' Corso finished.

There was silence as this sank in.

Wilding's face was a vision of shocked hopelessness. At last he managed to speak. 'If you knew there was a cult involved . . .' he said to Corso, 'if you knew that before I went to Wales, why the hell didn't you tell me? Warn me?'

Corso said nothing, just stared at one of the three enormous brass chandeliers.

'What's the connection between RAF Croughton and Brawdy?' pressed Wilding.

'The colonel was the deputy base commander at Croughton,' the prime minister said.

'Technically,' said Corso. 'I had just completed a tour of duty at another secret US research project codenamed SOSUS – the submarine tracking station in west Wales.'

'Brawdy.' The prime minister glanced at Wilding. 'And during your time at Brawdy, Colonel, did you ever meet this young man's family? Or his father?'

Wilding blinked and I saw him mouth the word 'What?'

'Not to my knowledge, no.'

'Then you had other reasons for divulging classified information to Mr Wilding. Personal reasons?' Her words hung for a second in the silence of the Cabinet Room. 'Go on,' Thatcher added cuttingly. 'Tell him.'

'A daughter.' Corso said in a hushed, faltering voice. He shook his head with painful slowness. 'Tessa Romero is – was – my daughter.'

Bitter understanding crept into Wilding's face.

'You have to understand,' Corso rushed to explain. 'I couldn't handle Araceli. She was young and wild, making impossible demands. And I – '

Wilding bounded to his feet, his chair crashing back onto the floor. 'She was seventeen!' he shouted. 'How could you leave her? Her parents were fucking satanists!'

And with Corso gaping up at him, he lunged and landed a punch on the soldier's face.

The prime minister sat silently through the chimes of Big Ben. 'If you are quite finished . . .?' she said after the last chime.

Gripped on each side by a burly policeman, Wilding nodded.

'All right, let him go.'

Wilding took a seat on Caxton's other side. Away from the red-faced Corso.

'Don't think this hasn't been a nightmare for me,' Corso attempted. 'I lost a daughter.'

'A daughter you never knew,' Wilding said bitterly.

'And now I'll *never* know her.' His jaw tightened and there was an uncertain silence. 'That awful hotel,' he continued at last. 'Araceli, her mother and father – all of them nuts! I didn't know how to cope. I had to get away!'

'But you didn't get away.' Wilding's voice trembled. 'The admiral saw to that, didn't he? That's why the sky spectres came to Croughton. They came for you. The admiral summoned them to revenge what you did to his daughter.'

'And I've been running ever since,' Corso said. He gazed blankly past the prime minister at the ornate fireplace, lost in his own past.

Thatcher fixed Corso, Wilding and Caxton with determined

eyes. 'Gentlemen, you have clearly endured a horrific ordeal, one that defies all scientific explanation. But not only are East–West relations rapidly deteriorating, the world faces a new enemy.'

'What are you going to do?'

'If these entities, these demons, can be manipulated, controlled . . .'

Horrified understanding broke on Wilding's face. 'The sky spectres are manifestations of occult power. They won't be controlled!'

'Unless we make a concerted effort,' she insisted. 'We intend to study these demonic intrusions.'

'Study them?' Wilding glanced feverishly at Caxton. The psychologist was frozen in his chair, his eyes like plates. 'We're talking about an ancient evil stronger than all of us. And you want to study them?'

'Prime Minister,' Caxton added, 'I would caution against this. It may indeed be possible to emulate Admiral Hill Bartlett's work or replicate Jack Parsons' experiments, but I implore you to take heed – the entities we encountered won't be controlled!'

The prime minister was unmoved. 'Britain needs the very strongest defences.' She nodded at Wilding. 'As your grandfather so succinctly put it, whoever controls the skies controls the world. We must understand this power and control it, before some other nation does.'

Rising from his chair, Wilding looked horrified. 'No, please. No, you can't!'

The prime minister also stood. In her heels she was just taller than him. 'You must admit the idea has merit. Imagine, a superior army of indomitable soldiers. Ultimate warriors. Do you agree, Corso?'

'You must take precautions,' he said. It was the last view he expressed before abruptly leaving the room.

Caxton was shaking his head. 'The study of the paranormal should be for good, to advance our knowledge about the human condition.' He had learned this, he told us, from his father's psychic research.

'Actually,' Thatcher said suddenly, 'it was the government who funded your father's work, Dr Caxton. The Security Service.'

'What? What do you mean?'

'Back in the 1930s. Your father's laboratory at Queensbury Place was under intense scrutiny by the government. Our files on his work are kept below the Cabinet Office in Room 800.'

'I don't believe you,' said Caxton, but he looked shaken.

'The Security Service took the view that we needed to know whether his work on the paranormal had produced results; whether we could learn about events at a distance, for example, or predict the future. The knowledge we gained was invaluable in the war. Your father's worldwide expeditions, his many visits to Germany, only increased its value.'

Caxton looked horrified.

The prime minister smiled. 'We can fund your work too.'

Caxton looked a little less horrified.

'Don't listen to her!' Wilding insisted.

Thatcher ignored him. 'The idea is to expose a group of young and impressionable service personnel to a sky spectre. We will devise the scenario, control the situation and observe the results.'

'You mean open a portal to hell!'

She nodded. 'Much as your father did before you. The site has already been selected. Remote and off limits to the public: the twin bases of Bentwaters and Woodbridge. Near Rendlesham Forest.'

Caxton was silent. He was staring at a document the prime minister had just laid before him. Finally he reached forward and picked it up.

'I won't sanction this,' Wilding whispered.

'It is not for you to sanction,' was the prime minister's cutting response. 'And as for your cooperation, I will not take no for an answer. You will help us or you will be arrested under the Official Secrets Act and detained.' She glanced at Caxton. 'The same applies to you.'

'My God,' Wilding exclaimed, his eyes rolling back in his head. Caxton placed a consoling hand on his arm.

'Young man,' said the prime minister, her tone softer now, 'your suffering has not been in vain, and your grandfather's sacrifice won't be forgotten, I promise. His memory and his work will live on.'

Wilding's eyes misted over.

'It is your duty,' Thatcher said to the man whose worst nightmares had once been proliferating warheads and his own spiralling obsessions. 'Tomorrow we face a new world. We must have the facts. And we cannot tell the people.'

'When?' Caxton asked, apparently resigned.

Thatcher's eyes glimmered. 'The date is set,' she replied. 'December 1980.'

'Next year,' said Wilding as if she'd said next week, next day, now.

'But in the meantime,' said Thatcher, 'we have need of your experience elsewhere. There have been other reports of . . . sightings, all over Britain. And abductions.'

Caxton looked at Wilding, who did not move, did not speak.

'What do you need us to do?' the doctor asked the prime minister.

She spread her arms wide. 'Everything in your power. Help us. Fight for us.'

Robert Wilding stared down at fingers that had begun to drum out a staccato rhythm on the tabletop, and I thought I heard him whisper, 'No more. Please. No more,' but his words were lost amid the tapping of his fingers on the table, three short beats, three long beats, three short beats. *Save our souls.*

THE END

Author's Note

This story is inspired by the wave of UFO sightings that occurred in the Havens in the winter of 1977. It is however a work of fiction. Thankfully the area did not flood that year or in 1963; there was no satanic cult and no mass suicide. I hope the residents of the Havens will forgive me taking liberties with events, geography and place names. Yet something very mysterious did happen at Broad Haven Primary School, and the children – now adults – who witnessed a UFO land in the field behind their school still maintain they saw something truly unexplained. And on the whole the residents of the Havens seem to believe them. The school keeps a scrapbook commemorating the event; it's packed full of written descriptions and drawings made by the children. But of what?

It surprised me to learn that in 1977 officials at the Ministry of Defence were asking themselves the same question. I say surprised because, while the British government was telling the public that it had 'no records of any unusual activity in the area', we now know – thanks to declassified documents – that officials were so concerned about UFO sightings in Wales that they asked the military police to conduct a discreet investigation. One document asks the military police to assess 'the volume of local interest and/or alarm and whether there is a readily discernible rational explanation, or whether there is prima facie evidence for a more serious specialist inquiry'. Intriguingly, the minister responsible at the time was deliberately kept in the dark about the investigation. The author of the mysterious memo writes, 'I have not even told the minister I am consulting you.' One can't help but wonder why our elected representatives weren't told what was going on, especially when they were making public statements about the events. How was this covert investigation handled? We may never know. Curiously, these documents have not been released.

In the hope of learning more I stayed in the area and interviewed witnesses. Not only did the people I meet believe they had seen strange lights in the sky, they described craft of unknown origin on the ground and in the air. They also described seeing giant humanoid figures in spacesuits in 1977 – figures that stalked the countryside at night. Was there an explanation? In the 1990s a practical joker confessed to dressing up in a silver suit and scaring a local woman, but his admission did not explain all of the sightings: UFOs around Stack Rocks and a nearby farm, giant figures staring through the windows of isolated houses, terrifying families.

That's when the idea for this story occurred to me. A story about belief. How do people respond to unexpected events? How do we interpret them? How do one man's paranoid interrogations of reality interact with our own understanding of the material universe? These were the questions I wanted to explore through my protagonists' eyes. Anxiety and compulsive disorders interest me; any syndrome that can cause someone to give themselves over to rituals that are self-destructive deserves scrutiny. What compels someone to do something without reason or evidence? The same question could be asked of anyone who believes in God, any supernatural phenomena or for that matter UFOs.

And the evidence for the existence of UFOs is persuasive. Reports come from credible and reliable eye witnesses – pilots, scientists and other professionals – describing objects that travel at quite fantastic speeds, buzz aircraft and outrun scrambled jets. They have been tracked on radar hundreds of times, they have left ground traces in the form of radiation readings and they have harmed witnesses.

Just one example. In 2015 Airman First Class John Burroughs succeeded in a legal bid to force the US Department of Veterans Affairs to pay for an illness allegedly caused by a UFO encounter in Rendlesham Forest, Suffolk, in December 1980. That month several members of the United States Air Force witnessed a strange craft near the base at close range. Shortly afterwards Burrows fell ill with symptoms resembling radiation exposure. Documents from the British Ministry of Defence confirmed that high levels of radiation were detected at the site where the UFO was encountered.

Readers may be interested to learn that most of my characters' experiences in St Brides Bay are inspired by actual reports. Stack Rocks has been associated with a great many UFO sightings, and there have long been mysterious reports of 'ladders' and 'doors' embedded in the rock surface. But there is no fort, nor any tunnels connecting Stack Rocks with the mainland.

I have chosen quite deliberately to present an alternative hypothesis to explain UFO mysteries firstly because this is a thriller whose purpose is to entertain, and secondly because I wanted a more original explanation than extraterrestrials. When I learned of a private report circulated among the British

Establishment in the 1970s warning that the forces controlling UFOs were dangerous and demonic, I found that hypothesis. It is based on the theory that before Satan can return to dominate the earth his way must be prepared by an elite group which either sympathizes with the Antichrist or has been possessed by demonic powers.

Something about that idea perfectly captured the Cold War paranoia of the times, as well as reflecting some historical accuracies. For example, although the rocket scientist Jack Parsons never visited the Havens, he was a student of satanist Aleister Crowley, who claimed to have opened a portal to another world through which UFOs and other demonic influences slipped through. There is also evidence that in the 1950s Parsons was studied by a secret US government group, the Collins Elite, which was concerned that his experiments had opened a psychic doorway allowing UFOs through from elsewhere. Closer to home, in the early 1950s a branch of the Air Ministry at the Hotel Metropole on Northumberland Avenue near Trafalgar Square was secretly studying flying saucers. This unit wasn't located underground as it appears in my novel but its operations were highly classified.

Do similar secret investigations continue to this day? The MoD says not, but then of course they have said that before. Readers can draw their own conclusions.

Acknowledgements

If this novel evokes a strong sense of place, that is possibly because much of it was written in the Havens, and I would like to thank everyone living in the area who assisted me with my research. Most of the UFO sightings that appear in the book are loosely based on factual reports.

I would like to acknowledge a number of people who have helped me with this book. At William Morris Endeavour, my fabulous agent and early supporter Cathryn M. Summerhayes; I appreciate you getting me started on this road and for your constant support in handling complicated rights issues. At Quercus thanks to: Andrew Turner for his avid promotional efforts, Louise Davies for structural edits, Mark Jones for his beautiful illustrations, Leo Nickolls for his stunning cover design and editor Kathryn Taussig for accepting the book.

I owe particular thanks to the many dedicated researchers who study UFOs, including Dr David Clarke and Nick Redfern, who have both played considerable roles in accessing and analysing official documents on the subject, and Nick Pope, a noted researcher who investigated UFOs for the Ministry of Defence. His experiences with the subject in the corridors of power were an early inspiration. Most importantly thanks to the late

Randall Jones Pugh, who so diligently investigated the wave of sightings that inspired this story.

Thanks to my friends: Guy Black, to whom this novel is dedicated, for supporting this project in so many ways, but notably by assisting in research by tabling parliamentary written questions in the House of Lords; Jon Harrison for his comments on an early draft; Craig Jarrett for his generosity; Guy Chambers for taking the trouble to accompany me on a research trip to the Havens in weather that was very far from ideal; and Robert Wilding for kindly allowing me to borrow his wonderful name (any other resemblances are purely coincidental!).

My heartfelt thanks to my family: my brother James Spring for his comments, contributions and extremely helpful revisions, and my wonderful mum Pamela Spring for sharing so many of the ideas that inspired the novel and for having the patience to hear me talking about them over too many years!

Last but by no means least I owe thanks to my partner, Owen Meredith, for his dedication and support.

Writing this novel has been a mysterious journey but a long one, and I am sincerely grateful that I have not had to make that journey alone.

The GHOST HUNTERS

Welcome to Borley Rectory, the most haunted house in England.

The year is 1926 and Sarah Grey has landed herself an unlikely new job – assistant to Harry Price, London's most infamous ghost hunter. Equal parts charming and neurotic, Harry has devoted his life to exposing the truth behind England's many 'false hauntings', and has never left a case unsolved, nor a fraud unexposed.

So when Harry and Sarah are invited to Borley Rectory – a house so haunted that objects frequently fly through the air and locals avoid the grounds for fear of facing the spectral nun that walks there – they're sure that this case will be like any other. But when night falls and still no artifice can be found, the ghost hunters are forced to confront an uncomfortable possibility: the ghost of Borley Rectory may be real. And, if so, they're about to make its most intimate acquaintance.